BLACK MOON PACK

BOOKS 1-3

HEATHER HILDENBRAND

Black Moon Pack Trilogy

To Hunt A Wolf, To Kiss A Wolf, To Keep A Wolf

By Heather Hildenbrand

Cover by Zhandre Dex G. (MC Damon)

Editing by Dawn Y & Lewis Books LLC

BLACK MOON PACK

HEATHER HILDENBRAND

TO HUNT A WOLF

BOOK 1

CHAPTER 1

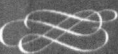

A dozen motorcycles are parked at the curb outside Inferno, each one painted with a fiery skull across the tank. The red and black gloss gleams underneath the flood lights. In this seedy part of town, nothing is sacred, but even out here where theft and vandalism are commonplace, no one touches the bikes. Not the ones with the skulls, anyway.

A lump forms in my throat as I study the painted emblem. Once upon a time, I rode shotgun on something very similar. Not anymore.

Never again.

Ignoring the pang in my chest, I scan the row again and then zero in on the one bike that matters. A black Harley with orange tassels hanging from the handlebars.

Bingo.

Looks like my mark has arrived, and that means it's show time. When I reach for the seat belt buckle, a dainty hand grabs my wrist with surprising strength.

"You don't have to do this."

I look over at my best friend, Kari, who sits in the driver's seat. Her curly brown hair is a mess after riding here with the windows

1

down. Dark brown eyes that remind me of Bambi for all their innocence stare back at me.

I look away again, unable to hold her soft gaze. Inhaling, I note how her SUV is new enough to still smell like stiff leather; a gift from Daddy for her twentieth birthday. I don't know what that's like—no gifts for me and no Daddy either—but Kari's never made me feel weird about how much economic privilege separates us. She's the only person in our entire pack I call a friend. She gets me. And she never makes me feel cast aside, not like the others.

Not like him.

She's also my complete opposite. I am my mother's daughter—tough, fearless, and reckless enough for us both. Kari, on the other hand, is kind, caring, and way too trusting for her own good. In this moment, the divide between us is very obvious, and it has nothing to do with the fact that she's the only one of us who currently owns a car.

With her hand still gripping my wrist, she tries again.

"I mean it, Mac. Inferno's a cesspool. You really don't have to go in there." Her brown eyes are so wide and intense that they gleam in the street light we're parked under.

I shake my head at her, resigned. "You know I do."

"Is this about the money?" she asks. "Because I know you're saving up to travel but—"

"Who told you that?"

She softens. "You suck at keeping secrets from me, Mackenzie Quinn. I know you too well. And I saw your browsing history when I used your laptop to look up when the next season of Euphoria comes out." I sigh. *Busted.* "If you need money, you know you can just ask me—"

"Absolutely not," I tell her. "Besides, it's nothing. Just a fun getaway I was thinking of."

"You're a terrible liar." She flashes a rueful smile, but it turns sad. "I know you want out. And you deserve so much better than this pack has given you. You *should* go somewhere. Start over. Forget this pack of assholes who've done nothing but hurt you."

She stops short of saying his name, and I'm grateful. Even after three years, I can't bring myself to admit he's the reason I want to disappear. Besides, Kari's forgetting one important thing.

"You know I'm not going anywhere," I tell her. "Not without you."

She hesitates. "I can't just leave," she says quietly.

I scowl. "I know you still feel loyal to your father."

"He's a hard man, but he's my family—"

"Your brothers are your family too, and they would kill you if they could," I snap, but even after a thousand arguments just like this one, I can see her mind is still made up.

If she won't leave, neither will I.

I can't abandon my friend to the cruelty of her family. But I don't know how to save her from them either.

I lean back again. "Your father's offer included too many zeroes to pass up. And I need to provide for my future—wherever that takes me." There. I can at least admit that.

She scowls, her nose crinkling in disgust as she lets me go and stares out the windshield. "My dad's a dick for making you do this."

"First of all, even if I wanted to agree, I'm abstaining since talking bad about my alpha will get me locked up," I remind her, noting the current pack law prohibiting alpha-bashing. "And second, this is my job, Kar. So, yeah, I kind of have to do it."

"You could tell him the mark left town."

Her voice is so hopeful it makes my heart hurt.

Kari might be the alpha's daughter, but she's the sweetest, kindest person I've ever met. Kind of crazy considering her father is one of the cruelest. Then again, I'm definitely no innocent, either.

"If I do that," I tell her, "Your dad will just order me to leave town to chase him down."

Kari huffs.

Neither of us presses that idea. We both know my presence here is the only thing keeping Kari safe these days. Her family is Grade-A psycho-pants when it comes to hierarchy and inheritances. Kari is third in line for the alpha seat, but that hasn't stopped her two older brothers from threatening her life in order to keep their spots secure. Their lifelong obsession with stepping on one another to climb to the top has only gotten worse as we've gotten older. Kari's friends have deserted her. Except me. I'm just crazy enough to stay and stand between her and them.

Yeah, the Black Moon pack is kind of a shit show. We're complicated, dark-hearted bastards, every one of us. Except for maybe Kari. If we're the monsters who slither in the dark, she's dawn's light. Except, one of these days, even she won't be able to chase away the shadows that lie in wait.

On a sigh, I unclip my seat belt and reach for the door handle.

"Mac, listen."

Kari's voice stopping me yet again elicits a groan. "I know, I know. You hate this," I say, but she shakes her head, her brown eyes pinched in worry.

"I do, but that's not what I was going to say. Listen, my dad's been weird lately. Angrier and grumpier than usual."

I snort. "That's saying a lot."

"I know. That's my point. Something's up. His security teams have been replaced twice in the last week."

"Why? Did something else happen? I mean other than…"

I can't bring myself to finish the sentence.

Kari's face falls, and I curse myself for being an idiot.

But she just shrugs and forces her gaze back to mine. "I don't know. But whatever's going on… Just keep your eyes open, okay?"

"Head on a swivel, got it."

She sighs. "I wish Vicki were here."

My chest pangs at her words.

If anyone else said that to me, I'd be offended. My mother's reputation as the best bounty hunter this side of the Mississippi leaves me as second best, no matter what I do. Growing up in her shadow wasn't exactly rainbows and unicorns. But on this, Kari and I agree. For once, I'd be happy to pass this job offer on to her instead. Except that we both know that wouldn't work.

"Your dad asked for me specifically," I remind her.

"Yeah." She tries—and fails—to give me a smile. Instead, it's a grimace. But I know she means it when she says, "That's because you're the best there is, Mac. Now go hunt bounty and stuff."

"Fine, but only because you asked nicely."

I grin as I climb out into the darkness. The air is cool. Early spring in the mountains has a sharpness to it that nips at my skin. My tank top and tight pants aren't just a costume to help me blend in; they're a staple of my wardrobe. Seriously, the day I show up in a dress is the day to check Hell for ice.

Propping the door with one hand, I turn to peer in at Kari. "Don't wait up, Mother."

She snorts and gives me the finger.

I shut the door and head for the club.

Behind me, I listen to Kari start her car and pull out of the lot. I don't exhale until I hear her make the turn onto the main road. Crigger would flip if he knew his precious princess came even this far with me. On this, we agree. Kari doesn't need to be involved in what I do.

Hell, I probably shouldn't be in this line of work either, but no one told my mom not to bring her kid on the job all these years, so here we are.

Inferno is a biker bar meets dive meets techno club. Except without the techno music. Instead, the owner, some biker chick named Rita, who apparently won the place in a poker game twenty years ago, only plays country music remixed to a dance beat.

The result is a weird mix of "my dog died but I'm going to shake my booty about it."

The bouncer at the door, a giant, hulking man in overalls—no shirt—

glares at me as I approach. His underarm hair is long enough to peek out from between his folded arms. Classy, dude.

"Got ID?" he says gruffly.

This close, I can already hear a George Strait club remix wafting out from inside. Cringing internally, I paste on a smile and hand over my ID.

He peers down at it.

"Mackenzie Quinn. Name sounds familiar."

"I get that a lot."

He squints at me, and I note the lines at the corners of his eyes. "You related to Vicki Quinn?"

"Depends. Are you going to let me in if I say yes?"

His gaze hardens. "You hunting tonight?"

I flash him my fiercest, most cunning smile and wink. "Does it matter? Long as it's not you."

He grunts then motions to the door. "You break anything, you pay for it. That's Rita's rules."

"Noted." I push past him and through the scarred door that is stained with things I would rather not identify or think too hard about. Wiping my hands on my pants, I let the door swing shut behind me and plant my feet so the force of the music doesn't knock me on my ass.

Rita loves her some bass.

The very walls pump and grind along to the beat.

It's impressive.

If it weren't paired with a crooning male vocalist desperate to win his lover back by explaining how pitiful he is without her.

I don't do love.

Or pity.

No one in my pack does.

So I guess that's irony for you considering there are nothing but Black Moon wolves here tonight.

When I've adjusted to the onslaught of sound and the dim lighting, I stalk slowly into the club's main room. There are two levels—the ground floor and one above it that's mostly just a balcony wrapped with a metal railing where people can watch the dancers below while getting their own groove on.

I pause along the wall and take it all in, using the moment to pull the ball cap from my back pocket and stuff it onto my head.

No one I recognize, though it wouldn't matter much if I did spot someone who knows me. Chances are, they wouldn't want to admit knowing me anyway. I'm not exactly Miss Popular among my pack. If my mother's reputation weren't enough, what Levi did to me all those years ago, the way I fell apart over it—it's something I've never recovered from. And it certainly never won me any friends.

"Oh, shit, it's Big Mac."

I stand corrected. Apparently, there is someone I know in here. Someone I really, really wish I didn't.

"Hilarious as always, Guy." I roll my eyes, but he's grinning like the stupid nickname is still just as funny as it was back in middle school. Guy is still just as immature, so I can see where he'd think so.

"You here to party, Big Mac? Because, I don't care if you're a Romantic, I'll party with you."

"Mac and Cheese!"

Before I can answer, another male swoops in, looping his arm around Guy's shoulders. Their movements are loose, fluid, like they've already had plenty to drink. Wolves tend to burn alcohol quickly, so these two must be really knocking them back for the effects to show like this.

"Lenny," I say, tensing at the sight of him and Guy together.

One of them alone I can handle. But both of them together have a knack for getting under my skin in a way that always leaves me miserable afterward. Maybe it's the fact that they were there— ground zero, front row seat—the day my life went to shit.

"You out here looking for a new mate?" Lenny asks, eyes gleaming with what is sure to be a joke at my expense.

"Nah, bro, she's a Romantic, remember?" Guy nudges him.

"I don't know, she looks like a Reject to me."

I ball my fists as the usual taunts are tossed at me. Their banter clearly amuses them, and I silently run through every curse word I know, willing them to get bored and give up.

Finally, they do.

"Rejects are what I do, Mac, don't forget that." Guy winks at me as he follows Lenny back to the dance floor.

I watch them go, breathing hard against the hollow pit in my stomach.

Fuck Levi Wild.

Fuck what he did to me.

And fuck those assholes for making me relive it every time I see them.

If it weren't for Kari, I would have left this town in my rear view long ago.

I refocus on the crowd, my eyes drawn upward mostly so I don't track Guy and Lenny as they retreat. The rope and duct tape I stashed out back earlier is meant for my mark but it can just as easily be used on them instead.

Let it go. They're not worth it.

From the balcony, catcalls are tossed out along with—is that? Yep, it is—a push-up bra. Red lace from the glimpse I get. It falls, disappearing among the dance floor crowd, and someone hoots like they've won a prize.

Gross.

But it's a successful distraction from the raging anger boiling my blood. My temper cools, and I shove all thoughts of Lenny and Guy aside.

My wolf hearing is on overdrive, thanks to the noise, but I force my senses to remain heightened and alert. Somewhere in this thirst trap is my mark, Dirk Fletcher. Wanted for crimes against the alpha. Whatever that means.

The charge itself is a broad bucket Crigger gets to fill with anyone who talks shit about him.

Honestly, the guy could have just called Crigger an asshole to the wrong bar buddy. These days, our alpha doesn't need much of an excuse to come after anyone. Kari wasn't wrong. He's on a hair-trigger, and we all know why.

Jadick Clemons is missing.

The heir to the alpha's throne. Crigger's firstborn. His pride and joy.

Right.

Jadick is a lot of things, but "pride and joy" aren't on the list.

I don't care if he never comes back except that, until he's found, Crigger is going to make all our lives miserable as hell, mine included.

Maybe bringing Dirk in will win me some brownie points.

I almost snort out loud at the thought.

Crigger doesn't even know what brownie points are.

Still, if I don't bring Dirk in, there'll be hell to pay.

Better get it done.

I scan the club again, concentrating this time.

It doesn't take me long to spot him.

As predicted, thanks to the intel I was given, he's at the bar, clinging to a longneck bottle. I watch from the shadows for several minutes, assessing. The crowd is older in this place. I'm probably the youngest by a decade. No one my age parties at Inferno—well, except for my high school bullies evidently—so it makes sense the bouncer recognized my mother's name. Most of these people will too.

I have to be careful.

Do this right.

My brain thrives on strategy and logic, and the next five minutes go by with me calculating possible exit points, counter-attacks, and contingencies. Every single scenario I run ends with me dragging Dirk's ass to the meeting point Crigger instructed. Though, one stands out as easier than the others. Fewer potential casualties.

The place is packed by the time I make my move—perfect for blending into the shadows. I weave in and out, head down. No one stops me. In my dark jeans and ball cap, I'm not eye-catching enough to become a target. Not with so many scantily clad women to choose from instead. I make it through the crowd with only two ass-grabs to my name. My wolf rears up at them both, pissed as hell and gunning for revenge, but I force her back down again.

Teaching these assholes a lesson about consent is not on the agenda for tonight.

Another time.

9

At the bar, a woman in a leather vest cackles loudly at something her friend says and leans into him. I use the opening to slide in between her and Dirk, deftly pulling my cap off and tucking it into my back pocket.

Despite the anticipation of what's to come—or what could happen if I'm caught—my heart thuds at a steady rhythm. My tendency for adrenaline, or worse, fear, died a long time ago. A drunk dissident at a bar isn't nearly enough to make me sweat anymore.

"Hey."

My voice is quiet against the chaos and noise, but in a club full of wolf shifters, it's enough.

"Hey, yourself, darlin'." Dirk's eyes are glassy and unfocused, but he manages to leer at me.

Perfect.

I lean in. Just a bit. Barely anything at all, really. Then I flutter my lashes. "Can you tell me where the bathroom is?"

Disappointment clouds his eyes. Then they spark again with exactly what I expected from a guy like him. "Kinda loud in here. How about I show ya?"

I nod, and he gets up from his stool, but not before he drains the rest of his beer. Waste not, want not, I guess.

Dirk leads the way, pushing through the bodies that stand between us and his destination. I quickly realize he is not, in fact, taking me to the bathroom. Mostly evidenced by the fact that we've already passed the doors marked with the restroom signs. He doesn't even try to hide the fact, either. Like he thinks I won't notice. He's either stupid or drunk—or both.

Finally, at the very back of the darkest hallway, he pushes through an unmarked door.

Night air washes over my skin, and I shake my head at the utter predictability. Not to mention the audacity. Don't get me wrong, I expect nothing less from Black Moon scum, but seriously? Is chivalry really this fucking dead?

The door shuts behind us, and Dirk whirls on me.

I widen my eyes and let my lips part in feigned surprise.

"Um, I think we took a wrong turn," I say.

Dirk offers what I think is supposed to be a disarming smile.

"Sweetheart, if this is wrong, I don't want to be right."

He sidles closer, and I back away, both of us doing this creepy dance until my back hits the club wall. When I can't go any farther, I hold my breath to keep from smelling him. Beer. Old cigarettes. And body odor that could peel walls.

Crigger really owes me for this.

"You ain't been here before, have you?" Dirk asks.

"Nope."

I shove the word out while trying not to let the stench in.

"Well, then, let me give you a proper Inferno welcome."

He leans in, and my knee slams hard into his groin.

"Argh." He doubles over.

I wrench away, mostly to avoid actual physical contact with the smelly parts of him, and bring my fist down on his back, sending him to the ground at my feet.

He sputters and groans, completely focused on his throbbing balls.

That makes one of us.

"What the fuck," he spits when he finds use of his voice.

I stand over him, a little disappointed he was so easy to take down.

"You were really going to force yourself on me, weren't you?"

When he looks up at me, I use my heel to shove him back down again. My eyes catch on the dumpster in the corner.

"Trash like you deserves to be taken out," I tell him. "Unfortunately for you, it's not going to be that simple. Come on." I nudge him. "On your feet, Dirk."

His eyes widen, and he peers up at me, hands still cupped around the goods. "How do you know my name?"

A bit of indignation—and maybe worry—creeps into his pained voice.

"Because unlike you, I do my homework on a mark before trying to drag them off and trying to assault them."

His eyes narrow, and I can't help but goad him. Any asshole who hurts women deserves a lot worse than a kick in the balls.

"I know several things about you, Dirk Fletcher of seven-forty-one Wichita Road, member of the Hellions biker club since age sixteen." At my words, he backs away, on all fours now. I let him. He's not going anywhere. "In fact," I add, "I know something you don't."

He glares up at me. "Yeah, and what's that?"

"There's a bounty on your head, Dirk. A pretty penny, too, which makes me wonder what in the hell you did to piss Crigger off so badly."

His expression twists. Anger. Righteous disbelief.

He realizes what I am; why I'm here.

Except judging from the look in his eye, he thinks I'm incapable of doing it.

"Fuck Crigger, and fuck you, girl. You won't take me in. And you're going to regret ever trying."

He thinks I don't see the shadow on my left, but I do.

A blur of movement. A silent attack.

Dirk's friends are fast, but I'm faster.

One, two, three; I put down the trio of Dirk supporters just as quickly as I did him. In the chaos, Dirk tries to make a run for it, but I drop his friends and then slide in front of him, blocking his exit.

His eyes are wide now, full of real fear.

"What are you going to do with me?" he asks.

"Well, I'm not going to do what you were going to do to me," I say dryly.

It takes me all of two minutes to knock Dirk on his ass again, and this time, I restrain him. He fights me, but it doesn't change anything. He still ends up as my prisoner. And his Hellion friends are still useless to stop me.

When I'm done, Dirk struggles against the ropes I bound him with like his life depends on it. Considering the mood I'm in, it kind of does. I finish him off by pressing a rectangle piece of duct tape over his mouth and then straightening. He looks up at me from where he's slouched against the dumpster.

"Mmorfghoh."

I roll my eyes at his attempt to talk through the tape.

"No questions until the end of the show," I tell him.

His three Hellion buddies are lying around us in varying states of consciousness. My right ribs still sting from the brass knuckles the last guy surprised me with. I nearly shifted right then, but in the end, my wolf wasn't necessary. I took these assholes down while on two legs like my mom taught me.

Four drifters for the price of one.

But I don't bother with Dirk's friends. Crigger doesn't care about them, so neither do I.

Dirk doesn't go willingly, though, and it's honestly more exhausting to drag his ass to the back of the alley than it was to fight him and all three of his biker gang friends.

Finally, I make it to the warehouse door.

It's non-descript and half-covered up with trash, old boxes, and a scrap of drywall beginning to blacken with mold. The area looks deserted at best. Dangerous at worst. We're close enough to Inferno to still hear a low hum of music, mostly bass. It covers any small sounds, including my footsteps and Dirk's muffled pleas. But underneath the music is a stillness that leaves an eerie chill in its wake. Nothing else moves. Nothing else even breathes in this place. Whether it's from the awful music or the sense of death hanging about, not even the rats come back this far.

This is why Crigger picked it.

No one will look for him here.

And that means, if this goes badly, no one will look for me.

A dramatic thought, but our alpha isn't exactly known for level thinking. And with Jadick missing and the fact that he requested me specifically for this job, I can't help but think there's more to this than just a shit-talking biker with a warrant.

I shove the door open, and it creaks on its hinges. Despite the inky darkness looming, my senses tell me what lies ahead is a large, empty space. Dirk's muffled attempts to cuss me out echo off the walls, the sound of his voice pinging back and forth only confirming my suspicions about the emptiness.

Somewhere in this old, forgotten warehouse is my alpha. And my payout.

My eyes slowly adjust, and I start forward.

I've gone several steps when a grunt sounds from deeper inside the space. It's followed quickly by a gasp and then a wet, gnashing sort of sound that makes me think of a blade scraping against bone.

I freeze.

Beside me, Dirk continues to struggle.

I punch him in the stomach hard enough to knock the wind from his lungs. In the ensuing quiet, I listen.

"You will not... get away with this... not this time."

The voice is pained and sharp—and fading.

It's Crigger, but not like I've ever heard before.

He sounds weak.

And very, very injured.

I drop Dirk, who is now wheezing, and race toward Crigger's voice.

As I run, a shoulder hits mine hard enough to make me stumble. The force of his body slamming into mine is enough to send me reeling, but it's more than that.

It's the scent.

I know that scent like I know my own reflection.

What it's doing—what *he's* doing—here now is a horrific question.

I catch myself and straighten, whirling toward the footsteps still racing away. They reach the door I came through a moment ago, and a figure steps into the opening.

He stops and looks back.

Behind me, Crigger's breathing is ragged and wet.

He's not going to make it. I don't need my wolf senses to tell me that. Death is all over this place. It's hovering over my alpha.

14

And reflected back at me in the gaze still holding mine from the exit.

Levi fucking Wild himself.

Speak of the devil, and the devil shall appear.

"Mac," he says, and the pain that scrapes over his tongue as he says my name is like a brand against my soul. "What are you doing here?"

When I find my voice, the words that spill out are full of condemnation. "Did you just kill the alpha?"

"Mac," he says again, this time in defeat.

The sound of another door banging open drowns out whatever else Levi might have said. I jerk toward it just as bright spotlights click on to reveal a dozen men pouring into the space. They fan out, combing the area with flashlights and headlamps. One of them sees Crigger and shouts for the others.

Dread curls in my gut as their eyes land on me.

"Stop," one of them shouts.

"Don't move," commands another.

Even though I haven't.

"The alpha's down," announces a third.

One by one, they begin putting pieces together.

Crigger on the ground covered in his own blood.

Me standing here like a deer in headlights.

Another man bound and gagged at my feet.

I don't have time to process how bad this will be before a familiar figure walks in behind the security team.

Thiago Clemons, Crigger's youngest son. He's a year older than Kari and me, just far enough ahead that I mostly escaped his torture in high school. I've heard the stories, though, and they aren't pretty. Not to mention everything Kari has told me. His cruel eyes assess the scene faster than the others. Not a shred of emotion registers on his stony face as he studies his father's now lifeless body.

"Is he dead?" Thiago asks.

"Yes, sir." The security agent who answers him manages to sound sad.

15

Thiago doesn't react to the news that his own father has just been murdered. His eyes rake me over, and he snaps at the men closest to him.

"Take her into custody," he tells them.

Fear grips me.

This is bad. Like really, horribly, life-threatening bad.

"It wasn't me," I say quickly. "It was…"

When I look back, Levi is gone.

CHAPTER 2

My wrists are bound—painfully tight—and before they even attempt to move me, I'm force-fed a strong concoction of wolfsbane to mute my wolf. I swallow if only to keep from choking. The deadly herb lacing the cold brew burns my throat. I fight panic, thinking of all the people who've overdosed and died from this stuff. But there's no stopping the liquid being poured into my mouth. When the cup is empty, I cough as my wolf strains to the surface one last time. She knows she's about to disappear, and she's pissed as hell about it. A snarl rips from me, and I lurch toward the guard. He responds by backhanding my cheek hard enough to drive my entire body sideways.

Pain explodes behind my cheekbone, radiating through my skull. It takes everything in me to remain upright and to keep from retaliating.

Instead, I bite my lip until I taste blood.

When I look back at the asshole, he smirks, which nearly shatters my control. But then he moves aside as Thiago comes to stand before me.

"Mackenzie Quinn, notorious bounty hunter," he drawls. "Oh, wait. That's your whore of a mother I'm thinking of."

I don't even think; I simply act.

My skull cracks his as I head-butt the bastard.

"Ugh." He groans in pain and backs away.

Unfortunately, the guard is back again, delivering one of his signature backhands. This time, I go down on one knee from the force of it.

Not good enough, apparently.

Thiago is there in an instant, recovered and way too pissed for my own safety. He shoves me to the ground with his boot and delivers a kick to my ribs that brings tears to my eyes.

From this angle, I can clearly see the door I used to enter. The one Levi fled through.

It's empty.

Just like my stupid heart where he's concerned.

Asshole.

Just like the rest of them.

"What the hell do we have here?"

The sound of Thiago's voice draws me back, and I twist my head around to see him standing over Dirk.

Shit.

I forgot about him.

Dirk's eyes go wide as he stares up at Thiago.

"What is this, little Quinn?" Thiago snaps at me.

He doesn't take his eyes off Dirk this time, which is fine by me. I'll answer his question if it means his focus is on something besides breaking my ribs.

"Your dad put out a bounty on his head," I say, the words scratchy and laced with pain. Behind my back, I work the ropes around my wrist, hoping to loosen them.

"For what?" Thiago demands.

"The order said 'crimes against the alpha.' That's all I know."

Thiago reaches down and yanks the duct tape from Dirk's mouth. Dirk chirps in pain then falls silent. He's not as stupid as he looks, I guess.

"What did you do to piss off my father?" Thiago asks him.

"I-I don't know."

Thiago hooks his thumb at me. "What about her?"

"Sir?"

Thiago rolls his eyes. "Did she kill the alpha?"

He over-enunciates each word, and I have to fight not to roll my eyes.

Dirk's eyes flash to mine, and in that split second, I know what he's about to do. He's about to screw me in the only way he can. And there's not a damn thing I can do about it.

"Yeah, she killed him," Dirk says.

"Liar," I scream, kicking my legs and trying to shuffle my way close enough to kick his balls into his asshole.

Thiago straightens and motions to the guards. One of them comes forward and jams a piece of cloth into my mouth. Another slips a black hood over my head. I begin to struggle. And then, something cracks sharply against my skull, and I'm out like a light.

THE FIRST THOUGHT I have upon waking is: Thiago is a dick. Not that I'm surprised. He's been nothing but a bully his entire life, especially to Kari. In that respect, nothing has changed since the last time I saw him back in high school, except that he's maybe worse now than he was then. Worse because, with Crigger dead and Jadick missing, he's now the reigning alpha of the Black Moon Pack. And that means he no longer has to answer to anyone.

I, however, must answer to him.

And he's given me the migraine of all migraines to remind me of that.

I breathe deeply then instantly regret it as my ribs scream in protest. Shallow breaths then. I take them slowly, listening intently to a steady dripping of water from somewhere I can't see. There are no lights back here where they've stowed me. Across the narrow space, I spot a dim lamp, but it doesn't offer much of a view beyond concrete walls. I inhale a damp, musty scent.

My instincts tell me I'm in a basement. Without my wolf senses, I have no idea which basement. Hell, I could be in another town, for all I know. But something tells me Thiago wouldn't let me get that far from his reach.

I don't have to wait long before he comes for me.

With my head still pounding, I manage to stand inside the small cell. My muscles ache and protest every move I make. Without access to my wolf, I won't heal any quicker than a human would. It also means my chances of fighting my way out of here are slim to none.

I'm at the mercy of a man-child who tortures squirrels in his spare time. Or, at least, that's what Kari told me once when we were kids.

"Good, you're up."

Thiago's eye twitches as he stops outside the bars of my cell. It isn't from nerves, though, judging from the twinkle in his eye. He looks excited. Like he's been waiting for this moment for a long time. The excitement scares me more than his anger would have. He has something up his sleeve.

Thiago watches me as if he's reading my thoughts.

I let my disgust and hate twist my expression.

Read that, asshole.

"Dirk had some interesting things to say while you napped."

Nap. Right.

My eyes track his hands as he pulls a rag from his back pocket and wipes his fingers on it. The fabric is stained red. My stomach knots.

"I didn't kill the alpha," I say.

"Dirk says otherwise."

"Dirk is lying so he won't be brought up on his own charges."

It's a classic maneuver on Dirk's part. Cliché even. But either Thiago doesn't see it, or he doesn't care.

The slow-curling smile he offers tells me it's the latter.

"Prove it, little Quinn."

His voice is velvety soft. A challenge. A dare. The look in his eye tells me he knows I can't.

"The pack is in mourning," he adds. "They're devastated over the loss of their alpha and demanding justice. What kind of alpha would I be if I denied them that? And with his murderer already in captivity?"

I glare at him, but fear slides beneath my skin.

"It wasn't me," I say, but we both know my words are hollow without proof.

"I see. And who was it then?"

I scowl, not offering an answer.

"I found you standing over his dead body. A Romantic with every reason to hate the man. Tell me, Mac, if you were in my position, what would you think?"

"I'd think I need to investigate," I say, but deep down, I can see his point.

I'm a reject with a broken heart. A Romantic, though I hate that label. I have motive, even though I'd never use it as a reason to kill in cold blood. That's not me, despite my rep or line of work.

Unfortunately, my rep and line of work are what make me a perfect killer. Thiago knows it, and I do too.

"The thing is, little Quinn. I'm in a tight spot here. On the one hand, vengeance must be had. On the other, you're Kari's best friend, and I know my little sister would be heartbroken if she had to watch you die publicly." He sighs like it's a real conundrum. Like he cares.

My veins burn with wolfsbane and rage.

His mention of Kari is a trigger. He's been cruel to her for years, always in secret. Always behind the back of his father. But now, there's no one to hide from, and that terrifies me more than my own fate.

"Leave Kari out of this," I say through clenched teeth.

Thiago smiles. Sort of. It's a dead kind of smile that turns my veins cold.

"Tell you what. You bring me who actually killed my father, and I'll let you live. For Kari."

I blink.

My surprise teeters dangerously close to relief before I realize what's happening. He believes me. Thiago knows I didn't kill his father. Otherwise, he'd never let me go. He's using me. Manipulating me to get what he really wants. I can't tell if what he wants is his father's killer—or me gone so he can mess with Kari unhindered.

"I'll give you a name," I say. "You can send your men to hunt him down."

"A name."

"Yes." My stomach twists even as I say it. The idea of selling Levi out is…horrific. But if I don't—what will Thiago do? "I saw the killer. He ran out right before your men stormed in. I'll give you his name. And you can let me go."

One glance at his hardened eyes and I know he's not going to go for it.

"A name is hardly a fair trade for your whole life, little Quinn."

"It is when I'm innocent," I shoot back.

Thiago glances back at where two of his security guards are stationed behind him. "Bring her in," Thiago says.

One of the men walks out and returns a moment later. In his grasp is Kari.

I grab the iron bars and hold tight, biting back a string of curses I already know will be pointless.

Kari growls at the guard. She struggles against him, but it's not enough.

He shoves her into the center of the room, and she stumbles to a stop beside Thiago.

"Hello, sister."

"Go fuck yourself."

"Oh, I have plenty of other options for that."

My hands tighten around the bars. "Stop this," I hiss.

"Mac?" Kari's eyes widen when she finally sees me.

My heart squeezes.

"What are you doing?" She aims the question at Thiago.

His eyes sparkle with an enjoyment that makes me want to cut them out of their sockets. "I thought you might want to attend this meeting since it involves your friend."

"Let her go, Thiago." Kari's voice is hard. She's trying to sound tough. But we both know she's nothing compared to Thiago. He's more than tough. He's cruel—and she can't match that cruelty. She doesn't have it in her.

"I was just about to do that." He turns back at me. "Right, Mac?"

I snarl at him.

"Mac, what's going on?"

Kari knows nothing is ever that simple with Thiago.

"They think I killed your dad," I say quietly.

"What?" She looks from me to Thiago. "That's bull shit. Mac would never—"

"He knows that," I say, and she falls silent.

I sigh, exhaustion setting in. I'm tired. And not just physically. Thiago has worn me down by bringing her here. And he knows it. "He says I can have my freedom if I hunt down the real killer."

"Then do it," Kari says.

I give her a look. "It's not that simple."

Her brows draw together in confusion. She doesn't understand, but she won't ask me. Not here. With him.

Thiago watches our silent exchange, somewhere between bored and impatient.

"Well, little Quinn? Do we have a deal? Or will you submit to the sentence your crime demands?"

"I..."

Kari looks away as if bracing herself for my refusal—and for what will happen after. I tell myself death is better than hunting the real killer. Levi Wild is a torture all his own. One I'd rather die than be subjected to a second time. The first time around was bad enough.

But I'm not inclined to explain that to my new alpha.

When I give my answer, I feel a little piece of my soul being chipped away. I'm honestly surprised there's any left at all by now.

"Fine," I tell him. "I'll hunt down the wolf who did this and bring him to you."

Triumph flashes across Thiago's face. Honestly, the fact that his expression registers anything but cruelty or amusement throws me off guard. But then he's snapping at his guards and moving aside.

The one who grabbed Kari earlier does so again.

"What the... get off me." She struggles, but he tightens his grip and drags her toward my cell. The second guard unlocks the door, and Kari is tossed inside with me.

"What are you doing?" I ask.

Kari reaches for me, but the guards are faster. They each take a wrist and pull me out of the cell. Thanks to the wolfsbane, I'm too weak to resist.

"Go," Thiago tells me as the cell door clangs shut behind me. Sealing my friend inside.

"Kari—"

"Will serve as insurance," Thiago says.

I stare at him in horror as every last piece of his twisted little plan finally falls into place for me. "You can't just lock her up. She's your sister."

"Return with the wolf who killed my father, and I'll let her go."

He doesn't wait for my answer before moving past me toward the door. The guards follow, dragging me with them.

"Wait," I say, desperation leaking into my usually steady voice. "You can't do this. She's an alpha-heir."

Thiago turns back, his thin mouth hinging in a calculating smile. "That's precisely why I'm doing it, little Quinn. Now, go hunt a wolf."

CHAPTER 3

Thiago leaves my wrists bound as he marches me up the steps and out the front door of the alpha house. It doesn't matter that I do my best to fight his thugs or demand one last moment with Kari. My panicked threats go unanswered and ignored. Thiago has decided, and that is that. Even before he was alpha, there'd been no reasoning with him. Now? I dread to think what pack life will be with him leading us. Crigger was bad enough. Tough. Unrelenting. He expected everyone to fall in line. Thiago will be worse, of that I'm sure. Hell, considering he's just locked his own sister in a cage, he already is.

Outside, sunlight temporarily blinds me.

I falter, but the guard behind me shoves at my shoulders. I'm forced down the steps, nearly tripping as I try like hell to get my bearings.

A crowd yells at the sight of me, and I flinch.

What the hell?

One by one, all of their eyes fasten on me. I swallow hard, forcing my back straight and my shoulders down. This pack has already taken enough from me. I won't let it take my pride.

"Thank you for waiting patiently," Thiago calls in a loud voice.

He is unsurprised at the sight of them, which means he knew they'd be here, waiting, watching, thirsting for blood. No wonder he's determined to make an example out of me. One look at the angry faces and I understand. Our pack is in chaos over Crigger's death. Without someone to blame, Thiago's power is precarious.

"I've met with all eyewitnesses from the place my father's body was found," Thiago tells them. "We have a suspect. A Romantic, of course. This fringe group has become a threat that will be dealt with. Our pack remains committed to strength through rejection. That will not change. These Romantics will be found, and when they are, they will answer for what they've done. As one of them, Mackenzie Quinn has agreed to hunt down my father's killer and bring him back here so that justice, no vengeance, may be served."

The crowd makes noise.

Some cheer. Others shout demands. *Lock her up.*

Romantics will ruin us all.

Thiago ignores them all.

I can't decide if he's helping me or damning me to something worse by letting me go when they all so clearly think I did this. Then I remember Kari. This isn't about me. It's about clearing the way for Thiago to lead unchallenged. It doesn't matter that Kari would never want to take his spot. His fear is bigger than his brain. Bigger even than his ego. Definitely bigger than his dick.

He nods at my closest guard, and the man reaches over to cut the bindings on my wrists. They fall to the ground, and I resist the urge to rub at the sore skin left behind.

Thiago leans in, his voice low, as he tells me, "You will bring me my father's murderer, or Kari will die for it. Do you understand me?"

"She's innocent, and you know it."

He shrugs as if none of this matters to him. "She's a threat."

Not for the first time, I wonder briefly if he had something to do with Jadick's disappearance. The older sibling had been next in line for alpha. Not anymore.

My hands fist, and my lips part to bare teeth. Thiago's sharp eyes flick over me, missing nothing.

"One last thing," he says, turning back to the crowd. "Until she brings me my father's killer, Miss Quinn is exiled. This is our justice but not our vengeance. Not yet. I swear to deliver you both, in time. Your alpha has spoken."

The crowd goes wild, and I'm shoved down the remaining steps and into a black SUV. A burly driver waits inside. The second the door shuts behind me. The man hits the gas, and we speed away. Within moments, we've left behind my pack, my town, and any chance of saying a proper goodbye to anyone I actually love.

WE MAKE a right and then an immediate left. I know where we're going without having to ask; we're headed for the boundary line. On a lone stretch of highway, I stare out the window and let my mind wander back to the town we've left behind and what it thinks of me. Blackstone, Virginia started as a railroad town. That was two hundred years ago, and it hasn't changed much since. Still small, still simple, still trying to convince the outside world that we're merely human.

But we're not human. We're liars. Always have been. And maybe our lie is justified. Protect our kind from all the things humans would do to us if they knew we existed. I can sort of understand it, this "us versus them" mentality. But then came the cruel rejection of our own.

A century ago, our alpha rejected his true mate and decided, for whatever stupid reason, that rejection made him stronger. Others agreed—because who would contradict an alpha?—and the practice stuck. Toxic masculinity, werewolf edition. Now, our pack prides themselves on the practice of ignoring fate, hormones and instincts be damned.

Can a wolf die from rejecting its one true soul mate?

Yes.

Does my pack see that as a problem?

Not as long as you live.

The ones who wither away from their choice are deemed weak anyway, and who wants weaklings in their pack?

Not Crigger.

And certainly not Thiago.

There is power in being a Reject. And zero glory in being a Romantic. In fact, those who believe in actually choosing your true mate are cast out. And now, they're also being blamed for Crigger's death. It's a political stunt, nothing more. Because Levi is a lot of things, but romantic isn't one of them. I would know.

If there's one thing I know for sure, it's this: The Black Moon pack is as black-hearted as they come.

And now, I'm no longer welcome in it.

Exiled.

Homeless.

Inevitably, I think of my father, but I shove the thought away. Wherever he is, he's probably happy and definitely better off without me. My mother, on the other hand… I don't know what she'll do when she finds out what happened.

She's not a predictable person.

Vicki Quinn is a firecracker.

That's what the people in town say.

She always dismisses them, smiles in that way she has, and changes the subject. I don't press it. I already know what I need to know. Once, twenty-one years ago, my mom said screw it and had an affair with a human. They were together fourteen months. Then I was born, and she took me and ran away in the middle of the night.

To protect him.

As far as I know, it's the only selfless thing she's ever done.

She's going to raise hell when she finds out Thiago exiled me.

The only comforting thought that gives me is that maybe she'll find a way to free Kari in the process. I don't need my mother to help me. But I'd find a way to be grateful if she helped my friend.

The SUV brakes, and the momentum sends me shooting forward hard enough to snap me out of my own musings.

"This is it, kid."

The driver pulls over onto the gravel shoulder, and I glance around. We're in the middle of nowhere. Not that I expected anything less. I have no money. No phone. No car. And no chance of getting his help with any of those things if his expression is any clue.

Great.

When I don't move fast enough for his liking, the driver turns in his seat and pins me with a nasty look. "Did you hear me, girl? I said get out. Now."

"I'm going," I mutter.

"One more thing," he adds. "Anything happens to Thiago, and we all have orders to eliminate Kari."

I stare back at him, incredulous.

Sure, the threat is Thiago's style, but the fact that this asshole would follow through is asinine.

"She's next in line," I remind him, but he only shrugs.

"I take my orders from the alpha."

Our stare-down only lasts a moment before he's waving me out again. "Now get going," he snaps.

Arguing is pointless.

I open my door and climb out, sliding off the buttery leather until my boots hit the gravel. The door barely clicks shut behind me before the asshole hits the gas. He pulls a U-turn, kicking up gravel in his wake, then accelerates back onto the highway in a cloud of dust.

I put up an arm to shield my face from the rocks and dust.

When he's gone, I lower it and stare at the retreating taillights until they vanish into the distance.

Then, I'm alone.

The wind stirs the ends of my tangled hair, and I'm struck by just how long it's been since I showered.

The scent coming off me is...ripe.

It takes me a long moment to realize the fact that I can smell myself so clearly is significant.

Finally!

My wolf is back.

She returns slowly, stirring lazily against what remains of the wolfsbane. While my blood burns through the last of it, I start walking, urging my wolf to fully wake. In the meantime, I plan my next move.

Somewhere out there is a killer. And whether I like it or not, I have to find him and bring him back to Thiago.

Levi was something to me once. But then, he betrayed me and became nothing. After that, I swore I'd never have anything to do with him again.

Unfortunately, in a pack like mine, promises are made to be broken.

It's Levi for Kari.

That's the deal.

I don't even let myself think about it. I just shift and point my beast's nose into the wind.

It's time to hunt a wolf.

CHAPTER 4

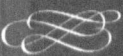

I hunt for three days before I catch a scent. It's long enough to fray my nerves over worrying about Kari. Twice, I retake my human form and find a phone, but the only number I know by heart is Kari's, and no one ever answers it. Until I can get my hands on Levi, there's nothing else I can do for Kari except keep going. Still, it shouldn't take this long to find him. My tracking power is better than anyone else I know, besides my mother, which means Levi's better at hiding than I gave him credit for.

Eventually, my hunting instincts win the battle and I catch a faint trace of him which sends me down the Blue Ridge into North Carolina. Lakeland, the sign says. Population a whopping 1402. The only bar in town, Quenched, has Levi's scent all over it. From the outside, the place looks like a complete shithole, which only makes me more certain I've come to the right place. This place feels made for people who want to be forgotten.

Only problem is I can't forget Levi. I've tried.

I wait for nightfall, using the hours in between to swipe clothes from a drying line in someone's backyard and trade a couple of hours of dish duty for a meal at some hole-in-the-wall barbecue joint. One perk of small towns is their willingness to trade for goods and services.

I'm tempted to work for another hour in exchange for making a call, but there's only one person left I know who'll pick up. The idea of talking to my mother is one I eventually dismiss. Even if she could find out if Kari's okay, I'm not sure she'd condone the deal I made. Vicki Quinn is all about looking out for number one; the exact opposite of what I'm doing by trying to save my friend.

In the end, I take the meal and forget the phone call.

By ten, Quenched is the place to be.

Its empty lot has filled with pickups and Harleys. I study the place from across the street, using my wolf senses to get a read on what I'll find inside. The door opens as a gray-bearded guy exits, and music spills out behind him.

Country.

And not the techno-shit they play at Inferno.

This is the classic kind. Patsy Cline, George Jones, and even some Johnny Cash.

I sigh but then immediately stiffen as a sense of awareness slams into me. I feel him before I see him. When my eyes finally catch up, my breath catches. A dark figure crosses the lot. His scent slams into me with the force of all the feelings I've spent three years burying.

Levi.

My chest tightens, making it hard to breathe, so I glance away. My eyes narrow as I study the person beside him. The recognition brings with it more feelings I'd rather forget, but not in the same way Levi does. Tripp Thompson was my friend once—until he chose Levi over me. Still, the sight of him doesn't make me want to saw my leg off rather than walk in there and face him.

I watch as they both disappear inside.

Then I blow out the breath I've been holding.

I count to ten, but by the time I'm done, I still can't think of a reason not to do this.

All I can think of is Kari.

And Thiago.

And clearing my name.

So, in the end, even though I'd rather poke my eye with a sharp stick, I go inside.

The room is hazy, thanks to a cloud of cigarette smoke that's probably been hanging here since Patsy Cline released her debut album. My eyes scan quickly, and my hands are twitchy with the possibility of punching something. Or someone.

The bar is nearly full. Older men with beer guts. Some in leather. Most wearing the insignia of whichever motorcycle club they belong to. And one sniff tells me they're all human.

I relax at that.

Humans are easy.

Harmless.

I don't see Levi, but that's probably better. It means, hopefully, he doesn't see me yet either. Cautious, I make my way to an open space at the far end of the bar. Somehow, everyone manages to stare without actually making eye contact.

Par for the course in a town like this one, I guess.

The bartender sidles up. A woman whose years behind the bar have toughened her into a hardened shell judging from the no-bull-shit look in her sharp eyes.

"What'll you have?" she asks. Not unfriendly, just impatient.

"Root beer," I tell her.

She doesn't even lift a brow as she turns away to pour my drink.

The sensation of a body pressing in close behind me has me gearing up for a sucker punch. Then I hear the voice.

"I thought I told you to lay off the hard stuff after last time."

Tripp.

Even before I've whirled to face him, I already know Tripp's expression will be fixed in a maddeningly charming smile. After ten years as friends, I know him well enough to predict his cheerful, teasing nature. Sure enough, his grin is the first thing I see when I look at him.

His boyish looks make him appear younger than twenty-one. That hasn't changed, I note. Neither has the shaggy hair he always insists on wearing long and unruly. He's my height, which puts us eye to eye. Great for punching, I think with a smirk.

"What the hell is a nice girl like you doing in a place like this?" he asks.

But I don't laugh. I can't.

"Tell me you're not here with *him*."

The words are out before I can stop them.

Tripp's expression twists. He rolls his eyes. "Don't start with me, Mac."

"Me? You're the traitor."

"You want to do this? Now?"

I bite my tongue to keep from delving into an old argument. But the pang in my heart is the same as always. After everything, Tripp remained friends with Levi instead of me—and that would always hurt.

"I need to talk to him," I say instead of beating a dead horse.

Tripp eyes me warily.

"Does this have anything to do with that trouble back home?"

I stare at him, not sure whether to pummel him or take his question seriously.

"If by trouble, you mean the part where I saw Levi murder Crigger, yeah, Tripp, it has to do with that." I dart a glance around the room, knowing full well Levi sent Tripp over here. Which means he's close.

I realize belatedly I've dropped my guard, and now I scramble to get it up again.

"You didn't see shit," Tripp says, and my hands ball into fists.

Behind me, the bartender says, "That'll be five-twenty-five."

"For a root beer?"

"Inflation," she says dryly.

"Here." Tripp takes a ten out of his wallet and tosses it onto the bar behind me. "My treat."

I open my mouth to argue with him, but the bartender snatches it up and walks off before I can say a word. Tripp looks back at me with a self-satisfied smirk.

"Levi went too far this time," I say, returning to the business at hand.

Besides, Tripp's already hurt me enough that I don't feel indebted to the guy for one soda.

"He's not going back, Mac."

"If that's what he thinks, he can tell me himself."

But Tripp doesn't move.

"Get out of my way, Tripp."

He looks at me, and I see something in his eye I don't like. Something that suggests he cares. Once, I would have believed him. Tripp and I grew up next door to each other. When my mom wasn't hauling me off to hunt criminals with her, I stayed at his house. We told each other our secrets. Helped each other learn to live in a pack that doesn't tolerate weakness. Now, he has Levi for those things. And I've been left behind.

I attempt to shove past him, but he grabs my wrist. "Mac," he says, his tone a warning. And somehow, an apology too, but I refuse to accept either one.

I wrench my arm from his grip and glare up at my former friend. "What are you, his bodyguard now?"

"He doesn't need a bodyguard, you know that." Tripp's voice is kind, which only pisses me off more. "He doesn't want to hurt you. Neither of us do—"

"A little late for that."

"But he's not going back."

I start to argue with him. Or maybe give in to the urge to punch him and satisfy the rage that's building in my veins. But the deep rumbling of an all too familiar voice stops me cold.

"Let her go, Tripp."

Tripp steps back, and my gaze collides with a pair of honey-brown eyes that are depthless in their secrets—and their wickedness. His hair is disheveled, same as it always has been. A wind-blown look that only adds to the air of danger that surrounds him. God, he looks even better than I remember.

I hate him for it.

And for the way my entire body reacts to him standing before me.

A fresh jolt of adrenaline spears through me, sending my heart rate into overdrive. I have zero doubt he picks up on my racing pulse, especially considering we're close enough to scent one another's dominant intent.

His pupils dilate, and a muscle ticks in his hardened jaw. He's tanned from what I assume is a lot of time outdoors. His muscles are lean though very evident through the thin t-shirt he wears. His strength isn't from any gym but from years' worth of hard labor and fighting his way through a pack who labeled him an outcast from the moment he was born into it.

We were similar that way.

Until we weren't.

At fifteen, I was the youngest in the pack to ever find my fated mate. Levi was sixteen, and he'd already had his share of girlfriends, but in his heart, he was a Romantic, just like his parents. We dated for three years, and back then, that felt like a lifetime.

Even without the mating call, I would have fallen for Levi Wild. But our pack thrives on the rejection, and in the end, that's exactly what Levi did to me. My senior year.

In front of our entire school.

"I reject you, Mac Quinn."

He'd spoken the words with enough intimacy that I still feel the sting of them three years later. He ripped my heart out with those words, mostly because I never saw them coming. In private, he'd told me he loved me. That our pack was stupid and cruel for rejecting their true mates. He'd told me we'd be the first to break the cycle. Change things for everyone. We were Romantics, and we wore it proudly.

But in the end, he'd become the exact thing he'd pretended to hate.

He'd broken his promise.

And he'd broken me too.

Despite my revulsion for him, my wolf and my own chemical

makeup betray me. Standing before him now, the urge to go to him is a force, unlike anything I've ever felt. The need to wrap my arms around his neck, to run my hands through his thick dark hair, to press my lips to his—it's a desire I feel everywhere.

Patsy croons about it over the jukebox, giving a soundtrack to my torment.

"Hi, Mac," Levi says, the sound of his voice a sexy sort of scraping that I feel right into the marrow of my bones. "It's good to see you."

"Bull shit," I say, but he doesn't flinch.

Out of the corner of my eye, Tripp looks worried. Levi ignores him. All of his attention is focused completely on me. It's stifling.

"Can we talk outside?" I say.

And even though he has to know my intentions are dark, he nods slowly. Every signal he's giving off is sinfully inviting, but I know better. Levi is at his most dangerous when he's thinking about sex. Or trying to make me think about sex.

He takes a full step back and gestures for me to go first. "After you."

"I don't think—" Tripp starts to protest, but Levi spares him a single glance that silences him.

I give Tripp a triumphant smirk, hopefully reminiscent of the one he gave me earlier when he tried to keep me from this moment. Then I shove past him and out the door.

My neck tingles with the danger, but I force my steps to remain measured and slow as I make my way outside. The moment I'm free of the stifling, smoky bar, I whirl.

Turning my back on Levi cut me to my core once.

I won't make the same mistake twice.

CHAPTER 5

Tripp doesn't follow us outside. I can only assume he's found a different exit so he can watch from the shadows. He'd never hurt me, so I don't bother looking for him. Levi, however, watches me like a predator about to take down its prey. It's a look I know too well, and even now, three years later, it leaves an ache in my chest that won't quit.

"You shouldn't have come."

He doesn't say it with any concern for me. Probably just pissed I've interrupted his good time.

"Believe me, I wouldn't have bothered if I had a choice," I tell him.

Confusion flashes, hardening quickly into resolve.

"You don't belong here."

"On that, we agree. But you dragged me into this, and I can't let you just walk away," I tell him. "I saw what you did to Crigger. And Thiago—"

"Fuck Thiago."

I cross my arms, mostly to hide the fact that my nipples are hardening. Ugh. It seems three years without laying eyes on Levi hasn't been long enough for the girls. "I don't disagree with your sentiment, but I'm not here to talk shit about him either."

"Then why *are* you here, Mac?"

His voice becomes a rough purr, and I immediately distrust it. Almost as much as I distrust my body's reaction to it. To him.

"They think it was me," I say, and the fact that not an ounce of surprise flickers in his gorgeous honey eyes only enrages me further. "But, of course, you knew that already, didn't you? The moment you left me inside that warehouse, you knew I'd take the fall for what you did."

Something flashes in his eyes. There and gone too quick to name. "It's a little more complicated than that."

I shake my head. "Right. I guess it wasn't enough to reject me. You have to ruin my life too. Let me get executed for your crime so you won't ever have to see my face again."

His eyes widen, the barest hint of shock. "Executed? But there's no proof—and you had a witness."

"Are you kidding me? The witness you saw was a mark I was hauling in for a payout. You think he owed me a shred of loyalty?" Levi doesn't answer. "That piece of shit sold me out the moment he had his chance."

"You got out though." The hardness has left his voice. I pretend not to notice because, if I so much as scent pity, I will kill him right where he stands.

"Don't look so relieved. Thiago's in charge now, and he's not one for mercy. Or second chances. Can't say I disagree with him there." He looks away. "If you must know, I'm only here because I can't go back there."

His gaze swings sharply back to mine. "He exiled you?"

"Actually, first, he charged me with murder, which we both know comes with a death sentence. When a better opportunity presented itself, he decided to send me out here to haul your ass back. Give me a chance to prove my innocence."

"I can't go back," he says quietly.

"And give him a chance to lock Kari up instead," I add.

46

He grimaces, and I see true hatred flash in his amber eyes. "Fuck—"

"Thiago," I finish for him. "Yeah, I got that."

He levels me with a look that sends heat up my spine. "Did he... I mean when they brought you in— Did he hurt you...in that way?"

I hesitate.

Part of me wants to lie and say yes. Or at least spare him the satisfaction of an answer. But the tortured look he wears plays tricks on me, so I tell the truth if only to end this horrible dance we're doing right now.

"No."

He blows out a breath.

To my surprise, he doesn't seem satisfied though. His boots crunch over gravel as he wanders a few steps away to pace. I watch as he runs a hand through his dark hair, sending it into a messy disarray that only makes me want to be the one with fistfuls of his hair in my hands.

When he looks back at me, his eyes are bright.

"You could stay gone," he says. "Make a new life. It's not like Blackstone has anything for you to go back to—"

"He has Kari," I remind him.

"She's his sister," he scoffs. "He won't hurt her."

"You know that doesn't matter to him. He probably had something to do with Jadick's disappearance, and now he's going to do the same to Kari—and use me to do it."

He doesn't answer, but he doesn't look happy either.

I know before he speaks what his answer will be, so I'm not surprised when his shoulders slump and he shakes his head. "There are things you don't know, Mac. I can't explain, but... I can't let you take me in. This is bigger than you. Bigger than Kari."

Rage burns hot inside me.

I glare back at him. "You don't have to 'let' me do anything. If I want to take you in, that's what I'll do."

He faces off with me. An invitation. And a sad sort of challenge. But it's his pity that sends me over the edge.

I'm already tensing in anticipation when he adds, "You can try."

His attack is swift, but, more than anything, it's fierce. I stumble, narrowly avoiding the leg he sweeps out in an attempt to level me. Barely recovered, I swing on him—and am met with only empty air.

My grunt is the sound of my own failure, but Levi doesn't stop there. He comes at me again, offensive and defensive blurring into one move. One attack.

His body is beautiful and deadly as it tries to put me down.

Levi has spent his life training to fight, but his training wasn't official like mine. His skill comes from experience. A lifetime of fighting to survive—literally. The scrapping he did as a kid has made him cunning and limber, a deadly combination, and I hate him for all the reasons my wolf wants to take him to bed.

When he finally sweeps my feet out from under me, I don't know if it's because my wolf has decided to let him win or my heart is too broken to stop it.

I look up at him from where I've landed on my back. His expression is impossible to read, but I swear I see regret flash before his mouth settles into a hard line.

"You're out of your league, Mac. Go make a new life for yourself. You deserve to be happy."

His boots scuff against the loose gravel. Then he's gone, and my rage is a burning inferno that demands to reduce Levi Wild to nothing but ash—if only I could do the same to my feelings for him.

TRACKING LEVI IS USELESS. Not because I won't find him but because, when I do, we'll undoubtedly repeat the little song and dance from earlier. I'm not in the mood to end up on my back for that man a second time tonight. Especially because if it happens again, I might just drag him down on top of me and give us both a different kind of ending to our little reunion.

Instead, I find a shitty motel and break into an empty room for the night.

After a hot shower, I pull on a pair of black leggings and a sports bra I found at the gas station grocery store combo on my way over here. I don't love the idea of stealing, but without money or credit cards, I'm a bit strapped.

Pressing a towel to my wet hair, I eye the bedside telephone.

It's an olive green thing with a cord that looks stretched beyond its capabilities.

I wander over and pick it up, surprised to hear a dial tone.

Wondering if I'll regret it, I dial the number and wait.

She picks up on the fourth ring. "Yeah?"

"Mom?"

"Mac." There's relief in her voice, but I can already feel her breezing past that to the business side of things. "Where are you?"

"North Carolina. You heard what happened?"

"Yeah."

"I need you to find a way to get Kari out of there."

"Honey, you need to worry about yourself right now. If you don't bring back a body, it's your head—"

"I know, Mom."

She falls silent, and I know she's irritated I didn't let her finish the lecture.

"Who's the mark?" she asks finally.

I swallow hard, heart pounding. "No one I can't handle."

"I'll help you hunt if you need it—"

"I didn't call for help with the mark," I snap.

Her tone hardens. "I don't see how being angry with me will help your position. You're the one who got yourself into this mess, not me."

Her words slice at me, but I force myself to relax. "Thiago has Kari," I say as calmly as possible. "If we can get her out, I won't need to hunt the mark."

"Kari isn't my priority. Getting you off Thiago's radar is."

"She's *my* priority," I snap. Forcing myself to calm down, I try again. "Look, I called to tell you I'm safe and I've got it handled on my end. If there's anything you can do for Kari—"

"There isn't. Not without getting myself killed."

I bite back a slew of curses. "Fine. I guess there's no reason for this call."

"Mac," she begins.

"Bye, Mom." I hang up before she can start in on why it makes more sense to abandon Kari and save myself.

If she won't rescue my friend, I'll have to honor my bargain with Thiago. The only person who can help me now is Levi. And, like my mother, he refuses to do a single thing that would benefit anyone but himself.

Asshole.

I flop onto the creaky mattress and flip through channels on the TV until my eyelids begin to droop. It doesn't take long before I'm drifting; caught somewhere between awake and asleep.

It's a skill I learned as a kid. My mother's line of work demanded a level of alertness that left me with what is quite possibly a serious sleep disorder. Upside—I can be awake and asleep at the same time. Downside—I'm never under deep enough to feel fully rested. Thanks to a lifetime of this habit, I know with absolute certainty that sleep hangovers are a thing.

Tonight, however, I fall nearly into a full REM cycle. My brain begins to blend fiction and reality until my dreams are full of cries for help from Kari with a background soundtrack of Dance Moms reruns still playing from the motel television.

A scraping noise, so quiet it's nearly not there, wakes me suddenly. As a wolf, sensory instincts aren't something you can turn off even in dreamland, and my inner beast screams at me to haul ass. I force my body to remain still while I try to work out what's changed. A lifetime of training is the only reason I can tell when the air inside the small room changes subtly. Another body being added to the space.

My eyes spring open just as a knife is plunged toward my chest.

My wolf takes over, heightened reflexes kicking in, and I'm out of the bed and racing from the room before my heart has fully completed another beat.

A wolf scent slams into me.

It's unfamiliar. Male. Aggressive.

I catch a glimpse of his face, and while I don't recognize him, the knife he wields sends a clear message. I don't wait around to find out why the hell he's decided to try to kill me.

Instead, I run, and the fucker chases.

I make it down the short flight of metal stairs and across the lot before I know he's going to catch up. I can't outrun him, not on two legs anyway.

Dammit.

Woods beckon across the empty road, and I sprint for the cover of the trees. The moment I'm inside, I shift. My newly pilfered clothing shreds right off my body as my human form bends and breaks itself into my wolf. I land on four paws and shove off again, sending dirt and leaves spraying out behind me as I haul ass for safety.

My breaths are short, my lungs burning, and still, the asshole is on my heels. I feel the moment he shifts, and the air around me changes to accommodate his new form.

He eats up the distance between us like it's nothing. And he never wavers, not even when I manage to duck around a thicket to throw him off. Somehow, he can sense where I've gone even without the benefit of sight.

Tracker.

My senses scream at me, and I curse myself for being so stupid. I should have known. And if he's a tracker, running is the worst thing I could have done. It's only stirred his bloodlust.

Without warning, I turn and face him. He's close enough to slam into me when I do. I use my claws, my teeth, and my lean, lithe body to my advantage and send him careening sideways.

Mostly, it's the element of surprise working in my favor because, as soon as he recovers, I realize fighting is almost as risky as running.

He's a dark wolf with sinewy muscles pulled taut over thinning fur. Patches are missing, and scars are evident in what looks like a body worn down from years of doing exactly what he's trying to do to me now.

Whoever he is, he's done this before.

Track. Kill. Repeat.

He's worse than a bounty hunter.

He's a hired murderer.

Where I stick to wanted criminals, a tracker will kill even an innocent if the payout is there.

But who the hell hired him to kill me?

I don't have a chance to ask before he launches himself at me. The force of his heavier body knocks me down, and I don't have a chance to wriggle away before he's pinned me.

His massive paw slashes down my shoulder, ripping me open. It's a narrow gash that burns instantly, and I renew my desperate struggle to free myself enough to roll away.

He doesn't budge, and when he pulls back again, I can see myself reflected in his glowing eyes.

This is it then.

Exiled only to be hunted down and murdered.

I bare my teeth, determined to go out with an attitude, and brace myself for the final blow.

But it's a blow that never comes. Not for me, at least.

Instead, my attacker is shoved off me as another wolf slams into him.

I jump to my paws and get ready to finish the tracker off, but there's no need. His grunt turns to a sharp yelp and then falls abruptly silent.

I peer into the shadows until I see him.

The tracker lies on his side, half-buried in a pile of leaves. His throat is ripped open, and his eyes are lifeless, aimed at the wolf who just took him out like it was nothing.

I look from my would-be killer to the wolf who just saved me, and the recognition slams into me.

Levi.

He looks back at me through too-large wolf eyes, and the breath is sucked from my lungs. On two legs, he's a human-like god. On four, it's all I can do to keep my wolf from rolling right over onto her back and showing him the goods.

She's all his, and he knows it.

I hate him. And her.

I hate this.

Mates.

It's stupid and archaic and a relentless wanting that burns in my stomach.

Levi stares at me so long that I eventually look away.

The moment I do, I know that's what he was waiting for. My submission breaks the spell, and he saunters off. The idea that he's going to walk away like this was no big deal sparks my temper.

I don't think about it, I just shift back and march after him in the murky darkness.

"Hey," I call out sharply.

He doesn't stop.

"Hey!"

Finally, he turns back.

When he sees me standing before him, he shifts too. I realize way too late what a horrible idea it was to provoke him because my gaze is instantly drawn to his chiseled abs and the perfect "V" that points like an arrow on a treasure map to what he has to offer.

Fuck me…

Literally.

Levi clears his throat, and when my eyes whip back to his, he's watching me with an arched brow. I bite my lip, terrified I said that last part out loud.

"Mac," he prompts, sounding smug.

I inhale sharply, not sure when my body stopped doing that without being told. And I'm just about to demand all sorts of answers to important, non-sexual questions, but then his eyes lock onto something on my neck, and he marches closer.

"What the hell," he growls. "You're hurt."

He reaches for me, and the moment his fingers brush my skin, I flinch and step back. He drops his hand like he's been burned. Our eyes lock.

"You're bleeding."

His voice is gentle. Kind.

My eyes burn with hot tears. Grief.

Because I know he's not gentle or kind. But dammit, I wish he were.

When I don't answer, he reaches for me again.

I wrench away and step back, crossing my arms in an attempt to cover up.

"You saved me," I say like it's an accusation.

"Let me guess. You had him."

I narrow my eyes at his sarcastic tone.

"Why?" I demand.

"Why what?"

"Why bother to save my life when I'm the only witness to the fact that you killed our alpha?"

Levi's expression tightens. Even in the darkness, I can see the familiar lines that appear at the corners of his eyes and the way his mouth turns down into a subtle frown.

"I don't want you to die, Mac."

The words are soft, almost like he means them.

"I don't believe you."

He stares back at me, eyes glinting. "Did it even occur to you that maybe I didn't kill Crigger?"

"Why are you following me?" I ask, refusing to answer his question. Or even consider it, really. An innocent Levi presents all sorts of problems, starting with the fact that we're standing this close without a shred of clothes between us.

My nipples harden in response.

Lie.

They've been pebbled since the moment he looked at me.

"I think the response you're looking for is 'thank you.'"

His answering smirk snaps my control, and I slam my fist into his stomach. He grunts, doubling over and backing away. Probably smart. I cross my arms, content to watch him struggle.

"Thank you," I say sweetly.

He straightens and glares up at me. "Next time, I'll let him rip your throat out."

I flash him a winning smile—and then promptly pass out.

CHAPTER 6

I wake to a burning sensation ripping through my chest. Gasping, I shoot up out of bed and then immediately regret the decision.

"Whoa, easy."

A pair of hands ease me back toward the mattress. Bleary-eyed, I look up at Tripp leaning over me. He meets my eyes and immediately frowns at whatever he sees in my expression. "Don't even think about punching me too, by the way. I'm *helping* you."

Helping?

My eyes flick around what looks like a hotel room. I'm lying in a queen bed covered with a floral duvet that has worn thin from use. On the cheap desk at the foot of the bed is a coffee maker along with a placard printed with the Wifi password. On my right, a sliding glass door leads onto a sunlit balcony—and standing at the railing, his back to me, is Levi.

At the sight of him, I lose all sense of physical pain in my own body. All that exists is the pain he caused my heart. I feel it—and him—like a punch in the gut.

His shoulders are tense.

He's worried—I hate that I know that.

Just like I hate that I have the distinct urge to go to him and massage the tension away with my hands.

Obviously, I'm unwell.

I can't help the pang I feel at knowing Levi is right out there but Tripp is the one at my bedside, making sure I wake up.

With that in mind, I tear my eyes away, back to Tripp, who hovers, concern lining his forehead. Probably still worried I'll punch him.

"Where am I? What happened?"

Tripp sighs. "You don't remember anything?"

"If I did, I wouldn't be asking."

"Fair point." He cringes like he'd rather nurse me into a quiet death than explain any of this.

"I remember a tracker trying to kill me," I say, squinting as I force my memory to return. "And Levi," I say before Tripp can fill me in. "Dammit. He took the guy out before I could question him."

The reminder irritates me all over again.

Tripp's eyes narrow. "He saved your ass."

I shrug then wince as sharp pain shoots from my shoulder down into my chest. "Ugh. What the..."

I lift my hand toward the source of the pain. My fingers brush over what feels like a bandage, but Tripp slaps my hand away before I can be sure.

"Don't pull the bandage off," he warns.

"What happened?" I repeat.

"The tracker used poison," he says warily.

"Poison?"

"Rattlesnake venom. They sometimes soak their claws in it."

My eyes widen. "That shit is deadly."

"Exactly."

"That son of a... I'm going to kill him."

"Too late," Tripp reminds me.

"Well, I'm going to find out who sent him."

I toss the covers aside and kick a leg over the edge of the bed. I haven't even pressed my foot to the floor before Tripp is shoving me back again.

"Tripp, get the hell off me," I warn.

When he doesn't back off, my fight or flight instincts kick in, and my wolf rears up, losing her shit faster than I can control her. My hands shove out, pushing hard against my friend's shoulders, and Tripp flies backward, crashing into the desk chair.

The noise brings Levi running. I'm still not even on my feet before he basically tackles me back to the mattress again.

"Get ... off me," I say, breathless and furiously struggling against his vise-like grip.

This close, his scent hits me hard, and my wolf goes ape shit for an entirely different reason. I force myself to keep fighting him, but in reality, all I want to do is hold him down so he can't let me go until I'm done with his ass.

Actually, it's not his ass I'm focused on just now. It's his rock-hard arousal currently pressing into my thigh. I stop struggling and, in a completely humiliating move, press myself into him, arching my back slightly to increase the pressure.

Levi stills and then removes himself from me, standing over me with a dark look that says he'll knock me out if he has to.

Honestly, it might be best.

My cheeks flame hot at what a fool I've just made of myself.

"Let me go," I say with not nearly enough conviction.

"You're weak," he says, and it feels like an insult rather than a medical fact. "If you get up now, you'll kill yourself from exertion."

"What do you care?"

His eyes narrow. "I've just wasted half a day babysitting your ass and this is how you want to thank me? By dying?"

"Thank you for what? Killing the only lead I had for who ordered a hit on me?"

"I saved your fucking life, Mac."

He sounds angry now too. Good.

"You also endangered it by letting me take the fall for Crigger's murder, and don't think this makes us even for that."

"This is bull shit." He cuts a look toward Tripp. "Talk some sense into her."

"Me? What am I supposed to say to her?"

But Levi just heads for the door.

His ability to walk away from me only enrages me further, and I lose all sense of self-control or filter.

"Seriously," I say, working myself into a nice little tantrum now. "Why bother saving me when my being alive so clearly inconveniences you? I mean, if not for me, you'd get away with what you did to Crigger, and you wouldn't have the whole salty, rejected female thing to deal with. Seems like an easy out to me."

He stops, his hand on the knob. His shoulders are stiff, his spine straight. But there's something like defeat in his eyes when he turns back to me.

"You're the only thing that makes it worthwhile, Mac. You'll never believe it, but that doesn't make it any less true."

His words silence me. Not because I believe him but because I can't think of a comeback that doesn't sound stupid and heartsick. Because I want him to mean it so damn badly.

He looks at Tripp. "Take care of her. Then meet me at Jade's."

Jade's?

Who the fuck is Jade?

An image of a faceless woman flashes in my mind. Jealousy stabs through me, and I duck my head to hide my feelings. Levi's personal life is his own. He made that clear. Unfortunately, my wolf didn't get the memo. Neither did my heart.

"You owe me for this, man," Tripp tells him.

He snorts, glancing back at me one last time. "Oh, I'm already paying, believe me."

Levi's out the door and pulling it closed behind him just as I fling the bedside Bible at the back of his head.

CHAPTER 7

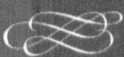

While we wait for my body to burn off the venom, Tripp doesn't let me out of his sight other than to shower and pee. Even then, he's at the door when I emerge. Clearly guarding against any attempted escape. But Levi was right. I'm weak. Too weak to make a run for it, at least for now.

"You hungry?" Tripp asks from where he's pulled a chair to the foot of the bed. He leans back, propping his feet on the wall so he can tip himself onto the back legs.

I don't miss the fact that he's blocking the exit.

"I could eat," I say grudgingly.

Tripp isn't bad as nursemaids go. The truth is I'm a shitty patient. Not that I'd ever admit it. For the last two hours, I've given him the silent treatment, but my stomach will no longer allow it. My insides are cramped with hunger.

Tripp orders food and then returns his attention to the episode of HGTV. It's the latest in a marathon, and I'm nearing my limit on how many times I can listen to these people complain about what they deem a "design flaw" in a house none of them had to pay for. If I have to watch one more housewife bitch about her first-world problems of a too-small dining room table, I'm going to let the poison take me.

"So, you work for Levi now?"

No answer. Tripp's trying to wait me out. Fine. But I'm way more stubborn than he is.

"Never figured you for much of a foot soldier," I add, knowing full well it's going to trigger my former friend way too hard to not ignore me.

But he merely cuts me a knowing glance. "That's the best you've got?"

"What are you talking about?"

"When you're bored, you pick fights. I haven't forgotten who you are, Mac."

I look away, cracking my neck side to side like I'm unaffected.

"Why are you so hell-bent on bringing him in, anyway?" Tripp asks.

I cut him a look because now I'm the one triggered. "He didn't tell you? Thiago's on a power trip."

He snorts. "When is he not?"

My eyes narrow. "This time, he's clearing the board of anyone who might threaten his newfound power. He's holding Kari hostage until I get back with someone he can make an example of for Crigger's death."

"Shit." All pretense vanishes from Tripp's expression. He looks shocked but not for long. Finally, he shakes his head. "I'm sorry, Mac. That's gotta be hard."

"I can't abandon her."

"Of course not. I would never suggest it."

"Levi did."

He looks away, his expression clouded with secrets.

"What aren't you telling me, Tripp?"

He sighs. "That's an explanation we don't even have time for."

I gesture to the shitty hotel room and my bandaged chest. "I'm not going anywhere—as you've made perfectly clear."

His glare doesn't have enough bite for me to take seriously. "Has anyone ever told you how annoying you are when you want something?"

I smirk. "You mean besides you?"

His lips curve. "You don't listen to me."

"I don't listen to anyone."

"Yeah, no shit." His smile fades quickly.

I bite my tongue, hoping he's going to tell me something. Anything. Because one thing I know for sure is that Tripp holds secrets. Some of them are his, and some of them are Levi's. And maybe if I'm patient enough, he'll spill a few.

He blows out a puff of air. "Do you know why Levi rejected you?"

I look away. "Because he wanted to look strong for the pack," I say quietly. "Because it was more important to keep with tradition and be accepted than it was to be with me."

Tripp scoffs. "You're an idiot if you believe a word of that."

Irritation—and wounded pride—have me grinding my teeth together. "Fine, what's your version?"

"My *version*," he says emphatically, "aka the truth, is that he did it to protect you."

I stare at him for a full beat before tossing the words aside like the garbage they are. "How does breaking my heart and humiliating me protect me?"

Before he can give whatever bull shit answer he'd planned, his phone dings with a text. I wait while he reads it, watching the way his eyes lock in on the words on the screen. His mouth turns downward in the barest hint of a frown, and then he blinks, and it smooths away.

When he looks at me again, there's no trace of any emotion.

More secrets.

Except, he's better at hiding them. Three years ago, Tripp wouldn't have been able to hide his feelings from me. And he wouldn't have bothered to try either. He's changed. We both have.

"Is your master giving you orders again?"

I can't help but goad him. It's the only thing I have left in my arsenal; if I can't fight with my fists, I can attack with my words. And I have to fight somehow. Otherwise, all I have left is the hurt.

He glares back at me. "I don't have a master."

"The way you jump when Levi tells you to says otherwise."

"That wasn't Levi."

"Then who was it?"

He looks away. "None of your business."

"If it has something to do with killing Crigger, it's my business."

"Crigger dug his own grave."

I eye him. "He had help getting put in it though."

He doesn't answer.

"Did you help?" I ask when the silence stretches.

His eyes whip to mine. "Screw you, Mac. We might have lost touch, but you know who the hell I am. And I'm not a cold-blooded killer."

"Nothing cold about it," I say, but he's right. I don't really believe he had something to do with Crigger's death. The problem is, I don't know if I still believe Levi did either.

"What was Levi doing there that night?" I ask.

I don't actually expect an answer. Like everything else I've demanded to know, I fully expect him to ignore me or change the subject. I almost fall out of bed when he says, "They had a meeting."

A meeting with Crigger. What the hell for?

"What were they meeting about?"

He hesitates, but I'm pretty sure if he shuts down now, I will brave the venom and a slow death if only to get up and kick Tripp's ass.

"Jadick," he finally says.

I blink, my mind racing ahead with what the hell Jadick and Levi and Crigger have in common.

"What about him?" I ask.

Tripp's phone dings again, and a second later, there's a knock on the door.

He rises quickly, his finger to his lips in a reminder to be quiet.

I roll my eyes. Someone just tried to kill me. As much as I hate being forced into this bed to recover, I'm not looking for a round two. So I don't plan on alerting anyone to my presence here.

I watch while he pads silently to the door and checks the peephole.

Satisfied, he opens the door and then closes it again, a bag of food in hand.

"Hungry?" he asks.

"You know me better than to even ask," I say, and he grins.

We dig into the food, and I proceed to eat just as much as Tripp does. He used to tease me about it until said teasing devolved into a wrestling match that, back then, wasn't an easy win for him. Eventually, sophomore year, he hit a growth spurt and finally managed to beat me, but I refuse to let him live down the fact that, for most of our childhood, I kicked his ass.

His eyes sparkle as he watches me devour my food, and I know he's thinking about all those fights just like I am.

"Don't you dare make a comment," I warn him. "I haven't eaten in two days."

"I wasn't going to say a word."

"Right."

"Here." He holds out two white pills.

"What are those?"

"It'll help with the pain."

I don't move to take them, and he rolls his eyes. "If we were going to kill you, we would have just left you in the woods, dumbass."

"Whatever." I take the pills and down them with the last of my soda. "Happy?"

"Thrilled."

We lapse back into silence for a while, but reruns of House Hunters aren't enough to distract me for long.

"Why was Levi meeting Crigger about Jadick?" I ask.

Tripp doesn't seem surprised by the question. He knows me too well to think I'd let it go.

"Crigger was hoping Levi could help find Jadick."

"Why would Levi help Crigger with a damn thing?" I snap.

The only person who hated Crigger more than me was Levi. That hate was part of the reason I'd easily believed he could kill the alpha himself. Seven years ago, Levi's parents vanished, and Levi's never stopped looking for them—or suspecting Crigger as the one behind their disappearance.

"That's a question for Levi."

Right. All that means is Tripp doesn't plan to explain.

I huff and lean back against the headboard, thoughts turning over and over with the bits and pieces Tripp has given me.

Crigger met with Levi right before he was due to meet with me. And Crigger was still alive when I got there. That meant if Levi didn't kill Crigger, he saw who did.

I had to find Levi again.

If I could shake the killer's name from him, I could hunt that person instead. Thiago wanted a killer. That's all that mattered to him. I hoped.

"Whatever you're thinking, don't."

Tripp's voice yanks me back to the present.

"I'm not thinking anything."

"Right." He snorts. "You're never not thinking anything."

"You're just pissed I always won at capture the flag back in high school."

He rolls his eyes. "You didn't beat me out of skill. You talk shit and get everyone mad enough to forget what they're supposed to be doing."

"Don't hate the player…" I laugh as he gives me the finger.

"How's your mom doing with all this?" he asks, and I don't bother to hide my distaste for his change in topic.

"She's pissed as usual."

"If we're lucky, she's already hunting Thiago and will have him taken out by morning."

"She's not pissed at Thiago. She's pissed at me."

A strange look crosses his face. "Why?"

"She thinks I should stop trying to hunt Levi."

"I don't disagree," he begins.

"She wants me to stop doing anything that might help save Kari. She says I should think about saving myself. That I should move on."

"Damn, Mac."

"You know how she is."

"She puts her own family first. I can't fault her for it."

"Well, I can," I say fiercely. "Kari is my family."

He doesn't say anything. Tripp has never liked Kari, and I've given up trying to figure out why. I used to think he was jealous, but the truth is, Tripp disliked her long before she and I became close. Besides, Tripp has never been like that; threatened by other people. We never let ourselves get caught up in that competition mentality. Not until he chose Levi over me, anyway.

"If it were you in that cell, I'd do the same thing," I say.

"Back at you," he says with zero hesitation.

I don't bother to tell him my mother would leave him to rot just like she plans on leaving Kari. Hell, she might even leave me if I'd been the one Thiago had locked away.

"My mom's not going to help," I say. "Levi's the only chance I have at clearing my name and freeing Kari."

"You really think Thiago is going to release her?" Tripp shakes his head.

"He has to."

"Thiago's never going to keep his word. Even if you bring him Levi's head on a platter, he's not going to do something that doesn't serve him."

I hate that he's right. And that I have no other options but to deal with a man whose default setting is cruelty.

"I have to try."

"Levi's not going to let you take him," he says.

"I don't plan on giving him a choice."

Tripp doesn't respond.

I try not to think about what will happen if my friend decides to stand in my way on this. I don't want to fight Tripp. But then, I don't want to turn Levi over to Thiago either.

The fact is, what I want no longer matters.

In the quiet, my full stomach makes me lethargic. Lazy. Or maybe that's the pain pills I took. I snuggle deeper underneath the covers. My injured shoulder stings with the movement, but it's not as bad as it was before.

"You hate him so much you'd turn him in to Thiago?"

The question is spoken softly, but my body reacts with a familiar pain in my chest, squeezing until it's hard to breathe.

"Don't try to make me feel bad about this," I snap. "Levi's the one who rejected *me*. He made his choice then. And he made it again the night he left me to take the fall for Crigger's murder. What happens now is simply a consequence of those choices."

When he speaks again, his voice is harder than I'm used to. It reminds me of Levi in that way.

"You don't know a damn thing about consequences, Mac."

I sit up a little straighter. "What is that supposed to mean?"

He's quiet for a long moment.

"Remember when Lacey Cartwright asked me to the spring formal freshman year?"

Okay, not the direction I expected him to go.

"Yeah. She was the only one brave enough to approach you. Everyone else thought you and I were together."

I almost smile at the old memory. Tripp and I have never dated. We played spin the bottle once in sixth grade, and when it was our turn to kiss, we both gagged and left the party rather than be forced to touch lips. There's not an ounce of attraction between us.

"Yeah, well, I told her no. Do you remember that?"

His humor is gone. He looks way too serious for some dumbass high school dance memory.

"No," I say. "I don't remember that. Why'd you tell her no? She was the prettiest girl in our class."

"Exactly."

"I don't—"

"Thiago wanted her. Everyone knew it. Even Lacey. And he'd already threatened anyone else who tried to date her."

"Thiago's a dick."

I hate quoting Levi but it's the truest response I can give.

"I still would have said yes," he goes on. "But that afternoon, Jadick found me in the locker room. He asked me to leave her alone. To not make her a target."

"Why would he have cared?"

"Because Lacey was his mate."

I stare back at him, sifting through memories faster now. Lacey Cartwright was the most popular girl in our class—until she was tragically killed in a boating accident the summer before senior year.

"Wait. Lacey was Jadick's fated mate? But Jadick never claimed her," I say.

"No, he didn't."

There's a lot to unpack in the way he says the word. Questions I don't even know how to ask.

"I don't understand. What does Jadick have to do with me hunting Levi down?"

"Jadick rejected Lacey."

"Yeah, and Levi rejected me. It's what this pack does. So what?"

"Sometimes, rejection is protection, Mac."

"Jadick rejected Lacey to protect her," I say, not quite sure whether I believe that. From what I know about Jadick, he's just as bad as Thiago.

Tripp merely shrugs.

"Okay, but Lacey died anyway. What the hell good did it do her in the end, to be rejected?"

His phone dings again. This time, he gives it his full attention and takes his time texting back. My patience threatens to snap, but even worse, I can feel the medicine really kicking in. Exhaustion washes over me, tugging at my eyelids.

I fight sleep, determined to get answers from this convoluted, bull shit story he's giving me.

I yawn.

"What does Lacey have to do with me, Tripp?"

He slides his phone away and looks back at where I've slumped hard against my pillow. "Hopefully nothing, kid. Hopefully nothing at all."

CHAPTER 8

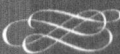

I'm groggy when I wake again, thanks to the pain meds, but the moment I open my eyes, grogginess is gone, replaced by horror as my gaze lands on the figure currently standing in front of the glass doors. Dark blonde hair is tied up in a no-nonsense tail, and her narrow cheekbones are too much like mine to be denied. Strong arms and narrow shoulders are crossed over a lean figure whose slight stature hides a formidable foe or a very capable ally. Not that she has many of the latter. I still, wondering if I can pretend to sleep until forever. Anything to avoid…this.

I have no idea how I slept through her arrival or Tripp's departure. One thing I know for sure: I'm going to murder Tripp when I see him again.

She looks up from her phone and right at me—as if I've called her name. And maybe I have. Maybe she can hear my breathing change. The woman has the senses of an ethereal being. I almost snort at that. More like a demon. They're ethereal too, right?

"Hello, Mother," I say when our eyes meet.

Hers are a dark brown color that never wavers, either in color or aim. Mine are hazel—always changing with my mood. Like my father's. People say my mother and I look alike, though. The high, narrow cheekbones. Sharp nose. Full mouth. I hope we don't share similar facial expressions. Hers are much more venomous than anything I imagine myself capable of being. Like the one she's giving me now.

"Oh good, you're up," she says.

No relief. No, "*I was so worried.*" Just a clear agenda. My waking is one more thing to check off the list.

"Nice to see you too," I say dryly.

She ignores both my words and the sarcasm dripping from them.

"I brought you some things."

I follow her nod to a small bag on the floor near the wall.

When I look up again, she glances down at the bandages covering my shoulder. "Venom?" she asks.

"The tracker's claws were coated."

"And you haven't healed it yet?"

I grit my teeth. "My wolf was muted recently, courtesy of Thiago. My healing's still a bit slow."

"You always were prone to accidents," she says as if this is somehow my fault.

Instead of replying, I toss the covers aside and swing my legs over. Unlike Tripp or Levi, my mother doesn't try to stop me.

My head spins for a minute then settles again. I'm faint. Weak. I probably need food and water and a couple of Aspirin. But I'll live.

Standing brings another wave of dizziness, but I push through.

There is no version of this where I remain in this tiny-ass room with my mother for company. Briefly, I wonder if Tripp called her simply because he knew it would get me moving again. Then I dismiss it. He's not that conniving.

Levi is.

I banish that thought too.

After finding and losing him twice now, I refuse to think about the man I'm supposed to be hunting.

When I can walk without swaying, when my mother's hot gaze isn't boring into the center of my back, I'll think of him then.

I snag the duffel bag by the wall and make it into the bathroom without further barbs traded. Just as I'm shutting the door behind me, I hear my mother call, "Don't take too long. We've got shit to do."

The door clicks shut, and I let the back of my head thud against it.

Deep breaths, Mac.

You faced down a tracker whose claws were laced with snake venom and survived.

You can survive her too.

I strip and stand in front of the mirror, waiting for the shower water to warm up behind me. I concentrate on the tape holding the gauze in place. With careful fingers, I peel it back from one side and study the skin underneath. It's already closed over with ugly scabs. A product of my wolf healing. But underneath the scabs and surrounding them, my skin is a disgusting shade of yellow.

The poison is going to take a bit longer to shake.

A smarter person would be resting.

Unfortunately, I don't have the luxury of rest.

The sting of ripping the bandage off makes me hiss. Tossing it aside, I look back at my reflection again.

My body isn't what I'd call beautiful. Strong, yes. But my hips aren't curved, and my breasts aren't full, and the tattoos I use to cover all my scars are a far cry from society's beauty standards. My fingertips trace my eyebrows, one then the other. They're sharp and angled like my face, little slashes over my hazel eyes that have a way of always making me look angry.

Or maybe I *am* always angry.

Like mother, like daughter.

On the other side of the door, I can hear her talking on the phone. Her voice is low, but I catch some of it anyway. Something about sending someone else. I'm surprised to realize she's being offered a job—and she's turning it down.

For the chance to babysit me.

Ugh.

Of all the ways Tripp could have sabotaged my plan to hunt him and Levi, this is the most underhanded of them all. I spend the rest of my time in the shower thinking up all the ways I plan to get him back for this.

When I'm done, I rifle through the bag and sigh.

The "things" my mother brought me leave a lot to be desired. The oldest shirt I own. A sleeveless, ripped thing I should have thrown out but it's the shirt I wore when I took down my first mark. Sentimental. Stupid. And the jeans are faded from wear and probably one good roundhouse kick away from shredding right off my body.

It's better than stolen leggings, I guess.

When I emerge, my mother tosses me a protein bar and a bottle of water. "Here," she says. "Take it on the road. We need to move."

I plant my feet, bracing for a fight. "I'm not going anywhere with you."

"Mac, now's not the time."

"Now's all I have," I toss back at her.

She rolls her eyes. "There's no need for dramatics."

"I haven't seen you in four months. And now you show up here and start tossing orders before I'm even out of bed. *That's* dramatic."

Her eyes narrow fractionally, and I know it's the only warning I'll get before she loses her temper. Most people are scared of a pushed-too-far Vicki Quinn. I'm not most people.

"It's been four months because I'm a working mother, and I will not apologize for that. Tripp called me because a tracker almost killed you," she says. "I came because you're my daughter. And now, we're going to find out who hired that asshole and why. And then we're going to kill them. Is that dramatic enough for you?"

I want to argue. To protest or put my foot down. To tell her to leave me alone. But her plan is my plan. And with her help, we'll get answers faster. I'm not ashamed to admit that my mother has contacts that I don't. Forty-five years' worth of them. If anyone can find out who sent that prick, it's the woman standing before me.

I need her.

Doesn't mean I have to like it.

"Fine," I say, hauling my bag over my shoulder. "Nothing like a little mother-daughter murder spree to bond us."

DESPITE THE BITE in the air, we ride with the top down. After two days cooped up inside that hotel room, I close my eyes and tip my head back against the seat, enjoying the feel of the wind in my tangled hair. My mother's Jeep is a growly thing that's been everywhere she has. It's scarred and scratched—like us—and one of the few fond memories I have from my childhood. Sleeping in the backseat of this thing. Climbing mountains and boulders in search of criminals. Hiding on the floorboard while she tagged them. Then, later, when I was older—helping her take them down.

I've lived a lot of my life in this Jeep.

My mother glances over at me as we barrel down the highway. "You can stop trying to scent his trail. The rain has washed it away."

"I don't know what you're talking about."

"Yes, you do."

I scowl.

The woman's a mind-reader. And she's not wrong. Any trail I'd hoped to catch of Tripp or even Levi is gone with last night's rain. It's like even the weather has decided to take their side. I have no way of knowing whether I'm driving toward or away from wherever they've gone. But for now, I can't focus on that. Or them.

Right now, all I want to know is who the hell tried to kill me.

We drive west for two hours before my mother takes an exit for some place called Indigo Hills.

I've never been, but I've heard of it.

And what I've heard isn't good.

I cut my mother a look, arching a brow. "Mafia territory?"

"They trade in information and that's exactly what we need."

Twenty minutes later, the open road gives way to signs of civilization. Industrial buildings. Warehouses. And then, offices and skyscrapers. Somehow, out of the fields and farmlands, a metropolis has sprung to life. I stare, a little open-mouthed at the impossibility of this buzzing city existing in what was literally the middle of nowhere five minutes back.

"How in the hell...?"

"Indigo Hills," she points out.

I see them in the distance. Not hills. Mountains, really. They're such a deep purple, they look nearly black, and form an almost perfect ring around this valley. And around the entire city we're driving into.

"The mountains were spelled by the Crescent Coven three centuries ago. From the other side, the shadows play off the light, and it sends any would-be tourist or traveler right around them instead of through."

"How'd we get in?" I ask.

She smirks. "You have me. And I know things."

I roll my eyes. My mother's a little bit aware of what a badass she is.

We park in front of a skyscraper taller than any I've seen in this state, but instead of going inside, my mother leads us directly across the street to an Italian restaurant. It's a bit out of place, considering the casual, family vibe it puts out. Especially amid the glitz and glamour of what could have been the Upper East Side of New York.

I went there once.

Dragged a werewolf with a gambling debt all the way back to Blackstone. Mom tied him to the roof of the Jeep like he was luggage.

"Stay close, and don't speak," my mother says just before pushing through the restaurant doors.

A place called Altobello's.

The scent hits me first, and my stomach cramps. That protein bar is long gone, and this place smells straight up like heaven on a plate. At the same time my hunger hits, I also notice this place is completely empty except for a single occupied table in the back of the room.

Stale cigar smoke hangs in the air.

At the center of the haze, four men sit around what looks like a poker game.

Beers and poker chips litter the surface of the table.

Like they've been at this a while now.

There isn't a single employee in sight.

Two guards emerge from the shadows. One from the left, the other on my right. My mother tenses but otherwise doesn't react to the threat.

"I'm here to see Franco," she says with the kind of authority only Vicki Quinn possesses.

The security guard on the left grunts as if he's about to object, but one of the men at the back table speaks first.

"Vicki Quinn, aren't you a sight for sore eyes?"

His accent is notably Italian.

He stands, and I see that he's in a rumpled dress shirt and gray suit pants. Even disheveled, he has the look of a man with deep pockets—and a stomach for violence if the rumors are true. He's old enough to be my father. Or grandfather. But the way his eyes see everything at once gives me pause. I won't underestimate him.

He comes forward, arms open, and she goes to him, letting him hug her. She kisses both his cheeks—air kisses but it's still more affection than I've seen from her. Surprised by their familiarity, I pause a few steps from where she's joined him in the center of the room.

"It's good to see you, Franco," my mother says.

Not quite warm but not chilly either.

What a weird day it's turning out to be.

"It's been too long, darling," he tells her.

She steps out of his embrace but allows him to keep his hand on her lower back as they both turn to me.

"And who's this beauty?" he asks.

Behind him, the three men at the table look on with mild interest.

I meet his gaze. "I'm Mac," I say.

"She's my—"

"Apprentice," I say, cutting my mother off.

I try to hide my horror at the fact that she was about to divulge our familial connection. Rule one of our work is that we never, ever tell business associates that we're related. *You don't hand your enemy your greatest weakness, Mac.* That's what she always says. And now here she is breaking her own rule.

What the hell?

Who is this guy?

"Apprentice," Franco repeats, brows raised. I wait for him to point out the physical resemblance between my mother and I, but he doesn't. "And what can I do for you and your lovely *apprentice?*" he asks my mother.

The way his voice catches on the last word makes me want to roll my eyes.

Fine, lying was pointless.

Whatever.

"Can't I just stop by because I want to see an old friend?"

Franco laughs. It shakes his ample belly. "If only I could ever believe you to be the kind of woman who would do something so romantic."

My mother smirks. "You know me well, Franco."

"That I do." He laughs again. "Come. Sit. Are you hungry? What can I get you to drink?"

He leads my mother toward his table. The three men make room. One of the guards pulls up a chair. I notice my mother's subtle wave at me to stay put. Fine by me. I do my best work by being underestimated and unnoticed.

Changing direction, I march to the bar and slide onto the last stool. The second security guard rounds the bar behind me, splitting my attention.

"What'll you have?" he asks.

He's young. Probably only a year or two older than me. Handsome too. If my wolf weren't mated...

But she is.

We are.

Dammit.

"What do you have to eat around here?" I ask.

If my mom can treat this place like a second home, it can't be that dangerous. And my stomach is painfully empty.

The guy smiles. "The best spaghetti and meatballs you've ever had."

"I'll take it. Biggest plate you've got."

His smile widens. "Coming right up."

He disappears through a narrow door along the back wall.

I refocus on my mother.

Franco is regaling her with some bull shit story about a high-stakes poker game he won. According to him, the pot involved a lot of money and a man they both knew who was wanted for embezzlement by some pack northeast of here. Franco took the man's money and made sure he was arrested by the end of the game. It's supposed to be funny, I guess.

She laughs when he laughs.

It's weird.

The guard brings me a plate of spaghetti that I have to admit *is* the best I've ever had. I stifle a groan of pleasure and honestly debate kissing him on the mouth in gratitude. Unfortunately, my mouth is only interested in kissing one person, and it's not this guy. Because that would be too easy; wanting someone who wants me back.

Ugh.

I wash the food down with water because, even though I'm pretty sure they won't poison me—I'm already poisoned, technically —I'm not stupid enough to lose my wits in a place like this.

The fact that it's empty at lunchtime speaks volumes about what these men are and what sort of business goes on in here.

"Franco, listen," my mom says as I polish off the last of my food.

Finally, we're getting down to business. "I need to know what you've heard about a tracker hired for a contract liquidation."

"Hm. Was the liquidation successful?" Franco asks.

My mother's gaze flicks to me. "No."

"I see."

And I can tell by the sharpness in Franco's gaze that he does see.

"Now that you mention it, I did hear something about an inside hire."

I straighten in my seat.

My mother doesn't react.

"Inside hire?" she repeats with a practiced sort of curiosity.

"Your new alpha. What's his name?" Franco snaps his finger. "Theo?"

"Thiago." My voice rings out clearly across the room. The men all turn to look at me, and my mother glares.

I told you to stay quiet, her eyes scream.

I ignore her.

My stomach churns with rage. Thiago spared my life only to exile me and try to kill me once I'd left his borders. It doesn't make sense. But then, I think of Kari, and, actually, it makes perfect sense.

He only spared me as an excuse to get to her.

With me gone, he has no reason to release her.

Ever.

This was never about Crigger's killer, this was about Thiago eliminating his own competition.

My mother's anger is a frequency screeching in my head. But I don't let her rules keep me from getting my own answers. This is my fight just as much as hers. More, actually.

"Thiago Clemons. He's the new alpha of our pack," I say. "Is that who you mean?"

"Yes, Thiago. Crigger's kid." Franco studies me. "He's making a power play of it, from what I hear."

"He's a dick," I say, and the guard who fed me snickers from where he leans against the wall not far away.

"He's got a lot to prove and not a lot of time to prove it," Franco says.

"He paid the contract," my mother says. "You're sure of it?"

"I could be sure. Depends on what you've got for me."

I have no idea what my mother has for him. Or what he'll want. But she's unruffled.

"Marco Gerardo," she says smoothly.

Franco stares back at her. "You sure about that?"

He sounds deadly serious now. In fact, all three men at the table are leaning forward. Whoever Marco is, they seem very interested in him.

"I could be sure," my mother says. "If you are."

"I am," Franco says without hesitation. "Your alpha paid the contract."

My mother nods. "Marco's your guy." She pushes to her feet. "Come on, Mac. It's time to go."

Franco stands, and the two guards snap to attention, closing in so they flank him as he walks my mother to the door.

"Thanks," I tell the one who fed me.

"Anytime," he says, and I can hear the undercurrent of attraction. He's flirting.

I want to flirt back. But something stops me. And it's not my heart's stupid relentless devotion to an asshole. Something else ties my tongue.

The mate call.

Alarm shoots through me as I realize Levi is here. With every ounce of self-control I possess, I keep my eyes trained on the guard as I smile tightly and then join my mother at the exit.

Franco says goodbye. My mother promises to "come by soon." And we leave. All the while, I'm hyper-aware of Levi's presence. Somewhere close by.

When we're back on the sidewalk, the feeling intensifies.

Still, I don't search for him.

I refuse to let him know I can sense him. Not until I know why he's here.

Whatever he's up to, he's not going to get away with it again.

CHAPTER 9

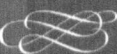

The street is crowded with traffic. It takes us several minutes to cross to where Mom parked the Jeep. The entire time, I feel him nearby. Levi. He's above me, that much I know. But I don't look up to see exactly where.

My mom is clearly oblivious to it. She marches straight to the Jeep and unlocks it with her fob. But I hesitate.

"Where are we going now?"

"Not 'we,'" she corrects. "Just me."

"Excuse me?"

"You're going to find a safe place to lay low while I handle this."

"You can't be serious. You want me to *hide?*"

"I want you to *live*," she snaps then reaches for her door handle and yanks harder than necessary. She's pissed. And now that Franco isn't watching, she's letting it show.

But I don't move to open my door.

"Get in," she says.

"No."

"Mac," she warns. "We don't have time for this."

"You're going to kill him, aren't you?"

She doesn't even pretend to be confused about who I mean. We both know I'm talking about Thiago—the asshole who paid to have me killed.

"He messed with my family," is all she says.

Like that's all the reason she needs.

Maybe it is, but it's not a good enough reason to shove me in a hole somewhere while she does all the dirty work. The words of that security guard ring in my head. If something happens to Thiago, that would make Kari automatic alpha. Would he really carry out Thiago's order to kill her? I can't be sure, and the thought of risking it—of letting my mother loose on him—makes me sick.

"I won't be left behind on this."

"You'll do what I say until I make it safe for you again," she says.

Her voice is more than a warning now. It's a promise that she intends to get her way even if it means taking me by force.

"He has Kari," I remind her. "And he's threatened to hurt her if something happens to him. Do your plans include making sure she *doesn't* get hurt?"

"I'll do my best."

"Not good enough," I all but yell.

My mother hesitates. "You're my daughter, Mac." Desperation leaks into her eyes. "What am I supposed to do?"

Vulnerability is only there for a second, and then it's gone. The mask is back. But even a glimpse is proof she's more upset than I realized.

Still, I can't let her make a bigger mess of what's already a shitshow.

"I can't let you do this," I say.

Instead of giving in, though, her expression hardens. "It's not up to you."

When I still don't move, I expect her to come at me, maybe even physically put me in this car. She can try, anyway. I've never come to blows with my mother, but for this, for Kari, I would.

But instead, she pulls out her phone and dials a number.

"Tell Franco Mac is staying here until I get back," she says.

"What?" My eyes widen. No freaking way she's dumping me with the mafia while she kills Thiago.

"Yeah, I'll owe him," she says in response to whoever's on the other end of the call.

She hangs up and glances at me one last time. "I can't not protect you, Mac. You'll understand someday."

In the next second, she climbs into the car alone and starts the engine.

She engages the door locks.

Then she drives off.

My heart pounds as I try to think. Franco's going to lock me in a room if he gets his hands on me. Been there, done that. Not doing it again.

I whirl and catch sight of the two security guards emerging from the restaurant. They search the sidewalk and street beyond until their eyes land on me standing in the middle of this parallel parking space.

They start for me, ignoring the crosswalk and the traffic, which somehow just knows enough to stop for them.

Shit.

Time to move.

I whirl and take off for the nearest alleyway at a full sprint.

My shoulder burns a little as the poison stirs in my blood now pumping faster than before. I don't stop or slow. And I don't worry about finding an exit. Instead, I follow the call of my mate.

Levi's already headed out, but I've still got a lock on him.

With any luck, he'll lead me away from these assholes and maybe even give me a chance to make good on my promise to haul his ass in. If I can get to Thiago before my mother, with Levi in custody, maybe I can still save Kari before shit hits the fan.

I run until my lungs burn and my chest threatens to cave in around the pain. Twice, I consider shifting, but there are too many people, and I'm sure a wolf in the city will be more noticeable than a strange girl. Even in a metropolis full of werewolves, there are rules about propriety.

Levi stays far enough ahead that I'm terrified I'll lose him at any moment. The only good thing about his superior speed is that I'm fairly certain he has no idea I'm following.

He finally stops when we reach the outskirts of town, at a retirement community complex of all places, and I hang back, catching my breath while I note the apartment he enters. At least I've lost Franco's men. For now.

The traffic is almost non-existent here, and while the neighborhood seems nice enough with the tiny manicured patches of grass and pretty white gate blocking access to non-residents, I can't help but feel a sense of eyes on the place.

I wait an hour, trying to assess what's going on behind closed doors. But Levi doesn't emerge, and no one else goes in or out of the place either. It's stupid to walk blindly into something like this, and if Levi were any other mark, I wouldn't do it. But staying out here is more of a risk considering the entire Indigo Hills Mafia is probably looking for me now.

I can either stay out here and wait for Franco and his guys to haul me in. Or I can use the element of surprise to apprehend Levi and trade him for Kari.

I head for the apartment, skipping the front gate and, instead, veering around the back.

Climbing the low wall, I dart between hedges until I'm right outside the apartment I watched Levi enter. It has a large front window covered in blinds. I bend low to bypass it and find a small fenced-in backyard around the side.

Scaling the fence, I drop to my feet on the other side and hurry to the back door.

Unlocked.

These guys are seriously sure of themselves.

I slide it open as silently as possible.

My shoulder burns. My heart pounds. My breaths are short and shallow, but I make sure to keep them silent as I walk through the back door and into a small kitchen.

A table and set of chairs sits between me and the rest of the house. My eyes land on a figure sitting at the table, and I stop cold. When I see who it is sitting before me, my jaw drops.

For a second, I forget all about Levi. Or Thiago. Or even Kari.

"Jadick?" I whisper.

My brain catches on the fact that I'm standing in the same room with our missing alpha-heir.

"Hello." His greeting is smooth and way too calm given I've just broken into his house.

"Holy shit."

Jadick Clemons is alive and well.

Shock is replaced by hope. The welling in my chest is over-whelming, and I don't know whether to laugh or cry or punch something. Namely him.

"You're alive," I blurt.

"That's a very astute observation."

My shock dissolves into fury.

"What the hell is the matter with you?" I demand. "Why are you hiding out here when your pack's fallen into the hands of your psychopath brother?"

"You must be Mac," he says in a deep voice that doesn't miss a beat, considering the accusations I've just spewed. "We've been expecting you."

Shit.

The realization I'm not as stealthy as I thought comes three seconds before someone grabs me from behind and hauls me off my feet. Despite my attempt to run, I'm tossed over a very broad, very strong shoulder and held down by an arm that is muscled to perfection. An arm I'd lick if I had any less self-respect.

Levi.

His scent slams into me, and I realize belatedly the shock of seeing Jadick here has dulled my senses. I never even saw him coming.

Dammit.

"Put me down." I try to sound tough, but when you're slung over someone else's shoulder like a sack of potatoes, it's hard to sound scary or intimidating.

To make up for it, I fight, kicking wildly until my toe lands solidly against the parts of him I accidentally sex-dream about at night sometimes.

"Ugh." He grunts and almost drops me.

Almost.

But not quite. When he adjusts his grip, tighter than before, I know fighting isn't going to work. Out of sheer desperation, I play the only card I have left.

I lick his arm, self-respect be damned.

"Did you just ... lick me?

"Damn right." I beat my fists against his back. "And there's more where that came from."

I'm pretty sure I hear Jadick snicker.

"She sounds like she means it," he says.

Levi sighs. "Mac, I swear, you're going to be the death of me."

He sounds mildly irritated, which is nothing compared to how I feel about him leaving me in that hotel with Tripp—and then my mother.

Abandoning the licking, since it will only lead to me enjoying my current predicament, I try another tactic. With every ounce of momentum I have, I wrench myself sideways and succeed in falling off Levi's shoulder. I land on the kitchen floor—right on my face. Probably should have thought that through.

The tile is cold and hard against my cheek, and I wince at the pain shooting through my cheekbone. When I pry myself up again, a pair of boots steps into view about six inches from my eyeballs. I follow them upward until I see Tripp glaring down at me. Beside him, Levi is still cupping himself in pain. Whoops.

Behind him, Jadick sits at the table, watching us all with an amused expression.

"When you said she fights dirty, you weren't kidding," Jadick says.

Levi glares at him, which is good because I don't think I have it in me to do it myself right now. Tripp extends a hand to help me up, but I ignore it and climb to my feet, gritting my teeth at the pulsing pain in my face.

"Damn, girl." Tripp studies the damage I've done to myself. "You kicked your own ass."

"And his." I smirk at Levi, and Tripp tries and fails to keep from laughing.

"She's got you there," Tripp tells him.

"Lucky shot," Levi grumbles, trying to look recovered even though I'm sure it still hurts. After all, it's only been three years since I last had my hands on the goods, and that's not something a girl forgets. Not that I've fully experienced it, but our make-out sessions came close enough and—

"I think I saw a pack of peas in the freezer," Tripp says.

I shake off the urge to daydream about the size of Levi's dick. Right now, he's being one, and that's what matters.

"Does someone want to explain to me what the alpha-heir is doing in a retired living community on the edge of mafia territory?" I ask. "Or why he isn't currently taking his rightful place among our pack?"

"Not particularly," Levi says.

This time, I do actually manage to glare. "I think you owe me an explanation."

"Hey, you're the one who crashed our party," Tripp says to me. "You don't just get to demand answers too."

"He has a point," Jadick says, but he looks like he's enjoying all the banter more than he wants to be a hardass about anything. "Maybe you could start with an explanation of your own," he says to me. "Tell us what you're doing here, and maybe we'll do the same."

"Yeah." Tripp crosses his arms. "I, for one, would love to hear that story. And where's Vicki?"

"Oh, you mean the babysitter you called for me and then dipped out because you're too chickenshit to tell me you called my mother on me?"

"Uh-oh," Tripp says, and his smirk vanishes.

"I am going to kick your ass for that," I tell him.

Before he can offer an apology—or claim temporary insanity—there's a knock at the front door.

No, a pounding.

A fist bangs against the steel door so hard it shakes the entire apartment.

We all fall silent. Judging from the wide-eyed stares the guys are giving one another, they have no idea who it is. My stomach tightens because there's a very good chance I brought this trouble with me.

"Mackenzie Quinn," an unfamiliar voice shouts from outside.

Dammit.

Make that a one hundred percent chance.

"Any idea who that is?" Levi asks me.

"Umm, possibly the mafia?"

His expression darkens.

I wince.

The voice calls out again. "Come out, or we're coming in. We don't want trouble," the man adds, and I can't help but roll my eyes at that.

Riiight.

Because banging violently on a front door just screams *peace and love.*

"You led the mafia to our doorstep?" Tripp hisses. "While we're housing a fugitive? Are you insane?"

I give him a look that's somewhere between admitting that I'm an idiot and straight-up fear. "Whoops?"

Levi curses.

I can almost see the urge to wring my neck playing across his delicious features. The banging comes again, and he blinks like it's snapped him out of whatever daydream of my ass-whooping he just experienced.

"Take Jadick with you," he tells Tripp. "Go to Jade's."

The name reignites a flame of jealousy inside me. I glare at them all, not even caring if it shows at this point.

"What about you?" Tripp says.

Levi looks back at me, his expression blazing just as hot as my own. "Mac and I are going to have a little talk."

CHAPTER 10

I don't argue. Mostly because I have my own reasons for wanting to be alone with Levi. None of those ideas involve talking, especially the ones I've forbidden my hormones from attempting. But mostly, I recognize this as my chance to finally apprehend him. With my mother racing off to murder Thiago, I don't have much time left to help Kari before she's caught up in the chaos. So, when Levi nods at me to follow him, I go willingly.

We scale three fences over to the backyard on the far end of the row before slipping out through the back gate. From there, Jadick and Tripp split off, and while it's tempting to follow them—Jadick being alive solves a hell of a lot more problems than hauling Levi in —I stick with Levi instead.

I refuse to admit, even to myself, that part of me needs to make sure he escapes the danger I've unwittingly put him in with the Indigo Hills mafia pack.

No one else is allowed to hurt my mate except for me.

And they damn sure aren't allowed to kill him.

Considering we ran all the way here, I fully expect to do the same for however long it takes to get wherever Levi has decided to take me. So, I'm surprised when he leads us to the back of the apartment complex and unlocks a creepy white van.

"Get in."

"Seriously? A kidnapper van?"

"It blends," he says simply then climbs in behind the wheel.

I slide into the passenger seat, wrinkling my nose because the inside reeks of him. Pine and spice. It's the best smell in the whole world as far as my wolf is concerned. I hate it.

"Have you been living out of this thing?" I ask, glancing in the back where a futon couch has been folded into a bed.

My stomach does a weird sort of somersault at the idea of Levi in that bed. Or me and Levi in that bed.

"Off and on," he says distractedly.

I face forward again as Levi hits the gas and hops the curb, bypassing the main entrance in favor of a service road behind us.

He's simultaneously watching the road in front of us and the mirrors showing our rearview.

Right. Danger. Not a good time to think about sex. Unfortunately, where Levi's concerned, I'm never *not* thinking about sex.

I roll my window down, hoping the fresh air will clear my head.

Levi gives me a look but says nothing. I have a feeling he can sense my arousal anyway. Stupid mate bond.

We ride in silence, both of us checking for some sign of a tail.

After several miles, it's clear we're not being followed. Satisfied, Levi loops us onto the highway and heads east.

The silence stretches, and inside me sits too many questions to even name. Finally, my brain can't contain them all, and I spill one.

"Are we going to talk about the fact that you've been hiding Jadick Clemons all this time while Crigger gets murdered and his pack goes to shit?"

Levi glances over at me then back at the road. "Are we going to talk about the fact that you brought the Indigo Hills Mafia to the doorstep of my safe house, ruining in one hour what I took six months to create?"

Touché, asshole.

Wait.

"Six months? Are you saying you and Jadick planned his disappearance? That he wasn't kidnapped or held against his will?"

Levi doesn't answer, and my temper spikes.

"You're telling me he's willingly sitting by while Thiago locks Kari in a cell and steals the alpha title out from under him?"

"I'm not telling you anything, actually."

"Fine. You know what, I don't want whatever explanation you might give. I'm sick of wading through your lies."

"*My* lies? You're the one meeting secretly with the mafia and then leading them to my doorstep. Wanting me dead is one thing. Selling me out to Franco Giovanni himself is another."

My jaw drops. Indignation is a bitter taste in my mouth. "I would never... But of course, you think everything is about you."

"What the hell else am I supposed to think? You come looking for me, and the next thing I know, you've led an army of wolves to the very place Jadick is hiding out. Maybe you're not running from Thiago. Maybe you're working with him."

I can't breathe against the rage that boils inside me.

The fucking nerve...

I look wildly around for some outlet, some weapon, some way to react to the insane accusations he's just lobbed at me. But in a moving vehicle, there isn't much to choose from.

Only one thing, in fact.

I unbuckle my seat belt and reach for the door handle, shoving the door open to reveal the highway pavement racing by underneath us at eighty miles per hour.

"What the hell!" Levi yells and swerves, the momentum slamming my door shut again before I can hurl myself out.

Admittedly, it was a reckless plan to begin with.

But when Levi manages to foil it, I only get angrier.

He swerves again, this time onto the shoulder, and then brakes hard enough to throw me forward against the dash. Unbuckled, I grunt as I'm tossed clear of my seat and flattened like a pancake against the glove box.

Levi climbs out of the driver's seat and hauls me up, dragging me to the back and tossing me onto the futon.

When I manage to roll and look up, his gaze is wilder than I've ever seen as he stares down at me.

"Are you insane?" he demands.

"I mean, yeah, probably. Kind of."

My answer seems to make worse whatever mental break I've just caused him to have. He leans down, nostrils flaring.

"I will not let you die, Mac, so stop fucking trying."

"The only thing I was trying to do was get away from you," I snap.

He doesn't answer.

"Oh, so you're the only one allowed to leave in this relationship?"

"What relationship?" he growls.

And the stab of hurt I feel at his words makes me lash out.

"I hate you," I spit.

He growls, grabbing my wrists and pinning them over my head. He's close now, his body pressing down against mine. "You can hate me all you want, Mac. But you will stop trying to get yourself killed, or you'll suffer the consequences."

It takes me a minute to respond, mostly because I'm too busy trying not to arch my hips into his. My nipples are a lost cause. They're already hard enough to cut glass, and I have a feeling he knows it.

Rather than continue to fight, I stop struggling and let my body relax. If it's a fight he wants, then surrender's going to really piss him off. Turning my head, I refuse to meet his eyes as I say quietly, "There's nothing you can do to me you haven't already done."

Levi's reaction isn't the victory I expect, though.

Instead of the insult I've braced for, he lets me go and turns around, balling his hands into fists and letting out a roar that comes from deep in his gut. A roar he's purposefully chosen not to aim at me. More like, he's aiming it at himself.

It jars me more than any retort I expected.

He seems tortured. And that doesn't make sense, not according to the uncaring asshole label I've given him. His emotional outburst makes me feel bad for him, and that's not an emotion I'm comfortable feeling.

I sit up and attempt a joke. A bad one. "We can go again, and this time you can jump from the moving vehicle."

He turns to me, not a shred of amusement on his pained face. He sits down beside me on the lumpy mattress.

"Mac, I know I've hurt you. Deeply. But you have to know that it hurts me too. If you can't trust me, trust your wolf. Trust our connection. I know you can feel the truth in that. What I did to you... it kills me. But it was the only way."

I don't pretend to understand his logic, but I'm done trying to argue it. At least for today.

"I didn't betray you," I say instead. "The mafia guys were there for me. It had nothing to do with you. And I'm sorry I got you tangled up in my problem."

"Why are they looking for you? What were you doing with Franco?"

I sigh. "My mom knows him. She asked him about the guy who hired the tracker to kill me."

His eyes darken. "Did she get a name?"

"Thiago."

Levi curses. His hands fist again, and I wait while he works to get control of himself. I can't understand why he's so angry about the idea of someone else trying to hurt me, but every time I ask, his answer gets more cryptic, so I leave it alone.

"What are you going to do?" he asks.

"My mom wants to go after Thiago directly."

"Don't you?" he asks.

"I want to save Kari. She's what matters to me."

"You think your mom's method will endanger Kari."

"I do."

"And the mafia?" he asks finally.

"She asked them to babysit me while she 'handles things.' I may have run off before they could lock me up."

He snickers. "They underestimated your stubbornness."

I decide to let that be a compliment. "Anyway, it had nothing to do with you or Jadick. Thanks for helping me get away from them, though."

I look away before he can see my true intentions for coming with him. But Levi's not an idiot, unfortunately for me.

"I'm not going back, Mac."

I let my desperation leak into my eyes as I look up at him. "Not even for Kari?"

"Kari's not safer with me dead," he says. "And we both know that's exactly what will happen if you turn me over to Thiago. I'd wager he'll kill you too when he's done with me."

"None of that would happen if Jadick goes with us," I say.

But Levi shakes his head. "Jadick's more at risk than either of us. Why do you think he went underground in the first place?"

"I get it. Thiago wants to clear out the competition and place himself on a throne of his own making. But if we all work together—"

"I won't ask Jadick to give himself up or put himself at risk for me."

"Kari's his sister. At least, give him the option to decide for himself."

He doesn't answer, and I bite back a slew of curses all aimed at him. There's something else going on, something he's not sharing. Otherwise, none of this makes sense.

"I'm asking for your help," I say, my words sharp.

He arches a brow. "Since when does Mac Quinn need anyone's help?"

I blow out a breath.

"You're not some damsel in distress," he adds. "And I know you too well for you to make me think you are."

"I'm not a monster either," I say, accusation dripping from my words. "Kari's life matters. Even with whatever secret plans you're cooking up, you can't just ignore her in all this. She's innocent."

He hesitates, and I wonder if he's actually thinking all this over or just pretending to.

"If I don't agree, you'll just keep hunting me, won't you?"

I smile sweetly. "Never give up on your dreams. You taught me that."

He could have punched me in the face, and I would have been less shocked than the response he gives me now.

He closes the distance, his mouth covering mine, and every nerve in my body ignites. His kiss is hungry. Like he's starving and I'm the last meal on Earth. His hands grab me, taking, claiming—like he already knows I'm his. And dammit if I don't kiss him back like he's right.

When his tongue brushes mine, I sink into the abyss where all my deepest wants are stored, every one of them named Levi Wild. There's no sense of logic or even time. Only Levi's mouth and hands —and the fact that we aren't naked yet.

A sob breaks loose from my throat, mortifying me the second I hear it. I break the kiss, chest heaving, eyes watering—and I don't know who I hate more. Him or what he's done to me. I can't even enjoy the thing I've spent three years dreaming of.

Levi's ruined me for everyone—even himself.

"I can't..." I say, my voice cracking. "Not like this. Not when... we're still on opposite sides."

Not when you still don't want me in the way that matters.

Instead of backing off, he leans in. His hand cups the back of my neck, and he presses his forehead to mine so I'm forced to shut my eyes or meet his so closely I can read his thoughts.

"Mac, I'm so sorry for all this. And for what's to come. I will never—"

"What's to come?"

I wrench away, staring at him warily. My fingers tingle where they touched his bared throat a moment ago. Every inch of me is still hot, but my brain is struggling to warn me through the fog of my own lust—and it's screaming now.

At the look in his eyes. At the way he shifts closer. Again.

Like he's trying awfully hard to distract me.

"There are things in motion." His fingers stroke my hair. "So much of this began long before you walked into that warehouse. If I could go back and change it—"

"You'd what?"

His eyes are steady on me. Too steady.

Too full of secrets.

Another sob builds. Because whatever this is, it isn't a reconciliation.

The back door of the van is torn open at the same moment the sliding door slams ajar. Both openings reveal men in ski masks. Their scents hit me—a dozen wolves, none of them Black Moon pack.

I jump to my feet. My adrenaline spikes, and my instincts scream at me to do whatever it takes to get away. The logical side of me knows it's already too late.

The thug at the back door reaches for me. I pull my leg back and slam my heel into his nose. He cries out, stumbling back. Hands shove at me from behind, and I career forward. Giving in to the momentum, I jump out of the van, determined to get free of this corner they've backed us into. But another attacker takes his place, and instead of landing on the ground, I'm plucked out of the air by a vise-like grip. Unfamiliar arms come around me, locking against my torso, bruising my ribs.

I scream, twisting my body in a corkscrew motion in an attempt to wriggle loose. But these guys are professionals. Another one grabs my ankles, neutralizing that particular threat.

When I twist again, I catch sight of Levi exiting the truck, and my heart literally stops beating for long enough that I think I might actually be dead.

If I am, this is Hell.

Because he's not fighting, and he's not being attacked.

In fact, he hops out of the van with an expression that might have shattered my heart had he not done that very thing to it already.

Levi doesn't look at me. That, more than anything, confirms my fears.

"You're late," Levi tells them.

"You missed the rendezvous point by three miles," one of the men snaps. He's the one I kicked in the nose, and I'm rewarded now by the sight of blood pouring from his face and dripping off his chin. "You might have mentioned she'd put up a fight."

"If you'd been on time, she wouldn't have," Levi says.

I stop struggling. The shock of awareness literally paralyzes me.

It's not the fact that he's just out-maneuvered me that's breaking me down. It's the realization that those stolen moments on the futon were all part of his plan to distract me from this.

He set me up.

"Load her up," Levi says, and the two men holding me like a sack of potatoes begin carrying me toward another van parked behind ours.

This one's newer, sleeker. Black with tinted windows. It looks professional like his team. They wear matching dark uniforms, and every one of them moves unlike any thugs-for-hire I've ever encountered.

Something tells me if they get me in that van, it's all over.

I start fighting again, redoubling my efforts. I probably look insane with the crazy-ass way I'm corkscrewing around, but it's the only way I know to break their grip.

It doesn't work.

They get me to the van and toss me in like garbage.

A hand reaches for me, and I catch it with my teeth, biting until I taste blood. The man barks out a curse, and I let him go, spitting his blood on the van's scratchy carpet.

"She's fucking rabid, boss," one of the goons complains.

"Tie her up," Levi says in a voice devoid of any emotion.

It takes three of them to hold me down while one zip ties my wrists and another my ankles. I curse them all using an old Cajun phrase I picked up from one of my mom's marks. The guy rears back, eyes wide through the ski mask he wears.

"What the hell'd you just say?" he demands warily.

"You'll find out in six months," I say sweetly.

He pulls his hand back like he's going to hit me. Before he can, someone else reaches over and presses tape across my mouth.

Assholes, I scream with my eyes.

"That's better," the guy with the tape grunts, eyes narrowed as he backs away.

When they're done, they secure me to a metal rack mounted to the van's interior. Then they slam the door shut.

Outside, I can still hear their muffled voices.

"What is the damned point of all this?" one of the men asks. "If she's this big of a threat, we shouldn't bring her back."

"She's a liability if left alone," Levi says.

"Then fucking kill her, and be done with it." Pretty sure that's the guy with the busted nose. Asshole.

Rather than answering him with words, there's a grunt and then a thud.

Everyone else goes silent for a long moment.

"Get him up and in the other van," Levi says. "Burnett, you take him and your team. Gregario, you're with me. You have your orders. Follow them. And don't question me again."

There's a chorus of "yes, sirs" and then boots on gravel as everyone moves away. Up front, the van doors open, and Levi and another masked asshole get in. The masked asshole drives. Levi doesn't bother to look back at me as we pull onto the road and head for wherever the fuck they're taking me.

I don't know what Levi's up to, but it's clear he isn't who I thought he was.

Not even close.

Levi's the monster here. And I'm officially the thing I've spent my entire life trying to avoid: I'm the damsel in distress.

CHAPTER 11

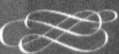

I wake up tied to a chair in a dark room that smells like
Levi, and I decide right away that, no matter how much
they torture me, the scent will be the worst part of this entire
experience.

Pine and spice fill my nostrils, stronger with every inhale.

It's Levi—and he's everywhere.

For a wild moment, I let myself wonder if they aren't piping it in
through a vent somewhere as part of some psychological torture
method.

The air is damp, and beneath the scent of my scorned mate is the
unmistakable musk of raw earth. I'm underground. Or close to it.

No windows.

And the zip ties around my wrists and ankles have been refas-
tened even tighter than before.

At least, they removed the duct tape.

The fact that I slept through it being ripped off worries me more
than anything else. Drugs. Somewhere along the way, I've obviously
been dosed. The last thing I remember is being tossed into the back
of a van and then—nothing. I search within and am relieved to find

my wolf still here. They haven't muted her, which gives me a shred of hope.

A hope that dulls with every new thought.

My mother has gone to kill Thiago. If she succeeds, Kari might die too. And I'm stuck in this underground room, forgotten, while the world burns down around me.

No one knows where I am. Not my mother. Not Tripp. And the list of people who might care, much less rescue me, starts and ends with those two people.

Levi claimed not to want to see me hurt, but clearly that's only because he was saving the job for himself.

My hope deflates like a popped balloon.

I'm so fucking screwed.

I HAVE no idea how long I sit in the darkness, only that it's long enough to make friends with the shadows. When the door opens, I'm not relieved, though. Especially when I see that it's Levi himself framed in the dimly lit opening. The sight of him jolts me—a thousand points of pain that prick all the way to my soul. Or what's left of it. After rejecting me, I thought his betrayal couldn't cut any deeper. I was wrong.

"You're awake." His voice is carefully controlled.

Mine, not so much. "Fuck. You."

He ignores me and turns to someone behind him. "Bring it in."

Another figure enters. One of his security team. Using the light coming in from the room beyond, I recognize his scent from their snatch-and-grab back on the highway. Not the one whose nose I broke, but there's still time.

The guy wheels a small cart into the room and parks it near the wall, still just out of my reach. If my arms weren't bound, that is. As it is, there's no way I can reach either of them, no matter how close they stand. I know. I've tried. And I have the bloodied wrists to prove it.

The guard leaves without a word.

Levi remains.

The door shuts, sealing us both into complete darkness.

A second later, a light clicks on, and I look over in time to see a small switch on the wall near the cart. Then I'm forced to look away, blinking furiously until my eyes adjust to the sudden brightness.

Levi grabs a foldable chair from near the door and opens it.

He sits, facing me several feet away from my own chair.

His eyes are steady on mine. Assessing.

"Whatever you're going to do to me, just fucking do it," I snap.

"What do you think I'm going to do?"

"Besides kidnap me and tie me up? I don't know. Torture. Kill. Whatever you want."

At the last part, something in his eyes flares. A hunger that sends heat curling low in my belly. I bite my lip. Maybe "whatever he wants" is a little suggestive, but if his goal is torture, taking me while I'm unable to touch him in return would definitely top that list.

As soon as I have the thought, I curse myself and shove it away again. Now is not the time to want him. Now is the time to hate him. Or better yet, kick his ass and get myself the fuck out of his presence.

He blinks, and that hunger is gone.

"I don't want to do any of this, Mac. But you left me no choice."

"Excuse me? Are we victim-blaming now? How in the hell is any of this my fault?"

"You hunted me," he says as if that somehow negates him taking me prisoner.

"You framed me for murder."

Anguish flashes. Maybe even regret. Then, like the hunger, it's gone.

"You're in over your head," he says quietly. "If I hadn't brought you here, you would have gotten us both killed."

"Brought me here?" I scoff. "You mean abducted me. Say the words, asshole."

His expression tightens. "If I untie you, will you run?"

"Of course not." I snort, and he relaxes. "I'll kick your ass, kill you, then I'll run, dragging your dead body along behind me to deliver to Thiago."

He shakes his head. "You still think he'll let Kari go if you bring me in."

He doesn't say it like a question.

More like I'm the idiot if I say yes.

Seething, I refuse to answer at all.

"He's using you, Mac. All he cares about is power. He has a little taste of it now. And he knows he has to eliminate the rest of his family to keep it."

"You'll say anything to save your own ass. You've already made it clear you don't care about Kari. Or me."

The tic in his jaw lets me know I've pushed him too far. He stands with enough force to send the chair toppling behind him. Then he closes the distance, grabbing the back of my chair and leaning down so that we're eye to eye.

"You have no idea who or what I care about. I've tried to tell you, but it's like you don't hear me. What the hell do I have to do to convince you?"

It's like my eyeballs detach from my brain. I drop my gaze to his mouth—just for an instant, but it's more than enough. Levi lets out a growl, and I gasp as his mouth crashes against my own.

My arms strain against the bindings. All I want is to get closer. Logically, I know I should use this opportunity to knee him in the dick, but the only thing I want to touch his cock with right now is my hand or my mouth. I arch into him, pressing my breasts against his chest. Scraping my nipples across the fabric of his shirt.

The friction is delicious. But I want more.

His tongue sweeps into my mouth, plundering.

Levi is taking exactly what he wants, and I can't bring myself to resist—because it's what I want too.

My teeth snag his bottom lip, biting down softly, and he groans.

I whimper, desperate for whatever he'll give me, and his body stiffens.

Instead of deepening the kiss, he pulls back. His chest heaves with labored breaths. The look in his eyes is pure, primal hunger.

I look back at him, uncaring that I've let my guard all the way down. He already has my heart at his beck and call; why not take my body too?

Whatever he sees in my eyes, it's not enough though.

He inches back a little more and exhales heavily.

"Focus on this moment, right here," he whispers, desperation replacing desire. "If you don't believe my words, believe this," he adds, his gaze dropping to my lips then flicking up again to search my glazed eyes. "I will protect you until the day I die, even if it means protecting you from yourself."

My temper stirs.

Desire cools.

This asshole just kissed me to prove a point.

Fine, two can play at that game.

I go with Plan B, driving my knee up and into his groin.

It doesn't quite pack the force I'm capable of, thanks to the bindings trapping my ankles, but it's enough. He doubles over but, unfortunately, recovers quickly. When he straightens, his glare is unyielding.

"If you don't believe my words, believe this," I say, throwing his words back into his face. "I hate you so much more than you seem to hate yourself."

His nostrils flare. "You're stubborn as fucking hell, you know that?"

"And you're a monster."

"You know nothing about what I am. Not anymore."

"You're right. Because you don't tell me shit. You run around with missing alpha-heirs and play ninja all day while everyone else pays the price. What else am I supposed to think?"

When he starts to answer, I cut him off. "You can't kiss your way out of an explanation," I add. "I'm not a man. I can think and have an orgasm all at the same time."

The faintest hint of a smile quirks his lips. "I'll keep that in mind. Though it might be difficult to achieve the latter without the use of your hands—or mine."

Before I can think of something snappy to say, he stalks out.

IT'S NOT long before I realize Levi's torture hasn't ended simply because he left the room. In the silence, I'm forced to acknowledge the presence of the food cart he left behind. The scents coming from it are making it impossible to forget how empty my stomach is. That plate of mafia spaghetti is only a memory, and whatever's hiding underneath the tray cover promises to make me forget it altogether.

But Levi doesn't return.

I get impatient. Then I get hangry.

Using my weight against the chair, I sort of hop my way over to the cart. If there are cameras on me, whoever's watching doesn't seem to mind if I help myself.

Fine.

I don't need Levi anyway.

Using my teeth, I pick up the tin cover and let it fall onto the hard floor. It crashes loudly, but still, no one interrupts. I stare down at the plate of lasagna and then let loose with a string of curses—every single one of them a creative alternative to Levi's given name.

Of course, he left me with no fork, no hands, and the only food I can't easily eat without them.

My stomach rumbles, and I seriously debate face planting into the thick pasta, manners be damned.

From the other side of the door, I hear voices. They don't belong to Levi, which means they must be his security team. My wolf hearing picks up just enough to concern me.

"...contain her."

"Levi tried. Clearly, she's not going to cooperate."

"She's a threat to the whole community."

"Drugging her is the only solution."

I look down at the lasagna with a new concern.

Fuck this.

I refuse to go easily, no matter how much of a monster Levi is to me.

Lifting my bound feet, I pull them in and then kick them both out, sending the tray careening backward. It topples over, crashing hard. The dishes break, and the echo of the destruction shatters the silence of my cell.

The door opens, and three guards race into the room.

They stop and take in the fallen cart and broken dishes. Then they each narrow their eyes on me.

"Rude," one of them says, which throws me off only because it's so much more civilized than the response I expected from them.

"Minnie spent a lot of time on that lasagna," says another.

Like it's an accusation.

Like I'm the bad guy here.

"I'm sorry. Where are my manners?" I say lightly then narrow my eyes as I add, "I must have left them behind when you abducted me from the side of the road."

One of the men growls. "You don't want to eat," he says. "Fine."

Instead of coming to kick my ass, he motions to his friends, and they all three walk out again. The door shuts. The lock clicks. And I'm once again alone.

This time with drug-laced lasagna all over the floor. Still, it's better than having it inside me.

I tell myself I won. Or this round at least. But the longer I sit alone in this room, the less I believe it. My hands and feet have long since gone numb yet somehow still ache. Other than that and the fact that I have to pee so badly I might not make it to a bathroom, the only torture happening now is self-inflicted. Over and over, I replay every moment since the one where Levi left me in that ware-house with a dead alpha.

The fact is that I never actually saw him commit that crime. And if I'd been a little less hung up on how hot he is and what a sucker I apparently am for rejection and abandonment, I might have gotten out of there in time too.

Instead, Thiago found me—and used me.

He never cared about justice for Crigger. He cares only for holding onto the power he finally has. Kari's the real victim in all this. Not me.

And I can either keep finding reasons to pick a fight with Levi. Or I can find a way to free her. But first, I have to free myself.

CHAPTER 12

I drift off, pulled under by exhaustion despite the discomfort of my position. No one returns. Not with food or even water. At first, it feels like a mind game. To show me who's boss. To make me compliant. But then I begin to wonder if they've forgotten about me altogether. Time feels unmeasurable in the dark silence. But I suspect at least a day goes by. Maybe two. My wolf begins to push back at being confined so long, but I don't shift. To do so would use the last of my strength, and I can't be sure the bindings on my wrists and ankles would actually break. They haven't yet despite my attempts. If they don't give during my shift, my legs will break, and that will be that.

Finally, the door opens, and Levi walks in.

Despite my exhaustion, my body reacts. A magnet being pulled to its opposite pole. Even dehydrated, starving, and numb, I can't help wanting him. It's science, not sentiment.

Or that's what I tell myself.

Words feel heavy. The idea of trading barbs is an energy I can't afford at this point. So I remain silent as he strides toward me.

Bracing for whatever abuse he wants to fling at me this time, I am in no way prepared for when he kneels, looks right into my eyes, and says, "I'm sorry."

What?

He produces a knife, and I flinch. He stops, gesturing to the ties that are now embedded against my wrists where they've cut through layers of skin. He brings the knife up and uses it to slice through my bindings. First, my wrists, then my ankles.

I'm too shocked at his apology and suddenly being freed to even use that freedom to fight him. Besides, my limbs are jelly, my circulation nonexistent. The moment I put weight on my feet and attempt to stand, my knees buckle, and I topple forward.

"Whoa." Levi catches me, his strong arms pushing me upright again. "Go slow," he says.

I stare at him in confusion, very aware of where his hands are still gripping my arms—and how nice it feels.

"I went through this in training. I remember how long it took to get proper feeling back into my legs."

"Huh?"

"You look confused," he says uncertainly. "I just meant... I know how you feel because of the training exercises I've done with the team..."

That's not why I'm confused. But I don't bother to contradict him.

Instead, I use the brain power I have left to confirm the suspicions that have been nagging me for days.

"Where are we?" I ask.

He hesitates. "In the mountains."

Something tells me this place matters.

I try a different tactic.

"You're in charge here."

"Yes. No. Sort of." He ducks his head, and I can't quite reconcile a humble Levi with the asshole who locked me up and basically tortured me. "Whoa." He catches me again and waits while I re-steady myself. It's slow going, and Levi seems more and more upset with my condition.

"Didn't they feed you?"

My gaze flicks to where I remember kicking over the lasagna. It's gone, the space clear of any evidence a food cart had ever been there at all.

Levi waits for an answer. I look up at him through the tangled hair in my eyes, too confused and dizzy to be upset. Playing games isn't even an option right now.

"No."

"Come on," he says, gripping my waist and hauling me to my feet.

Our closeness jumbles my thoughts again. We're hip-to-hip, which isn't exactly the most sexual of positions, but all I can think about is his hands gripping my hips, his body fitted against my own.

We take one step together, and I see stars.

Levi catches me even before I realize I've begun to collapse.

My head swims. Lack of sleep, lack of food—lack of a lot of things—makes it hard to think clearly. Maybe he was on to something leaving me alone so long.

In this moment, I'm too beaten to deny that he's won this round.

"I'm so fucking sorry for leaving you here this long. It shouldn't have happened, but there was an emergency I had to deal with, and I left—" He breaks off, calling out for one of his guys. "Burnett. Get in here."

A redheaded male in dark blue military fatigues appears in the doorway.

"Get her some water," Levi instructs him. "And something to eat. Now."

"Sure."

The guy disappears, spurred on by Levi's urgent tone.

He's not one of the trio from the lasagna incident, which gives me hope he'll actually do as he's asked.

"Come on." Levi grips me tighter and begins moving me slowly toward the door.

I don't resist. I don't even think I could if I wanted to. It's not just the physical aspect, either. His kindness, the apology, it's too weird.

Like I've entered some alternative universe that only exists inside this room.

We make it out the door and into the adjoining room, this one larger. It no longer smells like dirt. Instead, the scent of pine and spice slams into me. It makes my eyes water, and I chalk it up to nearly dying of hunger and thirst. But this smell, it makes me thirsty in a different way.

I notice a bed in the corner. It's nothing more than a mattress on the floor. And it's literally the only piece of furniture in the room. Beside it, a short stack of clothes is folded neatly on a concrete floor.

Levi turns me away from the mattress and helps me across the room. He stops outside another door, this one leading into a small bathroom.

"I'll be right out here if you need help," he says.

"I think I'll manage."

I push the door shut behind me and hurriedly do my business. It's not a big deal in the grand scheme, but I'm pretty sure it's the best pee of my life. When I'm done, I survey myself in the mirror. Tangled, dirty blonde hair falls over my shoulders, framing a face I almost don't recognize. Dark circles ring my eyes, and my cheeks bear traces of the scratches from my fighting frenzy when they brought me in. But it's the hollow look I wear that makes me shudder at my own reflection.

I look like a shell of the badass, capable girl who set out on this journey. I look beaten.

Averting my gaze, I try to remind myself who I'm here for.

Kari.

Not a single soul on this planet is fighting for her besides me. I have to stay focused. And that means I can't afford to kick Levi's dick into his stomach. Not yet.

When I open the door again, Levi's waiting.

"Here." He shoves a bottle of water at me.

The seal hasn't been cracked yet, so I take it and twist it open, drinking until I can't breathe and nearly choke on it. The liquid is sweet relief to my parched throat, but I pace myself. It'll do me no good to throw it up again.

Levi's security guy returns. Burnett. He holds out a protein bar. "Sorry, kitchen's closed, this is all I can find."

Levi frowns and starts to object but, I snatch it away. "It's perfect."

And still sealed.

I peel the wrapper back and break off a huge bite.

"Why wasn't she fed?" Levi demands.

"Grey was in charge of it," Burnett says with a shrug.

"Tell him to meet me after his shift," Levi snaps.

"You got it."

Burnett walks out, and we're left alone again.

I stand there and scarf down the entire bar then finish off the water without breaking our silence. By the time I'm done, I am mildly convinced I can walk unassisted. My feet and legs are tingling with the feeling of blood returning. My hands work well enough.

Still, Levi actually looks … sorry. Or something close to it.

"How long have I been in there?" I ask.

He hesitates. "Two days, give or take."

Two days.

Damn.

No wonder I'm coming apart at the seams. My mother trained me for all manner of fighting—offense, defense, and everything in between. But I've never trained for a scenario like this one. Capture. Torture. And the fact that Levi's my captor… I have no idea what to do or say next.

But he's watching me like it's my move.

"What's the matter with you?" I ask.

"What do you mean?"

"I don't know. You're being…weird. Apologizing, bringing me water, food."

He chuckles darkly. "You mean nice?"

"You kidnapped me and kept me in a locked room for two days without food or water. Let's not get carried away."

He sighs. "Look, I had to do something drastic to—"

"Don't say you're keeping me safe."

"All right." He gestures to the door Burnett left through, and, I suspect, whatever lies beyond. "I'm also protecting the people in this community."

I glance around what looks like a fallout shelter. "What community?"

He hesitates, clearly debating whether he can trust me. I don't give him any false hope, but finally, he nods anyway. "Come on. I want to show you something."

He leads me down a series of short hallways. We don't pass anyone else, but I can hear voices somewhere nearby. The building is squat with low ceilings and very few windows. "Compound" feels like a fitting word. It has a military feel with function prioritized over comfort.

But it's not cold or even dangerous.

Not like Thiago's house.

Maybe I've been left alone too long because I should feel endangered by a place that held me against my will, but more than anything, I just want to understand. What makes this place special enough that Levi would lock me away just to keep it safe?

And why in the hell does he think I'm a threat to it in the first place?

"What's this?" I ask as we pass a hall and I hear music drifting out from an open door.

Children's songs.

"A few of the families that live here have little ones," he says and then tugs me forward.

Children?

Families?

What the hell is this place?

We keep moving, and Levi quietly points out a few more areas.

"Rec room," he says, and I glimpse a ping pong table and video game console through the glass doors. "Gym, laundry, showers."

Community, the men had called it.

I see that now.

Up ahead, the hum of voices grows steadily louder until Levi stops me in front of a set of wide double doors. A security guard stands beside them.

"Sir," he says when he sees me. "Is this wise?"

"She's fine, Grey. No thanks to you."

"Sir?"

"We'll talk about it later," Levi says. "Move."

With a glare aimed at me, the guy pulls the door open, letting us pass.

As soon as I walk in, I stop and sweep the large room with wide eyes. My senses tell me there are at least forty, maybe fifty people seated around the long rectangular tables. A few are still finishing whatever dinner remains on their tray, but most have finished and are chatting with their neighbors.

The smell of food draws my attention, and I see a kitchen running along the right side of the room. True to the guard's word, it's closed now. The lights are dark up front near the serving stations.

A cafeteria.

And a crowd.

Every one of them is a wolf shifter.

Most are dressed in the same fatigues as Burnett.

Out of all the things Levi could have been hiding from me, an entire army of shifters under his command was the last thing I would have guessed.

Finally, I turn to look at where he's waiting at my elbow. He's watching me with an eagerness that looks disturbingly like hope. I don't understand it. Or him. Or any of this.

"Who are these people?" I ask.

He nods at the crowd. "This is my pack."

"Your...."

I can't even say the word. It's too busy punching me in the gut. The word "pack" suggests a bond closer than family. Closer than, in this case, a mate. And it stings even though it shouldn't.

"Your pack," I manage through gritted teeth.

He nods. "Mac, meet the Jades."

Another sucker-punch.

The Jades.

Not *a* Jade.

There is no girl he's running off to be with instead of me. I should feel relieved at the misplaced jealousy I felt back at that hotel. But I don't.

Somehow, I think this is worse.

Instead of one girl, he's traded me for a whole new family. He's truly moved on with his life, and the evidence is staring back at me, reflected in every face in this room.

CHAPTER 13

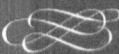

My eyes widen as I look out over the sea of faces. They've begun to notice me now too. Slowly and then all at once, conversation begins to quiet until the entire room goes silent and they're all staring back at me with some sort of expectation I already know I can't meet. Or don't want to.

"Everyone, this is Mac Quinn," Levi says. "Mac, this is everyone."

No one speaks.

"They're staring," I say to Levi.

"They heard you were hunting me," he says.

I whip my gaze to his. "You told your entire pack?"

He shrugs. "Our bond runs pretty deep. I couldn't keep it from them. Not when there was danger."

Their bond.

The words are a knife twisting slowly.

I stare back at every one of their curious faces, resentment simmering in my blood. It's not their fault Levi used them to hurt me. But they're going to feel the consequences. I couldn't reject him three years ago, but I can reject his people now.

"What are you looking at?" I demand of a woman closest to where I stand.

At my harsh words, she ducks her head and turns around.

Levi stiffens, but he doesn't comment.

Slowly, conversation resumes around us, but I can feel their edginess. Like they expect me to attack Levi right here in front of them.

I arch a brow at him. "You must think I'm dangerous if it means warning your pack about me—and locking me up to keep them safe."

But instead of hurling an insult or a threat, he grins, and my knees nearly buckle at the sight of it. After only a slight wobble on my part—and honestly, it's a miracle I don't crumple—Levi's grin turns to a smirk.

"Mac, you have no idea what kind of danger you put me in."

Something about the way he says the words makes me wonder if we're still talking about the fact that I want to trap his ass and then turn him over to our enemy.

"This must be the infamous Mac."

I look over as a woman I've never seen before strides up with two male guards close at her heels. One of them is the redhead from earlier, Burnett. I recognize the other male from the van-grab. The one who managed to wrestle me into submission. My expression tightens at the sight of him, but I force myself to focus on the woman who obviously outranks the two men, judging by their formation behind her. Her gray-blonde hair is cropped short and combed back to reveal a pair of steel-blue eyes that don't waver from my own. Her uniform is less "military" and more "manager" with black pants and a matching jacket. But her posture and stance don't fool me.

This chick can fight.

And she dares anyone to make her prove it.

"And you are?" I say, not in the mood for bull shit power plays.

"Frankie Dyer."

She doesn't offer any other greeting than her name.

Fine by me.

I don't bother to reply.

"Frankie," Levi prompts because she's clearly come with a message. When the woman hesitates, he adds, "You can speak freely here."

She doesn't look particularly agreeable to that idea, but she does it anyway. "The teams are on their way in now." Her gaze flicks to me. "Where should I have them debrief?"

"We'll meet them in the hangar," he says.

She looks even less thrilled about that, but she doesn't argue. When she walks off, her two shadows follow.

"She seems friendly," I joke.

"You want her trust, earn it."

His response is clipped.

I glare at him. "I don't want anyone's trust. I want to save my friend."

He hesitates as if putting aside whatever he really wanted to say. "Fair enough. First, don't you want to see what's in the hangar?"

I roll my eyes. "Sure. Hopefully, it's an armored vehicle I can use to run you over with and then make my escape."

"Without me?"

"Of course not. You're in the trunk in this scenario."

"Naturally."

He holds my stare, and for some reason, I have to make an effort not to smile. Asshole.

"Come on," he says, and this time when he leads me through the halls, I can at least feel my feet again.

"So, what team was she talking about?" I ask. He glances at me knowingly. "What? Just trying to make conversation."

"No, you're trying to gather intel while also counting doors and mapping exits." He points at a door before I can argue and says, "Let me help. That one leads to the roof."

"I wasn't—"

"And that one leads to the basement."

"You're an ass—"

"Oh, don't forget the janitor's closet."

I shove hard, slamming him into the closet door hard enough for his head to make a loud *thump*. He grunts at the impact, and I use the element of surprise to land a punch in his gut.

"I'm done playing house," I hiss. "You're coming with me. To end this."

He doubles over, but his recovery is faster than I anticipated.

Before I can bring him fully down, he's straightening and shoving me off him. He grabs my shoulders, twisting me toward the wall, and slamming my shoulders against it.

I struggle, but his grip is too tight to shake.

His eyes are like granite as he stares down at me. His chest rises and falls with labored breaths.

"Last warning, Mac. Try that again and I'll lock you up for a lot longer than two days."

I bite back the urge to scream at him. He's beaten me more times than I want to admit. But worse than the injury to my pride is the threat it poses to my friend.

"My mother is out there," I say, my voice cracking as my control finally slips. I am near tears, but I can't bring myself to care. There's no pride left in me where Levi's concerned. He stripped that away from me a long time ago. "If she kills Thiago, he's given orders to do the same to Kari. If that happens, it will be on you."

"Don't worry about your mother," he says. His voice is rough, clearly unmoved by my emotional display. Asshole. "And stop being rude to the people here. They've done nothing to you."

He steps back, releasing his hold on me, and I nearly crumple. My sense of urgency wars with the cold reality that I will never accomplish my task in time to save Kari. My mother has never failed a mission yet, and I don't expect her to start now.

Resigned, I hang my head.

Levi motions for me to walk with him again, and after another ragged breath, I obey.

He begins pointing out doors again as if the past few minutes' interruption never even happened. If he's bothered that I've just tried attacking him on his home turf, he doesn't show it.

"Conference rooms," he says, gesturing to a closed door. "And this."

He pushes through and I follow.

On the other side, I find myself in a large open area with high ceilings and enough space to park at least a dozen vehicles comfortably. The left side of the hangar already holds four vehicles. A Range Rover, a couple of older sedans, and a motorcycle, but the right side is empty.

At the far end, the large bay door is wide open. From here, I have a straight, unhindered shot to the outside world. I can also hear the distinct hum of several vehicles approaching, which means I have a feeling I wouldn't get very far if I tried to run.

Then again, why would I do that when my target is standing six inches to my left?

"The hangar," I guess.

He nods toward the opening as the first of a convoy pulls in. "And the teams," he adds.

We stand back while they all park, six vehicles in total. Four are dark SUVs like the one Thiago used to banish me from pack lands. The other two are armored trucks similar to what I've seen banks use to transport money.

"So, what, you decided to start your own mafia pack or something?" I ask, trying to understand what the hell is going on here.

Levi shakes his head. "Not quite. Although, the mafia pack used to be part of a larger pack and then broke off on their own, so in that, we're similar."

I shoot him a look that undoubtedly conveys my confusion. "You started your own pack. You're in charge here... Does that mean you're alpha?"

"Something like that." His smug smile makes me want to punch him in the mouth. "Impressed?"

I roll my eyes, turning away, because, well, yeah.

Becoming an alpha is about a hell of a lot more than just finding people willing to become your pack. You have to fight for it. To bleed for it. Making an alpha takes more than most are capable of giving. To survive the process is a feat in itself. The fact that Levi's done it and lived to tell me about it? Yeah, that's impressive as hell.

But he clearly knows that and just wants to hear me say it.

Like hell.

"What is the point of bringing me here?" I ask. "To show off? You're an alpha. You have a pack. A security detail. Expensive cars. Whatever. You don't need to impress me; you need to outrun me."

He turns to me, something slippery in his gaze now. Like he has a secret. Or lots of them. "I don't want to impress you, Mac. If I did, we wouldn't have left the room where I kept you. In fact, I wouldn't have untied you either."

His words are unexpectedly erotic, and the desire that punches me in the gut steals my breath.

Levi leans in, knowing full well what he's doing to me now.

"You're not impressed by status, Mac. I know what impresses you, remember? Or have you forgotten what it was like to have my hands on you? My mouth?"

"We never…"

He's so close, his mouth brushes mine when he says, "Not yet."

I nearly lean in and give myself over to the promise in his voice. The sharp sound of a car door slamming brings me back to the present moment.

I gasp as Levi sidesteps me and goes to meet whoever is coming this way. Voices sound behind me.

I take another deep breath to steady myself, except the air is full of his scent, so all it does is threaten to choke me with desire. I force myself to turn anyway—to look unaffected by what's between us.

The teams climb out of their cars and shout hellos to one another, to Levi, their alpha. My gaze sweeps past the dozen or so men headed toward where Levi waits. I spot a familiar face among them.

Tripp.

His fatigues are dusty, caked with dirt. And he looks tired as hell. He offers a weak smile when he sees me, but the worry in his dark gaze is too pronounced to ignore.

Beside him is another face I recognize.

Jadick.

He's back, and his swagger is stronger than ever, unfortunately.

He looks directly at me, and in that stare is a complete disregard for anything other than his own agenda. When I don't immediately avert my gaze from his, he cocks his head at me. Curious. Interested. Clearly not used to anything but cowering.

What a jerk.

Behind them, one last car door slams shut, and a lone female figure catches my eye. Her gait is hurried though it's not purpose or concern that has her cutting a quick path through the others and straight toward me.

No, this is anger, pure and cutting.

Vicki Quinn glares at me with all the fire she possesses. Her hair is mussed, and there's dried blood on her cheek, but otherwise, she looks unharmed. I'm shocked to realize I was actually worried about her.

Then I look around for anyone else they've brought.

But Kari isn't here, and for a moment, I can barely breathe around my own fear. Has she done it then? Has my mother killed Thiago? Did Tripp and Jadick help? But if so, why would Jadick come back here? Something else must have happened. But I don't get a chance to ask what before my mother's temper spills over.

"You and I need to talk, young lady," she says to me.

For once, I don't care that she looks madder than a hornet and prepared to aim all that ire at me. I'm too relieved to see her here in one piece. And hopefully, Kari is too.

"Hi, Mom."

I can feel Levi's eyes on my back, but he doesn't interrupt this little reunion. He orchestrated it after all. Instead, he stands a safe distance away, chatting with his men. With Jadick.

"Don't 'hi, Mom' me," she snaps. "You called me in to your little friends before I could complete the mission. What the hell, Mac?"

Relief hits first. Thiago's alive, and that means Kari is too. Then I frown, glancing at Levi then Tripp, who's standing on my left, far enough out of the line of fire.

"I didn't call you in," I tell her.

"If you didn't, then who did?" she demands.

Silence rings out across the hangar.

My mother's sharp gaze cuts to Tripp.

He looks a little nervous as he says, "Levi ordered your extraction. What was I supposed to do?"

Her eyes widen, and she pushes past me, marching toward Levi. I hurry to catch up, not quite sure where this is headed. My mother never quite warmed up to Levi, and now? I'm pretty sure all sorts of retribution are on the table.

"You ordered my extraction?" she demands. "Before I could put an end to that little shitbrick?"

"It was a hasty move, Vicki. One we can't afford at this stage, you know that."

"Mom, listen, I—"

"Hasty? Are you kidding me?" She jerks her thumb at me as she goes off. "You brought *her* here and are letting her walk around like she's one of us, and you're questioning *my* decisions?"

I flinch as if she slapped me.

Us?

Levi doesn't answer, but his face reddens. I can't tell if he's embarrassed or angry, but at this point, it doesn't even matter. I can barely form words around the brick pressing down on my chest.

"You know about this place?" I ask.

My voice is small. I hate it, but I can't help it any more than I can help change what they've clearly already done behind my back.

"Of course I know," my mother scoffs like it should be obvious.

I take one look at their faces—Levi, Tripp, even Jadick—and in this moment, it *is* obvious. They've all been working from a master playbook and never bothered to give me a copy. Or even tell me, we were playing a game.

I look away from my mother. From Tripp. And I don't even

attempt to look at Levi. Every face I see is someone else who has or will betray me.

It's disgusting.

I back away.

"Hey. Wait."

When Tripp reaches for me, I jerk away from him.

"Mac, don't be dramatic," my mother says, and it's the last thing I hear before I turn and run.

CHAPTER 14

Outside the hangar doors, the land is barren and empty. Far off, the horizon is dotted with purple mountains, but here, there is a valley's worth of dead grass and dirt for what looks like miles. Overhead, clouds mute the daylight, washing the sky in hazy gray.

I have no idea where I am—or where I'm going—but it's not enough of a reason to stop. Not after the betrayal of everyone I know waiting behind me. My wolf rises to the surface, carrying me faster over the hardened ground.

I push, pumping my arms, lengthening my strides.

My bones begin to creak, and I'm only a breath away from shifting when I sense someone coming up on my flank. My first instinct is to turn and fight. Even if it's Levi. Hell, especially if it's him. But then his scent hits me, and I'm too surprised to do anything but maintain my pace. Out of everyone who might have followed and attempted to coax me back, he is the last one I expected.

He matches me easily, his even strides putting us shoulder to shoulder. Instead of trying to stop me, he continues to run alongside me.

I look over.

Jadick looks back.

I debate shifting, trying to run for it, but what just happened back there has stolen my drive. Or maybe it's our "kidnapped" alpha heir running quietly at my hip.

Ugh.

I stop, chest heaving, lungs burning, and face him.

He stops too, but I see none of the frustration in his gaze that I know is in mine. Only curiosity. As if he's wondering what I'll do next. Although, I get the sense he doesn't care either way.

"You're a coward," I say, glaring at him.

His brows lift. "I'm not the one running away from my problems. Literally."

"Aren't you?" I shoot back. "You're out here, hiding, while your entire pack thinks you've been kidnapped—or worse."

"Touché, little Quinn."

"Don't call me that."

"But it's your name."

"My name is Mac."

"Fair enough. Why are you angry, Mac?"

"Because they lied."

"Ah. Right." He looks like he understands, but then he blinks, and the confusion returns. "And why do you care what Levi does?"

"I don't."

His lips twitch. Asshole. "Of course."

Something about his smug, know-it-all expression forces an explanation out that I don't even want to verbalize. Not to him. "My mother has controlled my entire life. Making me into some version of her while still making all of my choices for me. When she decided killing your brother suited her, there was no changing her mind. She actually tried handing me to the mafia for safekeeping." I put the word into air quotes. "And now I find out she's been in on Levi's little secret life this entire time? It's infuriating. If he doesn't want me in his life, he doesn't need her either."

"You care an awful lot about who he has in his life, considering you want to let my brother kill him."

His words grate on me, and I bare my teeth. "You know nothing about what I want."

He holds up his hands in surrender. "I'm just trying to understand. To help."

"If you want to help, go home, and knock your brother off his throne."

"Actually, I plan to do just that." His eyes glint, and I recognize his manipulation—but I'm too invested in what he's just said to care.

"You do?"

"Yes, and I don't mean to sound callous about your very real predicament, Mac—" He emphasizes the use of my actual name this time—"But I'm not out here to chat about your broken heart."

I bite back the urge to deny his accusation.

"Then why are you here?"

"Because I could use your help."

"You want my help," I repeat uncertainly.

Not because I don't want to offer it. But I can't imagine how I might contribute to his plans. Without Levi or Crigger's murderer, I have nothing.

"May I voice an observation?"

I shrug. "Sure."

"You are a fighter, mostly because it's what you were trained for. And what you know. But more than that, you are a strategist. You see the bigger picture, and you assess. I'd wager you're constantly assessing, in fact. Risks, rewards, exit points."

"You seem to think highly of me, considering you barely know me."

"Knowing you and understanding you are two very different concepts, don't you agree?"

The way he speaks… like he sees me in a way no one else has—it throws me off balance.

"If you think I'm such a strategist, what's my strategy for leaving now?" I ask, trying to regain my footing.

"I don't think you're leaving at all."

"No?"

"If I hadn't come after you, Levi would have. Or Tripp. And even if they hadn't, it wouldn't have mattered anyway. Eventually, your emotions would clear, and you'd realize the only way forward is to go back."

I hate that he's right.

"I don't care what you think of me," I say. "What I care about is saving Kari. I promised, and that's not something I take lightly."

"I don't intend to stop you. Your loyalty is the precise quality that makes you so valuable."

"So you say." I hesitate, biting my lip while I do the exact thing he probably expects right now: strategizing. In the end, I give him what he wants, though. Because it can only help me get what I want too.

"What do you need me for?"

His grin is a slow, victorious thing. Like I've just fallen into the center of his web. "Come on, Mac. Walk with me."

He reaches over and slings an arm around my shoulders as if we've just become besties. Then he angles me back toward the hangar and starts walking.

I don't resist when he leads me back toward Levi's little camp. Mostly because I'm curious about Jadick's plan, but there's a part of me that needs to see this place for what it really is.

To understand.

Levi gave up everything, his home, his life, his mate—for this. A fresh start with people he clearly cared more about than he ever pretended to care for me. I need to know why. Even though I'm pretty sure whatever I learn is going to make me hate him—and myself—even more than I already do.

"Thiago has always been blinded by his own ego," Jadick says as we walk.

I snort. "Tell me something I don't know."

"All right. Did you know he had my mate killed?"

Sympathy tugs at me. "I heard. I'm so sorry."

"My brother has always seen me as his biggest threat. And he's spent his life punishing me for it. Unfortunately, he didn't limit his ire to just me."

"Kari," I say.

"Yes, and our parents."

"You think he killed your father."

"Don't you?"

"I have my suspicions," I say. "But what about your mother?"

"My mother's death is unexplained to this day. A rogue tracker found her in the woods, yet no contract existed for a payout of her death."

"Trackers don't work for free," I say darkly, thinking of the one Thiago sent after me.

"No," he said, "They don't. But it would have taken someone with great power to cover their tracks. My father's alpha power couldn't penetrate the tracker's mind during interrogation."

"I never even knew he tried."

"My family worked hard to keep these details secret. If word got out there was this much bloodshed among us, we'd become a target for others as well."

"I get it, but... if alpha power couldn't penetrate the interrogation, what does that mean? Thiago's just not that powerful," I say, shaking my head. "Sure, he has motive but not necessarily means."

"You're as smart as they say," he says.

"Why do you sound so surprised?"

He laughs, which seems a bit out of place given the topic of our conversation. But then, he's spent his life under the weight of Thiago's hatred. Maybe he's learned to live with it. "Not surprised. Delighted."

He winks, and I look away, uncomfortable. But Jadick goes on, clearly unbothered by my reaction.

"I am skeptical myself," he says. "Maybe my brother is more powerful than I gave him credit for."

"Or maybe he's working with someone," I say.

He gives me an appreciative look as if I've somehow impressed him again. "Maybe," he agrees.

"Is that why you ran?"

My words have a bit less bite this time around, but the accusation is still there. I can't help it.

"I left because he tried to have me killed. And I realized I was no longer sure I could trust the people around me not to help him. Thiago's not a kind person, but he's convincing when he wants to be."

They have that in common then.

"He'll promise you whatever you want to hear if it gets him what he wants," he adds.

I think of Kari. Of the deal I struck to bring Levi back to take her place.

And I remember Levi's warning to me. That Thiago never intends to let her go. Not while he considers her a threat to his position.

"Okay," I say, "All of this history is interesting, but it still doesn't explain what you plan to do to stop him or to rescue Kari. Not to mention why you need me."

We're nearly back inside the hangar now. Close enough that I can see Levi still waiting for us where I left him. My mother and the others are gone along with Tripp. I don't know whether to be pissed about that or grateful that he's given me space. He and I will have our own sort of showdown later. But for now, I keep my eyes on Levi as Jadick goes on.

"The Jades were created to stand in the way of stolen power," he says.

"An army to overthrow Thiago," I realize, looking around at the faces of the men and women working to unload vehicles or transport supplies. At his words, I see them all in a new light.

Maybe I don't resent them after all. Maybe we all want the same things.

"Levi thinks we need bigger numbers, but I disagree," he says as we make our way to where Levi waits for us.

"What do you think?" I ask.

Levi scowls as we come to a stop in front of him. Whatever he feels about my swift exit, it's not showing on his face now. Instead, he looks solely focused on Jadick and whatever master strategy he's about to lay out.

"Thiago's ego has always been his downfall," Jadick goes on. "He'll show his hand soon, and when he does, we'll prey on that weakness. Use it as leverage to draw him out. He'll sabotage himself. He always does."

"Uh, he's managed to bypass his own father and you as the heir. And he's current pack alpha," I say. "I'd say that looks less like self-sabotage and more like success."

Levi looks like he wants to agree.

Jadick shakes his head, not bothered by my doubt. "Thiago's always been too rash. Too quick to act. He doesn't think things through. Take Levi for example. Or me. Coming for us only made us fight back that much harder."

"I don't follow."

"Look around you. Thiago thinks he chased us off. Meanwhile, we've been building a haven and collecting everyone he's ever pissed off." He winks. "Trust me, taking Thiago down will be easy."

"It would be a hell of a lot easier if we had the numbers," Levi mutters darkly.

"You worry too much, brother. Do you not have faith in me?" Jadick asks, and I wonder how he can't see the irony of accusing Thiago of a big ego.

"What do you think it'll take if not an army?" I ask him.

He ticks them off one by one. "Cunning. Wit. Patience. And you."

"Me?"

"Thiago expects you to return with a murderer, doesn't he?" Jadick asks.

"Yes."

"You are the only one of us who can walk right through the front door without resistance. When you do, bull's eye."

"You want me to draw him out and then what? You'll shoot him from a rooftop or something?"

"You have a better idea?" he asks.

"No, but... the rules of the pack say you can't become alpha that way. You have to challenge him. Fight—"

"Times are changing, Mac. Aren't they, Levi?" He looks sharply from Levi and back to me. "You all want change so badly. I'm willing to do whatever it takes to get that change."

Levi says nothing.

"So, you want me to do your dirty work," I say.

"We all must play a role."

"And saving Kari," I say. "Who's role is that?"

"This is ridiculous," Levi says. "She's not an assassin for hire. I told you, this is what the Jades are for."

Jadick waves him off and smiles at me. "Think about it, Mac. You'd be a valuable addition to our cause." Before I can answer, he turns to Levi and claps him on the back. "I'm going to turn in, brother. See you both in the morning."

He strides away, disappearing through the door leading back into the compound.

Then he's gone. And I'm alone with the guy I came here to kidnap, who actually, it turned out, kidnapped me instead.

Levi looks at me with an expression I can't read. "You came back."

"Jadick's convincing that way."

Something angry flashes in his eyes.

"Kitchen's open again," he says. "For the crew just arriving."

I think about going back into that crowded cafeteria, facing those people who looked at me like they want to kill me.

"I'm good," I say. "Where's Tripp?"

"Probably still eating."

"And the others?"

"Everyone else has gone to bed."

Bed.

For some reason, I think of that mattress on the floor, and my face heats.

"I had a room made up for you," he adds, and I wonder if he's read my thoughts somehow.

"I'm not staying."

He cocks his head at me. "Aren't you?" When I don't answer, he adds, "What about Jadick's plan?"

"Jadick said a lot of words without actually telling me anything."

His brows lift. "You seemed into it."

"Jealous?"

"Should I be? You stuck around and listened to him in a way you never have with me."

"He didn't publicly reject me and then spend years working with my own mother behind my back to accomplish the very thing you promised we'd do together."

His eyes narrowed. "Is that how you see this?"

"How else should I see it?"

His voice rose. I'd finally shaken his control. Good. "You could try seeing me as something other than the villain of your fucking story."

"When you start *being* something else, I'll *see* something else."

His eyes narrow, and he grabs my arm, walking me backward toward the wall. Unlike earlier, I realize I have a choice. He's not forcing me. But I don't fight it. Or him.

My shoulders thud against the wall, and Levi crowds me, filling my personal space until I'm practically breathing him.

"I think about you every day," he whispers, his voice strained. "My wolf still wants you just the same as it did before. No." He closes his eyes slowly, inhaling me so deliberately it feels erotic, despite the fact that we aren't doing anything but standing here. "He wants you even more."

His voice is ragged. Raw. He's barely holding it together.

I can smell his lust just like I know he can smell mine.

"I did all of this for you," he says.

"Bull shit," I whisper, and his narrowed eyes register hurt at my response. I'm too shocked at seeing it there—at knowing I caused it in the first place—to continue my argument.

"Every single day since the moment I turned you away has been torture, Mac. Why can't you see that?"

"Because you left me," I say, letting my own broken heart show in my eyes. "You did the one thing you swore you wouldn't, Levi. You rejected me. And you did it publicly. It was the worst day of my life. And I think about you every day too. About that moment. I'll be reliving that nightmare every single day—forever."

"I'm sorry," he says, bending low until our foreheads touch.

He means it.

I can feel the genuine desperation—the pain—radiating from him. His wolf hates this. So does mine. But it doesn't change what he did. Or what we are now, which is nothing.

He angles his face, his mouth inching toward mine.

He's going to kiss me.

And I want to let him, but I know instinctively that if I do, it'll be like forgiving him. He'll think it's okay, that I'm not mad anymore. That he's allowed to destroy me and then come crawling back. Maybe it would have been okay, but I know I won't survive it twice.

It takes everything in me to turn my head.

To push him away.

He stumbles back even though I've used barely any force.

The way he looks at me… it's exactly how I feel about him too.

"Mac," he says, and my name is a plea.

He's begging.

But I can't pretend he didn't break me once. And I'm too damn strong now, thanks to his cruelty, to ever let him do it again.

CHAPTER 15

Despite the late hour, my mother is sitting on top of a table surrounded by half a dozen soldiers when I finally enter the cafeteria. Even from across the room, I can tell she's in the middle of some exaggerated story of one of her more dangerous takedowns. The sad part is she doesn't have to exaggerate. My mom's a badass. She's the best bounty hunter I've ever met. She's just not great at feelings.

When I get close, she smiles at me but doesn't bother to pause her story. I'm not surprised, but that doesn't stop me from being pissed.

I stop short of shoving a few of Levi's guys out of my way. Instead, I cross my arms and glare at the woman in the spotlight.

"Can I talk to you?"

She stops her story and offers me a tight smile. "Sure, honey." She hops off the table, and the guys part ranks to give her space to pass.

A couple of them groan at the interruption. She winks back at them. "I'll finish later, boys. I always do."

A couple of them laugh.

My jaw drops, and nausea rolls in my stomach. "Mom, if you could wait until I'm gone to hit on the younger ones, that would be great."

"Relax, they're all at least old enough to buy me alcohol."

I grit my teeth. This was a mistake.

"You know what," I begin as we pass into the hallway, but she grabs my shoulder and steers me into the room across the hall.

"Come on, we can talk in here."

She flicks on a light to reveal a small conference room complete with a table and half a dozen rolling chairs. A whiteboard is mounted to the far wall, filled with a bunch of scribbles and acronyms. This is some sort of planning space for them. I eye the board, but none of it makes sense.

The click of the door behind me makes me whirl, and I start in immediately.

"I cannot believe—"

I don't get far before she interrupts me. "Mac, I owe you an apology."

"You do?" I can't help the suspicion. Years of experience.

"Of course. I know it must hurt to find out I've been in contact with Levi when he wouldn't so much as send you a Christmas card."

I stare at her.

This is her idea of an apology?

"The truth is, I stumbled upon his operation purely by chance about eighteen months ago while hunting down a mark. Once I realized what he was doing here, I knew it was smart to hedge my bets and offer what value I could."

"Hedge your bets?"

She shrugs. "I mean, you never know which way these things will go. But now that Crigger's gone, and Jadick's almost ready to make a move, I think they have a real shot."

I huffed. "Unbelievable. And does Levi know you were just playing the field until you felt his team had a real shot? Or does he actually think you're loyal?"

"Does it matter?"

"Of course it matters."

She shakes her head. "Oh, to be young again and have such conviction."

Her wistful smile only pisses me off further. "Oh to be old and not give a shit about anyone but yourself."

Her smile falls. It's not anger that flashes back at me but something more like resolve. "All right. You want to talk about giving a shit, let's start with Levi. He built this place from the ground up. Mostly as a haven against Thiago, who wouldn't stop hunting him when he uncovered Levi's plan to accept you as his mate."

"Wait, what?"

Thiago knew about our plans?

"Oh, you didn't know that part? Well, let me go on. Thiago's been screwing with anyone he deems a threat for as long as he could walk and talk. And honestly, the womb was probably no picnic either, but Delores isn't around to verify—which should speak volumes. Anyway, the point is that the entire family has one goal, and that's to survive one another." She pauses, finally noticing my stricken expression. "Are you listening?"

"Levi really intended to accept me?"

She rolls her eyes. "Why am I not surprised you're stuck on that?"

"Does Thiago have something to do with why Levi rejected me?"

"You'll have to ask him."

Tripp's words from the hotel come back to me. He *did it to protect you*. My thoughts race with the possibilities of what that might mean, but my mother steps closer, crowding me enough that she has my full attention.

"I need you to hear me on this, Mac. You can run off to your mate once I'm done, but this is important."

"What is it?"

"Hear me when I say that family has the same one-track mind."

"What is that supposed to mean?"

She speaks so low I can barely hear her. "Jadick is the same as his brother. He wants to be alpha by any means necessary. That puts him on our side right now, but don't think for a second it can't swing in the other direction. The wind always changes, darling. Don't forget that."

"You don't trust him?"

"Not with my daughter."

"We finally agree on something," I say in a low voice.

Instead of irritation at my tone, I get a, "Good girl."

She heads for the door.

"Mom."

She pauses, her hand on the knob as she looks back at me.

"Thank you," I tell her almost begrudgingly.

"I didn't spare Thiago for you," she reminds me.

"I know that."

She studies me carefully. "Will you be here in the morning?"

I look away. "Maybe."

"You still planning on trying to drag Levi back to Blackstone?" she asks wryly, and I realize she knows I've been beaten by a mark— for the first time ever.

"Depends on whether he leaves me a choice."

She looks torn. "I would have preferred to keep you out of this, but what's done is done. Don't forget what I said."

"I won't."

"And get some sleep. Whatever they're planning, it might not involve letting me kill Thiago, but you'll need all your wits for it, I'm sure."

She doesn't wait for my response before letting herself out.

Her warning isn't concerning.

I have zero doubt Jadick intends to use me. There's no mistaking the sweetness in his voice. The flirty smile he shoots me when I ask the right question. But I'm using him too.

I intend to survive his family. And I intend to save Kari from them too.

The only real sucker punch my mother gave me has to do with

the guy I just rejected back in the hangar for no other reason than wanting to hurt him the way he hurt me once.

His words from earlier ring in my head. *"You could try seeing me as something other than the villain of your fucking story."*

What if my mother is right? What if he's never been the villain at all?

CHAPTER 16

$\mathcal{M}$ ovement in the doorway startles me out of my spiraling thoughts.

"Tripp," I say, exhaling at the sight of him.

"Sorry, didn't mean to scare you." He runs a hand through his hair, expression tight. "Everything okay?"

"Yeah, fine."

The pause between us is awkwardly full. I want to say something —*anything*—that will bring back the friendship we once had. But that friendship didn't include secrets, and now we're so full of them that I can barely see him at all through all the words left unspoken between us.

"My mom's in the cafeteria, holding court," I say. "If you're looking for her."

"Actually, I was looking for you."

"Oh."

"Well," he says after a moment, looking everywhere but at me. "I'm sure you're tired. I can show you where you'll sleep."

I start to refuse, to tell him what I told Levi—I'm not staying.

But in the end, I give in and let him lead me back through the maze of beige-colored hallways. The turns are slightly familiar now, and I work on committing them to memory, once and for all. My mother is right. Whatever Jadick is planning, I can't afford to let my guard down.

The halls are empty of everyone but us. The only other people we pass are two guards stationed at the hangar door, which lets me know it's the only way out. They don't make eye contact with me as we pass.

Even walking right beside my former friend, I sense a distance between us that hurts my heart.

Finally, Tripp shows me into a small room.

"I made some room in the top drawer if you need to store anything," he says, gesturing to the dresser.

"This is your room?" I ask, surprised.

He shrugs. "There aren't any singles left empty so I figured… I'll sleep in a hammock in the hangar for now."

"Thanks," I tell him, unsure what else to say.

It's a nice gesture. But I'm not sure how to be "nice" to Tripp after everything.

"What was this place?" I ask, glancing around at the nondescript walls. "Before, I mean."

"A human army base," he says. "Training camp or something. One of the Jades had a connection and knew they'd shut it down, so we took it over. So far, no one's been the wiser."

"How long have you lived here?"

He eyes me warily. "If I tell you, are you going to punch me?"

His words sting, mostly because it's a valid question. But I can't bring myself to answer it seriously. Somehow, I think that would make it worse.

"I make no guarantees either way." I cock my head, showing I'm teasing. "You worried you can't fend me off, Thompson?"

He snorts. "Please, Quinn. You're lucky I've gone easy on you all these years."

"Oh, yeah, I'm super grateful for that."

Our smiles fade, and too soon, the awkwardness is back.

"There's a granola bar and water for you." Tripp nods at the dresser and then turns to leave. For some reason, the pre-wrapped food melts my heart. It's clear he understands my distrust of these people, and whether or not he agrees with it, he's willing to meet me halfway.

"Tripp," I call.

He stops, eyeing me with a gaze still full of secrets.

My shoulders sag.

"Good night," I say.

"Good night."

Sleep is slow to come.

I lie awake, listening to the silence and trying to ignore the isolation of this place. Or maybe that's just the awareness of betrayal.

If Levi really did intend to accept me, he's had three years to tell me the truth. Three years of no contact and then three days' worth of nonstop lies. I don't know how to pretend either of those things away.

I can't excuse it.

All I can do is hope this all leads back to Kari—and try not to get my heart broken all over again before I get there.

THE NEXT MORNING, I venture warily out of my room, only to find the hall notably empty of guards. Either they decided I wasn't going to run after all, or they didn't care either way.

The cafeteria is packed for breakfast. Despite the crowd, there isn't a single familiar or friendly face among them. No Levi. No Tripp. Not even Jadick or my mother is around.

One particularly harsh face steps into view, blocking my path. Grey.

The one who made sure I didn't eat or drink for two days.

My hands ball into fists. "What the hell do you want?"

"You shouldn't be allowed to roam alone."

"Are you going to stop me?"

He starts to answer, but a short barked order cuts him off.

"Grey. Back off."

We both look over to see Frankie cutting a path through the onlookers.

Her hair is still damp from a shower, and her uniform is freshly pressed. Her entire vibe is "don't fuck with me," which I appreciate, though I would have rather dealt with the asshole myself.

"Don't you have somewhere to be?" she demands of him, standing toe to toe with the asshole despite the six extra inches of height he has on her.

"She should have an escort," he snaps at her.

"Consider me it," she says in a voice that dares him to argue.

Grey looks me over, his lip curled in a snarl that makes it clear what he thinks of me. Then he turns on his heel and leaves.

"Don't pay him any attention," Frankie tells me.

The rest of the cafeteria slowly goes back to their own business.

I exhale, not sure whether to be relieved or disappointed I didn't get to kick the guy's ass.

"He tried to starve me to death," I say, "so, yeah, he's going to have my attention—at least until I can repay the favor."

Her brows lift. "I see. Does Levi know?"

"Yeah."

"And Grey's still breathing?" Frankie asks wryly.

I frown. "I'm not sure Levi cares quite that much."

She snorts, but her amusement dies at the sight of my expression. "Give it 'til end of day," she says. "If Grey's still walking around like he owns the place, you have my full permission and support to lay him out."

"Noted," I say.

She pats my arm. "See you around, Mac."

"Bye."

She disappears toward the food line, leaving me alone to navigate. Ignoring the glares and whispers, I manage to snag a plate of pancakes and a water before retreating back into the hall. My stomach grumbles at the sound of it and I realize how long it's been since I had a real meal.

The idea of returning to my tiny room is too unappealing. Instead, I duck back into the conference room from last night. While I eat, I try to decipher what the coding on the whiteboard means.

Behind me, someone knocks lightly on the open door.

I look up to see Levi standing there, and a hundred emotions wash over me. Even after hours apart, the look he gives me takes me right back to where we left off in the hangar last night. His eyes swirl with need, and I nearly give in and throw myself into his arms right here. Then a second figure enters behind him, shoving him aside so he can pass.

"Move, bro," Tripp grunts good-naturedly. He stops short when he sees me, though. "Oh. Hey."

I wrench my gaze from Levi and look at Tripp. "Hi."

The awkwardness reaches a new level with the three of us in the same room again.

"I was looking for my mother," I say lamely.

"She left early this morning," Levi says.

"What?"

"She didn't tell you?"

I sigh. "Of course not. Why would she?"

He hesitates. "I'm sure she was just busy with the details of whoever she's hunting down this time…"

"Don't defend her," I snap.

He falls silent.

In that silence, I only feel worse.

"We were just—" Tripp begins.

"Listen," I say at the same time, but then Jadick arrives, and I clamp down on whatever sentimental thing I'd been about to indulge in.

Pushing to my feet, I prepare to make myself scarce. Whatever they're here for, it clearly has nothing to do with me.

"Hey," Jadick says with a flirty smile. "Glad you're here. I was just going to look for you."

"You were?" I ask warily.

"We'd like to invite you to stay for a status update on the Thiago situation," he says. "Care to join us?"

My eyes widen, but Jadick doesn't react to my surprise. I look from him to Levi, waiting. But even if Levi's in charge out there, with the men, in here, it's clearly Jadick at the helm.

"Okay," I say, still off-balance.

But I'm not going to turn down information.

Levi rounds the table, and Tripp follows. They both take a seat. Jadick motions for me to take one too. I sit across from Levi. Jadick sits beside me.

I scoot away as much as possible without making it obvious.

"What's this about?" I ask.

"We'd like to make sure everything's on the table." Jadick smiles. "Pun intended."

Tripp rolls his eyes. "Terrible," he mutters.

"That sounds good," I say, doing my best to focus on the information he's offering to divulge. "We can start with who made the call to extract my mother and why."

"I made that call," Levi says.

I'm not surprised. They'd said as much yesterday. But his admission means I'm forced to meet his gaze. There, I find way too many layers of emotions to unravel. Instead, I shift my eyes to a spot on the wall just over his head.

"Why bother?" I ask. "Not that I'm not grateful, but she would have eliminated your enemy for you. We all know she's capable."

"Because of this." He sets his phone on the table between us and hits play on a voice mail.

Thiago's voice fills the room.

"Levi, brother, I hope you're well."

The smugness in Thiago's voice infuriates me, but I force myself to keep quiet and listen.

"You may have heard I've struck a deal with your little Reject. Quinn is on the hunt for a killer, and I've taken my sister as leverage until she brings me one. The people want justice for my father's murder, and I intend to get it for them. In the meantime, please

162

warn the little Quinn that should any harm come to me, I've left instructions that Kari should meet that same fate."

There's a blood-curdling scream that abruptly cuts off.

Thiago chuckles darkly, but I barely register the sound. My own heart has dropped to my stomach.

I look up at Levi.

He's already watching me.

"Sounds a bit like our previous arrangement, eh?" Thiago adds, clearly amused with himself. "In case there's any confusion, that deal also still stands."

Click.

The call ends.

My heart pounds.

"What deal?" I ask.

Levi doesn't answer.

"What deal?" I repeat, louder now.

"You didn't tell her." Jadick's tone is surprised.

I spare a glance for Tripp, who keeps his eyes on the table.

Every one of them knows something I don't.

"I will tear this compound apart, and then I'll run back to Thiago and sell all of you out if you don't tell me about this deal right the fuck now," I growl.

"Everyone out," Levi says.

His voice is barely above a whisper, but it's deadly.

Tripp and Jadick exchange a glance and then get up from their chairs.

"Don't be too hard on him, Mac," Jadick says.

Levi looks ready to punch him.

"Not now," Levi says in a tight voice.

I catch a twinkle of satisfaction in Jadick's eye, but then he ducks his head and walks out behind Tripp.

When we're alone, I push out of my chair and stand against the far wall. It's stupid, really. There's nowhere I can go Levi can't reach me. His hooks are in too deep.

He looks up at me, and the connection between us pulls taut.

"Thiago came to me three years ago," he says, voice devoid of emotion. "He knew what you and I planned to do... accepting one another as mates. Proclaiming ourselves as Romantics. He threatened you. He said— He said he'd kill you if I didn't reject you."

"You're serious?"

"I would never lie about this, Mac."

I don't know what to think. Everything I know about Levi— about what he did—paints him as an asshole. A villain.

"And you believed his threat?" I can't help but scoff.

"You think I'd risk it?" he asks, eyes blazing with intensity. Before I can answer, he adds, "I knew he'd do it because he did it to Jadick first."

"Right. Lacey." I almost forgot. "But Jadick rejected her," I say. "And Thiago still killed her."

"Exactly. Imagine what he'd do to you if we mated."

His words are laced with pain, and I know he's done exactly that: imagined all the ways Thiago would have hurt me. Still, I can't simply accept this explanation. After three years of hating him, I can't just turn it off.

"You could have told me—"

"I cannot lose you," he roars.

He's out of his chair in the space of a blink. Rounding the table, pressing rough hands to my cheeks. "I love you, Mac. I have loved you since the moment I first laid eyes on you in seventh grade when you punched Pete Bolling in the nuts for stealing Tripp's lunch money."

"He was a bully."

He smiles. Or tries to.

"You are more than my mate, Mac. You're my whole fucking heart. I couldn't possibly have done anything other than what I did. Telling you would have risked you. Defying Thiago would have risked you. Coming back for you would have risked you. Don't you get it by now? I will never, ever do anything that could hurt you."

"Except that you did."

His brows dip. Confusion mars his desperation.

I pull free of his grasp, and he lets me. His hands drop to his sides. He's never looked more lost. I've never felt so angry.

I fist my hands, pacing in front of the whiteboard now.

If Levi's not the enemy, who is? Because I have to find somewhere to put all this rage. I don't even have to ask. I already know. Thiago.

All that pain. My life, my happiness, my mate—stolen from me.

For what?

A family feud?

Power?

A fucking title?

"Jadick's going to challenge him," Levi says, obviously reading where my thoughts have taken me. "It's the only real way to end this."

"Jadick's right about Thiago," I say. "He has no honor. He won't fight fair. Not even in a challenge."

"Then we'll all fight," he says.

"Thiago already has Crigger's entire army," I say. "They've pledged their loyalty. They'll fight."

"I have an army too."

"That's why you created the Jades? To fight for Jadick?"

The name, it fits.

But he shakes his head. "I didn't create the Jades. I may have brought us together to this place, but I didn't create them. To be a Jade means you're tired of the way things are in Blackstone."

"Wait. They're all from our pack?"

He nods. "Some left years ago. Others joined us more recently. But we're all done with Crigger's rules. These people want change, Mac. Same as we do. And they're willing to fight for it."

"They're jaded," I realize, and he offers a rueful smile.

"Too on the nose?"

"Not any worse than Romantics and Rejects, I guess."

"I just wanted a place where I belong," he says, and I wonder if he's thinking of his parents. "Where maybe someday we could belong together."

His smile fades as he waits for me to respond.

He created this place, brought these people here, to fight back. Not for Jadick. For me.

My heart swells.

Hope.

It's almost too much to feel. I can't remember the last time I let it in. And the urge to shove it out again is so practiced I nearly do it. But then I stop myself.

Trembling, I close the distance he's put between us.

He's completely still as I come to a stop before him. Like he doesn't want to spook me. I don't blame him. But I also don't want to run. Not anymore.

"You never wanted to reject me?" I whisper.

I am terrified of his answer—of having this hope crushed.

"No, Mac. I never wanted to reject you."

My eyes fill with hot tears. I blink them back. His expression softens, and he reaches up to cup my cheek again. Slowly, he leans down, and my breath catches.

I don't move.

I don't even breathe.

If anything ruins this—

But nothing does.

His kiss is soft. Achingly gentle and more like a memory come to life. I melt against him, my hands reaching for his shirt, his skin, his hair. Whatever I can find. I need to feel him against my fingertips.

When I wrap my arms around his neck, he growls. It's a primal sound that wakes my beast, and I make a sound of my own—pure lust and need—and then the kiss is no longer soft or sweet. He grabs my hips, yanking me against him. Unsatisfied, he lifts me so that our bodies meet and meld in all the right places.

I cling to him, desperate and agonizingly hungry for more. His kiss is hot and rough, his tongue plunging into my mouth like a demand. He spins so that I'm pinned against the wall, and, with one hand cupping my ass to hold me steady, he slips the other hand beneath my shirt.

His fingers dip inside my bra, closing around my already hardened nipple and expertly flicking it until I'm squeezing my thighs in a silent plea for more.

"Mac," he groans, pulling his mouth from mine so that he can trail kisses down my throat.

My fingers are tangled in his hair.

My control is long gone. No memory I possess compares to the reality of Levi touching my body.

His hand releases my breast and dives lower, rubbing at my already soaked leggings. For once, I don't stop myself from grinding against him.

"Please," I whimper.

He snarls, mouth finding mine again and swallowing my sounds.

Still, it's not enough. There are too many clothes between us. Too much space. I want him inside me. I want him to consume me. Maybe then, I'll begin where he ends, and no one can ever come between us again.

The door opens.

It's a sound I'm only mildly aware of and honestly too worked up to even care.

But a voice shatters the breathless silence. "Levi."

He goes still against me.

His head whips toward the door.

I see Jadick standing in the opening, looking anything but ashamed at walking in on us like this. If anything, he looks weirdly into it. My face heats, and I lower my legs, sliding down the wall so that I'm standing on my own feet.

"What?" Levi demands, his arm still around me.

"There's been an incident." Jadick looks between us. "You're needed in the hangar."

"Fuck," Levi mutters, and Jadick glances at me one more time before leaving us alone.

I look up at him, unnerved by the afterglow of our little moment. But he stops me from pulling away, and instead of hauling ass for the hangar, he leans in and gives me a lingering kiss.

"What's that for?" I whisper.

"For later," he says and then steps back.

He grabs my hand; a clear message he has no intention of going back to pretending we hate each other. "Come on," he says. "They're waiting for us."

CHAPTER 17

$\mathcal{I}$n the very back of the hangar, a small security contingent forms a loose circle. Grey is one of them, but for once, he doesn't seem to notice me. He's too focused on whatever he's guarding. In the center of the circle, Jadick and Tripp stand over a man on his knees. It takes me until I'm three feet away before I recognize him through all the bruises and dried blood caked across his skin.

"Dirk?" I stare at him in complete shock. The sight of him alive at all is unexpected enough. But how the hell did he get *here*?

"You know this guy?" Tripp asks.

Dirk stares up at me with a bleak expression.

I tear my gaze from his and focus on Tripp, who's clearly waiting, along with Jadick and Levi, for an explanation.

"Not exactly. He was a mark. Crigger hired me to bring him in before…" I don't finish before I'm turning back to Dirk, eyes narrowed in suspicion. "What the hell are you doing here? And how are you alive?"

"He's here because this is where he lives." Levi's voice is soft but not gentle.

I turn to him, startled. One look at his face, and I realize my knowing Dirk has somehow shattered the trust we'd just rebuilt between us.

"Dirk is a Jade?" I look from Levi to Tripp and finally to Jadick, who doesn't seem quite so disturbed by my involvement with the bloody dude kneeling at his feet.

"Dirk has been working as an informant for us," Jadick explains.

"He went dark a couple of weeks ago," Tripp supplies.

A few possibilities dawn on me, and no matter which one ends up being true, I know I've stepped in some shit that makes me look like a real asshole right about now.

"Look," I say, "Crigger hired me to bring him in. I had no idea what for. I just needed the cash—and to stay on his good side."

"Because you cared so much what that asshole thought of you," Tripp says, and I glare at him.

"I care about staying alive and out of jail. Or have you been hiding behind these walls so long you forgot what it's like to survive in Black Moon?"

He doesn't answer.

None of them do.

But my temper is hot now, so I keep going.

"I brought Dirk in despite the fact that he and three of his friends tried to kill me for it."

A muscle in Levi's jaw twitches at that, so I decide to leave out the part about Dirk trying to force himself on me.

"You know I'm telling the truth," I say to him, "Because you saw me with him the night you left me in that warehouse to take the fall for Crigger's murder."

Tripp and Jadick look at Levi.

He sighs. "She's telling the truth." He flicks a glance toward Dirk. "I didn't recognize him that night."

"How could you miss that detail?" Tripp demands, but Levi shoots him a look sharp enough to silence him.

"I was distracted," he says simply, and no one argues.

No one looks at me like I'm the traitor anymore either, so I keep my mouth shut. Levi taking my side is too foreign for me to know how to react.

In the silence, I crouch so that I'm eye-level with Dirk. It's clear now that they haven't forced him to his knees out of some attempt to dominate him. He's simply too weak to stand.

"I thought Thiago would have killed you," I say.

"Been moments I kind of wish he had," he admits.

My heart pangs with guilt. Despite what Dirk tried to do to me, I can't help feeling like his injuries are my fault.

"Thiago tortured you," I say, and he doesn't answer.

He doesn't need to.

Levi's hand closes around my arm, and I let him pull me to my feet. Jadick moves into my spot and crouches in front of Dirk.

"You're safe now." Jadick places his hand on Dirk's shoulder. "But we need to know what you gave up, brother."

Dirk's expression crumples as he relives a pain I can't even imagine. "I held out as long as I could," he says gruffly.

"I know you did," Jadick says and nods in encouragement for Dirk to continue.

My heart begins to thud harder as my senses pick up the nerves coming from the others. They're worried. Levi's only ever played it completely cool with me. No matter how bad things were, he's never been worried. So, the fact that he is now puts me on edge in a way that makes my skin crawl.

I focus on Dirk, holding my breath while I wait for his answer.

"I don't know. It's a little fuzzy," he says, voice cracking.

"Try to think," Jadick says a little more forcefully now. His hand squeezes Dirk's shoulder.

Dirk winces. "Okay, fine, I told him about the Jades," he rasped. "I couldn't help it. My body gave out. My control was gone. He drugged me, and I just started talking—"

"Did you give him our location?" Jadick snaps.

His voice is a whip, silencing anything but the answer.

Dirk's broken whisper is a roar in my ears. "Yes."

~

LEVI STIFFENS. He doesn't look at me. No one does.

"Evacuation protocol?" Tripp says though it's not much of a question.

Jadick stands. He and Levi share a look.

"Do it," Levi says.

"Dammit," Jadick mutters, but he doesn't disagree.

"What about…?" Tripp nods at Dirk.

Jadick uses a two-way radio to call for medical support, and within moments, two Jades in scrubs arrive to help treat Dirk's wounds. I watch, wondering if they can see what I can: Dirk's physical wounds will heal, but judging from the haunted look in his glassy eyes, nothing they do will make him forget what he went through.

He was tortured.

Because of me.

"I have to make the rounds." Levi's voice is an anchor in my sea of chaos, and I force myself to pay attention.

"Rounds?" I ask.

"I need to be sure everyone's following protocol. Can you stay here? Wait for me?"

"I'll stay with her," Tripp says when I don't answer.

Levi hesitates.

"I won't take my eyes off her," Tripp insists. "Go."

Levi squeezes my hand once, and then he's gone, hurrying through the hangar and barking orders to everyone in sight. Jadick is already gone, I realize. And so is Dirk.

Tripp pulls me into a hug.

I let him, startled by the fact that he's shaking.

Not him, I realize.

Me.

I'm in shock.

Freaking out in a way my training usually prevents. But nothing has prepared me for this. I'm not worried for myself. I can handle whatever happens next. It's all the people inside these walls—their endangered lives—that fill me with a guilt so thick I can barely breathe through it.

Get it the fuck together, Mac.

Tripp finally lets me go, and I hate to admit that his arms around me helped steady me. He studies my face, his hands pressing against my cheeks so I can't escape his perusal.

"Breathe," he orders, which makes me wonder how much of my horror is showing on my face.

"I am," I say, but even I can hear the lie.

"In," he orders, and after a beat, "Out."

I follow his direction. After three deep breaths, I feel a little more like myself. Around us, people rush in every direction. Their energy becomes more urgent with every passing second.

"It's going to be okay," Tripp says, letting me go.

He glances at the vehicles currently being loaded with people. I can already see that there won't be enough room in them for all these bodies. And who knows what sort of threat is headed our way already. If we'll even make it out in time.

"No," I say, "It's not."

"Don't," Tripp warns, eyeing me knowingly.

"I did this."

His gaze hardens into a stony resolve. "No," he says firmly. "That prick Thiago did this. Don't let him get off that easy. He's the one who'll have to pay." He grips my shoulders. "And we *will* make him pay."

I shake loose of his touch, not sure I fully believe that anymore.

"Yeah," I say anyway. "Okay." I straighten. "What can I do?"

"Put her in the truck," Levi says before Tripp can answer.

I look up to see him leading a dozen men through the hangar, every one of them dressed in nothing but shorts.

"I'm not taking a spot in one of the cars," I say.

Levi frowns. I brace myself for an argument.

"Tripp, take them to the perimeter. Organize and start sweeps," Levi says.

"You got it." Tripp gives me a sympathetic look. "Don't do anything stupid," he tells me and then jogs off with the security team.

I turn to Levi. "I'm not going to argue about this."

"Good. Then it's settled."

My eyes narrow. "There isn't enough room as it is. I'm not taking up a spot that should go to someone else."

"The truck is armored," he says. "It's safer for you there."

"And what about all the women and children? Will they be safer?" He scowls. "Where will you be?" I press.

"Running with the others."

"Good. I'll do that."

He looks ready to argue or maybe even toss me over his shoulder and throw me into the closest trunk. I plant my feet, ready to fight him off, because there's no way I'm taking a spot away from a mother or her child.

"Let her run with us."

We both turn to look at Jadick. His hands are full of supplies.

"She's shady as hell," he adds when Levi doesn't answer. "Probably best to keep her where we can see her. Besides, we need her for the plan."

"I already told you that idea is too reckless," Levi begins.

"I'm in," I say quickly.

Jadick beams at me. "Atta girl. Okay, let's get these vehicles on the road. See you at the checkpoint?"

"Fine," Levi mutters, and Jadick strides away.

I try—and fail—to hide my victory.

"Don't look so smug, Mac. If you're running with me, that means I will tackle your ass before I let you do something stupid."

My response is muted by a horrific boom.

Around me, people scream, but I can't hear them through the temporary deafness in my ears.

Dust and rock rain down around us. Instinctively, I put my hands over my head, which isn't really necessary since Levi grabs me and pulls me down to the floor with his body covering mine. We land hard against the stone, and I grunt as Levi's weight settles against me.

A large boulder rips loose from the ceiling and slams into the concrete beside us. I jerk at the sight of it and feel the reverberation of its impact all the way through my bones.

I'm still recovering from it when Levi yanks me to my feet again. His face looms in front of me, eyes wide and urgent.

"Follow me."

His words sound as if they've come from underwater.

But I make them out, barely, thanks to the shape of his lips as he talks.

I nod, and he grabs my hand, pulling me through the hangar.

He shouts orders to the people around us, but I can't hear them.

The vehicles fill quickly as everyone climbs in, and Levi yanks me out of the way as each of them accelerates for the exit. Another explosion rocks the hangar. More stone tears loose from above and beside us.

Twice, I'm nearly crushed but manage to jump clear of the falling debris.

My feet barely keep me upright, thanks to the shaking ground. Beside me, a woman falls. Her cries are cut off as she lands face first in a pile of rubble with a boulder as large as a car on top of her.

I glance behind me and see others also pinned or lying still and bloodied in the broken piles of stone and debris. My chest squeezes, and I falter, wanting desperately to turn back and help. But Levi's expression as he yanks me toward him—toward the exit—makes it clear that's not an option. And deep down, I know it won't do any good. They're gone. And if I try to go back, I'll die with them.

More explosions sound above my head. Boulders fall, and the walls shake with the force of their impact. Every inhale draws another cloud of dust into my lungs, and I choke as I leap over the uneven ground. The hangar is crumbling, falling apart with us still inside it.

If I didn't know what this was, I'd assume an earthquake.

But this is no natural disaster. We're under attack.

Thiago has found us.

Dirk sold us out. And I put him in the exact right place to do it.

The remaining Jades sprint through the hangar opening with us. One by one, they all shift into their wolf, and we pour out of the doorway into the dusty air. In the distance, red taillights are fading as the convoy drives off. Levi steers me toward the trees, and we run with the others, shifting as we go.

My clothes tear away from my body as my limbs lengthen and pop. One second, I'm a human, and the next, my wolf is eating up the ground with her long strides and massive paws.

Behind us, the Jade compound continues to crumble as more explosives detonate topside. I have no idea how many men Thiago has sent to kill us, but I have no doubt that's what will happen if we don't fight our way past them.

We're all being hunted now.

CHAPTER 18

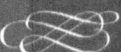

We make it to the base of the mountains before Thiago's men catch us. In the gorge, at least a dozen men appear and begin to drop from above, repelling off the craggy rocks and blocking our escape. As the first few hit the ground, we fan out. I bare my teeth, muscles bunched and ready as I square off with a man still tethered to his drop cord. He produces a blade and cuts the cord then immediately shifts. Before I can sink my teeth into him, Levi is there, cutting past me to take the man down into the hard dirt.

I growl, mostly out of the need for a fight of my own, and look for another opponent. The wolves who came with us are nearly all engaged in fights of their own. We're closely numbered. Unless reinforcements show up for Thiago's men. A likely scenario, considering the damage they've already done to the compound itself.

We need to win this fight, and we need to do it fast.

Another man drops from above.

I meet him before he has time to complete the shift, my teeth ripping into his shoulder and tearing a chunk away. His blood and tissue coat my mouth, but I spit it back at him before darting in for another bite. This time, I come away with his throat, and his cries of pain die out at the same time he does.

I spin and look for another.

Levi appears, breathless and with a hard gleam in his eye. He nods for me to follow him away from what's left of the fight. Reluctantly, I do.

We haul ass through the gorge, increasing our speed only when the rest of our ranks finish with the enemy behind us and catch up.

I do a quick count as I run.

We've lost two more.

As much as I want another chance for vengeance, I find myself hoping we don't run into any more soldiers. Every life lost is another life I feel responsible for losing.

Thiago wanted this.

He planned for it.

But I gave him the opportunity to make it happen.

At nightfall, we finally stop to rest.

We're deep in the mountains now. My wolf senses are alert for threats, but aside from that first attack in the gorge, we've met no one else. Up here, the air is colder. A crisp scent of pine and dirt. My wolf enjoys it—or she would if we weren't here because Thiago was hell-bent on killing us all.

The others gather around as Levi takes his human form again. "We'll rest in this system of caves," he tells them. "Start again in the morning."

"Jadick will worry," one of the men says.

Grey.

I've managed to keep my distance from the asshole all day, but now, I want to take a bite out of his jugular. My temper still rages beneath the surface, and I have nowhere to put it. He seems as good a place as any.

"Jadick will worry more if we're reckless," Levi says. "We still have men out there patrolling to make sure we aren't followed. I won't leave them behind."

Grey doesn't argue.

I force myself to relax.

"Burnett, Grey, take first watch," Levi adds. "Wake me to relieve you."

Returning to wolf form, the two men begin climbing for the high ground to take up their positions. The others disburse as well, breaking off into groups of two or three and disappearing into the shallow caves we've found lining this ridge.

Still in wolf form, I wait, watching Levi.

He looks back at me with exhaustion lining his expression. The shadows have gathered, making it hard to see details, but this close, I can't ignore his naked body. Even my wolf finds his human appearance attractive.

It's a weird sensation.

Finally, the silence stretches too long, and I wonder if I've mistaken his interest. When I turn to go, he stops me.

"Will you stay with me?"

I try to think of a reason to refuse him, but in the end, I follow him into the darkness of an unclaimed cave.

Inside, the shadows are thick, the darkness so complete it takes a few minutes for my eyes to adjust.

Levi remains human.

He ducks out again, leaving me alone so long I give in and lie down. My eyelids begin to droop, and by the time he returns, I'm fighting sleep.

I watch with lazy focus as he goes to work building a fire. When the flames are crackling, he approaches me and holds out a patchwork of leaves someone has strung together with vines.

"For you to sleep more comfortably," he explains.

He sets it down in front of me and backs toward the fire again.

I watch him go, wide awake, thanks to his sudden closeness.

"We'll have to hunt for something to eat in the morning," he adds.

My wolf is interested at the prospect, but my human side grimaces. Nothing like taking down a rabbit for brunch.

Levi stares at me from where he's perched on the other side of the fire.

"You can shift back if you want," he says.

But I don't move.

"Seriously, Mac. I know you don't love staying in this form for this long at one time." He hesitates, looking away before adding, "I'll keep you safe tonight."

His words pierce me, and I give in to the need to be human again.

"I can keep myself safe," I say quietly.

His eyes snap back to mine, and his expression softens. "Hi."

"Hi yourself."

"Are you okay?"

"I'm not injured."

"That's not what I meant."

I bite my lip. Honesty isn't my first instinct, not with Levi. But tonight, I find myself trying it for the first time in years. "I'm sorry," I say quietly.

"For what?" he asks, startled.

"For letting Dirk be taken. For...what happened at the compound."

"That wasn't your fault," he says.

"That's nice of you to say." I shake my head. "But I had a hand in it."

"I saw Dirk with you that night. I'm just as much to blame as you are for his capture and torture." "Besides," he adds, his words almost a challenge. "I would have thought you'd be glad to see the compound go. You weren't exactly welcomed into it with open arms."

"I can still appreciate what it meant to you. That place was your home. The people who were killed were your pack—and now they're gone."

At my words, whatever mask he'd worn before drops away. Raw grief shines in his eyes, and I feel the depth of it like a punch in the gut. I realize too late what a gaping wound my words have uncovered. For all his stoicism and leadership today, he is broken by this.

His expression is bleak as he says, "You would think I'd be used to loss by now, but it doesn't really get easier."

His voice is ragged. He won't look at me.

I find myself blinking back tears.

"Levi..."

Despite everything between us, my heart hurts at the sight of his pain. At knowing I helped cause it.

"I didn't set out to create a new pack, you know. I didn't mean to become an alpha either. It just... I went looking for my parents."

"Is that why you left town?" I ask. "I always thought it was to escape me."

He finally meets my eyes. "It was," he admits. "But only because of Thiago's threats. His blackmail meant I couldn't afford to give in to temptation. And I knew if I stayed..." He sighs. "Well, I think we've already proven we can't keep our hands to ourselves when we're in the same space."

He tries for a smile, but it's more of a wince.

"Did you find them?" I ask, needing to change the subject. To talk about anything except the tension between us. Even now, in this cave, with the threat of an attack hanging over us all, I can't think about anything except the sight of Levi's ripped chest in the firelight.

Thankfully, the rest of him is hidden in shadows, or my self-control would have dried up long before now.

"Your parents," I add when he doesn't answer.

He blinks as if breaking through his own distractions. "No," he says. "I found Grey. And Frankie. And then more and more of them. All of them used to be Black Moon. And all of them wanted their lives back." He smiles. "Then one day, Tripp showed up, and it was all kind of a smooth slide into pack life after that."

"Tripp has a way with people," I say.

"He's sneaky," Levi agrees. "In a good way."

I don't answer. I want to agree, but then I think of how he kept the truth from me. How they all did. Even my mother.

"Where will you all go?" I ask instead.

"Tripp and I have a few possible locations scouted," he says.

"You planned for this."

"We planned for contingencies." Something about his words trips something in me.

"You knew this might happen."

"I'd be an idiot not to consider it. And the possibility became more likely when Jadick joined us. So I had Tripp look into a few places. There's an abandoned shopping mall outside of Wythe. Looks like the city planned to reinvest and revamp but ran out of money, so it's just sitting. We can go there at least until we figure something else out."

I don't respond.

The silence stretches between us with a thousand words left unspoken. I try to accept it. That this night is our last together. That no matter what, in the end, he'll choose the Jades, and I'll be left alone to fulfill my promise to Kari. I try to accept that tomorrow we'll be enemies again.

But just for tonight, I can't help enjoying that what's between us now feels something like friendship.

Tonight, we're on the same side. Just for a little while.

"You could come with us," he says, and I stare back at him, surprised he's said the words aloud. We both know my answer won't be yes.

"I promised Kari," I say simply.

"You need a plan, Mac. Somewhere safe to figure out what's next. Wythe is safe—"

"I won't hide."

"Is that what you think I'm doing?" His words are sharp now. "These people rely on me. Women, children. They have nowhere else to go."

"They chose to leave. That's not on you."

"Every single person here is a victim of Crigger's toxic way of life. Since the moment we became a pack underneath a black moon, we've been doomed to choose between death or a life of misery. We've been enslaved by Crigger's twisted ideas. These people are risking everything to escape that."

"You want to talk about choices, Levi? Give me a break. I didn't even have that. You made my choice for me. And when you left, Kari was there for me. Not you. Not Tripp. Not even my mother. I don't put my life above hers because, without her, I wouldn't be here. So, maybe these people risked everything to escape. But for me, there is no escape. The pack doesn't trap me. My feelings for you do that all on their own. So, fuck escape. I'll risk everything for loyalty. At least, I still have something to fight for."

CHAPTER 19

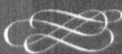

I regret my words the minute they're out. I don't deny they're true, but the look on Levi's face as I say them weighs me with guilt. Knowing the truth and speaking it are two different skill sets. He is silent for a long moment; long enough to make me feel like shit. He's already grieving, and I've basically kicked him while he's down.

Finally, he pushes to his feet. "I better relieve the guys for watch," he says, turning away before I can respond. "Get some sleep," he adds.

Then he shifts and slips out of the cave, leaving me alone with the fire and my own hollow regret.

I sleep fitfully, which is pretty normal for me, but between bouts of actual rest, I have nightmares of Levi running off and leaving me to wake up alone on this mountain.

The morning is drizzly and cold, but contrary to my dreams, Levi is still here. The others are already assembled and in four-legged form when I emerge from the cave as my wolf.

True to Levi's instruction, we hunt first, and then, when our bellies are full of rabbit, we make our way to the meeting point where everyone else will be waiting.

The checkpoint Jadick mentioned turns out to be a campground in Virginia that feels dangerously close to Blackstone's town limits.

Jadick and the rest of the convoy are already there when we arrive. Through a break in the trees at the top of a ridge, I spot tents and canvas rooftops already erected. A cooking fire makes my stomach rumble in response to the aromas. The only other scents on the air are those of the Jades. And my mother. Even so, Levi makes us do three loops around the perimeter, checking for some sign of a trap before he's satisfied it's safe.

When we descend, Jadick is sitting near the fire, surrounded by women. I have to remind myself it's because most of the men are with us, but still—it paints a picture that has me rolling my eyes.

On the fringes, I spot Frankie, and when our eyes lock, I get the impression she agrees with me about Jadick's…methods.

"You made it," Jadick says as Levi and I walk through the camp to where he sits. He doesn't look worried, but that's Jadick. Confident. Too sure of himself to worry.

I tell myself that's the mark of a winner.

But I can still remember my mother telling me during training sessions, "Cocky equals dead."

I don't even realize Levi's shifted back to his human form until he speaks. "Run into any trouble?" he asks.

"None." Jadick's gaze lands on me. "You?"

"A few scouts in the canyon. Nothing we couldn't handle."

"Sounds like a fun story." Jadick snaps his fingers at one of the Jades sitting nearby. Some girl who watches Jadick like he's some sort of god. "Felicia, be a sweetheart and get them something to wear, darling."

"Sure."

She jumps up and hurries to hand over a couple of plastic grocery bags. Levi takes them, and it's all I can do not to bare my teeth at the way her skin brushes his.

Mine.

My wolf is about three seconds from either peeing on him or clawing her tits off. Anything to stake her claim.

Levi turns away from her and gives me a knowing look.

"Come on," he says.

Feeling stiff after our fight last night, I follow him back to the thicker trees and take what clothing he dumps at my feet. He leaves me alone to change, and I listen as he divvies out the remaining clothing with the others who arrived with us.

I listen as he asks about the rest of our men and the answering reports that they've all arrived ahead of us. Everyone who survived is here.

My relief is mixed with sorrow for the lives we lost.

Wind tugs at the ends of my tangled hair as I hurry to pull on the secondhand jeans and t-shirt. The jeans are tight as hell, and the shirt is stained, but I'm not complaining. I'm grateful for anything that lets me eat food that's been cooked over a flame instead of hunting another rabbit.

When I'm finished, I step out from my little changing area to find my mother waiting. She wears the same thing she always does —fitted cargo pants and a long-sleeve Henley. There's a small cut across her cheek that's nearly healed.

"Tripp called me. I came as soon as I heard." She gives me a quick once-over. "You're okay?"

It's more of a statement. We both know "okay" equals alive to her. Anything else can be healed but not if you're dead.

"I'm fine. You?"

I expect her to brush off my concern, but she doesn't. Instead, she hesitates, and in that brief pause, I see it—something has happened. Something besides the Jades compound being compromised and destroyed. Something besides the lives lost before they could escape with us.

"What is it?" I ask, adrenaline pumping.

As usual, my training kicks in, and my heart rate remains steadily calm in the face of danger.

"It's Kari," she says.

"What about her? Is she—"

She puts up a hand to stop me. "Come. See for yourself."

I follow her back to the fire where Jadick still waits. His entourage has left, and now it's Levi and Tripp sitting with him.

"Did you tell her?" Tripp asks, glancing from me to my mom.

"Only that it's about Kari," my mom says as she takes a seat across the fire from Jadick.

"What happened to Kari?" I demand, refusing to sit.

Jadick doesn't meet my eyes. Levi looks just as confused as I am, which means they haven't told him either.

Tripp sighs. "Here."

He holds out his phone, and I take it, noting he's queued up a video. Levi comes to stand beside me and leans over my shoulder to watch. I press play.

Kari's face fills the screen.

She's gagged, and her cheeks are flushed red and tear-stained.

I draw a shuddering breath then hold it as the camera zooms out to reveal the rest of her. She's tied to a chair. Her hair and clothes are dirty. But there's no blood that I can see.

Not yet.

A sign rests in her lap.

On it, someone has scrawled words in black marker: *Dear Mac, Will trade for Jadick Clemons. 24 hours or this deal dies.*

After a beat, the camera pans around to reveal Thiago. He offers a sadistic sort of wave that's friendly if you're into serial killers and narcissistic assholes. The camera focuses on him until the picture goes black and the video ends.

"Fuck," Levi says and moves away to pace.

"When was this sent?" I demand.

"About three hours ago," Tripp says.

Forcing myself to breathe, I look at Jadick. "Dirk gave you up."

"It seems that way."

"He put my name on it," I say, "which means he knows I'm with you."

"It also means you have a target on your back as big as his," Levi practically snarls.

"Relax, man," Tripp tells him. "It just means he's using her friendship with Kari against her."

Levi rounds on him, but my mother interrupts.

"Tripp is right. Thiago knows using Kari as bait only works on the people who care about her most. And that's Mac."

I want to be mad, but my mother's right, and all that matters now is Kari.

"What are we going to do?" I ask, desperation leaking into my voice.

"We're going to give him what he wants," Jadick says.

I watch him, skeptical and wary about what he actually means.

"And what's that?" I ask.

He shrugs like it's nothing and says, "Me."

"So, you're going to challenge him?" I say.

"Don't be naïve, Mac. It's a trap."

"So, then what—?"

"Relax. He's showing his hand like I said he would."

"And what hand is that?" I ask.

"He's obviously decided I'm more valuable to him than Kari. Now we know he's willing to do anything to get to me. We can use this."

Jadick sounds so confident, so smooth. I'm not sure whether to find comfort in that or be even more worried about how this will end.

Levi is tensely silent and hasn't taken his eyes off the fire for long enough that I wonder if he's hypnotized by it—or maybe he's that determined to tune us out.

"So, you challenge him then," Tripp is saying when I force myself to tune back into the conversation, "winner becomes alpha."

"If it were that simple, I would have challenged him the moment our father died," Jadick says.

"Jadick's right," Levi says, finally joining in the conversation though he doesn't look at me. "Thiago has no honor. He won't fight fair."

"Then neither do we," I say.

My mom nods because, in this, we agree.

Jadick merely grins.

"You have an idea," I say.

"Of course." He glances between us all, and I can see that he enjoys keeping us on the hook like this.

"Well?" my mother demands. "Spit it out."

"Thiago will be expecting a direct assault because he knows we *do* have honor," Jadick says. "Instead, we use the Jades to infiltrate the city. I have a small contingent of men still loyal to me there. Informants, soldiers—they'll help. We'll neutralize the men we already know my brother will have positioned out of sight, ready to shoot us in the back."

Levi doesn't answer. Something's wrong. I can see it every time he looks at Jadick. I just don't know what.

"We don't have the numbers," Tripp says, shaking his head to dismiss the idea. "We were already outnumbered before, but we lost too many in the attack. Not to mention morale... We lost women and children, man."

His quiet outrage speaks volumes. I can feel the heat of my own fury coursing through my veins. I remember the faces of those I watched fall as the hangar caved in around us.

"Then we'll get the numbers," Jadick says.

He's still so calm, and my rage points at him now.

"From where? And when?" I demand.

"Vicki has mafia contacts," Jadick says, "And I have some friends in Hawley pack who might—"

"Hawley pack doesn't even exist anymore," I say. "They're all Lone Wolf pack now. And their alphas are a day's drive from here."

"We'll send teams," he says. "One to the Lone Wolf alphas. Another to the Mafia pack."

"We don't have that kind of time," I say, frustration mounting. "Kari needs us now. Thiago won't wait around. We have to respond before the deadline, or he'll only up the stakes, which means hurting Kari or worse. You have to let me bring you in."

"I'm not going to just walk into a trap," Jadick says, condescension dripping from his words. "That might be how you do things, but it's not smart enough to win this war."

My hands ball into fists.

Before I can use them on his privileged little face, Levi stands. "I'll go."

I stare up at him, confused. "What?"

He looks at me. "Thiago sent you to hunt down who killed his father. He said he'll let Kari go if you give him that person. Take me in. Trade me for Kari."

"Levi..."

It's what I wanted. Or what I set out to do, anyway. But now, after everything that's happened, I can't imagine turning Levi over to Thiago. Or to anyone.

"I can't let you do that," I say, pain twisting my words.

"We can't ignore his message," he says. I'm too torn to appreciate that he actually agrees with my plan—for the first time maybe ever.

"You're not *letting* me do anything," he says, his words an exact reminder of the ones I'd tossed at him that first night I tried to take him down.

But I can't find humor in it.

"You'd be walking directly into his trap," my mother says. "He'll have snipers ready."

"Vicki's right," Tripp says. "That's the stupidest move we could make. We need to be smart about this."

"We need to stop sitting on our asses," Levi snaps, except that he's glaring at Jadick as he says it.

Jadick gets to his feet, his air of nonchalance gone. Now, his jaw is hardened, and his eyes are obsidian stones. "I'm the alpha heir, and I'll say when we go."

"You're not an alpha yet," Levi says.

There's a tension between them that feels bigger than this conversation. Tripp catches my eye and gives a small shake of his head, basically telling me to stay out of it.

"Are you really going to cut me out of this, brother? After the partnership we've had? After everything I've done for you." His gaze flicks to me. "She's alive because of me."

"What?" I ask.

Even my mother looks confused now.

"Mac's not your concern any longer," Levi says in a hard voice.

"She's clouding your judgment," Jadick says. "Distracting you from our real goals."

"Our goal has always been about saving innocent lives," Levi says. His voice is rising now. His temper leaking out through cracked edges. "Your own sister is that innocent life in this scenario, and yet you continue to sit around pretending you've got everything under control."

"Watch it, Levi. I'm not one of your Jades you can just order around."

"That's right," Levi snaps. "*My* Jades. *I* am their alpha."

"You serve at my leisure," Jadick says.

I can't help wondering what the hell that means, but Levi's eyes flash, and he leans closer, getting in Jadick's face.

"Leisure is the perfect word, isn't it? All you do is sit on your ass while everyone else does the dirty work."

"You are an alpha for the sole reason that I never challenged you," Jadick says coldly. "Remember that, and remember what you're fighting for. Or who."

This time, it's Levi who glances at me.

"Believe me," Levi says, "I haven't forgotten."

Then he walks away, disappearing into the darkness that's fallen around camp.

Jadick lets him go without a word.

Finally, he takes his seat again, clapping Tripp on the back and sliding right back into his cheery persona. "Who wants a beer?" Jadick asks.

Tripp doesn't answer.

"I'm going to bed," my mother says and abruptly stands and walks off.

She doesn't go after Levi. I wonder if I should follow her.

"Mac?"

I look up to find Jadick holding a can out toward me. Tripp eyes me across the fire. I can't read his expression—or more specifically, I can't figure out who he's frustrated at most right now. But I don't wait around to find out.

"See you tomorrow," I say and leave Jadick and Tripp to strategize a plan I never plan to follow.

CHAPTER 20

*L*evi's long gone by the time I try to catch his scent. The tracker in me could still hunt him down, but after what just happened back there, I need time alone to think. Especially now. Turning away from Levi's trail, I head into the woods, crashing through brush, uncaring where the path leads. The sliver of moon overhead provides a dim light, though my wolf can see the way easily enough without it.

I walk until I come to a wide creek. The rushing of the water echoes around me, and in the chaos of that noise, I search for clarity.

Adrenaline pumps, my thoughts consumed by the video. Thiago's demand replays over and over in my mind. If I don't deliver Jadick, he'll hurt Kari. I know it. Just as I know I'll never convince Jadick to come back with me.

There has to be another way.

But the only other option is Levi, and I can't bring myself to ask him to sacrifice himself. Not even for Kari. Maybe a few days ago, I could have done it. But too much has happened since I left the pack. Too many crimes have been forgiven between us. I can't lose him again, not this way.

A branch cracks, and I whirl to see Tripp coming toward me in the darkness.

He holds up his hands in mock surrender.

"Just me," he says. "Don't shoot."

I turn back to the creek, staring at where the water breaks over a rock. "I figured you'd still be at camp, plotting war games with Jadick."

"Your mother agreed to go to Franco in the morning. To ask for backup." He sighs. "Jadick's gone back to drinking with his fan club. He considers it settled for now."

"I bet he does."

"It's not going to work."

I frown. "What are you talking about?"

"You have that look in your eye. The one you get when you think you can just talk someone into something. I'm telling you, Mac. It won't work. He won't do this—not for you and not for Kari."

I turn to look at him. "She's his sister."

"He's out here trying to strategize how to kill his own brother. Do you think family ties matter to any of them?"

"They're not all like that."

He doesn't answer.

"I know you don't like her," I begin.

"I don't trust her," he corrects. "There's a difference."

"Is there?"

"It's not personal. I don't know her well enough to not like her."

"Exactly."

He sighs. "If an entire batch of something is exposed to poison but only two of the three become contaminated, which results do you suspect—the majority or the minority?"

I shove him playfully. "She's not a science experiment, you nerd."

But he doesn't let up with the somber expression. "Exactly. These are people's lives we're talking about. And I don't fuck around with the lives of my friends."

"Kari's different," I say stubbornly. "You don't know her like I do."

He doesn't answer, and I know we're just going to agree to disagree—again. I might have argued if I didn't want to be past all this once and for all. To have my friend back.

"Anyway, Jadick's a dick, but he's not out here trying to kill us like Thiago is."

Tripp looks entirely unconvinced as he says, "He's a Clemons, Mac. They all are."

CHAPTER 21

Tripp walks me back to camp in silence. Deep down, I know he's only making sure I don't do something crazy like run off to save Kari alone. But he doesn't say as much, and I'm grateful. It lets me pretend he's just here to be my friend instead of a babysitter.

He stops in front of a large tent. "Your mom made up a sleeping bag for you," he says.

I nod. "Thanks for walking with me."

"Sure." He hesitates. "See you tomorrow."

"See you."

He doesn't leave until I climb into the tent and zip it closed.

My mother's already asleep. She stirs as I climb into the extra sleeping bag.

"You okay?" she mumbles sleepily.

"Fine, Mom."

She mumbles, "The enemy of my enemy is my friend, Mac. Remember that."

I hold back a sigh. Even in her sleep, she's quoting cliches at me like some kind of wise woman.

"Good night, Mom."

"G'night."

I listen to the symphony of night insects and do my best to count time as it passes. The longer I lie here, the more resolved I become to my crazy-ass plan. Offering myself in exchange for Kari is possibly the dumbest move I can make. It's also futile.

Thiago will never go for it.

He doesn't want me.

The only person he'll let Kari go for is Jadick.

And maybe Levi since he knows Levi will lead him to Jadick. That's why he let me go after Levi in the first place. Torturing Dirk was only the prelude—a show of what will happen if I dare bring him my mate.

But... if I can make the exchange public—offer myself in front of the pack—I might have a shot at making it work. It'll mean confessing to Crigger's murder, which carries a death sentence. But I can't think of another way. I meant what I said to Levi last night. He took my choices away. At least now, as bleak as the options are, I can choose my fate. Even if it means dying for that choice.

I spend what feels like hours lying here trying to think of something else.

In the end, there is only me.

My death for Kari's life.

It's horrific but it beats carrying the weight of her death on my shoulders for the rest of my life. I can't bear it, and I know that because the deaths of the Jades we left behind already threaten to consume me.

I can't take one more.

My mother's snores offer more than enough noise to cover the shuffling sounds my clothes make as I dress and slip outside. She doesn't stir as I move past her and into the night air. How that woman can sleep so heavily in her line of work is beyond me. But tonight, I'm glad for it.

I pause long enough to press a feather-light kiss to my mother's cheek.

I love you.

I don't dare speak the words aloud. It'll have to be enough that I kept her safely out of the conflict. Even as I think it, though, I know the opposite will be true. She'll be angrier that I did this without her than the fact that I did it at all.

Guards are stationed around the camp. I can't see them, but I can sense them.

My wolf catches their scents easily enough on the wind, and I pick my way slowly through the camp to avoid their detection.

After what feels like forever, I leave the last of the Jades behind me.

Ahead, a narrow trail snakes its way through thick forest. The road would be faster. But it's too risky.

I can take this until dawn.

By then, I'll have enough of a head start to—

A figure looms before me.

"Going somewhere?"

I swallow a scream and lock eyes with Levi.

"Dammit," I hiss. "You almost gave me a heart attack."

"You're the one sneaking around camp in the middle of the night. Shouldn't I be the one scared?"

Tears burn my eyes at the sight of him. I had hoped to spare myself this particular goodbye. In fact, looking at him, I know I can't bring myself to say it.

"I'm not stopping you," I tell him. "Scream if you have to."

Doing my best to seem unaffected, I start for the trail, but he falls into step beside me.

"I think I'll just walk it off."

"What are you doing?" I ask sharply.

"Coming with you. What the hell do you think?"

I stop and turn to face him. "Levi, you can't." My voice nearly breaks on the words.

"Why? Because Jadick said so?"

He's angry, but I know it's meant for Jadick and not me.

"I don't know everything that's happened between you two," I start.

"And you don't need to. All you need to know is that I agree with you about answering Thiago's demand."

"Jadick wants to wait," I remind him.

"Jadick is a coward," he snarls. I blink at the vehemence in his words. He straightens and calms. "But we don't need him."

"What are you going to do?" I ask, finally realizing what he means by joining me.

"I'm not doing anything," he says. "*You* are going to hand me over to Thiago, get Kari back, and then tell the others what I've done so they can come and get me out of there, hopefully before Thiago cuts me into tiny pieces."

"You're counting on Jadick to rescue you? I don't know if that's such a safe bet."

"No, Mac." He takes my hand, squeezing it and sending a zing of pleasure through me at the simple touch. "I'm counting on you."

I shake my head, ready to refuse his insane plan. "It's impossible," I say. "We haven't had time to plan it or think through all the ways it could go wrong—"

"Oh? And what was your plan?" he asks.

I don't answer.

"Run back there alone? Beg him to let Kari go out of the kindness of his heart? You have no leverage without me, Mac."

"I have myself," I say quietly.

He looks stricken, and I know he's realized what I meant to do.

"You were going to die," he says, his voice hoarse.

"I was going to save Kari," I say. "And end the standoff. Buy you all more time to do … whatever it is you're going to do."

He stares at me like I've just slapped him. Finally, he shakes his head, snapping out of it. "Thiago would never go for it. He'll throw you out on your ass. Or maybe kill you for fun, but it wouldn't help Kari."

"It would if I made it public," I say. "Confess," I shove the word out, and he goes pale. "Tell everyone I killed Crigger."

"Make it impossible for him to do anything but execute you," he says, his voice rough with anger. "You really are insane, you know that?"

"If it were you in that cell, I would do the same," I say quietly.

"If it were me in that cell, you would leave me and never look back," he says. "Because that's what I would want for you. To be safe. Happy."

"That's the problem, Levi." I stop walking and face him, "Don't you see? I could never be happy without you."

His gaze softens.

He steps closer, pressing his warm palm to my flushed cheek. I lean into his touch, closing my eyes and trying to block out the horror of what has brought us together again. For just a moment, I want to pretend it's just us, finding our way back.

When I open my eyes again, the reality of what lies ahead is too harsh to pretend away. A single tear slips down my cheek, and he brushes it away with his thumb.

"I'm going to make this right," he says. "You have to let me do this. For you. For what I did—before."

"You were protecting me," I mumble.

"Let me protect you now," he says.

And I can only nod and give in. I've never been any good at telling Levi no.

WE SHIFT and walk until dawn as wolves. Mostly to access our senses more fully, avoiding patrols and getting through the boundary line undetected, but it also keeps me from saying or doing something drastic. My wolf whines at being told to keep her paws to herself, but giving myself over to Levi now will only make every-thing harder. I can't afford to give in to my emotions, no matter how badly I want to. Once we have Kari back, maybe then I can figure out where I really stand with the man beside me.

The journey to Blackstone isn't far, but it's painfully slow. We stick to the high ground and the thickets, using all our senses to be sure we aren't tracked or spotted by scouts. I have no doubt Thiago's got all of the pack lands on high alert after that video he sent us.

The closer we get, the more I start to wonder if the others were right; this plan is insane. We're so far past outnumbered, it's pathetic.

But it's not about numbers, I remind myself. Not when it comes to Thiago.

Levi sticks close, his fur brushing mine often as we make our way. I can feel his worry, but more than that, I feel his resolve. He's all in. With this plan. With me.

I think of what Jadick said to him last night. About me clouding his judgment. And I cross my fingers I'm not leading him to his doom.

The outskirts of town come into view just as the sun clears the treetops. We crest the final hill overlooking the valley of Blackstone, and Levi stops. He nods at a stand of trees, and we shift back to our human forms and put on the clothes we've carried in our mouths.

"Here." Levi holds out a length of rope.

"What's this?"

"I'm your prisoner," he says. "We have to make it believable."

"Levi…"

"Don't overthink it, Mac." He comes to stand in front of me, his hands squeezing my upper arms. "This will work. Kari will be safe."

"What about you?"

"We talked about this." His voice is gentle, reassuring. And I hate it. "Wait until you and Kari are safely away, and then we'll figure something out."

"I can't do this," I say, my voice breaking. "I already got enough people killed—"

"No," he says. "Those deaths are not your fault, Mac. Thiago did that."

"I was the one who hunted you—"

"And he used that to hurt the people around us. Thiago's fucked up choices are his, not yours."

I sigh.

He cups my cheeks, wiping at the place where tears would have fallen if I'd only let them. "Stop blaming yourself," he whispers. "Besides, I was a dick for rejecting you. Being tortured by Thiago is the least of what I deserve, right?"

His lips curve at his own horrible joke, and I feel a smile tugging at my mouth in spite of it all.

"Actually, in my revenge plot, I'm the one torturing you."

"Oh, that sounds way more sexy," he says, leaning in to trail kisses along my throat.

"Exactly." I close my eyes at the intensity of pleasure but force my voice to remain light. "Torture's only sexy if you let your prisoner go to the bathroom before things get messy."

"Noted. I will try my best to remember that for next time," he says, breath tickling my neck as he continues to kiss his way closer to my mouth.

"And maybe consider a menu other than drugged lasagna," I tell him.

He pulls back to frown at me. "What are you talking about?"

I roll my eyes. "Okay, we're still pretending."

"Mac," he says, very carefully. "None of the food was drugged. Or at least, not by me."

I stare at him, trying to decide whether I believe him. I kind of hate that we've come far enough to make out but not far enough for me to know if he'd lie about something like that. "Well, someone did," I say.

He lets out a growl and then steps back and punches the tree beside him. His knuckles crack against the bark, but the only one who comes out injured is him. Blood coats his knuckles, and he paces away, shaking his head against the pain.

The outburst is out of place, which only makes me worry.

"Whoa, chill. It made sense. The Jades don't trust me," I start to say, but he cuts me off.

"I questioned Grey extensively before we left the compound. None of the Jades were ever alone with your food. The only two people who were are sitting around that campfire trying to talk you out of doing exactly what we're about to do."

My blood ices over, and my heart threatens to crack at the possibility of what he's implying. Jadick, I can accept. He's a cocky douche who's only looking out for himself. And I'm sure, if I think hard enough, I can come up with a hundred reasons why he'd think killing me would help serve his cause.

But Tripp?

I can't even fathom the idea of that kind of betrayal.

"Tripp would never," I whisper.

Levi groans and runs a hand through his hair. "We don't have time for this kind of suspicion." He closes the distance, his energy chaotic now. "Mac, listen, we need to keep moving. We're too exposed out here. Let's just get Kari, and then we'll figure this all out, okay?"

"I can't rescue you without help, Levi. And if I can't trust Tripp—"

"Go to your mother. She has contacts you can use. People outside our group."

"She has business associates. My mother doesn't have friends, Levi. Why do you think she allied with you guys, knowing Jadick Clemons is running the show? She hates him. But she doesn't have anyone better to support."

He squeezes his eyes shut, and when he opens them again, I find a desperation I've never seen in them before. "We'll figure it out. We just have to keep moving. If we're spotted here—"

A shot rings out, and sharp pain lances through my shoulder. I gasp, and Levi roars, shoving me down. I hit the ground with a thud that I feel all the way down my spine, but even before I can open my mouth to cry out, the heaviness descends. My limbs weaken, and my tongue becomes a lead weight in my mouth. I can't even summon up the energy to be afraid as I watch Levi jerk in sudden pain and fall beside me.

He lands on his side, a dart protruding from his neck, and our eyes meet as scouts rush in to surround us.

"Targets down," someone says. A male voice I don't recognize.

A scream echoes inside the confines of my own mind. I am paralyzed against everything except my own emotions.

Fear.

Frustration.

Defeat.

Exhaustion presses heavily against my eyelids. Levi tries to speak but only grunts. I look back at him, unable to form the words to tell him how much I love him before the pull of darkness sucks me under and sweeps me away.

CHAPTER 22

J wake chilled to the bone and very aware that, underneath
the thin sheet someone has draped over me, I'm naked.
Inhaling sharply, I open my eyes and sit up, scanning the room
where I've woken. It's bland and sparsely furnished. Not a bedroom,
despite the narrow bed I'm lying in. Stainless steel shelving and a
bedside tray to match are the only furniture beyond the thin
mattress. Across the small room, a closed door leads… I don't know
where.

Through a hazy mind, I try to think. To get my bearings.

The last memory I can summon involves being shot with a dart
laced with a drug strong enough to drop me where I stood. Not an
easy feat when your target is a werewolf whose metabolism runs
three to four times faster than a normal human. And then, men
crowding around us, shouting at one another to take us into
custody.

I don't know who they are, but my bet is on a certain douchebag
alpha with a soft spot for sibling torture.

What I do know is I'm alone.

Levi isn't here.

That realization leaves a hollow fear coating my insides.

I scramble up, tossing the cover aside. Nudity isn't a new concept. And I have far worse problems than lack of clothing right now.

The door's locked, but I'm not deterred.

Stepping back, I call on my wolf.

She stirs slowly. I breathe a sigh of relief that they haven't bothered to mute her like Thiago did to me the last time he had me drugged. But before I can call my beast to the surface and shift, the lock clicks, and the door swings open.

I back away as Thiago walks in.

He looks me over, his gaze lingering on my breasts until I'm more uncomfortable than I am angry. He plants himself between me and the door. Behind him, a trio of guards waits just outside.

"Move," I say, my voice hard.

"Sure," he says breezily. "But first, maybe you'd like to explain to me where my brother is hiding. My men have searched high and low on those slopes and turned up nothing besides you and your lovesick little runaway."

"What have you done with Levi?"

Just the mere mention of him has me twisting in knots. My wolf surges, ready to show herself and rip Thiago to shreds if he's done something to harm our mate.

But just like I am singly focused on Levi, Thiago's clearly not ready to let the subject of Jadick go.

"You tell me where Jadick's hiding, and I'll take you to Levi," he says. When I don't answer, his grin broadens as if he's telling some sort of inside joke as he adds, "I'll show you mine if you show me yours."

"If you've hurt Levi at all—"

"I haven't yet," he snaps, smile vanishing. His expression strains as he snarls, "But refuse to answer me and that can change. Now, where is Jadick hiding, and what is his plan of attack?"

I stare back at him.

"He's not here," I say, and Thiago laughs harshly.

"Stop lying," he hisses.

"I'm not."

"We can do this the easy way or the hard way."

"Jadick isn't here," I repeat, louder this time.

Frustration heats my skin until the chilled room doesn't even register anymore. Thiago looks just as angry, if not more. He isn't convinced.

"He didn't come with us," I say. "We did this on our own."

It's a hard truth to admit, mostly because it means we're idiots. A failed plan with no backup and no rescue in sight. Thiago has us now, and he can do what he wants.

Except he never wanted Levi. Or me.

That much is clear from the disappointment clinging to him now.

"All right," he says, straightening and squaring his shoulders as if accepting something unsavory. "The hard way it is."

He turns to the guards. "Bring her in."

I back away, returning to the bed and grabbing the sheet. Wolves are used to nudity, but only when it means we're shifting. I don't exactly want to negotiate for my life—or Kari's—with every bargaining chip I own on full display.

Better to leave some of the mystery alive.

Wrapping the sheet like a makeshift dress, I tuck the ends together and then stand ready for whoever Thiago has summoned.

Kari steps into the open doorway, and I forget all about the sheet or trying to hide my vulnerability.

She's here. Alive.

That's all that matters.

"Kari," I breathe, relief threatening to buckle my limbs. I rush forward and wrap her in a tight hug. "I was so worried. Are you okay?" I pull back to study her. The dark circles underneath her eyes. A scratch along her left cheek that's just beginning to scab over. And a bruise along her jaw that's faded to a dark purple. All of these are recent. They have to be, considering how fast wolves heal.

"Did he—"

I can't even finish my sentence. My rage for Thiago is so completely beyond the ability to form words.

"I'm okay," Kari says.

Behind her, Thiago closes the door, offering us a moment of privacy. I'm surprised by the generosity, but then my worry for Kari takes over, and I drink in the moment, knowing it might be my last. Or hers.

"Come here." I pull her back to the bed, and we sit. "Tell me everything. I saw the video he made. He tied you up. I just... I'm sorry I took so long getting back here. But I found him."

It makes me sick to say the words—like they're the solution instead of an entirely new horrific problem.

"Who?" she asks, eyes lighting with hope.

"Levi," I say, cringing at what I'm offering here.

But seeing Kari battered and bruised at the mercy of a monster like Thiago leaves me no choice. I can't just leave her here. She doesn't deserve this. No one does.

"Levi?" she repeats, frowning.

"Yes, Thiago said I had to find your father's killer. He's the one I saw in that warehouse."

"Levi didn't kill my dad."

Her words startle me. How would she know? "That doesn't matter. Thiago has to honor our arrangement," I say. "He'll let you go."

"And what about you?"

"What about me?"

Her hands grip mine tightly. She leans in, eyes beseeching me. "Thiago wants Jadick," she says. "If you just give up where in the city he's hidden himself, when he plans to strike, I know Thiago will let you go."

"He doesn't plan to strike," I say.

"Mac," she says, her chin wobbling with the threat of tears. "I don't know what he'll do if you keep lying to him."

I shudder, my gaze flicking to the bruise along her jaw.

He'll do that and worse, I have no doubt.

"But I'm not lying. Jadick wouldn't come. He said it was too risky. That we needed more time, more men—"

"Dammit, Mac." The hardness in her voice stops me more than the words. "Don't you want to save me?"

I stare at her, shocked. "Of course I do. That's why I brought Levi—"

"Oh, screw Levi. He's as hell-bent on protecting you as you are of him."

I stare at her.

The flicker of darkness that flashes in her eyes isn't something I recognize at all.

"How do you know what Levi is hell-bent on doing?"

She scowls.

"Kari."

My heart pounds.

A slow dread crawls over my skin. It creeps beneath the sheet I've wrapped so tightly around me, hooking its claws into my flesh. I know its name even before I find the courage to voice it: suspicion.

Kari doesn't waver.

Her spine is straight, her gaze sharpened to a razor point.

It's that directness stabbing straight into my heart that makes me want to weep.

"How do you know what Levi is doing?" I repeat, my voice cracking as my heart begins to break. "And where did you get that bruise, really?"

She starts to answer, another lie clear on the tip of her tongue.

"I gave up my freedom for you," I whisper, and she finally drops the mask.

Her expression twists.

Gone is the terrified desperation. In its place is cold cruelty far beyond anything I've witnessed from Thiago. She stands and, eyes still locked on me, calls over her shoulder, "She's not going to give him up. I'm done here."

The door opens.

Thiago reappears, flanked by guards.

I stare, wide-eyed and disbelieving of the realizations threatening to drown me.

Thiago smirks. "I'm nothing compared to him, you know," he says.

I blink, confused. "You mean Jadick."

Kari backs toward Thiago, a clear alliance. Even so, I can hardly believe what I'm seeing.

"He's a monster," Thiago says. "Why else would we be going to such lengths to stop him. You could help us."

"No, I think you're much, much worse," I say, my voice hoarse.

This can't be happening.

Levi.

I have to get to Levi.

"You must not have spent much time with him, then," Thiago says.

It's a taunt.

He wants me to protest, to argue that I have spent plenty of time with him and know exactly where Jadick is now. I almost give in to it. There's no reason not to. I owe the man nothing. Less than nothing, in fact, for his abandonment of us. Of his own sister. Though, I wonder if he knew what I didn't all along.

Still.

He's sitting in a camp with my mother and Tripp and the rest of the Jades who trusted him enough to follow him here.

And I won't sacrifice them.

Not even for Levi.

Not even for myself.

"You're all monsters," I say, glancing at Kari.

The Kari I knew would wince. She'd be hurt at the accusation. But this one merely rolls her eyes and turns to Thiago. "If she isn't going to give us Jadick's location, we're done here." She turns to the security team waiting in the hall. "Dispatch more teams. Keep scouring the woods. Widen the perimeter. He's out there, and I want him found. Today."

Her voice is cold and demanding.

"All this time, you were helping him," I say. "Not a prisoner. A willing participant."

Kari turns to me, impatience dripping from a sour expression I barely recognize on her face. "I'm my father's daughter, Mac. What did you expect?"

"You were my best friend."

Something passes over her face. Regret? Sorrow? I try to identify it before the darkness creeps in again, but I can't read her like I used to.

Actually, I never could, I realize now.

"That's the thing, Mac. I was never the girl you thought you knew."

The truth of this moment—of Kari's deception—is a knife in my back. It hurts so much worse than anything I've been through up to this moment.

"I won't help you," I say, my chin lifting in a resolve that's unnecessary. They've already realized they'll get nothing from me. Not willingly, anyway. But I have to take a stand against the pain of Kari's betrayal.

"You don't have to be willing in order to help," Thiago says. "Remember the warehouse?"

My eyes snap to his. "What about the warehouse?" I demand.

Kari sighs.

"She can still offer information," Thiago tells Kari, ignoring me. "There are other ways of taking what she doesn't want to give."

Torture.

Kari pauses, and my throat constricts as I realize how quickly the tables have turned. Now, she holds my life in her hands. And I wait while she decides whether I'm worth saving.

Finally, she shakes her head, flicking a dismissive hand in my direction. "Turn her loose. Maybe she'll lead us to Jadick, though I doubt she's stupid enough to fall for it."

"And the mate?" Thiago asks.

Levi.

Kari looks me over, still considering. "Hang on to him. He is the leader of a rebellion, after all." She looks at me. "You're going to leave and never come back, do you understand me? Because if you do, you'll collect your mate in pieces, limb by severed fucking limb."

CHAPTER 23

My gut feels as if someone's punched a gaping hole through it. I can't wrap my head around what's happening. Kari has betrayed me—betrayed us all. Everything I thought I knew about her—about all of this—is a lie. She isn't in need of saving. Hell, she isn't worth saving. She's the villain in this story. I can see that now as I stare between her and Thiago. He's a monster; there's no question about that. But he's following her lead. That means she's in charge here. A Clemons, through and through, considering the lengths she's gone to try and lure Jadick out. To manipulate me into bringing him to her.

Out of all the siblings, Kari's the one I should worry about.

And I've just delivered Levi right into her hands.

The one person she knows she can use to control me.

Otherwise, I'd wrap my hands around her throat and squeeze until her eyes popped out of her skull. If only to end this.

Now, all that matters is saving Levi.

Regardless of what's happened in our past, I refuse to leave him here, in the hands of these monsters.

My wolf rises swiftly to the surface, tearing my skin apart in her haste to get free. My bones pop and lengthen, and I drop to all fours, baring my teeth at both of my captors.

If Kari thinks I'm going to just walk out of here without a fight, she never really knew me at all either.

Thiago grins—he, at least, saw this coming.

His shift is nearly as fast as mine.

I snarl and lunge for Kari, but Thiago is quick. The moment his paws settle on the cold floor, he shoves me back. My claws rake over his fur, opening shallow gashes along his right side.

He doesn't even flinch as he counters my movements and goes on the offensive. He's trained well—but I'm better.

Unfortunately, he has an entire team of soldiers on his side.

Our fight spills into the hall, and I do my best to keep from becoming surrounded. Unfortunately, that's a losing battle with so many opponents.

Thiago's the only one of them who fights me as a wolf. The rest of them use guns, and I can only hope they're still armed with sleeping darts rather than actual bullets.

One of the men fires.

I turn to look at where the shot went, and Thiago rams into me, sending me careening. I crash through a wall and shake myself against the dazed feeling it leaves behind. Aches and pains scream for attention, but I force myself up again.

I cannot let him beat me.

Behind him and his wall of brutes, Kari watches us.

She doesn't look invested in the least. More curious than anything. Maybe even bored. That ignites my fury all over again, and I crouch at Thiago, ready to spring past him toward her.

Before I can move, a roar fills the air. Something moves beside me.

Levi.

He leaps from his bed and shifts. Thiago doesn't even wait for him to complete the change before he strikes. I'm forced to intervene, knocking Thiago away from Levi before any damage is done.

Then, Levi and I are both dodging darts along with Thiago's teeth.

"Don't shoot Thiago, you idiots," Kari snaps at them.

The men stop firing.

We escape into the hall, and Kari backs away, clearly unwilling to join the fight.

Fine.

I'll give her no choice.

With a snap of my teeth, I slip past the closest guard and charge at Kari. My own blood pulses in my ears as I accept what I'm about to do: kill my friend. But Kari slips out of reach, dancing away and then running for a door at the end of the hall.

I chase, listening to the sounds of Thiago and Levi fighting behind me. Thiago snarls, and then their claws click on the hard floor as they follow my lead.

Kari slams through the door, and I tumble out behind her, narrowly missing her calf as we both pass into bright sunlight.

I glance around wildly, trying to get my bearings.

We're on the steps of the alpha house, far left of the main entrance. A side door with more than enough visibility from the street where a crowd has gathered.

At the sight of us, their voices lift in screams and cries for justice.

I falter, confused.

Kari stares at them, just as bewildered, and it takes me a long moment to realize they aren't here at her bidding.

If she didn't do this, who did?

Something slams into me from behind.

Not something, someone.

Thiago's teeth latch onto my hind leg, and I howl in pain as he rips me open. My legs give out, and I tumble hard against the concrete.

Thiago comes in for another bite, and I manage to fight him off. Over his shoulder, I watch as a dart strikes Levi in the hind leg. His eyes widen, blazing with surprise—and pain.

Then he snarls and comes for Thiago, ripping him off me with his claws.

Another shot hits Levi.

His eyelids begin to droop. His movements slow.

The crowd roars, and through the blood pumping in my ears, I have no idea if they're cheering for us—or for them.

A third dart hits Levi.

He falls, hard, eyes closed before he hits the ground.

I whimper, pulling myself to my feet, wincing at the pain from the wound Thiago gave me.

If I don't do something, they'll put me down next.

The shift hurts this time. When I return to my human form, I'm covered in blood, and not all of it's mine. Healing will be much slower this way, but there are more important things than my torn body.

"You all came for a killer," I scream at the crowd.

They're closer now, pressing in toward us with angry expressions. Some carry signs scrawled with words like "Justice for Crigger" and "Death to Romantics."

At my words, they roar back at me, urging me to give them what they want.

"There," I scream, pointing at Thiago, who's already stalking toward me like a predator ready to finish off its prey.

He halts, mid-attack.

The crowd turns to him, shock muting their cries.

"*He's* responsible for Crigger's death," I yell at them. "And he's not the only one."

My gaze swings to Kari. Our eyes meet.

I can't help the pain in my chest as I summon the words that will condemn her, once and for all, to our entire pack. Words I can never take back.

I look back at the crowd through eyes blurred with tears.

Movement ripples through them. I don't have time to see what's caused the sudden chaos of bodies being abruptly shoved aside. It doesn't matter anyway.

This is all about to end.

Before I can speak, a loud crack splits the air, and I whip my head toward the sound. Thiago falls at my feet, his massive form a mess of blood and flesh and tissue.

Then I look up, past him to where Kari stands with a gun.

No darts. Just bullets.

She meets my eyes.

There's not a shred of remorse in her gaze.

I don't move.

I can't.

Behind me, someone screams my name.

"Mac!"

It breaks the spell, and Kari blinks. She turns to the crowd.

"Mac is right," she tells them in a voice I've never heard her use before. Cold authority rings out in every note. "As you know, she was given the incredible task of hunting down my father's killer. And now, thanks to her, we know the truth. My brother, Thiago, has been working against my family for some time now. He had my father killed and even imprisoned me so that no one could challenge him."

The crowd ripples with unease.

I stare at the gun Kari still holds at her side, heart thudding. On my left, Levi lies still from the darts. Considering how well they worked the first time, I know he won't be getting up anytime soon. But if Kari so much as raises that gun in his direction, I won't hesitate to put myself between them.

"Mac is a hero," Kari declares.

The crowd cheers, pulling my attention back to them. To her.

What is she doing?

She meets my eyes with a sly smile that is more foreign than frightening. Who is this girl? Where is my friend?

Gone, her eyes seem to say.

"Mac deserves a hero's reception," she adds.

The crowd responds in kind, clapping and reaching for me now.

I back away from them, toward Kari.

227

She says something to her guards. I can't hear the words over the crowd, but they move toward Levi, and my heart leaps.

"Get away from him," I scream at them.

They ignore me, and I take a step forward, ready to fight them off.

The crowd has pressed in close now. Hands grab at me, and I shake them off. A strong grip closes over my wrist. I yank, but the voice in my ear stills me.

"Mac, it's me."

Tripp

I twist to look at him. "What are you doing here?"

My breath catches, and I start to glance around for the others. For Jadick.

"Getting you out of here," he says in a low voice.

"We have to get Levi," I insist.

"Get him inside," Kari yells, and I look up to see the security team hauling Levi's unconscious wolf back toward the door.

I struggle to free myself from Tripp's grasp, but Kari turns and pins me with a look that stops me cold.

"Remember what I said, Mac. Don't come back here. Not unless you want your mate returned in pieces."

The crowd doesn't hear her, they're too busy yelling about Thiago and Crigger and whatever lies Kari has made them believe about all of this. Tripp pulls me away. I stumble, my eyes flinging from Kari to Levi and back again.

A cry lodges in my throat.

I can't leave, not like this. Not without him.

"Mac," Tripp warns, his voice sharp.

Kari glances upward at something behind her and nods.

Still struggling against his attempt to move me, I shriek as the concrete beside me suddenly cracks open with the force of a bullet.

"Mac!" Tripp's grip on me tightens as a second shot whizzes past my ear.

Someone in the crowd screams.

Tripp doesn't ask again. Instead, he grabs me and lifts me off my feet, carrying me off into the throng of people. They part for us, letting us pass, but not before a third bullet finally finds its mark.

Pain explodes in my shoulder.

I jerk violently, and Tripp nearly drops me.

He curses, but I barely hear it over the roar of voices—and my own blood pounding in my ears.

Pain spreads, paralyzing me, until I hang like a sack of potatoes over Tripp's shoulder. He hisses out a strained breath and breaks into a run, shoving people aside.

"Move," he yells at them.

I can only hang limply and watch as Levi's body disappears inside the alpha's house. Kari follows without a backward glance.

She's the enemy now.

If I live to face her.

~

The story continues in
To Kiss A Wolf

TO KISS A WOLF

BOOK 2

CHAPTER 1

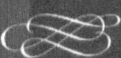

Flames rip through my body—the pain pulsing to the beat of my erratic heart. I am not awake, but I'm certainly not asleep either. Time hangs suspended as venom burns through my torn flesh. Days, weeks, hours—I have no idea how long I lay trapped in this state. I only know that, more than once, I wish it would end even if that end means my death.

In the absence of clear thought, my mind is awash with color.

Bright red for the blood spilled on the steps of the pack house, not just from my own body but from Thiago's as well. Black for the back-stabbing betrayal of someone I considered my closest—and only—friend.

White. Kari's gleaming teeth as she smiled at me—SMILED AT ME—as she ripped out my heart and watched it bleed at her feet.

She played me. Captured Levi. Killed her own brother.

Betrayal is a painful poison.

Desperation is a green cloud. Not envy, exactly, but a twisted rage that coats my mind like fog. Tripp carried me away from Blackstone, and with our escape, he's stolen any chance I might have had at taking Levi with us. I'm angry that he chose me over my mate.

That's a betrayal too.

Eventually, I am brought back to awareness as if by a sharp slap. I wake suddenly, wincing at the blinding glow of white light that shines against my closed lids. And the pain. Vicious pangs that sing through my veins like a banshee's song. Venom. So much venom.

"She's coming to," someone says.

Male. His voice is vaguely familiar, though I can't place it.

"I can't believe you just slapped her," says a second voice.

Tripp. I recognize his voice immediately.

"It worked, didn't it?"

My mother.

My muscles tighten.

Their voices, Tripp's especially, are not a welcome sound, not after everything. Not after my failure—and theirs.

"Just keep her still."

My mother again.

"Jadick," she adds, and the name itself is so buried in my own psyche that I don't recognize it. Not at first.

"Here, this should do it." Jadick's voice is firm, confident.

A sharpness pricks my inner arm, and my eyes fly open, sweeping the space in calculated panic.

I'm on my back. In a small room with bare walls. Three faces hover above mine. My mother, Tripp, and Jadick Clemons, alpha heir to the Black Moon pack. They look down at me with expressions full of concern. The sight of them here together fills my throat with bile. I don't want this.

I don't want them.

Behind them is a door.

If I can just get there, I can find Levi, put all this right again—

"Whoa, easy." Jadick blocks my attempts to sit up.

"Dude, you don't want to put your hands on her," Tripp warns.

"She'll rip her stitches if she tries to—"

I catch Jadick in the jaw with a clumsy fist. Tripp grabs him, holding him up while he gets his bearings. My mother steps in, shoving me down again with hands that are not nearly as worried about my stitches as they are about being obeyed.

"You stay right where you are, young lady," she warns me before I can try anything stupid. Her eyes are hard, and her voice is full-on "lecture mode" as she waits for my compliance.

Not likely.

But my attempts to struggle become slow, my limbs suddenly too heavy. I search for my wolf, but she's too far out of reach. I can't shift. Clearly, whatever Jadick injected me with is meant to subdue me. And it's working. Instead of wasting my energy on what I hate to admit would be a losing battle, I go still and put all of my aggression into the glare I aim at Vicki Quinn.

"What happened to me?"

"Kari ordered her security team to shoot you. One of the bullets found its mark."

Memories of gunshots swim in my mind. The gunfire echoes like a sound still buried in my eardrums. But I don't remember whose bullet it was—laced with venom, of course—

until they say the words. Kari. Not her team. She's the one who shot me. Now, I pretend it doesn't sting way down deep in my heart to know it's true.

"Where am I?" I ask quietly.

"Fountain Mall," she says.

Right. The mall. "In Wythe," I say, remembering what Levi told me.

"In Green Hills, actually," she says.

I stare at her.

Green Hills?

That's halfway across the state. Nowhere near Blackstone.

Nowhere near Levi.

"I thought Levi said the mall was in Wythe." My brain is still foggy, working too slow to make sense of this. How many malls did they scout, anyway?

The three of them exchange a look.

"Levi didn't know about this one," Tripp says finally.

235

His voice is tight. I can't tell who his ire is aimed at, though.

I close my eyes slowly, absorbing it all, then open them again. Jadick has recovered and is standing beside my mother, watching me warily. He rubs gingerly at his jaw, and I take that as a sign of victory.

Tripp stays well out of reach near my feet.

Smart.

I focus on my mom again. "How long have I been out?"

Small lines pinch around her mouth. She's pissed.

Join the club.

"Two days."

Two days.

I want to scream.

Levi could be dead by now.

Instead of arguing with her, I look at Tripp. "I can't believe you."

"Me? What the hell did I do?"

"You left him there."

His eyes soften. He stares down at me sadly. "I made a choice, Mac. You can't fault me for that."

I avert my gaze before any of them can see the tears welling.

"You chose wrong."

Awkward silence hangs until Tripp clears his throat. "I'll be outside."

His voice is sad, but I can't bring myself to comfort him. Instead, I listen to his footsteps shuffle out.

"Mac."

My mother's voice is softer now—almost compassionate.

I blink back angry tears and look over at her.

"What?" I snap.

"You have to go slow."

"Not the first time I've been poisoned this month," I remind her.

A tracker with claws coated in venom got ahold of me not long ago. I'd only just recovered when I was shot by my best friend. *Former* best friend. The girl I showed up to save is the one we all need saving from.

I swallow hard at the realization.

"This is worse than last time," my mother says. "If Tripp hadn't brought you back when he did, you would have died."

Her words are pointed—meant to make me care about the risks of pushing too hard—but I don't. The only thing I feel bad about is surviving.

"It would have been no less than I deserve."

Her eyes widen. She glances at Jadick.

"Let's give her some space," he says, "to rest."

My mother sighs but gives in. I can't help but wonder how Jadick has managed to give Vicki Quinn an order—and have her follow it.

"I brought you some things. They're on the counter when you feel up to moving around." I glance over and see the bag in question. It's a "go bag" my mom always kept in her Jeep. One for each of us. Just in case Crigger finally turned on us and decided we were more valuable dead than alive. Or at least, that's what I always assumed they'd be for. My mother never qualified it, she just liked to say "just in case" like the rest of the sentence didn't need explaining. I guess today is that "in case."

The bag holds mostly clothes. A few toiletries. No food because we'd always have our wolves for hunting. No fire either. Not when the cold is a non-issue for beasts like us. The only other survival item the bag contains is a pre-paid cell phone. Not that I have anyone left to call.

When I look back at her, my mother hesitates, at a loss for once. It makes me wonder if she's thinking the same thing about the sad state of my life. Of both our lives. "For now... get some sleep, Mac." She pats my arm and then walks out without waiting for my response.

Jadick follows her into the hall but leaves the door cracked. From here, I can see them huddled together, their whispers not nearly low enough.

"You really think she's going to be all right," my mother says, her words more of a question. For the first time since I can remember, I hear real worry leak into her voice.

"Physically, yes." Jadick's words come slowly as if he's chosen them carefully.

"What does that mean?"

"She's been betrayed by the one person she trusted most in the world. She's going to need more than a shot of anti-venom and a few stitches to heal from that. She has to *want* to heal."

"Then make her want to," she snaps.

He's quiet for a moment then says, "You realize what you're asking."

"You did it once before," she says.

"Precisely. You want to owe me again? Knowing what payment I'll expect this time?"

My mother hesitates. "Is there nothing else you want?"

"You know there isn't."

My heart pounds as my instincts scream for her to end this conversation. The words they're exchanging sound more like a negotiation than a request to help nurse me back to health.

Finally, she sighs. "Mac's life matters more," she says quietly. "Do what you have to do."

I miss what they say next as sleep pulls me under, willing or not.

WHEN I OPEN my eyes again, Jadick is lounging in a chair with his hands folded lazily across his abdomen. He smiles at me—a slithery kind of smile that turns my stomach. Until I remember how I got here and who's missing from this moment. Then, it's the kind of smile that makes me want to punch something. Jadick should not be here instead of Levi. And he shouldn't be smiling about it either.

"You look better," he says.

I stretch my limbs then immediately regret it when the pain sparks to life. Hissing through my teeth, I say, "I feel like death."

His smile slips. Worry crowds his eyes, crinkling the corners as he leans forward. "The anti-venom should have worked by now."

I don't know how to answer that. Discussing my medical condition is an unwanted prospect considering I don't trust this man as far as I can throw him. Besides, a quick check-in with my wolf reveals she's still MIA. And I refuse to admit how weak that makes me feel.

"What are you doing here?" I ask instead.

"I've been worried about you."

"And Levi?" I ask. "Are you worried about him?"

"Of course."

Liar.

"What are you doing to get him back?"

"Mac," he says, and in that word, I hear the truth: nothing. He's done nothing.

"He gave himself up for these people," I snap. "For you. And you're just going to abandon him?"

"There's a lot to consider," he says, but I don't want to hear his bullshit.

I sit up, blinking past the black spots that dot my vision. The room spins, but I ignore that too and glare at the pretty boy alpha heir. "Tell me what you're considering."

His smile is almost indulgent. "I don't think it's the right time to discuss battle strategy—"

"It's a rescue mission, not a war," I snap.

"He's the leader of a rebellion, Mac. An uprising. That's why Kari wants him. Regardless of how I feel about my sister—" I try to hide the fact that even the mention of her hurts me. "—the reality is, he's a traitor to her and will be treated as such. To even attempt to rescue him will likely ignite a full-scale war. I have to keep that in mind. I have to think of the lives here counting on me."

So, he's taken command then.

I figured as much.

"*Levi's* counting on you. You're supposed to be his friend." I nearly scream the words.

He frowns, silent in the face of my outburst.

Outside the door, footsteps approach.

The door opens.

My mother peers inside.

The sight of her reminds me of the cryptic conversation I over-heard, and immediately my defenses go up.

"You're awake." Her relief is clear, but it gives way quickly to suspicion when she sees my expression. "What's wrong? Are you in pain? I can get another dose of—"

"I don't want more medicine," I snap. "I want to know what you're doing to rescue Levi."

"Mac." My mom eases into the room. Her expression is gentle, but that's the problem. I brace myself for the sugar-coated refusal she's obviously about to give me. "Levi gave himself up willingly."

"We thought we were dealing with Thiago," I say. "I didn't know—"

I didn't know Kari was the villain instead of the victim.

The unsaid words burn my throat.

"Regardless, you two didn't have clearance to do what you did. You disobeyed direct orders, and you did it when we were as yet unprepared to launch any kind of rescue mission. We're doing all we can, but these things take time. Planning. We can't just walk up to the alpha house and ask for his release."

"Of course you can't. I'm not an idiot, Mother."

My tone is sharp enough to quiet her.

I look at Jadick. "Kari's not cruel without motive, at least. She wants something from Levi. Right now, it's you. The Jades. This place. And she'll torture him until she gets it out of him. He's not safe there with her."

"I agree," he says, which in itself shocks me into momentary silence. "Unfortunately, your mother is right about not being ready to launch a rescue mission," he adds.

"Forget it, I'll go my damned self." I start to get up, but the room sways. I clutch at the edge of the mattress. Jadick and my mother exchange a look.

"Tripp told us Kari ordered you not to return," my mother says.

Fuck.

She's right.

I hate when she's right.

"You'll only get him hurt if you show up there," Jadick says. His words are not a warning—they are salt in my wounds.

"We can't just sit around with our thumbs up our ass," I snap.

Jadick and my mother share a look that feels ominous.

"What the hell are you two plotting?" I ask.

"Mac, I know you're upset," my mom begins, but Jadick interrupts.

"Don't sugarcoat it, Vicki. She's a big girl." His expression is harder now. Not angry, but whatever gentle approach he'd used before is gone. At least *he* can see it won't work to coddle me. "Levi wouldn't want to risk the Jades for his own safety. I know because he told me so. Long before you ever showed up and created this mess."

"Me?" His words hit their mark. Guilt pings in my chest.

I created this mess.

"Levi's in Kari's custody because you decided to answer her call," Jadick says. "It was a trap, Mac. And you walked right into it, dragging Levi alongside you. I am glad you were brought home safe, but I won't risk everything Levi has worked for in order to satisfy your hormones. He knew the risks when he decided to go with you that night."

My hands curl into fists.

"He gave himself up for you," I tell him, a repeat of earlier. Mostly because I don't know what else to say right now.

Jadick shakes his head. "That's where you're wrong," he says, "He gave himself up for you."

CHAPTER 2

*T*he tile designs on the ceiling of my room swirl before my tired eyes. Maybe it's the vertigo. Or, you know, the poison. Either way, Jadick's words echo in my head, making rest impossible. *He gave himself up for you.* Our conversation was hours ago, but I am still trembling with rage. With the need to aim it somewhere, anywhere other than at myself. Jadick has refused to help rescue Levi. My mother's clearly on his side. Tripp can't be trusted—not until I know for sure whether he's the one behind drugging me when I was first brought to the Jades.

I have no ally here, not really.

That means it's up to me alone. Knowing they've abandoned Levi to a murderer pisses me off, and it's that rage I cling to now. Anger is an energy I can't afford to lose, not when I have nothing else left to fuel me.

Alone, I sit up, this time with less dizziness.

The pain in my left shoulder continues to burn steadily, but it's more bearable than before. Not by much but it's enough. Carefully, I peel my shirt back—it's clean and not the one I was wearing when I came here—and then do the same to the gauze taped to my skin. My stomach roils at the sight of the jagged stitches. Yellowish liquid oozes from beneath the sutures. It's not a great clean-up job, but then I didn't expect much considering Tripp's only training came from our first aid elective sophomore year.

Apparently, the Jades have no doctor. Or not one willing to treat me.

But I'm in fresh clothing. Fresh bandage too from the looks of it. That means one of them saw me topless. Ugh. It better have been my mother and not Jadick.

I press the tape and gauze back over the wound and try not to think about how much of my veins contain poison and how much is blood. Considering my wolf is still out of reach, I'd say the poison is still winning.

I move slowly. My parched mouth leads me first toward the counter where I find an unopened bottle of water. A granola bar sits next to it. I snag both and then uncap the water, drinking until my stomach churns. Capping it again, I tear into the granola bar, scarfing it so quickly my stomach roils. Next is the bag my mother brought me. Inside is a change of clothes and a few toiletries. The idea of a shower is appealing, but since none exists in this room, I leave the travel-size shampoo and soap alone. Rifling through, I find a flashlight and a bit of rope. No phone. Either she doesn't trust me, or she doesn't think I have anyone left to call. Either way, it sucks.

With a sigh, I shuffle over to pull the door open.

On the other side, a short hallway opens into what looks like a larger space.

Standing between me and that space is Grey, Levi's guard.

His cargo pants and black tee are a little wrinkled, but that's the only indication of the fact that he and all of the people he's sworn to protect here—the Jades, as they call themselves—are on the run and living in an abandoned shopping mall. I don't feel very sorry about his wrinkly uniform, though. Grey's never liked me. Then again, he's never pretended otherwise, so that's something.

"What are you doing?" he asks.

"Going to get Levi." I take a step toward him, gauging my physical strength against his right now. "What are you doing?"

He straightens and plants his feet. "Stopping you."

I snort. "I really, really wish you'd try."

He glares as if he actually might, but then his shoulders drop, and he shakes his head. "Too easy." He lifts his chin, a brutish gleam in his eye. "You look like shit, you know."

"Back at ya. Then again, I was shot with a venom-laced bullet. What's your excuse?"

His mouth pulls into a tight frown, and he marches over, looming over me. He wants to intimidate me. He has no idea I've seen too much to be scared of something so obvious as him.

"You might not want to talk shit without Levi here to protect you," he tells me.

"I don't need anyone's protection."

His brow lifts. "You sure about that? You're the reason Levi's not here in the first place. I'm not the only one who knows it either." He cocks his head. "Why do you think Tripp had to stitch you up?" He doesn't wait for my answer before he says, "The doc refused to treat you. The people blame you and rightly so."

My response stalls.

I try to catch my breath but can't.

He's right. This is all my fault. I—

"Grey."

A raspy female voice slices through our little stand-off.

Grey takes a single step back, eyes still locked on mine. The look he wears says this is far from over.

Frankie walks up, her gaze sharp.

She still wears the same no-nonsense expression as the day I first met her back at the compound. Her uniform today is navy blue overalls with a red anchor for a crest. I have no idea where she got the clothes or the crest because I've never seen it on any of the other uniforms, but she carries it off with an air of absolute authority.

"Is there a problem?" she asks.

"Just explaining how things are to our guest." Grey's voice twists on the last word.

"And exactly how are things, Grey?"

He looks away, clearly not wanting to explain it to her.

Something tells me she doesn't need him to.

Instead of pressing it, she looks at me. "You mind if we walk a bit? My knees need stretching, or they're going to petrify right where I stand."

Her request is a distraction; a delay in my mission. But I don't see how I can refuse. She's clearly making herself my ally by coming here and as much as I am itching to go after Levi, something tells me I'm going to need Frankie in my corner to get it done.

"Sure."

"Ma'am," Grey begins. "I'm supposed to keep an eye on her. Jadick's orders—"

"Do you think your *eye* outranks mine?" Frankie demands.

"Well, no, ma'am, but—"

"Then get the hell out of the way. And you can tell Jadick that was an order too if it makes you feel better."

She all but shoves Grey aside and saunters past.

As I pass, I offer him a smile that I'm surprised doesn't get me punched in the mouth, considering the dark look he flashes back at me. Grey might not have been the one to drug me back when Levi made me his prisoner, but it wasn't for lack of wanting to.

I follow Frankie into the larger space at the end of the hall and realize it's an abandoned department store. Which means my room is nothing more than an old store manager's office. Out here, empty clothing racks gleam underneath the lights. Behind us, the main exit has been boarded up tight. In front of us, plastic clothes hangers lie scattered across the faded carpet. Frankie steps over them and leads me out into the mall corridor.

The emptiness of the hallway is eerie.

No shoppers. No kiosks.

Well, there's one kiosk, and from here, it looks like someone spray-painted dicks all over it, but that only adds to the eeriness.

"You're looking a little pale. Should we stop?"

I shake my head, pushing my body to keep moving, but the

farther we go, the worse I feel. What was a slow walk a few moments ago is now a tilted hobble thanks to the burning pain radiating from my shoulder all the way down my legs. My lungs burn, and my breaths are labored. My mother was right. This time is worse. I am in no condition for a rescue mission—but what choice do I have?

"So, you're still in charge?" I ask, trying to get a sense of where things stand now.

"I'm head of internal operations," she says, using her fingers for air quotes around her title.

"Huh. I figured Jadick would have appointed his own people now that he's taken over."

"He has. Apparently, Gregario and Burnett have no spine or moral compass. They're his lap dogs now. And a few others have decided to be loyal to the new regime as well."

There's more she's not saying, but I can't let myself be distracted by Jade politics.

Silent, I scan the corridor for some sign of an exit. If I'm going to get out, I need a plan. But none of the doors are marked. Either there's no way out of this hall, or the signs have been removed. Far down at the other end of this wing, I can see a few people crossing from one corridor to the next. No one comes even close to where Frankie and I make our way, and I wonder if I'm kept apart from the other Jades for my safety or theirs.

"Interesting living arrangements," I say.

"It's better than a tent."

"Was that the other option?"

"Jadick doesn't give other options."

She's clearly not a fan of his.

"Levi mentioned a mall," I say quietly. "But not in Green Hills."

Frankie doesn't respond, but I catch her eye, and I know she understands where my thoughts have drifted.

"Kari tortured Dirk for the first location," I say. "Don't you think she'll—"

"That's why Jadick picked this place."

Jadick. Of course. Does that mean he's had plans of taking over leadership here all along?

"Is there even a mall in Wythe?" I ask.

She gives me a look. It tells me all I need to know. "Before you get upset about our leader being kept in the dark, it was for his own good. Levi doesn't know anything about this place, which means he can't give it up."

"Isn't that the problem, though? When he can't tell her where we are, she'll only go harder on him until—"

"Don't think too hard about things you can't control."

I swallow back the rest of my question along with the tears that threaten. She's right. Giving in to the mental image of Levi being hurt will only distract me from my goal.

Frankie steers me toward a small doorway next to a water fountain and ushers me through. In the short, narrow hallway on the other side, she pauses to lock the door behind us. My internal alarm starts blaring as I realize how isolated we've become.

"Where are we going?" I ask, noting the flickering light at the end of the hall.

The flashing creates weird shadows, and I just realized if Frankie's trying to double cross me, I've walked right into her little plan. But she turns a corner into a small office, and when I follow, I'm surprised to find Tripp waiting inside.

"You didn't tell me he was here," I say.

Frankie shrugs. "If I had, you wouldn't have come."

My surprise turns quickly to irritation.

"No shit," I snap. "Are you two working together now to ruin my life?"

"We're working together to understand what Jadick's really up to," Tripp says. "And whether his intentions are going to get us all killed."

I cross my arms, mostly to hide the fact that standing so long is making me sway. "What happened to Jadick being your golden boy? I thought he was like the Jades' mascot or something."

Frankie's eyes flash with disgust, but neither of them contradicts me.

"Jadick was always our golden ticket," Tripp says. "That doesn't mean he deserves to lead us."

"I'm leaving," I say, spinning for the exit.

"You sure?" Tripp calls. "If you do that, you'll miss the chance to listen in on Jadick's secret meeting."

I pause, my hand braced on the doorframe.

Dammit.

He has me.

I turn slowly, noting the small bank of monitors on the counter beside where Tripp stands. On the grainy screen, I can make out Jadick seated at a conference table. My mother sits across from him. Stationed behind him against the wall are two of Levi's personal guards, Burnett and Gregario. The latter is the asshole I sucker-punched when he first kidnapped me and tossed me into a creeper van.

I shouldn't blame him. He was only following Levi's orders.

But my anger isn't rational.

A fact Tripp is probably acutely aware of in this moment.

"Why can't we just attend the meeting in person?" I ask.

They exchange a glance.

"Let's just say Jadick has tightened up his inner circle," Tripp says.

My shoulders sag as I realize that circle doesn't include me. Or them, apparently.

"I thought you said you're in charge of internal operations," I say to Frankie.

"Fancy name for dorm mother," she says with a derisive snort.

"Jadick's playing nice with all of Levi's previous leadership," Tripp explains quietly. "But Gregario and Burnett are in his pocket. Always have been, apparently. As for strategy, he's doing things differently now that—"

He stops, and I look away because I know exactly what he was about to say. *Now that Levi's gone.*

I remind myself Tripp and Levi are assholes. Or were assholes. I was kidnapped by their people on Levi's orders, after all. It doesn't really ease my guilt, but it distracts me well enough.

Finally, I look back at Tripp. "And you're out too?"

He shakes his head. "I don't think I was ever in."

I want to argue, especially considering he's Levi's bestie, but I let it go. Maybe that's exactly why he's out.

Frankie nods. "It's starting."

We all turn back to the monitors. I shuffle forward for a closer look.

"Who's that guy he's meeting with?" I ask.

"Name's Vale," Frankie says. "He's one of our spies in Blackstone."

Blackstone.

My attention sharpens.

Jadick is meeting with a spy from pack lands. Maybe he's doing something after all.

I nod at Tripp, and he reaches over and turns a knob beside the monitor. Jadick's voice spills from a crackly speaker.

"...any trouble?" Jadick asks.

"The alpha house is on high alert, that's for damn sure," the man, Vale, drawls.

It's hard to make out specific features, thanks to the grainy image on-screen. These monitors are clearly from a bygone era. I wonder where Tripp even found them. But I don't complain, it's better than nothing.

"But no trouble," Vale adds.

"And the message?"

"Here. Read for yourself." He passes Jadick something across the table.

Jadick unfolds it and reads it to himself.

Then he smirks.

"Well?" my mother prompts.

Her nails drum against the table impatiently.

Jadick glances up at her then refolds the paper and hands it up to the security guards behind him. Burnett steps forward and pockets the paper then steps back again.

"It seems my sister has decided to accept my request for a video conference," Jadick says. "But only on one condition."

"What's that?"

"She wants Mac to join us."

"Absolutely not." My mother's response is swift and firm.

A pain that feels like the blade of betrayal twists in my chest.

"She can't handle this," my mother adds. "You know what she's been through."

"She's a liability," Vale adds, and my anger pulses.

He doesn't even know me.

"I don't disagree with either of you," Jadick says. "But we'll let it play out. You never know. It could work to our advantage."

"She's barely on her feet," my mother protests, clearly not ready to lose this argument.

Jadick pins her with a look. "You said the venom would only take a day or two to clear her system."

"Yes, well, it's an estimate. She's tough," my mom says uncertainly.

"Exactly my point." He presses his palms to the table and stands. "It's settled then. I'll let her know."

"I'll tell her," my mother says, standing quickly.

I don't wait to hear Jadick's response.

I'm out the door before Tripp or Frankie can stop me.

In the main hallway, I hesitate, unsure which way to go from here.

From the far left, I see my mother striding this way. I shrink back against the wall, sliding into an alcove beside the water fountain. She passes by then disappears inside the empty clothing store where Grey probably still waits for me to return.

I don't wait for her to figure out I'm gone.

The moment she's out of sight, I hurry toward the door she exited. It's near the end, just before this corridor opens into a kind of atrium where all of the hallways converge. In the center, a fountain has turned green with algae. Jades stroll around it on their way to or from various places, including a few dressed in guard uniforms. When I get close, several of them spot me, and I increase my pace before they realize I shouldn't be out here. Running is painful, so I end up doing more of a power walk. But eventually, I make it to the door my mom left through—and find it locked.

Determined, I bang on it.

"Open up," I yell.

My behavior draws a few stares from the Jades at my back. I face the door and bang harder.

"Jadick, I know you're in there. Open this door!"

The door clicks open, and Gregario scowls at me from the other side. Over his shoulder, I see a short hallway with doors lining either side. Jadick's in one of them.

"What are you doing out of your room?" Gregario demands.

"Tell Jadick I need to talk to him."

"He's busy." Gregario glances at someone over my shoulder.

I turn to see Grey and my mother approaching.

Dammit. Busted.

"Tell him," I repeat, "Now."

"What's going on?"

Jadick steps out of the last door on the right.

"She insists on talking to you," Gregario explains.

"Well then, let her through." Jadick waves me forward.

I shove past Gregario before my mother and Grey can catch up. Then I slam the door behind me and stride toward Jadick.

"We can talk in here," he says, ushering me toward the door at the end.

The conference room I saw in the video feed. It's empty now, but it still feels full of listening ears, especially since I know Tripp and Frankie are probably watching this entire thing. Despite that, I whirl on Jadick, angry that I'm not sure I could actually kick his ass in my current condition.

"Did you know?" I demand.

He shuts the door and walks to the chair at the head of the table.

Then he drops into it and folds his hands like I've seen him do when he wants to appear open and approachable.

"I know a lot of things," he says. "Maybe you could be a tad more specific."

I press my hands to the table. "Did you know it was Kari? All this time? That Thiago was just her partner? Her puppet?"

"You look winded, Mackenzie. Sit down."

He gestures to a chair, but I ignore it.

"I didn't know," he says finally. "I, of course, suspected. Thiago's always been easy to manipulate." His expression darkens. "And Kari's always been a fucking brat."

I stare at him, breathing heavily with the weight of my rage, waiting for him to go on. To give me something more. But he's clearly uninterested in this line of conversation. "There's going to be a conference call later this evening," he says instead. "With Kari." He pauses to see how I'll react.

I don't.

"I'd like you to be there for it," he adds.

But I'm not ready to let him off the hook. "If I find out you knew and didn't tell me—and now Levi's trapped there... I will kill you."

The door swings open, and Burnett and Gregario enter, crowding toward me until I'm backed into the corner.

"Get away from me, assholes," I warn.

They don't move, and I ball my hands into fists. I might not be up for this challenge in my current state, but I damn sure don't plan to back down either.

"They're only responding to your blatant threats," Jadick explains. "If you fight them, I'll have no choice but to restrict you to your room."

Jadick's voice is maddeningly calm.

He doesn't care which I choose.

He only enjoys watching it all play out.

"If I fight them, you'd be next," I say.

In response, Burnett grabs my arm and growls.

"Let me go, or I'll rip your arm off and beat you with it," I warn him.

"If you fight them, you won't attend the call with Kari. Which means you won't get a chance to lay eyes on *him*."

Jadick's words stop me.

Levi might be on the call.

I yank out of Burnett's grasp. He reaches for me again, but I growl at him, baring my teeth as if I'm an animal even on two legs.

Maybe I am.

"Back off, I'm not going to fight," I say, my words ringing with regret.

Burnett and Gregario take a grudging step back.

It's barely enough to give me space to breathe.

"Boys," Jadick says pointedly, and they finally retreat, positioning themselves on either side of the table—directly between me and their boss.

I look at Jadick lounging in his chair.

His eyes gleam with interest, and I have to force my hands into fists so I don't leap across the table and claw his eyeballs out of their sockets.

"You've always been strong, Mac," he says, "And I admired you for it. But now, in this hour of grief, you are breathtaking."

I don't know what to say to that. He's turned on by my heartbreak?

"Give me a team," I say, focusing on my goal.

"For?"

"To go after Levi."

"You're hardly fit enough for battle," he says.

Considering my breaths are labored from that small scuffle a moment ago, I can scarcely argue. But admitting it is out of the question.

"Then send the team," I say, desperate for something. "Frankie can lead them, or even my mother—"

"I will not risk lives recklessly."

I lift my chin. "Fine. I'll go alone."

"I can't allow it. Not when you're still recovering."

"Do you intend to keep me here as your prisoner?"

"Of course not." He looks surprised then hurt.

I have to remind myself it's all an act.

His charm is so convincing.

"I'm on your side, Mac. You and I have been allies since that moment in the canyon, have we not?"

I grit my teeth.

Allies.

Is that what he was to me when he made some backroom deal with my mother earlier?

"Besides, this call is a chance to negotiate. To decide all of this peacefully and diplomatically. Don't we owe it to ourselves—to Levi —to try diplomacy before we engage in any more violence?"

He's right, of course.

And he makes it all sound so easy.

So neat and tidy that to argue would make me the asshole.

"Fine," I say quietly. "I'll stay for the call."

"I'm glad to hear it." He beams, and I know I've lost this round even if neither of us is winning the battle.

CHAPTER 3

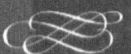

I'm sent back to my room to wait out the afternoon. Part of me wants to refuse or put up a fight, but something tells me I have to pick my battles wisely. This isn't one I can win, anyway. The line between guest and prisoner gets blurrier and blurrier. And my strength is still shit. After a failed push-up that nearly leaves me unconscious, I give up on physical training. Instead, I spend a few hours trying to sleep on the thin cot, but it's useless. Every time I close my eyes, I see Kari with the gun. Her betrayal cuts deeper than almost any pain I've felt. The only pain worse was Levi's rejection, but even that doesn't sting quite so sharply anymore. Not after knowing it was Thiago's blackmail that forced him to do it.

Before he was taken, things had changed between us. It felt like we'd been moving toward something. Maybe even toward each other. Finally.

Now that he's gone, it seems like a daydream.

I've hated Levi for so long—wanting to save him is foreign. But I can't deny I feel responsible. Besides, even when I loathed him, I'd never wish for his torture. Not at anyone else's hands anyway. For some reason, I think about my conversation with Kari that night outside the club. About wanting to leave. To travel. Anything to escape the toxic pack life with an alpha like Crigger. And I'm struck with the realization that I'm free. Right now, I could leave. Walk away from all of this. No choosing sides. No more being caught up in the Clemons' family feud that only ever seems to end in bloodshed for the people around them. And my heart is tempted, if only to find a peace I've never once in my life truly experienced. But then I think about everyone I'd leave behind.

The Jades, who only ever wanted a better life for themselves and their families. Tripp, who once stood by me in a way no one ever has. Who also left to fight for our futures even when that meant leaving me behind. And Levi, who gave me up—rejected me—to protect me. To save my life.

I can't leave them knowing it's all headed toward more violence. Leaving Levi wouldn't bring peace; it would be cowardly. And I'm no coward.

Besides, I'm the reason he's where he is. I'm the one responsible for this mess, just like Jadick said. My thoughts drift to Levi, where he is now. Probably the dungeon. Or one of those hospital-like rooms they put us in before. I wonder if he's angry about it. Or if he'll ever forgive me for getting him captured.

I wouldn't.

The guilt presses in until my chest is tight with it.

I have to stay. To make this right.

Hours pass in excruciating stillness.

No one comes for me.

I half-expected Tripp or even Frankie to show up after my show-down with Jadick earlier, but they've clearly left me to my own devices. That's its own kind of torture too. I don't trust them, but I find myself wondering if I might like their company—if only to keep from being stuck with nothing but my own thoughts.

Finally, there's a knock at my door.

My mother enters with her hair pulled back in a sleek bun that's more practical than elegant. She wears her usual utility pants and tank top. I look down and note my attire is nearly identical. The apple didn't fall far when it comes to our sense of style.

"We're assembling for a video call with Kari," she says. "Jadick has asked you to join us."

I get up, my heart already pounding at the thought of seeing Kari on-screen. Or worse, seeing Levi. I need to know if he's all right, but there's a good chance he's not—and I'm not sure if I can handle it.

My muscles scream in protest at my movements. I grimace and shove to my feet anyway.

"Are you sure you're up for this?" My mother eyes me worriedly.

"I'm fine."

"Would you like something for the pain?"

"No."

"We gave you the highest dosage of the anti-venom we could. But... you've already had one dose, and these things become less effective with each application."

"Does that mean it's not going to work?" I ask, startled at the thought. I'd assumed it would be like last time. A couple of days of exhaustion and then boom, back to normal.

"The dose we gave you should help take the edge off, but your body still has to do a lot of the work itself. It'll take some time to burn off the rest of the venom naturally."

Great. So, I'm going to be useless for even longer.

Sighing, I can't help but ask the question that's been bothering me since I woke here.

"Why did Kari shoot me?" I ask.

She blinks, startled by the question. Then her expression tenses. "Do I really need to explain? Kari played you, Mac. She—"

"I get that." I wave her off. "But at the end, she was letting me leave. She told me not to come back, or she'd hurt Levi, but she was letting me walk. Then all of a sudden, she was shooting at me. What do you think changed her mind?"

"I have no idea, Mac." She sounds exhausted as she says the words. Like she can't even summon the strength to consider my question.

I think about her cryptic conversation with Jadick and bite my lip. Part of me wants to ask what it meant. What kind of deal did she cut? And how fucked am I for being used as collateral? But I know my mother too well to think she'd answer me outright. Anything she wants me to know, she's already told me. Which is nothing.

"I know Kari hurt you," she says, stumbling over her words. Her tone is soft, but since that's not a voice she ever uses on me, it sounds unnatural. Awkward. I stare at her, unsure what's happening here. "And it must be hard—accepting everything that's happened because of your rash decision—"

Irritation flares hot at that.

"—But I want you to know I'm here for you."

"Please don't."

She frowns. "Don't what?"

"Do this. Try to talk about feelings. It's not us."

"Mac, I'm worried," she says. "You should be stronger by now even with the anti-venom losing its punch. You have to want to get better."

"Do you think I'm too depressed to heal myself?"

She doesn't answer, but for a moment, her mask drops away, and I can see the worry she's trying to keep buried.

"I'm going to be fine," I tell her. "I don't want to die, okay?"

"If you did have dark thoughts, you wouldn't be the first. There's no shame in a mate rejection affecting your psyche—"

"My psyche is fine."

"Mac, you know as well as I do—we hurt the most when the rejection process is at its height. For most, that pain only lasts a short time, but for you... This has gone on long enough, don't you think?"

"You want me to reject Levi," I say flatly.

"I want you to be strong."

I stare at her, stunned. "You really think that's what makes us strong?"

She doesn't answer.

I shake my head. "I never pegged you for a Reject, Mom."

"I'm not a Reject," she says, exasperated.

"Well, you're certainly not a Romantic."

"I'm a mother," she snaps. "That comes before a stupid label about my love life. It always has."

"Is that why you left Dad? Because you hate labels?"

"I loved your father," she says, eyes flashing. I've struck a nerve, but I don't care. I'm sick of being talked to like everything is my fault.

"Leaving is how you show love," I say, my words dripping with acid. "Now it all makes sense since you were always leaving me for some job or another."

"I did what I had to in order to survive." Her body trembles, and I'm not entirely sure it's mere anger rolling off her now. It feels more desperate than that. "You would have been ostracized if your father and I had stayed together. No, worse." She shakes her head vehemently, her eyes blazing now. "You've seen what our pack does to Romantics. The lucky ones are here—the Jades. They got out. Survived. The rest... Crigger wore them down until he ground them into dust. And now that bitch of his will continue to do the same. You might not like my methods, but I will always choose the side that protects you, Mac. That's all I care about. You can hate me for it—as long as you're alive to do so."

She falls silent, and I blink at her, a little stunned at her passionate monologue. Parts of it are so familiar that I could recite them. Reminding me what the pack is like. How she's sacrificed for me. But the part about choosing the side that protects me... It makes me think of her whispered conversation with Jadick. Their deal. And I realize that's exactly what it's about. My mother has agreed to whatever price he wants if he'll protect me. And while I don't agree with her methods, I understand. Because I'd do the same damn thing for Levi right now.

It sucks, feeling like a hypocrite. Especially in front of her.

"Okay," I say quietly.

She blinks, clearly shocked at my easy acceptance.

"Okay," she says on an exhale.

She looks like she wants to say something else but thinks better of it.

"Come on. We don't want to be late," she says.

Without a word, I let her lead the way.

Grey isn't outside my door, and I wonder if he's given up on keeping me locked away. But then I spot him waiting on the other side of the empty store. It makes me wonder if my mother asked for privacy. And more specifically, why he'd bother to agree.

We pass him, and, without a word, he falls into step behind us.

When we arrive at the offices, Burnett is there, holding the door to let us pass. Before entering, I glance at the Jades in the atrium, noting the stares that turn hostile when they see me looking. Then I duck inside and leave them behind.

As we near the conference room, my limp slows me down, and I can feel Burnett and Grey pressing in at my back. Their loathing is a current I can feel against my shoulder blades. But I force my steps to remain even as I turn the corner into the conference room. Being hated is nothing new, and neither is ignoring it. The only difference is that, this time, maybe I deserve it.

Jadick is already seated at the head of the table, right where I left him hours ago. On his right is Vale, the spy he met with this morning. I meet Vale's eyes, but he shifts his gaze away from my face, giving me an appraising once-over instead.

Prick.

"Welcome back," Jadick says, flashing me a smile.

I don't return it.

He motions to the chair on his left. "Have a seat. We're just about to get started."

Out of the corner of my eye, I watch my mother falter. She was clearly about to take the seat he just offered me. Instead, she recovers quickly and sits in the next empty chair. The set of her mouth tells me she won't forget Jadick's dismissal of her, though.

Good.

Maybe it'll snap her out of whatever has her acting like his lapdog.

I sit but only because I'd rather save my energy for Kari than argue over a seat.

Burnett and Gregario take positions behind Jadick. Grey stands near the door, a tablet now in his hand. His brows furrow as he studies it in concentration. Behind him hangs a large projector screen.

A moment of silence passes as we all settle in to wait. None of the guards look at me. Vale does, though. I look up and find him staring openly.

"You sure don't look like much," he says.

"Back atcha, buddy."

"You sure you're the one they're all fighting over?"

"Excuse me?"

Fighting over?

"Enough."

At Jadick's order, Vale falls silent, but his slight smirk tells me he's not impressed with me. Likewise.

"The call's coming in, sir," Grey says.

He glances up expectantly from the tablet in his hands.

"Accept it," Jadick instructs him. "Send it to the big screen."

Grey hits a button.

A second later, Kari appears onscreen.

My stomach clenches at the sight of my former bestie. Blonde hair falls softly around her shoulders, and her makeup is flawless. She looks like she's spent time on herself, and I feel that detail like a smack to the face. Not because I care about my own appearance but because I recognize the point she's making. She's not worried about retaliation or war for what she's done. She's so sure of herself, she's spent the day concentrating on nothing more than looking pretty. Meanwhile, I've spent mine agonizing over who I can really trust—and finding out the answer is no one.

"Brother," she says flatly.

"Kari, you're looking well." Jadick's tone is, of all things, affectionate, and I have to bite my tongue to keep from screaming at how revolting this feels.

Instead, I study her background view. She's in the alpha house library. I recognize the bookshelves. This used to be Crigger's office. Now, it's hers. It's a room she's always claimed to despise. I'm not sure if that was a lie too or if she's chosen this room to make another point.

Finally, I realize no one is speaking, and the silence has become tense.

"I agreed to this call because I thought you might actually have an offer for me," Kari says. "It seems I was wrong."

"You agreed to this call because you want what I want," Jadick says.

He doesn't look anxious about her threat to hang up. If anything, his eyes glitter with exhilaration. He's enjoying this.

Ugh.

"And what is it you think I want, brother?"

"Power. And to eliminate any threat against it." Jadick speaks like the answer is obvious. And Kari doesn't disagree. In fact, the hunger in her eyes is unmistakable. It makes me feel even more stupid that I couldn't see it before.

"If you know that much, then you also know the only thing that threatens my power is you." Her eyes are flinty now, proof of her hatred. It guts me to see her wear such a hard expression. To know she's really this monster underneath it all.

"Of course," he says smoothly. "Unfortunately for you, I have tradition and law on my side." Her eyes narrow as he goes on, "I am the alpha heir. You're Daddy's little princess who was overly spoiled for too long and has grown into a full-size brat."

She bats her lashes, disgust and amusement twisting her features. "What are you going to do about it, big brother, punish me?"

Jadick's expression tightens. "I'm going to give you exactly what you deserve."

"Is that so?" Kari's amusement vanishes, and I flinch at the violence in her tone when she says, "I've already eliminated one brother. I won't hesitate to do it again."

"Thiago was weak," Jadick says dismissively. "And stupid. I'm neither."

"Prove it. You know where I am. There's no need for these silly video calls. Just come and get me. If you can."

"Oh, I plan to. But first, I'm going to take everything else from you until you're alone and defenseless. Until I possess everything that matters to you." His eyes flick to mine then back to the screen. "That's when I'll come for you, dear sister. I hope the anticipation kills you."

"Oh, this is adorable," she croons. "You think I care about Mac?"

He shrugs. "You left her alive when you could have easily killed her. Why bother unless you have affection for your friend buried somewhere down deep in that dead heart?"

"I left Mac alive because I knew she'd run to you," Kari snaps. "And distract you with demands for a rescue. Which I sincerely hope you fall for because I'd love nothing more than to kill every Jade, one at a time, as you attempt to sneak them in through the back door of the alpha house." Her eyes gleam, and I realize she's telling the truth. This is exactly what she hoped for. We're playing right into it. I'm that predictable.

"You also shot her," my mother says, and Kari smirks.

"What's your point?" Kari asks.

"Well, you either wanted her alive or not. Which is it?" my mother demands.

Kari rolls her eyes as if this whole line of questioning is so obvious that she's bored. "The only one of you even remotely capable and competent enough to stop me is Mac," Kari says. "Or she would have been. Before the venom sang through her blood and knocked her on her ass. Now, I have no worthy enemy to worry about."

My mother glares at her. "Oh, I wouldn't go that far, you little bitch. Who do you think Mac learned everything from?"

"Please. Vicki, you know as well as I do; you've already made whatever deal you can with my brother. And now, he owns you. And trust me when I tell you, he's not going to let you kill me. No, the egotistical bastard is probably thinking he'll save that honor for himself. If only he were strong enough. But alas, he has no mate to reject, and without that process, he's just another over-inflated toxic male asshole whose daddy told him he could be somebody."

No one else says a word.

One glance at Jadick's face and I can see she's struck a nerve.

Then I remember Tripp mentioning Jadick's mate. Lacey. She died in a boating accident senior year of high school. Before Jadick could claim her. The way Kari talks, he never planned to. And judging by the death stare he's giving his sister, she isn't wrong.

"Rejecting a mate isn't the only way the magic bestows strength to our pack," Jadick says.

His words, the way he says them, make me wonder what he's really planning. Like he knows something we don't. Kari doesn't seem to notice. Her hatred of her brother is so complete that she can't see past it now. I can't blame her. Years of bullying and torture at his hands have made her single-sighted. All I can hope is that will distract her long enough for us to find a way past her defenses.

"You're right," Kari says. "Not without a changing of the guard. The Clemons dynasty has been nothing but a bunch of narcissistic bullies passing the baton of oppression and torture for decades. That stops with me."

"You know nothing about ruling a pack. Nothing about how to make people follow you," Jadick tells her.

"Sure I do. Demand respect, and kill anyone who doesn't give it. You taught me that, big brother."

Jadick's hands fist on the table. He stares up at the screen like he wants to launch himself straight through it. "You'll find it easier said than done. Especially with the army coming for your head. Your actions have started a war, and we will take no prisoners in our quest to right the balance you've destroyed with your little power play. The pack has you to thank for their slaughter. Anyone who stands in our way will be cut down. And the trail of blood will lead me straight to your doorstep, where it ends with you."

She comes out of her chair, leaning toward the screen in a snarl.

"I am the alpha of the Black Moon pack, you piece of shit. I won't listen to threats. And I won't allow a rebellion to rise, not while I'm in charge. You will regret ever standing against me."

"The only rebellion here is yours."

Jadick's tone is unmoved.

Kari, however, is coming undone. I can see the moment her temper snaps. When she speaks again, her voice has softened, but it's that fake sweetness that unnerves me more than anything.

"Speaking of rebellion, how are things going in paradise without your right-hand man?"

My breath catches. I've been waiting for her to mention Levi, but now that she's this angry, I'd almost hoped she'd forget him entirely. There's no telling what she'll do to him when she can't get to Jadick.

"Bring him in," she snaps to someone on the other side of the camera.

I hear a moment of shuffling and then a grunt. A second later, the camera pans over and settles on a figure strapped to a chair.

Levi.

I barely recognize him through the cuts and bruises marring his skin. His eyes are swollen so badly that they're barely open. Blood drips from the side of his head and down his temple. He's gagged and bound at the wrist and ankles.

There's a desperate sort of cry, and it takes a minute for me to realize I'm the one who uttered it.

"Levi's been a bit tight-lipped about the details regarding your new location," Kari says. "But we're breaking down all his defenses bit by bit."

She stands beside him, visible from the waist down. My chest tightens as I watch her grab his jaw and yank his face up toward her.

"Isn't that right?" she coos at him.

Then she pulls her arm back and punches him directly in the mouth.

He grunts, his face driven backward with the momentum of her fist. Blood leaks from his newly busted lip, soaking the gag and dripping down his chin.

"Don't fucking touch him," I scream, jumping out of my chair before I realize I've moved at all.

Jadick's hand closes over my wrist. Gregario looms behind me, hands on my shoulders with a firm grip.

"Sit," my mother hisses from my other side.

When I don't obey, she grabs the back of my pants and yanks my ass back into the chair. Gregario helps by shoving my shoulders downward. My body gives in way too easily though. Stupid fucking venom.

Onscreen, Kari drags her chair over so she can sit beside Levi. "He's not saying much just yet," she says, "But we'll get him talking eventually."

"He doesn't know where we are," Jadick says.

Kari shrugs. "I guess we'll know for sure eventually."

Now I do look at Jadick, my expression pleading.

He leans back in his chair, considering. "You're willing to trade for him, I assume."

"Of course. You're welcome to take his place anytime, brother."

But she's not looking at Jadick now. She's staring right at me.

I bite my lip to keep from screaming as Jadick continues to sit silently.

He's not going to agree to her demands, clearly, so what was the point of this call?

"Take me." I push to my feet, desperation hammering out a rapid beat in my chest. "Let Levi go, and take me instead. I'll be your prisoner."

Kari shakes her head, pity clouding her gaze. "Wow, Mac. You've always had an inflated sense of self-importance, but this is bad even for you."

"I'm offering myself to you," I plead. "I know things. You could torture them out of me and—"

"You're not who I want." Her smile slips, her lip curling as she looks from me to Jadick.

Still, he says nothing.

"Kari, please," I choke on the words, begging, but I can't even bring myself to care.

She rolls her eyes. "You're embarrassing yourself, Mac. Let it go."

I turn to Jadick. "Do something."

He looks at Kari, and I realize, not once has he spared Levi a glance. I want to scream at him. To blame him for it all. But his words from earlier ring in my ears.

He's there because of you.

He's right.

He's right, and I have no bargaining power to stop it.

All I have is Jadick, and he's not interested in saving Levi. Not when it means sacrificing himself. He's a Clemons. They all are. Tripp was right all along.

"We won't stand for this," Jadick says. "You've broken pack law, Kari. Too many to name at this point. Your sentence is death. And your executioner will be me."

As threatening as it sounds, he's offered mere words in the face of action—horrible, torturous action—and everyone here knows it.

Kari smiles. "Well. As fun as this has turned out to be," she says, "you're wasting my time. You wanted proof of life, you got it. But you won't get him back with a pulse unless you take his place. And even that offer has an expiration date."

"Take the offer," I plead with Jadick, uncaring who hears me at this point.

Jadick leans forward, ignoring me. "Enjoy your time as alpha, sister, however fleeting it may be. I'll be the last thing you see before you die. You can count on that."

He nods at Grey, who ends the call before Kari can respond.

I watch the screen darken, my heart sliding into my stomach.

Every time I close my eyes, I see Levi bruised and broken.

Because of me.

"Come on," my mom says quietly. She nudges me to my feet. "Let's get some air."

I let her lead me from the room, but I don't bother to tell her it's impossible. Levi is my air, always has been, and I'm slowly suffocating without him.

CHAPTER 4

My mom is awkward in the presence of my tears, and by the time we reach my room again, I can tell she's itching to get away.

"Just take some time," she says in a soft voice that doesn't sound like her at all. "You'll feel better when you've had some rest."

I look at her incredulously. "Levi is being tortured while we all sit here on our asses. I don't think rest will make me feel better."

"I only meant we need to keep our heads," she says, and it feels as if she's scolding me for crying. Like I'm the one in the wrong.

I grit my teeth, doing my best to not lose it completely. "Is that so?" I snap. "Because you're pretty cool-headed right now, and yet you insist on sitting on your hands."

"Mac, I'm not the bad guy here."

"No, you're just sucking up to him."

Her eyes narrow. "You're upset about Levi. That doesn't mean you have to take your feelings out on me."

"You don't know anything about my feelings."

Or any feelings at all.

"I'll come back when you've had a chance to calm down."

She lingers long enough to find me a box of tissues and a bottle of water, and then she's gone. In her absence, I immediately feel less stabby, though not much. I blow my nose and take a deep breath, and when that's done, I've made up my mind.

Kari was wrong.

I'm not the one with an inflated sense of self-importance. That would be our new self-appointed leader. But Jadick isn't alpha, and that means he's not the final word.

If he won't get Levi back, I will.

It's not going to be easy getting past Kari's security, but I'll figure it out. I have to.

Besides, I've fought alone my whole life. Why stop now?

I ease my door open, bracing myself for a run-in with Grey. But there's no one guarding my room. Instead of exiting through the store, I turn a hard right and creep farther down this short hall of former offices. There are three other doors besides mine. I shove open the first and find a storage room with wall-to-wall metal shelving. The shelves are stacked with boxes, but I don't bother with them. Closing the door again, I move on to the next.

Inside the second room, a counter along one wall holds a microwave and mini-fridge. A scarred white table sits alone in the center. I shut that door and move on to the third, heart pounding. Once upon a time, the adrenaline of a mission calmed me rather than left me breathless. Now, it's all I can do to keep my breathing even and steps silent.

This is about more than hunting a mark.

This is my life I'm fighting for now.

Maybe that's what makes me so desperate to succeed.

The third door is locked. I double back to my bedroom and rifle through the bag my mother brought me. There, in the small pocket, is a lock-picking kit I'd almost forgotten about. With tools in hand, the locked door gives way almost too easily. Within seconds, it opens to the outside, and my knees nearly buckle in relief. Sliding the tools back into my pocket, I step out.

Night air washes over me, humidity clinging even in the slight breeze. For a moment, I'm numb with shock that I actually found an exit.

My heart thuds. Half-expecting someone to grab me and yank me back, I glance right and left to get my bearings and get the hell out of here. I'm in an alley tucked between two larger wings of the mall. To the right, dumpsters and empty boxes litter the pavement.

The only way out is to my left.

I push away from the door, trying to break into a run that turns out to be more of a jogging hobble. Damn this venom and my weak-ass body.

I grunt, fury driving me. Up ahead, I can see where the alley opens to a large, deserted parking lot. Street lamps dot the asphalt, and I'm already strategizing which way to go so I can keep out of the light.

I'm so caught up in my own thoughts that I don't see the figure leaping from the shadows until it's too late. A body tackles me to the ground, and I go down on my hip hard enough to make me cry out.

Thick fists swing down at me, and I swing right back.

Every kick and punch I land hurts me almost as badly as it—hopefully—hurts my assailant. Maybe worse because nothing I do seems to deter them. A male grunt sounds from beneath a dark hood as my attacker swings a leg out and pins me between his thighs.

Broad shoulders rise up in the darkness.

A fist slams into my jaw.

"That's for Levi," the male voice snarls.

I see stars and not just because I'm on my back staring at the night sky.

Before I can recover, strong hands grab both my wrists, pinning me. Groaning, I blink furiously, determined to get my bearings before—

Something sharp slices through my skin, and I scream.

My back arches against the sudden pain then releases. I go limp as my eyes catch on the hilt of a blade sticking out from my thigh. My attacker's hand closes over it, and he yanks it free, dragging a string of curses from me along with it. The pain nearly paralyzes me. For a second, all I can do is grit my teeth against it.

Venom.

The fucker has tipped the blade in poison.

Just what I needed.

Struggling for strength, I watch as my attacker raises the blade again, this time with its tip aimed at my heart.

Fuck that.

I am not dying in a mall parking lot.

I try to shift before remembering my wolf is still out of reach.

Fine.

We'll do it the hard way.

My human teeth catch his wrist as he brings the knife down again. I bite as hard as I can and am rewarded with a sharp yelp. The knife clatters to the pavement just out of reach. He tries to jerk away as his blood hits my tongue, but I don't let up. A second later, his muscles go suddenly lax, and my powerful body twists out of his hold with ease. Disarmed and bleeding, my attacker stumbles away from me, scrambling to his feet.

I let him.

He's not going to get far.

I stalk slowly, toying with him. Also, my ability to move quickly is non-existent, but he doesn't have to know that. My rage and frustration from the last twenty-four hours pours into this one moment.

Even without my wolf, I'm the predator now.

The man backs away, no longer sure of himself. Of his kill. His jerky movements cause his hood to fall back. I stop at the sight of him, startled to recognize him as one of the Jades. I don't know his name, but I've seen him around, mostly hanging onto the fringes of the security teams, though I don't think he's one of them.

Then again, how else did he know where to find me?

Is this why Grey wasn't posted outside my door?

Was it a setup?

"Who are you?" I demand.

"You won't get away with this," he says, glaring at me.

We're almost out of the alley now.

The glow of the street lamps wash his face in orange, but the angry twist of his brows is only magnified in the light. He hates me enough to kill me. He doesn't even know me.

"You're the one who should be thinking of escape," I say. And I mean it. After what he's just tried to do, I won't feel guilty ripping him apart.

"I don't want to escape," he snarls. "I want your blood on my hands, bitch."

I keep moving toward him. "We'll see who spills blood next."

"Levi only ever tried to help, and you got him killed," he accuses.

That brings me up short.

He hates me because he blames me.

And why shouldn't he?

Some of my rage fades. Guilt sets in.

When he suddenly turns and runs off, I can't quite bring myself to follow.

Killing him now would only prove his point.

To him, I'm the bad guy.

Maybe he's right.

"Mac."

The sound of any voice out here is startling, but the fact that it's Jadick himself makes me whirl in panic. He's so close that I have to catch myself to keep from stumbling into him. He puts his hands up as if to help or grab me, but I recoil at the idea of him touching me right now.

His expression is tight, but there's no animosity. Not like the man that just ran off. And he doesn't carry a weapon.

Still, I eye him warily.

"Where are you going?" he asks.

His calmness is infuriating, so I simply stare back at him, very aware of how weak I am now. The new dose of venom pumps through me faster, and the sting of it steals my breath, but I refuse to let on.

"You're in no condition," he says as if I've offered an answer.

Then again, it's not hard to guess my intentions.

We both know what I want.

"You'll never make it past her guards," he adds.

I growl.

He sighs.

"Please come back inside so we can talk about this."

I deliberately turn away and begin walking across the parking lot.

Okay, limping.

"I'll get him back," he says, and I stop walking. "If that's what you want."

Slowly, I turn to face him, aware of the venom burning me from the inside out. But I ignore it and study Jadick, trying to decide whether he's lying. Or if he's not, what he wants in return. Whatever it is, I'll probably give it—and he knows it.

I hate him for that right now.

But I find myself making my way back to where he stands.

And now I hate myself.

He doesn't gloat. Somehow, that still feels like gloating.

Instead, he simply turns and leads the way back through the door I exited earlier. Then, down the hall and into my tiny room. Everything is how I left it a few minutes ago, which makes the whole thing feel like a dream.

Or a nightmare.

The only difference is that Grey is back, standing like a sentry between me and freedom. Beside him is Burnett, and beyond them are at least half a dozen others.

I ignore them all. So does Jadick.

"The man who attacked you will be dealt with," he says.

"What if I don't want that?" I ask.

"It's not up to you anymore." He doesn't bat an eye as he says, "You'll never see him again. Don't worry. You're safe."

Safe.

The idea of that word belonging in Jadick's mouth is ridiculous. I don't respond.

"Get changed," he says, glancing down at me. "I'll wait outside."

I look down at myself and realize my pants are torn where the knife caught me. And my shirt is in tatters where it's been stretched and ripped during the fight. My bra is on full display. If only that were my biggest concern right now.

Jadick is halfway out the door when I say, "Don't bother."

My leg burns hotter, and my head swims with the pain, but I don't care. I need to know what this is.

What he wants.

"Tell me what I have to do," I say.

He has the audacity to look confused. "I don't know what you—"

"Yes, you do," I say. "You'll rescue Levi, but it won't be free. Tell me what you want in return."

I am tempted to reach for the counter to steady myself. My knees are trembling with pain. But I resist. I refuse to let Jadick see me weak.

His confusion disappears, replaced with reluctant admiration. "You always impress me, you know. You're clever. Intuitive. Strong. It's a pleasant surprise."

"I don't want your compliments."

"Consider them part of my request."

Request.

Right.

This is extortion, pure and simple.

But I don't argue. I wait.

"I'll get right to it if that's what you prefer." He meets my eyes and says, "I'll rescue Levi. And in exchange, I would request your hand in marriage."

CHAPTER 5

$\mathcal{M}$arriage.

The word hangs in the air between us, and for a moment, my head swims with the shock of it. I want to refuse. I want to laugh in his face or throw something at his head. But all too soon, the reality of my situation—and the desperation that comes with it—comes crashing down around me. And I know I can't do any of those things.

Jadick knows it too.

He has the decency to look unsure.

Or maybe that's part of what makes him such a snake.

"You can't be serious," I manage.

But we both know he is.

"You're strong and clever and capable," he says. "More than anyone else I've known."

"You want to piss Kari off," I say.

His lips twitch. "An added benefit, I won't deny it."

"And Levi?"

He shrugs. "He would be free."

"But he would be rejected."

"And stronger for it." His eyes glitter with challenge. He's daring me to argue. "Our pack needs strong leadership, Mac. Practical choices. A head for logic and strategy. You have all of that." I don't say anything, so he adds, "Great responsibility requires sacrifice."

Bullshit.

There's only one of us sacrificing anything here, and it's not him. Not unless you count the fact that he's sleeping on sheets with a thread count below three thousand right now.

"What is this about, really? You don't need a mate to rule as alpha."

He shuts the door behind him with a soft click and then turns back to me. "You're right." He closes the distance between us, his voice quiet. "I don't *need* a mate. But I *want* you."

I shudder, which he apparently takes for interest instead of disgust.

He leans closer. "Join me, Mac. With you at my side, we can take back the pack and build an empire our ancestors only dreamed of."

"What makes you think I want an empire?"

"You want freedom, and that only comes with power."

"I don't—"

"You don't take orders from anyone," he finishes. "Believe me, I know. But if you agree—if you join me—you'd never take orders from anyone again."

My brows lift at that. "You mean anyone except you."

He smirks. "Of course. I am the alpha after all."

He says it like it will impress me. And that's what makes me snap.

"Jadick," I say softly, and I see the hope leap into his pretty eyes. "Hear me because I only want to say this once." I pause and then say very deliberately, "Fuck. You."

His eyes flash with anger that fades quickly. Too quickly.

He steps back.

"Take some time to consider," he says quietly. "Without me, I'm not sure there's much hope for poor Levi."

He walks out before I can find something to chuck at his egotistical head.

The door clicks shut behind him.

In the silence that follows, I try to ignore the fact that Jadick has just played an Ace I never saw coming, but the burn of the venom in my bloodstream is nothing compared to the searing wound to my pride.

Jadick is right.

Without him, Levi is trapped.

Whether or not I agree to his offer, I'm trapped too.

Finally, I cross to my bag and pull out the fresh shirt inside. Peeling off the tattered remains of my old one, I let the fabric fall to the floor. By the time I'm done pulling on the clean tee, I'm exhausted.

Forgetting the pants, I drop onto the cot and close my eyes, imagining myself wrapping my hands around Jadick's throat and squeezing until he never breathes again.

The door opens, but the scent of this newest visitor is recognizable instantly, so I don't bother looking up. Not yet. If I do, I'm not sure I can stop myself from unleashing my rage on my former friend. Even I can admit he doesn't deserve it—not for this.

Unfortunately, a few deep breaths don't do much to calm the storm raging inside me. When I finally force my eyes open, Tripp slouches against the closed door.

"Hey," he says warily. "I thought you might be sleeping."

"I'm not." I stare up at the ceiling, waiting for him to get to the point.

"You okay?"

"Why wouldn't I be?"

"Your leg is bleeding."

I look down and note the blood soaking my pants. It's not bad enough to worry about, but it's already stained the sheet underneath me.

"I was stabbed."

He straightens and steps closer. "What the fuck? Are you serious? When? Was it Jadick?"

I snort. "Yeah, right. If you think that asshole could get the drop on me, you don't know me at all."

Besides, Jadick doesn't stab with knives.

"Then who—?"

I turn to look at him. "What's it to you?"

Hurt flashes, but it's gone quickly. He steps back again, his expression shuttered. "I take it that didn't go well. With Jadick."

"It went the way Jadick wanted it to."

My head swims. With pain. And overwhelm. With venom.

Tripp snorts. "No surprise there."

I spare him a withering glance, hoping he'll take the hint and leave.

Instead, he holds out a banana—and a granola bar. "I brought you this."

It's the same kind as the one I found here when I woke before.

My pride wants to refuse it, but I can't bring myself to risk eating anything else. Not here. Especially not after the attack in the parking lot.

"Why bother?" I ask but snatch it anyway.

He doesn't react to his victory, which saves him from a throat punch.

"I know you're wary of the food here," he says.

My chest squeezes. I stare back at him.

Does he know because he's the reason behind it?

Someone tried to drug me when Levi first brought me to the compound. The suspect list is down to Jadick or Tripp. At first, I'd refused to believe Tripp could have done that to me, but I'm not so sure of anything anymore.

I unwrap the bar and shove a piece into my mouth.

We sit in silence while I chew.

The food helps me feel slightly less out of it.

I'm vaguely aware I'll need to dress this wound soon, but for now, ignoring it is the best I can do.

"I'm sorry I left him there," Tripp says, and my gaze whips back to his.

The desperation and suffering in his eyes are almost enough for me to let him off the hook. Almost.

"I hate myself for it," he goes on, his voice barely more than a whisper. "So I don't blame you for hating me too."

I want to tell him I don't hate him, but the words won't come.

"Help me get him out," I say instead.

He stares at me, clearly surprised. Then he's nodding like he's just been waiting for me to ask. "I swear it. Whatever you need, just name it."

"I don't know what I need yet," I say, and the admission takes something out of me. Or maybe it was my song and dance with Jadick. Either way, I feel like crying, and that's not something I intend on inviting Tripp to watch.

He seems to sense the conversation is over and moves to the door.

"When you figure it out, I'm here," he says.

I make no promises as I watch him close the door between us, maybe for good.

CHAPTER 6

I don't sleep so much as pass out. It's unusual for me to let myself sink so far into unawareness, but the poison makes anything else impossible. When I wake, the venom is a simmering burn that warms my skin from the inside out. The sheets are wet beneath me, and I realize I've sweated through my clothes.

Fever.

It wracks my body with bone-deep chills. I wonder how much is too much when it comes to the poison I can't seem to stop getting injected with lately. My wolf stirs, though, and it's the first sign of healing I've felt in days. It boosts my strength but mostly my morale. I can do this. I have to find a way to get Levi on my own. Jadick's offer is a dangling carrot—a rancid, vile, rotten carrot that I can't allow myself to reach for.

I won't.

There are worse ways to be poisoned than this damned venom in my veins.

Propping myself up on an elbow, I survey the room.

Nothing is out of place, but I can't shake the feeling something is different.

I force myself to sit and then stand. Crossing the room, I find my legs are shaky, my knees weak. My wolf surges in response, but even she can't seem to heal me any faster against the poison swimming in my bloodstream.

All I can do is wait.

But time is the one thing I don't have.

My door is unlocked, but any surprise I feel at that fact disappears the moment I pull it open.

Grey is waiting, standing sentry between me and the outer hall. Not unexpected, but the fact that he's no longer alone is. To my right, three more guards are stationed between me and the exit I used before. Even from here, I can see there's no need for them. The door itself has been boarded shut.

How did I sleep through that?

"Tell my mother I need to see her." My throat is scratchy, but I pretend it's not more evidence I'm falling apart.

"She left," Grey says.

What?

I pause, not sure what that means, but I can't bring myself to ask. Mostly because I don't trust him to tell me the truth.

"You look like death," he says.

I look up and realize he's studying me, assessing.

I scowl. "I'm sure you're disappointed it's only a look."

"Whatever that means."

I limp up to him. And stare him in the eye despite the fact that he's nearly a foot taller than me. "Play stupid if you want, but if you want me dead, you're going to have to try harder than that untrained wannabe-soldier asshole you sent for me last night."

His expression twists in confusion. "I didn't send anyone."

"Right." I shove past him.

Instead of stopping me, he follows at a safe distance. Close enough to tackle me if I try to run for it. Not that I can do much running right now.

"If I wanted you dead," he says from behind me, "you would be."

His words send a trickle of unease down my spine.

I look up as Frankie strides toward us, a woman on a mission.

Her expression is tightly clamped, and I can't tell if she's pissed or merely preoccupied. She stops when she sees me and fails to hide her surprise. Like she isn't expecting me to be out of my room. Her gaze zeroes in on my bloody pant leg.

"Mac," she says. "How are you feeling?"

"How do I look?" I ask.

"Like you could use a drink," she says. Her eyes flick to Grey then back to me. "Come on. Let's find you one."

I don't argue.

We both know a drink won't help, but if it gets Grey off my back, I'll go shot for shot with the woman.

Grey follows us all the way to the door beside the water fountain, which lets me know whatever she and Tripp do back here, it's not a secret. She pushes it open and then turns back to Grey, ushering me past before blocking Grey from following.

"There are no exits through here, and you know it," she tells him. "You can wait here."

He frowns but says nothing, which is just as well because she slams the door in his face. "Come on," she says, leading me down the hall. "We can talk back here."

I search warily for Tripp as we pass the other rooms, but they're all empty. At the end, she turns into a small space that has a desk set against one wall and a small cot against the other. Between them, facing the desk, are two camping chairs.

Frankie gestures for me to take one as she takes the other. Reaching into the bottom desk drawer, she holds up a bottle of Jack and two plastic cups.

"You were serious about the drink?" I can't help but ask.

"The wound on your leg," she says flatly, "Was it venom?"

I nod.

She shakes her head grimly. "Yeah, I'm serious about the drink. And you should be too. It's the only painkiller I've got."

"Good point."

"Mall security had it right," she says, uncapping the bottle with a sigh of appreciation.

I snort as she pours.

"Cheers," she says, handing me a glass and holding hers out for a clink.

"To new friendship," I say.

Her eyes sparkle, and I know she realizes damn well what I'm up to.

"To the future," she says, and we both drink.

The alcohol burns my insides. Not unlike the venom, but at least this time, there's a pleasurable buzzy after-effect.

"Another?" I ask.

She pours me a refill but leaves her own glass empty.

I shrug and knock it back. Day drinking isn't usually my thing, but then, this isn't a usual day, either. I almost go for a third but then remember the conversation this opportunity presents. Frankie doesn't say a word, clearly waiting on me to start.

I like her.

"Do you know where my mother is?" I ask.

Frankie hesitates. "Here, have one more."

She pours me a third drink and hands it over.

I shake my head. "I'm good."

She sighs and sets the drink aside on the desk. "Your mother went to see Kari."

"What? Why?"

"She went to negotiate your involvement in all this."

My involvement. Not Levi's.

My heart sinks at the same time worry takes over.

Kari has already proven she's just as likely to kill my mother as she is to agree.

"Does Jadick know?" I ask.

"Yes."

"And he just let her go?"

"He's not happy about it, believe me. If he didn't want you to like him so much, I think he would have locked her up instead."

I study her. "You know he proposed."

"I thought he might. Tripp and I have been listening to his meetings for a while now, and they're almost exclusively about you now."

I blow out a breath, enjoying the way the alcohol has begun to numb the pain. That third drink is sounding better and better.

"Does my mother know?"

Her brow arches. "Why do you think she went to see Kari?"

I stare into my empty cup.

"You're surprised," she says.

Finally, I drag my gaze back to hers and shrug. "My mother's not one to throw herself in front of a speeding bullet."

"Not even for her own daughter?"

I snort. I can't help it. The alcohol is eating at the filter I usually keep locked in place between my brain and my mouth. "Especially then."

"You underestimate how much she cares about you."

"She cares, but she doesn't understand. She'll risk herself to negotiate for me, but she won't even attempt to help Levi."

"She's a mother. Her priorities are different than yours."

"Do you have any children?"

"I did," she says, a shadow crossing her features. "Once."

Something about the finality of her tone tells me not to press her further. But it makes my heart hurt all the same.

"Do you think she'll succeed?" I ask instead.

"Do you? Kari is your friend."

"*Was* my friend. And no. I don't. Neither does Jadick, or he wouldn't have let her go."

She nods. "You're perceptive."

"He doesn't want to win," I say. "Why?"

"He does," she says, "But he's waiting for something."

"What?" I ask.

She hesitates and then says, "Have you ever heard of a hexerei named Rina?"

"No. Should I have?"

"Maybe not, but Jadick has sent men searching for her. I think she's part of his plan."

"The name's not familiar to me. Why would he need a hex? You think he plans to use magic against Kari?"

"It's possible, but the hexes haven't dealt with us in decades. I don't see why they'd start now."

"You mean since the curse."

She nods grimly.

"No one talks much about the curse," I say. "Only that we have to reject our mates in order to be strong. I'm not sure what it has to do with the witches, though."

"A century ago, a hexerei cursed the pack underneath a black moon. She decreed that fated mates would be our weakness. Then our alpha rejected his fated mate to become stronger, and the hexerei have been pissed at the loophole we found ever since."

Hmm.

And now Jadick suddenly wanted to find a witch.

"What did my mother say about it?"

"We didn't share it with her." She watches my expression and adds, "It's not that I don't trust her, but I know where her priorities lie. And I know how a mother thinks. She'll use anything I give her to fight for you."

"I don't blame you for not sharing. What do you think Jadick wants with this Rina woman?"

She sighs. "I wish I knew."

I pick up the glass and gulp down the third drink after all.

Frankie studies me for a long beat.

"Will you accept his offer?" she asks.

There's no judgment in her gaze when she asks. But there's a challenge. Like she wants to know how hard I'll fight. I wonder if accepting Jadick means I'm fighting harder or not at all.

"Jadick is a solution that only brings more problems," I say. "If I accept him, I'll be rejecting Levi, and even after everything Levi did… it's a betrayal I'm not ready to commit. If there's another way, I owe it to him to find it."

"I figured you'd say that. Jadick will try to stop you," she says.

"He already has." I glance at the stab wound. "One of the Jades decided to avenge Levi."

"You think Jadick put him up to it?"

"I don't know. At first, I thought it was Grey, but his denial was almost convincing."

"Grey?" she echoes.

At her expression, I cock my head. "You don't think it was him."

"I'm not saying he isn't capable," she says.

"But?"

"Grey isn't the type to delegate that sort of thing."

"I get that impression. But that only leaves Jadick, and I'm not sure he'd try to kill me if he meant to propose after."

"Love hurts," she says, and I attempt a laugh, but it's too sad and too bitter.

"You're telling me." I bite my lip. "Hey, will you do me a favor? Don't tell Tripp. About the proposal."

"It will break his heart."

"I know. I want to spare him a bit longer."

She nods, and we sit in silence with our own thoughts for a moment.

"He won't break," she says quietly, and I look up at her sharply.

She means Levi.

"I know," I say, the knowledge heartbreaking. It means his torture will be that much worse. "But I will."

"Yes, unfortunately, I think that's what both Clemons are counting on."

CHAPTER 7

Frankie's words stay with me long after I've left her and returned to my room. I've been so busy nearly dying that I hadn't seen it before. I wasn't sent away from Blackstone simply because I was useless to Kari's plan. She never meant to show me mercy. She also never intended to kill me with that bullet. She meant to use me. And so far, it's working.

I hate her.

Once, I loved her like a sister, but now, I can think only of wrapping my hands around her throat and squeezing until there's no breath left in her body.

Kari Clemons is dead to me.

And if I have anything to say about it, she'll be dead to the rest of the world soon enough.

Alone in my room, I peel my bloody pants off and inspect the stab wound on my thigh. It's mostly a surface wound. Minimal blood loss. No major arteries hit. Mostly, it's the venom I have to worry about. I use the First Aid kit left over from when they first stitched me up and bandage the area. Unfortunately, there's nothing I can do about the dried blood coating my thigh. I could ask Jadick for a place to shower, but my pride dismisses that idea outright. I'm not asking him for shit.

Besides, the granola bar Tripp brought me earlier is long gone, and I can't remember the last time I ate a real meal. If I'm going to heal from any of this, I need food.

Grey scowls when I step back into the hall. I ignore the other three assholes guarding the boarded-up exit. Refusing to look at them does little to calm my ire, but it's something.

"Take me to the dining hall," I tell Grey.

To my surprise, he doesn't argue.

We walk in silence, and the closer I get to the crowded atrium at the end of the hall, the harder my heart pounds. I scan for possible threats, surprised to find the attack in the parking lot has left me on edge. I'm not one to cower or hide, but these people outnumber me. Thanks to my wounds, I'm a sitting duck in their midst.

Still, hiding in my room will get me nowhere. Or worse, it could get me killed.

When we reach the center of the atrium, I stop and consider my options. The mall's food court has been reopened with Jades running a couple of the eateries that line one side of the space. High above us, natural light streams in through the angled glass ceiling. People mill about, chatting, horsing around, eating at the tables scattered throughout.

It almost looks like an actual mall experience.

Then Grey pokes me in the back, and I remember just how far removed from the real world I am.

"What do you want to eat?" he asks.

"I can order it myself," I tell him.

"You sure you want to interact? You don't exactly have a lot of friends here."

"No shit. I'm not letting someone dose my food again. I'll order for myself, or you can take me back to my room and tell Jadick you let me starve."

He rolls his eyes. "Come on then," he says, shoving me impatiently toward the pizzeria.

At the register, a girl with spiky blonde hair takes my order.

"Cheese pizza," I tell her, my stomach rumbling at the scent of the fresh dough wafting out from the kitchen.

"How many slices?" she asks, gesturing to the New York-style slices of plain cheese waiting under the heat lamp.

I glance over at the four pieces left and then back to the girl. "All of them."

She smiles to herself and plates them then hands them over. "Anything else?"

"Not yet," I tell her, and she laughs. "What about you?" she asks Grey.

"Sausage and pineapple."

"I think I have some in the back," she tells him. "Hang on."

She walks away, and I stare at him in disgust. "Seriously?"

"What?" he demands.

"Nothing." I take my pizza and then realize I have no idea where to sit.

There are no empty tables, and I realize too late that means we'll have to double up. Scanning, I check the faces of those already seated. I don't see the man who attacked me last night, but that doesn't mean he isn't here. Or that some of these people wouldn't do the same to me if given the chance. My muscles tighten, ready for a fight.

Grey is unaffected, however. Pizza in hand—pineapple. So gross —he nods at me to follow him. We end up in the very center of the crowd where half a dozen uniformed security guards have claimed the largest table.

Largest and loudest.

"Grey," one of the male guards calls out. His voice booms over the noise of the room. "Where you been, asshole? Come sit."

The guy has a full auburn mustache with no beard. It's a look that's always creeped me out. Or maybe it's just him. He looks like a walking billboard for how not to pull off the look.

"Wheeler." Grey takes a seat beside his friend without sparing me a glance.

Mustache notices me, and his smile slips. "Didn't realize you were still on duty," he tells Grey, glancing quickly away again.

The others around him give me sour looks.

I ignore them and round the table, taking an empty seat between two security guards. They immediately get up and leave. But their insult is lost on me because all that matters in this moment are the four slices of New York pie stacked on my plate.

I take a bite, and a small moan escapes as the hot cheese melts against my tongue.

When I look up, the guy seated across from me is staring with raised brows.

In fact, they all are.

"Good pizza," I say, heat rising to my cheeks.

I am not easily embarrassed, but an entire ops team watching me foodgasm—especially when every one of them probably wants to kill me—is a bit awkward.

"You're not wrong." Wheeler's lips twitch. "Well, except for Grey's pizza. That shit is disgusting and morally offensive."

Everyone laughs.

I focus on my pizza. Shoving another bite in my mouth seems easier than trying to figure out why that guy was just nice to me. By my third bite, the rest of the table has returned to their own conversations. I let their voices wash over me, content to sit among them even if I'm not actually one of them.

Again, I think of the Jade who attacked me last night. And while I still have my guard up against another attempt, my rage has faded to guilt. These people see me as their villain. What did I expect?

"Mac, right?"

I look up and find the guy across from me, the one with the judgy eyebrows, staring back.

"Or do you prefer Mackenzie?" he asks when I don't answer.

"It's Mac," I tell him.

"If you want more pizza, I can talk to Lauren."

"Excuse me?"

"The pizza. We're rationing because of the perimeter being closed, but I'm sure I could put in a good word."

I look down at my plate and realize I've already inhaled three of the four slices. My appetite is sated, and my wolf already feels stronger. I feel like an asshole at the realization I've taken more than my share. But then his words sink in.

"Why is the perimeter closed?" I ask.

He looks at me like I'm slow. "The mines have been set. Kari's scouts will pass within range soon. We—"

The female beside him smacks his shoulder. "Bruce," she hisses. "Don't be an idiot."

He falls silent and ducks his head.

I study her. She glares at me.

A few others have stopped talking again to listen in.

"You're going to take out her scouts," I say, glancing at their faces. "It will be war."

"She already declared war when she took Levi."

My hands tighten into fists, so I tuck them under the table. "If you kill her men, she'll know we're here."

"She knows now," one of them snaps. "Why else would she send scouts?"

I shake my head. "She's fishing. Probably sent trackers with skills that could have found us even if we'd teleported here."

I know. My first dose of venom came from just such a tracker.

"She has Levi," Wheeler says as if I need to be reminded.

"Levi would never talk," I snap back, my voice rising.

"He shouldn't be there to begin with," the girl chimes in. Vicious. Ugly.

The tables near us fall silent too.

Everyone's watching, waiting.

I swallow hard. "Look, I know you blame me for what happened, but I'm not your enemy," I say quietly.

"You're the reason Levi was taken," the girl says.

I nod, which seems to surprise them. "You're right. He went to Blackstone because of me. Because he wanted to fight for me."

"And you wanted to fight for Kari." The girl's voice twists when she says Kari's name. She's disgusted.

I grimace, but I won't deny the truth either. "Obviously, I got played there," I tell her. "But aren't we all fighting for someone? Aren't you a Jade because you refused to reject someone important to you? A mate? A family member?"

She exchanges a look with the guy beside her. I realize they must be fated mates. My senses are just too damn dull to read their bond.

No one speaks.

They also don't try to kill me, so I keep going.

I have no idea why.

There's no agenda, no benefit to convincing them not to hate me. Hell, I deserve their hate. I *am* the reason Levi was taken. But I keep going anyway.

"Levi went with me to Blackstone because he didn't want to be a Black Moon wolf anymore. He didn't want to survive at the cost of someone else dying. I don't either.

"You're not a Jade," someone says.

A few murmurs go around, but not everyone joins in.

Some of them look more curious than angry now.

"Believe me, none of you hate me more than I hate myself for what happened to him. But, for the record, I didn't leave him. I was dragged away while being shot with venom-laced bullets. Otherwise, I would have taken his place in a heartbeat. I still would. But Kari knows that. And that's why she sent me back here. Not for mercy, for torture. The kind that comes from knowing I'd kill to get him back and so would you."

A few of their expressions shift as they realize what I mean.

"She wants us focused on kicking your ass instead of kicking hers," Mustache says.

He's smart—even if he does look like a douchebag.

"If you think killing Kari's scouts will somehow avenge him, you're wrong," I tell them. "She doesn't care about me—her supposed best friend—so what makes you think she cares about her scouts?"

The girl across from me is the one to speak first. "I mean, we have to do *something*."

The others offer nods of agreement.

One by one, their gazes shift to me, and I'm startled to realize they're waiting for me to tell them what that something is. More than a few are still aiming hostile glares my way, but the rest? They want to hear what I think.

I try to come up with the answer.

"We're doing plenty."

Jadick's voice cuts through the thick silence, and the moment melts away.

His hand lands on my shoulder, and it's all I can do not to jerk away.

"Grey, I see you've made sure Mac is welcomed," Jadick says from behind me. "Thank you."

"Yes, sir."

"Mac, might I have a word?"

It's not a request. I wonder if the others can hear the steel lining his voice or if it's just me. Refusing would be a waste of time, considering the number of guards at this table, so I get up and follow him away from the crowds. He doesn't return me to my room or to his offices and instead leads the way down another hall entirely. His way of showing me I'm no longer expected to stay locked away from the others. Probably trying to win me over by giving me my freedom.

He still thinks I can be bought.

Instead of pointing out his mistake, I focus on the hall—on what I need to know of the Jades. What I can use against him later.

We pass a shoe store that's been turned into barracks and a tuxedo rental shop whose leftover mannequins have been set up for what looks like training exercises. The nude torsos are beat to hell along with what can only be stab wounds marring their plastic exterior.

I turn to Jadick with raised brows.

"Necessity is the mother of invention," he explains with a shrug.

His careless attitude trips a switch inside me. I think of the bombs waiting for those scouts, and my anger blots out reason.

"What is wrong with you? You're leading these people to slaughter."

"I'm leading them to war because that is what Kari has declared."

"She's declared war on you, not them."

"She wants to rule us all with more control than my own father did," he says. "If we're going to stop it, we must come together."

I stare at him. "Have you brainwashed your own psyche so that you actually believe these things you say? Or are you that good of an actor?"

"I am not like my sister," he says. "The Jades see that. I wonder why you can't."

"No," I say, "On that, we agree. You are not like Kari. She doesn't bother to hide her self-serving agenda."

His eyes twitch, narrowing a fraction before his expression smooths out again. "I have just learned the Mafia pack refuses to ally with us for our cause."

He changes the subject so swiftly it takes me a moment to catch up. I blink, surprised to learn he'd even asked them.

"The Mafia pack doesn't ally with anyone," I say.

"Yes, well, I'd hoped your mother's relationship with Franco—"

"Gross, do not say relationship."

His lips twitch. "Very well, connection?" I nod. "As I was saying, I'd hoped her connection to Franco would prove useful to us in our request, but they've refused."

"And the Lone Wolf pack?"

If he's asked the Mafia pack, I know damn well he's asked others. It's the reason he claimed we needed to wait before Levi and I decided to say fuck it and storm in on our own.

"They've also opted to remain un-involved."

"You mean they turned you down." I snort. "How does it feel to be rejected?"

He doesn't answer, but from the ticking in his jaw, I can tell I've struck a nerve. "We're waiting on another strategic project to come through."

The hexerei. Rina.

I have no idea what he wants with her, but I can't come out and ask, either. I need more information.

"Can I go now? I have things to do."

"Your mother has missed her check-in," he says, and again, I'm caught off guard by the swift change in topic. It takes a minute for his words to process. Not to mention everything he isn't saying.

I stop walking. "What do you mean missed her check-in?"

"Protocol is a check-in every four hours when on a high-risk mission—"

"I thought she went against your orders by trying to see Kari."

"She knows how I felt about the attempt," he says in a clipped voice. "But we agreed she would check in with me directly for safety reasons." His gaze flicks away from me toward the beaten-down mannequins. "I knew you'd be worried, and I wanted to be able to reassure you."

His eyes find mine again. There's an authenticity to the concern in his eyes that startles me. I find myself tempted to believe him. It would be so easy to accept that he cares about me this much. But then I remember his proposal—and the terms. Not to mention that conversation with my mother the other day.

"One missed check-in doesn't mean anything," I say, refusing to give in to the panic he so clearly wants me to feel.

"She's missed three."

I blink.

Panic claws its way further into my chest. My heart squeezes as I try to shove aside mental images of my mother subjected to Kari's true nature.

"We'll send a team after her," I begin, but Jadick's expression hardens, and I know that's not where this is going.

I bite back a scream as he says, "We can't spare the men, Mac."

His voice is gentle and full of regret. It's such a lie.

"My mother is worth twenty of your men, at least," I snarl, but it's no use. I can already see he won't budge. Not because he doesn't agree but because saving her won't help him win.

It's all a game to him.

And we're all pawns.

"She knew the risks, Mac. I can't—"

"You can, but you won't," I say viciously. "Just like with Levi."

"Unfortunately, even Levi is out of reach," he says.

I step back, eyes wide. "Does that mean you're rescinding your offer?"

"I have to be realistic. We lost too many at the compound, and our numbers aren't enough—"

"If I can get us more men to fight, will you send a team for her?"

I expect him to refuse outright. Or worse, dismiss me as silly or stupid. But he cocks his head, studying me thoughtfully. Jadick is a lot of things, but he takes me seriously, and in this moment, I am glad for that at least.

"How?" he asks.

I cross my arms. "Do you agree?"

Amusement flashes in his eyes. "If you can get us more men to fight, I'll send a team for your mother."

"What about Levi?"

"You know where I stand on that."

"You're telling me that if I agree to marry you right now, you'd rescue Levi but leave my mother to rot?"

"I've told you what I want from you, Mac. And what I'm willing to negotiate to get it."

He's asking me to choose—Levi's freedom for his happiness. We both know even after Levi's free from Kari, he'll never be happy again if I marry Jadick. It's a lose-lose for us all.

I want to scream.

Or to bury a knife in his dead, dark heart.

Instead, I say, "I know where we can get more people to fight on our side. And we can hit Kari where it hurts at the same time."

"I'm listening."

I sigh, hating my choices—the ones I'm making now and the

ones I'll make before this is over. First, I'll save my mother because it won't cost me my self-respect or my soul.

"The scouts," I say. "Don't blow them up."

He opens his mouth to argue, but I cut him off. "Set the explosives on another location as a decoy. But only after we've captured the scouts and brought them in. Kari will think they're dead, and she'll have the wrong location, which will give us the advantage of enough time to gain their trust."

"And what do we need their trust for?"

Dread crawls through me as I outline my idea for him. It's a solid plan. One that could win us back the pack before we've even faced Kari again. But that's what scares me. Handing this strategy over to Jadick all but ensures his victory, and I'm not sure he's a better choice than Kari. But I do it. For my mother. For Levi.

"Once we have the scouts on our side, we use them to get the rest of the pack," I say.

I watch as Jadick realizes what I mean. But skepticism clouds his excitement.

"You really think they'll turn against her and fight with us? Just like that?"

"I think you have no idea how much our pack hates your family." He scowls, and I roll my eyes at that. "That hatred will work in your favor now. The Jades are Black Moon pack. Or they were before they defected. But the people here aren't the only ones sick of the way things have been for us."

"And what way is that?"

"Being forced to reject our mates," I say. "Being forced into everything. No one gets to choose their own lives anymore."

My voice rises because it's beyond irritating that I should even have to explain this to him. Is he so buried in his own self-involvement and twisted ego that he can't see the pack's suffering?

"You're asking me to rescind the law." His expression darkens as he realizes where this is going.

"I'm telling you what you need to do to win the people's favor," I say. "It's the only way everyone will rally behind you."

He's quiet. Brooding.

Not thinking it over. Not really.

I can practically see the wheels turning in his head as he tries to find another solution. Another political promise he can make to these people that will get them to choose him. But there's nothing. We both know it.

Finally, he says, "And if I do this, the pack will turn against my sister?"

"Everyone back home wants change. If they believe you are that change, they'll fight. Hell, they're fighting already. The difference is now they'll do it with actual hope."

CHAPTER 8

*J*adick assures me he'll think about it. With nothing but his tone of voice, he manages to acknowledge I might actually have a good idea while still making me feel inferior. Prick. By the time he leaves me alone, the food sits heavily in my stomach, and exhaustion weighs down every movement. Back in the atrium, I watch Jadick and his entourage disappear inside their offices, my heart squeezing as I think of all the power he has and all the things he's choosing not to do with it.

He will if I marry him.

Ugh.

Not happening.

"Are you okay?"

I whirl at the voice and find a girl around my age watching me with concern. She's tall and slender with blonde, spiky hair. The pizzeria cashier from earlier. Lauren, someone called her, I think.

"Fine," I say and start walking.

I have no idea where I'm going, but I know I'm sick of standing in this fishbowl where all eyes are on me, hoping I'll do something interesting—or worse, humiliating. To my surprise, Lauren falls into step beside me.

"What are you doing?" I ask.

"You look like you could use a walking partner."

I study her, trying to decipher what that means.

"Your limp," she explains. "I heard you were shot with a venom-laced bullet."

I glance back and see Grey shadowing us. His perma-scowl remains, but I'm fairly certain he'd intervene if someone tried to kill me right now. And he hasn't carried me off to my room yet, so this moment is suddenly the closest thing to freedom I've had in a very long time.

I start walking again. "The bullet hit my shoulder. The limp is from the stab wound," I say wryly.

"No shit?"

I glance over to see her eyes widen. She looks down at my leg then back at my face. "You should have that looked at."

"Right."

My closed expression and flat tone make it clear how I feel about that. And her.

"I can take you to the doctor if you want."

I sigh, exhausted by this whole exchange. "Look," I say, pulling to a stop and turning to face her. "Maybe you haven't been paying attention, but the doc here doesn't want anything to do with me. This," I say, yanking the collar of my shirt down so she can see the shoddy stitches on my shoulder, "was done by the only one of you who actually cares if I live or die, and the only medical training he had came from an elective we took in high school so we wouldn't have to take band or home ec."

She frowns. "Doctors take an oath," she says, clearly ready to argue with me.

I roll my eyes. "If you think it's as simple as that, you're more naïve than you look."

Her expression tightens. "If you insist on judging all of us based on a select few douche nozzles, you're more naïve than you look," she shoots back.

I don't answer.

Arguing would be futile, but also, we've begun to draw attention. A few Jades nearby have stopped their own conversations in favor of listening to ours. Though, as I consider Lauren's words, I realize they don't all look hostile either.

The moment from lunch comes back to me. When they all paused to hear my ideas for what to do with this war. It's unsettling. And more than that, I'm unsure of myself. It's a foreign feeling, one I don't like. So, I turn away and begin limping again—back toward my room.

Lauren remains beside me.

I consider punching her. Whatever she sees in my expression makes her smile brilliantly. "I'm pissing you off."

It's not a question, but I grunt my agreement.

She glances back and then whispers, "We have a shadow."

I glance back too. Grey.

"Keep your enemies closer," I say.

"Ah."

I shoot her a pointed glance. She laughs.

Laughs.

We've passed Jadick's offices and are basically alone in my hallway now.

"Look, I don't really do friendships," I say uncertainly.

"You were friends with Kari," she says.

"Exactly."

Her smile drops. She lowers her voice. "Look, you need allies, that much is clear."

My brows go up. "Maybe. But why should I trust you? I don't even know you."

She cocks her head. "You don't remember me?"

"Should I?"

I wrack my brain, thoughts whirling now, but I can't place her.

Her expression softens. "Eight years ago, your mom brought in a drifter who'd wandered onto pack lands. He had a wife—his fated mate—and a daughter."

"They were living in their car." The memory comes back along with a vague recollection of the child. A blonde. Small features, way too skinny. Holy shit. "You're the daughter."

She nods.

Small world.

"So your parents are here?" I ask, trying to make it all fit together. My mom was already training me back then, but there were certain aspects of the job she wasn't ready to show a twelve-year-old. She waited until I was at least thirteen before she let Crigger know I was her little protégé. I was fifteen when he hired me for my first solo job. My mother had been so proud.

Lauren's expression falls. "My mother's here. She stays out of the spotlight. Helping in the kitchen mostly."

"And your dad?" One look at her expression and I know it's not good.

"Four years ago, Crigger killed him for being a Romantic. Levi got us out. Helped us find the others. Eventually, we became...this." She gestures to the mall around us, but it's not just the mall she's talking about.

The Jades.

This is what Levi created. Not Jadick.

"I'm sorry about your dad," I say. "But... doesn't that mean you should hate me? I helped get him caught."

And killed.

"I don't hate you. We were starving. You helped bring us into the pack, and those first four years in Blackstone were pretty great. I mean, I started eating regularly. Made friends. My point is: I owe Levi my life. And I want to help you get him back."

I hesitate, mentally listing all the reasons this is a terrible idea.

Finally, I feel my resistance crumbling right along with what's left of my strength. My vision blurs, and spots dance. I need to get off my feet. Damn this venom.

"Come on," I say.

Lauren smiles again, this time at full wattage.

She talks a mile a minute at my back as I lead us through the empty store and down the short hall to my room. All about her pet iguana Harry who's here somewhere because she couldn't bear to leave him behind when they fled Blackstone. And her short stint as a dental assistant before one of the patients freaked out and bit her and she punched him for it.

If I weren't so damn suspicious of anyone wanting to befriend me, I'd laugh right along with her when she tells the story. Including the part about getting fired and then the patient himself asking her out while still bleeding from his busted lip.

Lauren is easy to like.

Considering Grey's lack of a scowl as he pretends not to listen in, I think he likes her too.

My head swims as I push open the door to my room. At some point, I'm going to have to admit the anti-venom isn't working and give in to the need to rest. Even as I think about it, my stubbornness refuses. If I don't stop Jadick from whatever he's really doing, who will?

The swing comes out of nowhere.

One second, I'm walking into my tiny room, and the next, a figure steps out from behind the door and cracks my skull with some kind of blunt weapon.

Pain explodes, and I land on my face—hard.

The chair beside my cot crashes to the floor as I land on top of it. Someone screams. Behind me, there's a grunt and then another crack!

By the time I roll over, Lauren's already lying beside me. Her eyes are open but frozen. Lifeless.

Blood trickles from her nose and ears. Only a small drip that's already slowing to a stop. I stare at her already pale face with a sick feeling in my gut.

She's dead.

I know it even without my full wolf senses.

In the doorway, a masked figure is swinging his bat at Grey. He misses cleanly as Grey ducks, but the second attempt lands clumsily against Grey's upper arm. Grey uses his other hand to punch the guy in his jaw.

I try to get up, to lend a hand, but my muscles give out before I can even manage to sit. The venom inside me screams beneath my stitches and stab wound.

Grey roars, his fist slamming into the face of the masked attacker.

The asshole drops his weapon. It clatters as he staggers backward into the hall. Then his knees give out, and he falls onto his back. Grey is on him in seconds, pounding his fists into the guy's face. He doesn't bother to remove the mask until blood is oozing out from beneath the eye holes.

I finally manage to sit up, wheezing and in pain. "Grey," I call out sharply.

It's not a yell but it's enough to get his attention.

"We need him alive," I remind him.

He finally stops pounding the guy, and his shoulders sag. He peels off the mask and stares down at the face of the guy who just tried to kill us.

No, me.

With Lauren, he succeeded.

I don't look at her. I focus only on Grey and the man he's just put down.

"Who is it?" I ask.

Grey stands and drops the bloodied mask on the guy's chest. "It's Vale."

"Son of a bitch."

He crosses to where Lauren lies beside me. His eyes dance quickly over her and then back to me. He offers his hand. I take it, letting him pull me to my feet. The look in Grey's eye is still murderous. Behind him, Vale hasn't moved, and I have a feeling I know why.

"He's dead, isn't he?" I ask.

"So's she," he says, his voice rough.

I don't think about that. I can't. If I do, I'll feel the hole that's just been ripped into my gut. She died for being friends with me.

"Will Jadick be mad?" I ask. "About Vale?"

"Fuck Jadick," Grey says, surprising me with the vehemence in his voice. He stalks toward the hall, past Vale's body, before turning back to me. "You coming?"

"Where?" I ask.

He looks like he's about to say something then thinks better of it. Finally, he shakes his head. "Anywhere but here."

CHAPTER 9

Frankie takes one look at me and Grey and ushers us both into her room. The space is tight—tighter still with all three of us inside it. Grey doesn't look uncomfortable, though. He looks like he wants to kill someone. Again. I can't blame him. But instead of rage or violence welling inside me, it's guilt. And the growing sense of certainty that *I'm* the poison. Not the venom inside me.

"You, sit," Frankie orders, and I realize with a start that she's talking to me. That she's been talking to me for several moments. I didn't hear a word.

When she points to the cot against the wall, I sit, trying not to give away how badly I needed to do that.

Frankie shoves a couple of pills and a bottle of water at me.

"What's this?" I ask.

"Your head's gotta be ready to explode, considering the size of that damned lump," she says.

Gingerly, I run my fingers over the back of my head. Wincing, I realize she's right. A lump the size of a golf ball has already formed. I take the pills and the water.

"What happened?" Frankie asks.

"Ambush," Grey says grimly. "Apparently, Vale was working off his own agenda."

"I knew that asshole wasn't to be trusted, but Jadick wouldn't listen," she says.

"Now you have proof," Grey says grimly. Frankie glances at me as Grey adds, "But it wasn't just us."

Frankie's head snaps back to Grey. "Who?"

He hesitates. "Lauren Moore."

Alarm widens Frankie's eyes. "Where is she?"

"Dead," Grey says flatly, and the grief that fills Frankie's otherwise stoic expression tells me she liked Lauren too.

Shit.

I close my eyes and lean my head softly against the wall behind me. It's not hard to let their voices fade away. In fact, drifting is as easy as just letting go. Not sleeping. I don't know if I'll ever sleep. But this is easier. Lighter. I can just pretend none of this is happening. Even better… then none of it's my fault.

All too soon, the sound of the door closing snaps me back.

"Where's Grey?" I ask, noting Frankie and I are alone.

"He went to report what happened," she says.

I start to get up. "I should be with him. Jadick's going to be pissed about Vale."

"You aren't going anywhere." She all but shoves me back again, standing in front of me to block my escape.

I look up at her. "I don't want Grey punished for protecting me."

She sighs and pulls over one of the chairs then drops into it. "Jadick trusts him," she says. "He'll be fine."

Right. I have to remember, regardless of how protective Grey is, he's only doing it because Jadick ordered him to. And Levi before that.

Still.

I pull my knees up, hugging them to my chest. "I don't want anyone else to become a target because of me."

The words are barely more than a whisper, but they physically hurt to say.

Frankie nods knowingly.

"It's tempting to just close up, isn't it?"

"What do you mean?"

"When everyone you're close to is hurting—or worse—it makes you want to stop caring at all."

I look away. She's practically seeing into my soul.

"My daughter was eight when she was killed."

Her words are enough to make my head snap up again. Our eyes meet. Hers are soft, twinkling with something I can't name but have damn sure longed to see in my own mother's gaze.

"Emilia. She was beautiful. And smart as a whip," she says.

"I bet she was tough as hell," I say. "Like her mother."

She smiles. "Tougher."

A beat of silence passes between us. I know what she's doing. Where this is going. A sort of morbid pep talk. But I ask anyway. "What happened to her?"

"Crigger happened. His thirst for power. For violence. I don't have to tell you that man ruled with an iron fist. On this particular day, that fist decided to stamp out an entire apartment building. They started a fire to smoke out a man they'd been chasing for weeks. Harley something or other."

"They unhooked the gas lines," I say, shutting my eyes to the horror of what she's describing. But I can't forget the name. Nor the scene. Not ever.

"They said they cleared the building," she adds quietly.

I open my eyes again, mostly because all I see is the smoke pouring from the windows. Kari and I had seen it while driving home from school. Crigger and Jadick had stood out front while emergency workers struggled to put out the flames. Neither alpha nor his son looked remotely remorseful as the first responders wheeled out two gurneys, each with a body bag.

One bag had been smaller than the other.

Frankie is watching me. But the murderous look from earlier is gone. Now, the softness has won out. It guts me.

"She was sleeping and never heard the knock on the door," she says. "I was at work. A professor at the war college."

I'm not surprised. The war college is about twenty miles outside of town. A boarding school for students, though some of the teachers live off campus. Only the most elite soldiers and spec-ops recruits get sent there. Frankie as a professor makes total sense.

"I'm sorry," I tell her. "Your loss… I can't imagine."

"You can," she says. "Maybe not the way a mother loses a child. But something tells me you can certainly imagine something close to it."

I don't answer.

"Tripp and I have known each other almost his entire life," she adds. "Did you know that?"

I shake my head. A tear tracks down my cheek. Then another. I don't bother to wipe them away.

"His mother and I were neighbors for a few years when he was little. I babysat him when she had the late shift. And now, well, I guess I'm still babysitting him in a way."

I look up at her through wet lashes. "I know what you're trying to say."

"And what's that?"

"You lost your daughter and still found a way to care. You want to make sure I let people in. Not close myself off."

"Is it working?"

"Kind of," I admit.

She snorts. "You're making me work for it then."

"My mom says I'm difficult."

This time, she grins. "All the strong women are."

I shake my head. "I'm not strong," I tell her.

"What would you call it?" she challenges.

"Wrong place at the wrong time?"

She narrows her eyes, giving me a look that reminds me of my own mother's. I can practically feel the lecture coming on. "What happened to Lauren isn't your fault. Neither is what happened to Levi." When I open my mouth to argue, she cuts me off, her voice

318

taking on a firm edge meant to chase away my own doubts. "I know you're hell-bent on saving him, and that's fine. I'm not here to talk you out of it. But you can make it right without blaming yourself for what went wrong."

I sigh. "Is this your way of saying I should forgive Tripp?"

"I think you already know the answer to that."

FRANKIE LETS me sleep on her cot. Or, well, she doesn't wake me up once I've passed out. In fact, when I finally find my way back to consciousness, Tripp is sitting in Frankie's chair. And Frankie is gone. I snort. Real subtle, lady.

"What day is it?" I ask, rolling over and wincing as my shoulder flares with the movement.

"Wednesday."

I realize belatedly that tells me nothing since I didn't know what day it was to start with.

"How long have I been asleep?" I ask.

"A few hours."

I try to sit up and groan through the process. Everything hurts. Even breathing.

"My ribs are not okay with this," I say.

"The venom's pretty strong," he says quietly.

I arch a brow at that. "It probably wouldn't have been until that third dose."

He shakes his head. "You're a magnet for trouble. Always have been."

"Back at ya," I mutter.

He grins and sits back in the chair, watching me struggle as I attempt to find a more comfortable position. But that doesn't exist.

Finally, I give up and wallow in my pain.

"Frankie left you here so we could be best friends again, didn't she?"

Tripp snorts. "Something like that."

319

"She really cares about you."

"She's good people."

"Is that why you brought her with you?"

I try not to let it hurt—again—but it does.

He senses where my question is going and winces. "I would have come back for you too, Mac. But if I'd failed… if anything had gone wrong… Thiago would have killed you. You know that."

"I know." I wave him off, not wanting to pick at the wound.

"Do you? Because I mean that. You are one of the most important people in the world to me. I need you to know I'd never do anything to hurt you. I hate that you think I abandoned you."

I sigh. "Logically, I know the truth about why you and Levi left me," I say. "But my heart isn't so quick to catch up."

He nods.

Silence falls between us, and I try to collect my thoughts. To know where to start. Frankie wants us to patch things up, and there's a part of me that wants that too. A big part. But how do I go from here to there? We can't ever go back, and I don't know how to move forward.

"Did Jadick say anything?" I ask. "On the camera, I mean. About Vale."

"He was definitely pissed," Tripp says with a sort of grimace, and my heart lurches.

"At Grey?" I ask, eyes wide. "I knew it. It wasn't his fault. He—"

"If he was pissed at Grey, it was only because Grey stole the kill. When he heard what Vale tried to do to you… I've never seen him like that. Not even when Levi was taken. Believe me, if Vale wasn't already dead, Jadick would have done it himself."

"Oh." I sit back again, unsure what to say to that.

"And Lauren?" I ask.

His expression falls. "There will be a service for her. Tomorrow night."

"I want to come. If… I mean, if you think it's a good idea."

"I think Lauren would have wanted it."

I bite my lip as my eyes fill with more tears. Ugh. I want to do something. Anything. Sitting here and weeping doesn't count as *something*. But my body isn't capable of anything else, and it's infuriating. Then again, even if I were healed, I wouldn't know where to begin anymore.

"Well, I better get back," I say, scooting toward the edge of the cot.

"Mac." Tripp's voice stops me. A note of something serious. "There's something you should know."

"What is it?"

"Jadick took your advice. About the scouts. He had them captured and brought in. And apparently, some explosions just ignited in Wythe. In the exact location where Levi thinks we were headed."

I stare at him, his words sinking in slowly. Not the words. The meaning behind them.

"You think Levi finally broke?"

"I don't know." He shakes his head. "You did tell Jadick to move the explosions. Maybe he did."

My eyes narrow. "How do you know what I told Jadick? We were alone for that conversation."

He hesitates and then says, "Grey."

"Grey," I repeat.

He waits for me to process that.

"He's working with you," I realize. "Does Jadick know?"

"Of course not."

I blow out a breath. "So he doesn't hate me?"

"No idea. But he's a soldier, and Levi is his general. And he doesn't trust Jadick for shit. So that helps."

Right.

So he probably hates me. But he hates Jadick more.

"Okay, so Wythe exploded. Either because of Levi or Jadick," I say. "And the scouts are here."

He nods.

"Has Jadick spoken to them yet?"

His gaze is meaningful as he says, "He's decided not to."

I deflate. So he's rejected my idea of rescinding the law. Even beating Kari isn't worth him giving up control over us all. I expected it, but it's still a blow to realize, no matter what, nothing will change.

Tripp watches me. I feel his gaze zeroing in on my shoulder.

"What?" I demand.

"Those stitches giving you any trouble?"

"Not as much as the poison is," I say.

He snorts. "Even poisoned, you're a hellion, Mac." He looks away, adding, "I guess I'm surprised you're still here."

"It's not like I have anywhere else to go."

Another pause, and then he says, "He's never going to challenge her outright."

"No," I agree. "He's planning something else."

"Frankie told you about the hexerei, Rina?"

"Has he found her?"

"Not that I've heard," he says.

"And my mom?"

He shakes his head, his expression offering a small glimpse of the worry I feel before he smooths it out again. "Nothing."

My expression must give away some of my worry because Tripp says, "Hey, if anyone can take care of themselves, it's Vicki Quinn."

"You're right," I say, not sure I believe my own words.

Tripp reaches out and squeezes my knee in comfort.

"Ugh." I bite my lip, thinking. And trying not to freak out about my mom.

Without her, and without the strength of my wolf, there's not much I can do. Jadick knows it too, which has my fists balling in fury. He's backed me into a damned corner. I can't even get the Jades on my side. Not after what happened to Levi. And Lauren.

All I have are the scouts.

"You have a plan," he says a moment later.

"I have…the scraps of a plan," I admit.

"Tell me what I can do."

I don't answer.

"I know you don't trust me. And I know there's nothing I can say to change that. But let me earn it, Mac. Shit, let me sink or fucking swim. Give me something—anything. Because I'm losing my damn mind just sitting around on my hands, waiting for that asshole to get us all killed."

"If that's how you feel, I'm surprised *you're* still here."

"It's not like I have anywhere else to go."

My lips curve in a crooked smile. "Touché." The smile vanishes quickly as I think about what he's asking me. And he's right. He deserves a chance. Besides, he's already trusted me with the information he's just shared. "All right," I say. "The scouts we're holding. I need to know where they are, and I need access to them."

"I'm on it."

He rises and heads for the door.

"You really think you can make that happen?"

He turns back, a slick smile turning up the corners of his mouth. "You're not the only one playing a long game," he says and then slips out.

"That's what I'm afraid of," I mumble into the empty room.

CHAPTER 10

ripp returns an hour later with no information. He seems frustrated, and I can only assume he's not used to coming up empty-handed, but Jadick's made it clear Tripp isn't part of the inner circle anymore. Still grumbling, he promises to keep digging, and I head back to my room to wait. It's all I do anymore—*wait*—but unless I want to take Jadick's offer, I can't think of another way.

Despite my best efforts to convince Jadick to rescind the stupid mate rejection law, he hasn't done jack shit. Going to the scouts directly—bypassing Jadick—is my best shot at getting Levi the help he deserves. I can't leave his fate in Jadick's hands. Not when those hands would sooner choke Levi to death than save him.

Grey is waiting for me when I exit Frankie's wing. He straightens when he sees me and offers what might be a look of sympathy. Or it could be disgust. I can't be sure anymore.

"Did you miss me?" I ask with mock sincerity.

When in doubt, sarcasm.

"Jadick is asking for you," he says, refusing to take my bait.

"Why?" My stomach does a weird somersault at the possibilities.

Lauren. The scouts. My mother. Levi.

So many things hang in the balance. Or hang over my head. On my shoulders.

Grey merely shrugs. "He's called a meeting. Something about a delivery."

Tripp and I exchange a glance where he still hovers in the doorway behind me.

"Go," he urges me, "I'll be watching."

"Actually, he wants both of you," Grey says.

"This can't be good," Tripp mutters.

He pulls the door shut behind him, and we all three head for Jadick's office. Tripp and Grey walk on either side of me. Grey's quiet, but at least, he's no longer walking behind me like some skulking henchman.

"Tripp says there'll be a service tomorrow night," I say, glancing sideways at Grey. "For Lauren."

His mouth tightens as he stares ahead. "Yes."

He doesn't offer anything else, and I can't think of any words that don't sound hollow in this moment. Tripp remains silent, but his hand brushes mine in comfort before swinging away again.

We're friends again, I think.

Or the closest to friends we can be with so much baggage between us.

Inside Jadick's offices, there's a frenzied vibe among the security team hurrying from one room to the next. Grey gestures for Tripp and me to enter the conference room at the end of the hall.

I round the corner and stop short when I see the table already nearly full of people. Jadick sits in his usual place at the head. Gregario and Burnett hover behind him, each of them texting on their phones with looks of concentration. It takes every ounce of self-control I have not to make fun of them. Their fat thumbs are hilarious to watch as they attempt to type something coherent.

Frankie nods at me then looks away again, unwilling to give away how close we've become. The guy with the mustache is here too. And the girl, his mate.

They don't look surprised to see me. If anything, they look disappointed.

"Mac," Jadick says, looking up from an open file that's laid out on the table in front of him. His eyes flicker with something, but then it's gone, and he's all business. And impatient.

"You wanted to see us?"

"Yes. Have a seat—both of you."

He waves toward the table dismissively, but I don't move.

"What's this about?" I ask.

"You'll see," he says. "We're waiting on the arrival of one of our spies. Dirk—"

A sound in the hall draws my attention, and then Grey pokes his head in. "He's here," Grey says.

"Finally," mutters the girl.

"Send him in," Jadick says, and then to me, "Sit."

He pats the table, gesturing to the empty seat beside him. I make my way past the others and lower myself into the chair, wary now that he's mentioned Dirk. Tripp sits at the opposite end, next to Frankie. Our eyes meet, and I know he's just as nervous as I am.

Dirk was the asshole mark I was hired to hunt down the night Crigger died. I managed to bring him in despite his attempts to fight me off (not to mention force himself on me—gross), only for us both to find Crigger dead in a pool of his own blood. When Thiago stormed in, Dirk sold me out to save himself, thus setting all of this chaos in motion. Not to mention the fact that he was the one who gave up the location of the first compound. Under torture, but still.

He might be a spy for the Jades, but he's the last guy I want to see right now—and the one I trust least. Besides Jadick himself.

I can't help it. I lean over and hiss at Jadick, "I can't believe he's still working for you. After what he did?"

"Everyone deserves the chance to redeem themselves, Mac." Jadick gives me a pointed look. "I would think you, of all people, would agree with that sentiment."

Dirk walks in—smelling of rotten food and streaked with dirt and blood. The already silent room turns tense at the sight of him but he waves off the concern. "I'm fine," he says even though no one asks.

"What the hell happened?" Jadick demands.

"Ran into a few scouts coming back. Obviously, the pickup was a trap." Jadick grunts like they all expected it. I wonder briefly if that's why Jadick sent Dirk on this particular errand. Because Dirk is so expendable. I wonder if Dirk has figured that out yet.

"Anyway, assholes couldn't get the drop on me. I come bearing gifts." Dirk holds up a small cardboard box and sets it down in front of Jadick with a flourish.

Jadick wrinkles his nose, and Dirk retreats to the front of the room. Everyone on that side of the table reacts to his stench with varying responses.

"Where did it come from?" I ask since everyone else in the room seems to know already.

"Kari sent a message," Mustache tells me. "She left it in North-side. After—"

"That's classified," his mate hisses, and he falls silent.

Kari.

I eye the box with a new wariness.

"What's inside?" Jadick asks. He makes no move to touch the box.

"A message." Dirk's expression tightens until there's a hardness in his eyes—a fury.

My muscles tense at all of the possibilities that await us inside it.

Dirk takes an empty seat at the far end of the table.

No one speaks.

My heart thuds erratically. I want to scramble to open it, to end the suspense. But I also never want to look. To let it be real.

Finally, Jadick pushes to his feet, reaching for the flaps on the box. He pulls it open and peers inside. I watch his expression for some clue and note the way his mouth presses into a grim line.

His gaze flicks to me, and my stomach drops.

"What is it?" I ask, my voice small.

Fear licks its way up my spine and into every open crevice of my mind. This is it. Levi's heart or his eyes or a hand—

"A tooth."

I blink and watch as Jadick holds up a small bloodied molar for closer inspection.

He sets it on the table, and my eyes follow the movement. It's impossible to look away. My mind is filled with images of what it would have taken to remove this from Levi's mouth. How he would have struggled against it. How badly it must have hurt. Because I know for sure Kari wanted it to hurt.

"There's a note," Jadick says, and I glance up to see him holding a slip of paper marred with streaks of blood. He scans it quickly and then, frowning, hands it to Mustache. He scans it, grunts, and hands it to his mate. I nearly scream at them out of impatience. The girl glances at me then reads it aloud:

I've decided to return Levi to you after all.

Piece by piece.

If you want to end this, bring me my brother.

You have three days.

Next time, it'll be his tongue.

We'll see how well he leads a rebellion then.

I swallow against the bile that rises in my throat. Beside me, Tripp snatches the letter and reads it for himself while muttering curses. Then he hands it over to Frankie. One by one, the others scan the message. To verify? To search for hidden clues? I'm too busy holding my shit together to bother with any of that. I look at Jadick, who's staring at the tooth like it holds the secrets to the damned universe.

The others set the note in the center of the table.

People shift in their seats.

Whispers sound, and still, Jadick stands quietly.

The longer he takes to respond, the angrier I become.

Finally, he looks at Dirk. "And Northside?"

Dirk glances at me then Tripp.

"You can speak freely in front of them," Jadick says.

"Burned to the ground," Dirk answers grimly.

"Survivors?" Jadick asks.

Dirk shakes his head.

"Dammit!" Jadick slams his fist against the table.

"What's Northside?" I ask.

Dirk doesn't answer. Neither does Jadick. That only makes me more nervous.

"An outpost," Frankie says after a beat.

I meet her eyes and see everything I need to know. Worry. Sadness. Loss.

"Our people," I say, and she nods.

"They were handlers," she adds. "For our spies in Blackstone."

I wait for her to say more, but she doesn't. Then I look at Jadick. His expression is darkening by the second. My thoughts race. This doesn't look good. It looks like Levi gave up Northside.

"Levi didn't do this," I say.

Jadick's head snaps toward mine. He's looking for a target, and I just gave him me. "No one else knew," he points out.

"No one outside this room," Tripp says and earns a death stare from Jadick.

"Levi didn't do this," I repeat, my heart pounding.

"That's our last outpost," Dirk says, cutting off Jadick's reply. "We don't have any more connections to our spies in town. And with me spotted at Northside earlier, I'm burned."

"There's only one man left," Mustache says. He's still glancing at me like he's not sure if he's allowed to talk about this in front of me.

Frankly, I'm still wondering about it myself. Maybe Jadick has too many secrets. Maybe he's willing to give up a few if it means winning me over to his side. Maybe all this was just a way to twist the knife and make me give in to his demands.

I look at the tooth again then back at Jadick.

He's silent, thinking. I watch as his chest rises and falls with angry breaths. "Send a team for our spies," he snaps at Dirk, and then to Mustache, "Choose our best six. Tell them to camp in the highlands. Over state lines. See if they can make contact."

"Will do," he says.

Jadick's gaze sweeps the room and finally lands on Mustache again.

"Lorenz, you'll lead them," he adds.

"Yes, sir."

Mustache—Lorenz—straightens in his chair, obviously feeling himself for being chosen to lead the team.

"Everyone is dismissed," Jadick says.

A few people begin to stand. Frankie remains where she is.

"Sir," she says. "The note says three days. Do we have any plans to meet that timeline?"

I swallow hard, wondering the same thing.

"We don't negotiate with usurpers," Jadick says.

Frankie frowns.

"You're just going to let her keep doing this?" I ask before Frankie can respond.

Jadick pins me with a look and then says in a sharper voice than before, "You're all dismissed. Dirk, get showered. The rest of you, we'll talk again once Lorenz and his team are ready to go. Mac stays behind."

Frankie looks like she wants to press it, but Jadick cuts her off, adding, "This is my final decision."

The others rise and begin to file out. I watch as Frankie heads for the door, her spine rigid. Tripp pushes back in his chair. He hesitates, and I know he's waiting for me, but I can't tear myself away from Jadick. This changes things. The orders he's giving—they feel like a different path. If he thinks Levi is giving us up, he'll abandon him in a heartbeat. Even the Jades won't be loyal to a narc.

I stare at Jadick, panic rising. "You can't do this," I say.

"Calm down," Tripp begins, but I push to my feet, stepping out of his reach.

"You can't abandon him there," I repeat.

"I have to protect these people," Jadick says.

"You're protecting no one but yourself," I snarl.

"Tripp, give us a moment," Jadick says.

Tripp doesn't move.

"Tripp, go," I say, and then to the remaining guards, "Get out."

Rage ripples through me. I reach for my wolf. She won't rise, not fully, but I'll take whatever strength she can offer me now.

If Jadick means to kill Levi, I'll kill him.

Right here, right now.

"Do as she asks," Jadick says, and I realize the guards never moved on my order.

Assholes, all of them.

One by one, everyone else files out. Even Tripp, though he doesn't look happy about it.

Alone together, I stare at Jadick, my skin practically vibrating with the rage coursing through me now.

"I'm sorry for what Vale tried to do to you."

"And for what he did to Lauren, right?"

"Of course. If Grey hadn't ended him, I would have done it myself just like I did with the first one."

"The first one?"

His gaze flicks to the stab wound on my thigh. "I told you he would be dealt with, and now he has been."

I stare at him, not bothering to offer a response. He's just admitted to killing a man for what? My honor? What do I say to that?

"I'm not your enemy," he adds.

"True. You can't be my enemy if you're dead."

"Mac."

"Levi didn't do this."

"She pulled his tooth."

"He's stronger than that."

"Have you ever been tortured?"

I'm tortured now.

"Have you?" I shoot back.

And then I realize what he's really saying. He fully believes Levi talked under duress because that's exactly what Jadick would do.

"You think he's weak because you are," I realize. "If you were the one being tortured, you would have talked—and it wouldn't have taken a pulled tooth, either."

His expression hardens. "You have no idea what it's like to lead people," he says. "To hold their lives in your hands. To have them look to you for survival. I have to do what's best for them."

"You do what's best for you, Jadick. And no one else."

"That's not true."

"Then prove it. Challenge her. Right now. End this."

"It's not that simple."

"It *is* that simple. You're just a coward."

His strike is so swift and unexpected I don't have a chance to block it. My cheek explodes in pain as the back of his palm collides with my face.

"My mother said the same thing, and look where that got her." His voice is cold as ice, but there's no lie in it either. And that startles me almost as much as the slap.

I drag my gaze back to his and force a smile, gritting my teeth against the pulsing of my own heartbeat inside my cheekbone. "Your brother hit much harder."

He bares his teeth at me in a predatory snarl. "My sister is determined to kill us all, and yet you worry for one pathetic life lost."

My pride wants me to hit him back but that would be useless. In fact, it would only serve to kill Levi faster. I know that as well as I know the heartless look he wears now.

"Please," I whisper instead, my eyes searching his for some small shred of decency. "You are the only one who can stop this. You're the one she wants."

"You're wrong, Mac. You've always been wrong about her. She won't let him go if I take his place—she'll kill him just to spite us both."

"She won't need to kill him if she has you," I nearly scream.

"*Need* has nothing to do with it, you stupid girl." He steps closer. "If you think Kari still possesses a shred of mercy, you are more naïve than I thought."

"She left me alive," I say, refusing to give in. Or give up.

Even though it's getting harder not to agree with him.

"My sister left you alive because she thinks it will make me weaker to have you in my ear, begging for his life."

"Caring for a person doesn't make you weak—"

"Doesn't it?" He cocks his head, his warm breath washing over my face. "Where are all the people you care for, Mac? Are they here with you now? Are they safe?"

"You're a monster," I whisper, nearly choking on the words. On the reality that he won't budge an inch on this. He'll let Kari slaughter us all if it means he lives another day. We're not his people —we're his shields. And he doesn't care; I can see it written all over his pretty face.

"I'm not nearly as bad as she is," he says, and my hands ball into tight fists.

I feel the skin break against my palm where my nails have dug too deep, but I don't care. There's no other way. He knows it. In fact, he made sure of it.

"Fine," I say, all the breath escaping me with that one word. My chest deflates, and my shoulders sag. My self-respect evaporates into the air like nothing but fine smoke. "I'll do it."

His eyes light with victory. "You'll do what?"

"You know what," I say through gritted teeth.

"A deal such as ours deserves your honor, Mac. I need to hear you say it."

"I'll marry you," I say, shoving the words out of my mouth like garbage down a chute. "And in exchange, you'll free Levi. You'll face Kari before the three days are up."

"A happy bargain," he says, smiling.

Smiling.

In the face of such horrific cruelty.

He leans in, and I realize with disgust that he means to kiss me.

"No." I press my hand to his chest to stop him.

He straightens, frowning. "A proper bargain must be sealed."

"What the hell happened to a handshake?"

"You have agreed to be my wife," he says, arching a brow. "Surely, you understand the semantics of a marriage—and what's required."

"We're not married yet," I growl.

"How about this? When I've beaten Kari and freed Levi, we will stand on the steps of the alpha house and announce our engagement. And on that day, in front of our pack, you will let me kiss you."

I don't answer.

My stomach roils with the idea.

"You will have to do much more than that once we're married," he adds as if that somehow makes my decision easier.

"When you make the announcement, you'll also rescind the rejected mate law," I say.

He scowls.

"Final offer," I say, squaring my shoulders. If I can't have my mate, I'll make sure everyone else can at least have theirs. "Rescind the law. Let everyone choose their fated mate. And I'll marry you."

His hesitation becomes a slow, reluctant nod. "Fine. If that's what you want."

"It is."

He extends his hand. I take it, and we shake. His eyes glitter as he says, "We have a deal."

His grin is broad and empty of a single shred of decency. He's gloating, and it doesn't matter to him at all that he's doing it at the expense of Levi's survival. I want to kill him so badly I can't see straight.

But I love Levi more than I hate Jadick.

And that's the only reason I say, "Our bargain is sealed. You'll have your kiss like you said."

CHAPTER 11

By the time I leave Jadick's offices, I don't know the plan, exactly, but I believe him when he says we'll leave soon for Blackstone. For some reason, he wants me. And he'll do anything—even risk himself—to get me. It doesn't make sense, but I don't waste time trying to understand the mind of a psycho. What matters is that we're ready when the time comes.

I need to train.

I need to get well again.

The venom is a low throb in my shoulder and a constant burning bite in my thigh. It's done ribboning through my body apparently, and now it sits stagnant at the sites of my still-healing wounds. I can't afford to wait until I'm back to full strength. I won't be left behind when this rescue mission kicks off.

My face has to be the first one Levi sees.

Guilt twists its crooked knife inside me at that. I know very well why I need to get to him first. So I can explain. But it won't matter in the end. I've signed away my soul and his with my bargain to Jadick.

There's no coming back from it.

Only forward.

So, when I leave Jadick's offices, I tell Grey to take me to the training rooms.

He doesn't argue.

When we arrive, the tuxedo shop is full.

A line of Jades has formed at least twenty deep, each waiting their turn with the mannequins set up against the wall. Apparently, word has spread that Jadick is finally taking action.

I watch as someone sends a blade flying. It notches in the hard plastic between ribs—if the mannequin had any. The crowd parts, and I glimpse a female with short hair standing at the throw line. The guy behind her claps her on the shoulder for a job well done. Then the crowd closes in again, and I lose sight of them both.

Closer to where I stand, mats are laid out along the main hall, each with a couple of soldiers sparring. They don't use weapons beyond brute strength and hard fists. Grunts and curses echo against the high glass above our heads. It's a soundtrack that is darkly comforting.

I turn back to Grey.

"Find me someone to fight."

He eyes me shrewdly. "You're not healed."

"What do you care?"

He grunts and then turns away. I expect him to wander off to find a volunteer, but he returns a moment later, dragging a mat with him. He sets it in place out of the walkway and then gestures for me to step on it.

When I do, he joins me.

My brows shoot up. "You're going to fight me?"

"Do you prefer an easier opponent?"

"Fuck you."

He grins, but it's a deadly sort of thing—and then he launches himself at me.

I duck and retaliate. He arcs backward, and I miss.

For the next few minutes, we dance this way. But it doesn't take long for him to land a punch, thanks to my slow reflexes and injured body. He hits me square in my stomach, knocking the wind from my lungs. I go down on one knee, choking.

He steps back, giving me a moment to catch my breath, which surprises me more than anything. I look up at him through sweaty hair that's fallen into my eyes. "You could have finished me," I say once I find my voice again.

"Too easy."

Asshole.

I don't know why I expected him to say something friendly.

Getting to my feet sucks, but at least, I can breathe again.

Facing off with Grey, I plant my feet and get ready to go again. He studies me with an expression I can't read.

"Ready?" I ask when Grey doesn't move.

"Nah. I'm done." He turns to walk away.

"I'm not," I call out stubbornly.

He doesn't turn back.

Clenching my fists, I have to fight the urge to chase him down and put him on his ass. Losing sucks. Having him walk away from me like this is something else entirely.

I'm not even angry with Grey.

I'm angry with myself.

"I'll step in."

I look over to see the female with short hair. The one who threw the blade with such precision. Now that she's standing before me, I can see it's the same girl who's mated to Mustache, Lorenz. Great.

"Nely," she offers, stepping onto the mat.

"Mac."

"I know." Her expression is slightly friendlier than earlier, though not by much.

Lorenz is notably absent. Gathering his team, no doubt.

I look back at Nely and take a deep breath. Why the hell not?

"Let's do it," I say.

She bends her knees, falling back into a crouch. We circle one another, and I study her movements, trying to get a feel for her style. Out of the corner of my eye, I'm aware of others watching.

339

We've drawn a crowd, but I ignore them. It's Nely I need to watch now.

She attacks first.

A punch with a swinging arc that would have caught my temple. Or my jaw. Instead, I yank back, and she catches only air. She retreats and circles again.

When she comes this time, I expect another punch so I swing my foot out, but she lands a kick in my injured thigh before I swoop her other leg out from under her. I hiss in pain, and we go down on our asses together.

She raises up onto her elbow and grins back at me.

"Again?" she asks.

She's having fun.

I grimace at how easy this must feel for her. Meanwhile, my thigh hates me. "Again."

Twice more, Nely puts me on my ass. By the time I'm back on my feet for a third, the venom is pulsating pain throughout my body, and I have new bruises from Nely to add to the sensation. At the edge of our mat, the crowd has gotten involved, shouting their support—mostly for Nely. I don't mind. I can't hear them over my own blood pounding in my ears anyway. And I don't have enough pride left to care that they've witnessed me lose. Jadick took that from me earlier, and I've already given up hope I'll find a way to earn it back.

"Again?" Nely asks.

I'm surprised to realize her enthusiasm doesn't feel mean. More...hungry for the chance. But I shake my head. "If I go again, you'll be scraping me off this mat."

"What's wrong with that?" says a male voice. It's unfriendly and all too familiar.

The crowd falls silent.

Nely's smile vanishes.

I turn to see Burnett at the edge of the crowd. The look in his eye is unmistakable. He sees this as his chance.

"How about it?" he asks. "You want to go a round with me?"

I want to refuse. But I don't.

"All right," I say.

He steps out of his boots and saunters over.

I expect Nely to walk away, but instead, she moves to my side and plants her feet.

"What the hell is this?" Burnett asks.

"Evening the odds," Nely says with a shrug.

"How do you figure?"

"She's injured. And you're top-ranked. Both of us against you seems fair." His eyes narrow as she adds, "Unless you're worried you can't handle it?"

The challenge lands squarely in the bull's eye. His eyes gleam, and he cracks his neck side to side. "Let's fucking do this."

The crowd starts up again, and Burnett takes a fighting stance.

"Are you sure about this?" I ask Nely.

"Just watch his left. It's his strongest—"

She doesn't get to finish before Burnett roars and charges.

Nely's right. His left is strongest. I barely have the energy to dodge his blows. Even with Nely's help, I am not going to make it out of this without getting my ass kicked. I can only hope to last long enough that he's too tired to do real damage when he finally lands his hits.

Nely is like an insect, flitting around me and using her speed to distract him.

But finally, brute strength wins out, and Burnett catches her off guard.

His fist slams into her shoulder, knocking her off balance. She grunts and tries to regain her stance, but he's already winding up for what I know will be a knockout. My breath catches. My voice stalls. And my brain screams at me to stop him.

All I can see is Lauren all over again.

Launching myself forward with every ounce of energy I possess, I don't even know if I've moved fast enough until his fist slams into my temple and I'm driven straight down to the mat.

The crowd goes wild.

Nely curses, and blood pumps harder in my ears, drowning out everything else.

Voices rise, two indistinct figures clouding into my line of sight. They sound angry. At me? At each other? I can't tell.

My head feels as if it's splitting in two.

I could probably stand, but what's the point? No part of me wants to invite a follow-up, so I stay where I am. On my stomach, cheek pressed against the dirty mat that smells like feet.

"Mac, you okay?" Nely's voice is low above my ear.

"Ugh. Fucking peachy," I manage.

"Come on." She tugs my arm. "Can you stand?"

"Not if there's a round two."

"It's over," Nely says firmly.

The arguing somewhere above me grows louder. I let Nely pull me to my feet and see Grey and Burnett shoving each other. Burnett yells at Grey to "stay the fuck out of it," and Grey shoves him back—away from us. A few others join them until the crowd closes in around them, and I can't see what's happening.

"Here."

I turn to see Nely holding out a bottle of water. I take it gratefully and tip it up, chugging until dark spots cloud my vision. Then I lower it again, gasping. I swipe at my mouth and come away with blood. The tangy aftertaste of the water is coppery in my throat.

"Thanks," Nely tells me.

She's watching me like there's something to see. Like she expects something. A few others have stayed behind to watch us too. It puts me off balance almost as much as that punch.

"For what?" I ask warily.

"You didn't have to do that," Nely says quietly.

"You were on my team," I say.

She looks like she wants to say more, but then Grey is there, shoving me away from her. Away from everyone.

"Come on." He tugs my arm so hard I stumble and am forced to follow if I don't want to face plant.

342

"Where's the fire?" I snap, tasting more blood on my tongue as I try to talk.

He glares at me, leading us both away from the crowd. "With you, it's never far."

I gape at him. "How is this my fault?" I demand.

We're walking so fast we might as well be running. Past Jadick's offices. Down the empty hall toward my room. The crowd and their noise echo behind us, muffled until we turn into the abandoned store and the sound fades entirely.

"Grey," I say when he doesn't answer.

I glance up at him and see the angry twist of his mouth, but it doesn't make sense. When we reach my bedroom door, I step inside and jerk away from him, ready to fight if it comes to that. But he lets me go, blocking the exit with his body as he glares down at me.

"You don't have to keep protecting them from me. I'm not going to hurt anyone. Apparently, I couldn't if I wanted to," I add darkly.

"I'm not protecting them, you idiot. I'm protecting you."

Then he pulls the door shut, slamming it in his own face and leaving me alone.

CHAPTER 12

Grey returns shortly with food, which I eat, mostly because I have to do what it takes to regain my strength. The thought of him slipping something into my food crosses my mind, but it doesn't feel like the truth. Not anymore. Somewhere along the way, I started trusting Grey. And I believe him when he says he's protecting me. Maybe I'm being careless or naïve or any of the things Jadick thinks I am. But I can't do this alone. I need allies. And trust goes both ways.

After I eat, some of the pain eases, and my muscles loosen enough to allow me to move easier. I find myself waiting—again. For Jadick to come yell at me for fighting with Burnett. Or Tripp or Frankie to lecture me about smart choices. Part of me even half-expects my mother to turn up. She's never been MIA for this long. Not ever in my entire life. It worries me more than I can admit to anyone. Even myself.

But no one comes.

My thoughts drift to Levi's tooth. Kari's deadline. Jadick's marriage deal.

The harder I try to find a way out, the more the walls seem to close in around me.

I pace my room until the space feels more like a prison than a safe haven. Despite Grey's words—and the fight with Burnett—I'm not sure the danger is worth this. I've never hidden from my enemies. Run, maybe. But I don't back down when cornered.

Then again, isn't that exactly what I've done by agreeing to Jadick's bargain?

I refuse to allow my mind to draw parallels.

What's done is done.

Retrieving a discarded tennis ball from the corner, I settle on my cot with my back against the wall and toss the ball at the back of the door. It hits then bounces back again, and I catch and repeat.

Hit. Catch. Repeat.

The monotony helps shut off the constant stream of angry, worrying thoughts.

It helps me forget to punish myself about Levi for a little while.

Without warning, the door opens, and Tripp lets himself in, narrowly missing a tennis ball to the face. I catch the ball as it springs back at me and lower it to my lap.

"You want to watch where you throw that thing?"

"You're the one barging into my room," I point out, sitting up straighter.

"Heard you got into a fight with an ape," he says, his expression darkening as his eyes zero in on my mouth.

I touch it gingerly, remembering this particular injury actually started when Jadick back-handed me. But I don't say so.

He turns his head, and I notice the purple bruise along his cheekbone.

"What the hell happened to you?" I demand.

"I found the scouts."

My chest lifts. "That's great. Where?"

"They're being held in a music store at the end of the west corridor."

I frown. The west corridor is the only place I haven't been allowed to visit. For good reason apparently."

"Did you ask to see them?"

346

"Sure did."

"And?" I prompt.

He points to the bruise. "Gregario said no."

My muscles tighten with tension and the need to punch something.

"Jadick's hiding something," I say. "Even after everything."

"Of course he is. He's a fucking snake, Mac. You can't believe a word he says."

"You're the one who let him into your little rebellion," I say.

It's not nice, but my mood is darkening by the second. I need to yell at someone.

"Yeah, well, I have regrets."

I snort. "Don't we all?"

"Any word from your mom?"

"No." I sigh. "Although I'm not sure Jadick would tell me if there were."

"He likes you best when you need him," he says darkly. "That's for sure."

I tilt my head. "Why do I always feel as if you know more about him than you're saying?"

"Not *more*. I just recognize the evil in him." He shoves his hands into his pockets and looks me over. "Speaking of evil, I heard about your showdown with Burnett. You okay?"

"Fine." I don't bother to hide my scowl, and I know full well he's already caught sight of the raised lump on my head. "Bastard's lucky I'm not at full strength."

"Let me ask you something. Serious question. Are you *trying* to get yourself killed?"

"What the hell kind of question is that?" I snap.

"I know you're beating yourself up over what happened with Levi."

"You don't know anything."

"I know you're making some shady ass deal with Jadick, probably selling your soul."

Forcing myself not to flinch, I say, "I figured you were watching the whole thing earlier."

"Unfortunately not." His expression darkens. "Lorenz interrupted to ask me about joining his little team."

"What did you say?"

"Unless Levi's the mission, I'm not interested."

"Right." I blow out the breath I've been holding. At least, Levi didn't overhear my little proposal.

"Anyway, Jadick's a lying sack of shit who'll probably stab you in the back before it's all over. Whatever deal you're making with him, just remember that."

I look down at the tennis ball, mostly so I don't have to look at him. "I'm not telling you what I promised him."

"All that does is reassure me I'll hate it."

"Yeah," I say quietly, "You will."

He crosses the small space and sits on the opposite end of the cot, facing me. "What else can I do to make you trust me again?"

It hurts to realize there might not be *anything* he can do. Maybe we've come too far. Instead, I lean my head back against the wall and stare up at the paneled ceiling. The answer comes so suddenly; my whole body jerks with the effort of leveling my gaze on his again.

"Help me talk to the scouts."

"I already told you, they aren't letting me through—"

"I know how we can get to them."

"Whatever it is, I'm in." His answer is so immediate that I want to hug him for some crazy-ass reason. Maybe because even in the face of my distrust, he's still here for me. No matter what.

Instead, I smile slyly. "How do you feel about tight spaces?"

TEN MINUTES LATER, we're both wedged into the ventilation shaft. Tripp's heavy breathing might be funny—if it wasn't threatening to expose us.

"Quit breathing so loud," I hiss.

"I'm sorry, is my need for oxygen annoying you?"

"Getting caught will annoy the shit out of me."

He doesn't answer, but I can hear him trying harder to breathe more evenly.

Imagining his face scrunching up with the effort makes me almost smile. Unfortunately, the walls pressing in around me and stuffy air clogging my throat make smiling kind of impossible. As I shuffle forward on hands and knees, my shoulders slide along either side of the narrow ventilation shaft. I'm pretty sure Tripp's broad shoulders are hunched even more than mine, which is probably contributing to his mouth-breathing situation. A nicer person would probably be more understanding. I'm not nice.

Up ahead, the tunnel splits, and I take a left, hoping my sense of direction isn't off up here. We crawl in silence for what feels like a ridiculous amount of time to be shuffling around in a tiny-ass tunnel.

Finally, I stop, straining to listen to what sounds like Gregario's grumpy voice somewhere below us. "... no one in or out. I'll relieve you after I've finished dinner."

"Got it," says another voice, this one unfamiliar.

"What is it?" Tripp whispers, his voice no more than a breath.

"Shift change."

I wait until Gregario's footsteps recede.

When he's gone, I move forward to give myself room and then slide the ceiling panel silently aside. It's a small room from the looks of it. Another store office maybe. The angle is wrong, so I can't see the faces of the prisoners. But I can see two sets of legs each tied to a chair. Directly below me, a guard leans against the wall, staring down at his phone. I get a fleeting second to make out his face—not one I've met before—as I drop down to the floor in front of him. Then, my fist is slamming into his throat, cutting off his air supply and the ability to yell for help.

Tripp drops down beside me and grabs the guard from the back, choking him. The guy struggles wildly then falls limp, unconscious. Tripp lowers him to the floor.

The whole thing takes no more than six seconds.

I hold my breath, listening for any sounds outside the door. But there are none. I have no way of knowing if or when someone will come through though, which means no time to waste.

Tripp steps over the fallen guard, blocking my view of the prisoners just as I turn to face them. I wait, but he doesn't move aside. In fact, he seems frozen in place.

"You've got to be fucking kidding me," Tripp says.

"What?"

"These are the scouts?"

I shove around him and stop short at the sight of the two men bound in the center of the room.

Not men. Boys.

Dumbasses, more accurately.

Two of them.

And we know each other all too well for this to go the way I thought it would.

"Lenny," I say in defeat. "Guy."

I look them over, trying not to think about how fucked up this is. My biggest bullies from Black Moon—now, my only hope.

CHAPTER 13

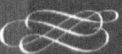

$\mathcal{A}$t the sight of me and Tripp, recognition dawns in their eyes, followed quickly by wild desperation. Their wrists and ankles are secured together, but they proceed to wriggle hard against the ties—to no avail. The sight of them tied to a chair brings back the memory of when I was in their shoes. For a moment, I can't move. All I can do is remember what it was like to sit in a room just like this one for days on end, wondering if I'd live or die. From behind a very unhealthy amount of duct tape, they attempt to call out, and that futility is what brings me back to the moment.

I roll my eyes and march over to them, ripping off the tape over Lenny's mouth without bothering to go easy.

"Fuck," Lenny says.

"Shut up," I hiss at him. "Or you'll bring the other guards."

Beside him, Guy motions for me to undo his tape.

Gladly.

I pull it off as hard as I can, enjoying the small pleasure of him groaning in pain.

Just because I need them on my team now doesn't excuse everything that came before.

"Big Mac," Guy says the moment the tape is peeled free.

My shoulders sag.

Disappointment. Dread. Disgust.

Memories of being stuffed into lockers assault me. Tripped in the halls. Cat calls. Name calls. Anything they could do to humiliate me. And that didn't count the rumors. These assholes spread everything from my moonlighting as a prostitute to Levi abandoning me for not being able to satisfy him properly. It was never bad enough to involve the principal, but their relentless commitment to fucking with me ate at me so slowly that I never realized they'd won until it was too late. Until I shrank away from their attention. Until I lost the will to fight back.

Seeing them here now, hearing them call me the old nicknames, is almost too much. I fight the urge to climb back into the vent shaft and leave the way I came in. But before I can do that, Tripp grabs Guy by the shirt and punches him square in the mouth.

Guy's head lolls to the side. I can see the marks from where the guards have already gone a few rounds in the same manner. Tripp glares down at him, though, unrelenting.

"What the fuck was that for?" Guy demands.

Blood leaks from his lip when he looks up again.

"Call her that again and I'll break your nose," Tripp says.

"But that's her name," Guy says.

"No, her name is Mac. Just Mac. Or Mackenzie. Do I need to repeat myself?"

Tripp raises his fist again, and Guy flinches.

"No," Guy says quickly.

Tripp steps back so he and I are shoulder-to-shoulder then crosses his arms.

"Are you here to rescue us?" Lenny asks hopefully.

"No," I say.

"Then what the fuck—"

"They're going to let you go soon," I say.

But Guy scoffs. "Are you insane? They're going to kill us."

"If they wanted to kill you, you'd already be dead," Tripp tells them.

Guy falls silent, scowling.

"Then what do you want from us?" Lenny asks.

"We're here to offer you something," I say, and I watch as Guy's scowl turns to suspicion. I can't blame him. We aren't exactly besties.

"We're not exactly in a place to accept gifts," Lenny says.

I exchange a withering look with Tripp. "Why would she choose them?" I demand. "You're telling me this is the best she could find?"

Tripp shrugs. "We have to work with what we've got."

I look back at my high school bullies, not sure whether to waste my breath. But Tripp is right; I don't have another option.

"Look, Jadick is going to send you back to Blackstone soon."

"You're serious?" Guy asks. "He's really going to let us go?"

Now that I know it's them, I'm tempted to rethink it. To make sure they never walk out of here.

"Yes." The word tastes sour in my mouth.

"Why the hell would he do that?" Guy demands. "Especially when we know where you're all hiding?"

"Because he's going to ask you to spread the word about us to the rest of the pack. About what we're fighting for. He's going to ask you to join our side."

Guy snorts. "And what side is that exactly?"

My eyes narrow. "The side that's going to kick Kari's ass."

"So, what? You want us to trade one Clemons for another?"

Clearly, Guy's going to be a pain in my ass about this—just like he's always been about everything.

"That's why I'm here," I say. "You're right. Jadick's just as bad as Kari is. That whole damn family is toxic, and I don't plan to let any of them lead our pack."

"But you just said you want us to help you defeat Kari," Lenny says uncertainly.

"Listen to me, dumbasses." My temper is straining, and I struggle to keep it in check. "Levi's being held prisoner in the alpha house right now. He's the real leader of the Jades. In fact, he's their alpha, and he could be yours too."

"You want us to help make Levi Wild the new alpha," Guy says.

"I want you to spread the word like Jadick asks," I tell them. "And when we return to Blackstone and Jadick challenges Kari, tell every Black Moon pack member to stand down and let it happen. That's it. You don't even have to fight because we're all on the same side here. Once Kari's gone, I'll free Levi, and he'll become the new alpha."

"You make it sound so easy," Lenny says.

"Simple, yes. Easy, no," Tripp tells them.

"Why should we do what you say?" Guy asks. "I mean, what's in it for us?"

And there it is.

I knew the moment I saw these two it wasn't going to be straightforward.

"What's in it for you?" I hiss. "Fucking freedom, that's what. No more looking over your shoulder to make sure you didn't accidentally catch a death sentence for crossing the street wrong. No more being told who to mate with or how to live."

They exchange a look.

"Is that it?" Guy asks.

I start forward, but Tripp puts his arm out to stop me.

"What else is there?" Tripp asks.

Guy shrugs. Or tries to. It's not smooth considering all the ropes binding him. "Lenny and I aren't really into the whole mating thing," he drawls. "And if I'm being honest, the exodus of you Romantic pussies left me and Lenny in a pretty advantageous spot with our new alpha. Sure, she's a woman, but I've decided not to hold that against her. We scored sweet-ass promotions when Kari stepped up, and at this rate, we'll be running shit by the end of the season."

"Just let me kick his ass," I say, but Tripp shushes me.

"I guess what I'm saying is I'm not really interested in losing what I've got," Guy finishes, "Unless the price is right."

The price. Of course.

He's going to extort us.

Unless I decide to say fuck it and kill him after all.

"Mac, go wait in the tunnel," Tripp says quietly.

"Why the hell would I do that?" I demand. "We're not finished."

"I'm going to have a private chat with our friends here," he says pointedly.

"If you're kicking their asses, I'm staying," I tell him.

He sighs. "Fine. Help me out then."

He bends down and retrieves the discarded duct tape beside Guy. Then he holds it out to me.

I take it and press it back over Guy's mouth. Guy shakes his head, struggling to resist, but he's got nowhere to go, and the tape sticks easily to his reddened skin.

I step back, and Tripp moves in.

"What are you doing?" Lenny asks from beside us.

Tripp doesn't answer. I don't even see the knife in his hand before he's plunging it between Guy's ribs. Guy moans beneath the tape, his entire body jerking as if to get away from the weapon. The tape keeps the noise to a minimum, but it's clear he's in pain.

Tripp slides it free and steps back, wiping the blade on Guy's shirt.

"What the fuck, man?" Lenny's voice rises, and I tense, hoping we haven't been overheard.

But Tripp merely stares back at Guy. "If you don't do as we ask, I'll find you and kill you in your sleep. And if you think for a second I can't do it, I'll remind you Mac is the most gifted bounty hunter in our entire pack. And she has every reason to want you dead."

Then he rips the tape off Guy's mouth, giving him one last chance to redeem himself.

Guy glares up at him. "You won't get away with this," he says roughly.

"I just did."

Tripp walks to the vent opening and jumps, catching the edge of it and hoisting himself easily into the space. I follow Tripp to the vent, looking back at Guy one last time. He stares at me with open hostility, and I try not to think about all the times he's tried to break me down.

"Kari doesn't give a shit about you," I tell him.

"No one does," he grunts, and I don't bother to argue before climbing up into the tunnel and leaving him behind.

CHAPTER 14

When we're back in my room, Tripp doesn't ask me if I think Lenny and Guy will come through for us. I think it's because we both know they probably won't. But I appreciate that he doesn't make me say it out loud. In the wake of my disappointment, I am in no mood to talk. Tripp takes the hint and makes himself scarce.

Grey is stoic as ever in the hallway.

I have no idea if he heard us sneak into the ceiling earlier, but I don't much care anymore either. Either he's on my side, or he's not. Simple as that. Part of me wants to tell him to get some damn sleep, but then I realize he'll probably just stay awake to spite me for saying it.

Instead, I shut my door and flop onto my cot.

My thoughts drift inevitably to Levi, which is a dark and twisty rabbit hole that makes my chest ache with fear and guilt and sorrow. Marrying Jadick might free my mate, but it won't make him mine.

Levi and I were a mess even before he was taken prisoner. That moment we had on the hill outside town…it feels like a lifetime ago.

It also feels like it could have been an ending just as easily as a beginning.

We still have so much between us. And just like with Tripp, I have no idea if the chasm is crossable anymore. Hell, maybe he'll hear I'm engaged and not even give a damn. Either way, I can save Levi, but I can't have him.

That last thought twists like a knife in my gut until hot tears burn my eyes.

My only consolation is in giving him the thing he wants most. I have to make him alpha. He's the only one who can change things for our pack. Even if I'm not around to see it happen. Because I have no illusions about the depth of Jadick's wrath when he learns I mean to double-cross him. He'll kill me for sure, but hopefully, I can take him with me in the end.

It's the least I can do for the pain I've caused.

And it's the only way to truly be free.

Hours later, I'm still wide awake and strategizing when Tripp bursts in. He's fully dressed all the way down to boots, but his shirt is untucked and his hair is a mess.

I sit up quickly. "What is it?"

"Guy and Lenny," he says.

I can't help but scowl. "What about them?"

"They're gone."

"What?" I demand.

But he's already back out the door, leaving it wide open for me to follow. I grab my boots and hurry to catch up. Grey is gone from his usual post at the end of my hall. That more than anything sets me on edge.

In the main corridor, we turn a sharp right for the atrium. It's still empty as ever down here, but up ahead, the other Jades are hurrying from one wing to the next. Purposeful. Urgent.

Security teams of two and three streak past the others, intent on their mission.

Guns are strapped to their waists.

My urgency drives me faster.

At the door to Jadick's offices, Tripp slows. I spot Burnett emerging and watch as his features twist at the sight of me. My head hurts at the sight of him, and I'm hyper-aware of the knot on the side of my head.

"What the hell are you doing out?" he demands.

"I came to help," I say.

For a second, I think he'll tell Grey to take me back. But for whatever reason, he doesn't.

"Get in here." He grabs me and yanks me into the darkened interior. Then down the hall and into the first room on the left. Tripp is right behind me, but Burnett stops him from entering at my back.

I don't turn as they argue viciously.

I meet Jadick's eyes instead. Something about the cold calculation keeps me from demanding answers.

"Let him in. Search them both," Jadick says without breaking my stare.

Burnett goes from telling Tripp to get lost to grabbing him and shoving him face-first against the wall. Tripp curses him, but he doesn't resist. Not even when Burnett begins patting him down, starting at the shoulders.

I brace myself for what he'll find. The knife Tripp used to stab Guy. We obviously didn't let them escape, but the stab wound is evidence we were there, and that won't go well for us.

Refusing to break our standoff, I hold Jadick's eyes and concentrate on breathing evenly. My training has given me the skills to control my nervous system at will, and I'm thankful for it now. He won't see me flinch.

But if he finds that knife he's so clearly expecting on Tripp, this is going to get a lot worse.

Burnett finishes the pat-down empty-handed.

"Let him go," Jadick says.

Burnett shoves Tripp toward the exit. "Get out of here," Burnett snarls at him.

I can feel Tripp's hesitation, and very deliberately, I turn and nod at him. "It's okay," I say. "Go."

"I'll be right outside," he says with a pointed look at Burnett.

Then he saunters out. No one speaks until the door closes behind him. When he's gone, Jadick looks at Burnett. "Now her."

I don't realize what he means until the asshole's hands land on my upper arms and I nearly lose my shit. Grabbing his wrist, I whirl, twisting his arm violently until he cries out. He goes down to one knee before gritting his teeth and grabbing for me. I leap just out of reach, managing to keep his arm in a tight grip.

He makes another sound of pain, and I crouch, ready to drop him onto his back.

"Stop."

Jadick's command echoes off the walls, and I curse myself for conceding. I tell myself it's his alpha blood that makes me obey. Not fear.

"Let him go," Jadick tells me.

Scowling, I do as he says.

Burnett whirls, looking at me with pure contempt.

"Leave us," Jadick tells him.

Burnett shoots Jadick a look. First angry then surprised. Like he thinks he's being robbed of his revenge.

"I won't repeat myself," Jadick says.

"I'm going." Burnett scowls and slams the door as he walks out.

When we're alone, Jadick stands in front of me. "I'm going to search you for weapons."

"Like hell," I growl.

"I'm going to search you, and you're going to let me. Otherwise, I'll have Burnett put a dart in your neck, and you can sleep through the entire process. Either way, you'll be patted down. I think you'd prefer to be conscious for it."

I take a minute, remembering the way Tripp slid that knife into Guy's gut—and replace Lenny's face with Jadick's. It's almost comforting enough for what's about to happen.

Finally, I plant my feet and hold my arms out wide. "Hurry up," I growl.

But of course, he doesn't hurry. Slowly, he takes a step

forward, closing the distance between us. His eyes are intent on mine, his breathing heavier all of a sudden. He brings his hands up and presses them to my body just beneath my arms. He lingers there, watching me like he's waiting to see how I'll react.

I try to keep the revulsion off my face, knowing it'll only make it worse.

With slow, unhurried movements, he drags his hands down my hips and around my waist. His eyes are locked on mine, and he's standing so close I can smell the spicy aftershave clinging to his skin. I force myself to hold his gaze, disgust curling in my gut as his hands venture upward once again; this time, running down the front of my chest.

The air crackles with tension, but it's not pleasurable. Not for me.

I can see his arousal though, pressing against his pants. It's all I can do not to drive my knee into it. And judging from the look he wears, he knows I've seen it. Maybe even knows what I want to do to it.

When his palms reach the downward slope of my breasts, he pauses, cupping them and squeezing lightly. Pure rage lights in my veins, and I know it's crept into my expression. He smiles—fucking smiles—and then drops his hands lower, running them down over my abdomen—then lower still.

When he gets to my thighs, he kneels in front of me. His exhale of hot breath washes over the front of my pants. I force my feet to remain where they are. Fists too. He looks up at me, his eyes shining with an expectation I recognize instantly.

He's turned on.

He wants me turned on too. But he also wants me to hate this.

With a sickening twist in my gut, I force my expression to neutral. Bored even. And I ignore the way his warm hands trail around my inner thighs. His thumb brushes my sensitive spot, and I flinch.

"Do that again and I'll kill you," I snarl.

I'd step back, but there's nowhere to go. Instead, I press myself into the wall and breathe.

His hands finally reach my ankles, and he finishes his exploration—because that's exactly what this was. Not a search. A discovery.

Bastard.

Finally, he pushes to his feet. His cheeks are flushed. His erection even more obvious than before as he looms over me. I was right; he wants me to fight back.

So, I don't.

My shoulders press hard against the wall in some attempt to put space between us. But he just leans in closer, refusing to give me an inch.

"Can I go now?" I ask, putting every effort into sounding unaffected.

His expression falls, and I know I've managed to resist giving him what he wants from me. "You're all clear," he says.

I turn for the door, hating that I'm slinking away instead of shoving him back. But he refuses to back off, and I can't stand here any longer without committing a murder that would doom Levi to the dungeons forever.

"Pack your things," he says just as my hand closes around the doorknob.

I look back at him sharply. "Are we leaving for Blackstone?"

"Soon," he says. "In the meantime, I want you close. You can move your things into the office across the hall. I'll have your cot moved as well."

"No."

His expression tightens. "Excuse me?"

Just the thought of it. Of him putting his hands on me whenever he wants...

"I'm not sleeping across the hall from you."

"You're not in a position to refuse me."

"You're the one who wants me badly enough to barter for a man's life," I say. "I think that means I'm exactly in a position to

366

refuse you."

His eyes narrow. "Negotiating is one thing, Mac. Disobedience will have unpleasant consequences."

"You are an unpleasant consequence," I tell him and then let myself out before he can say another word.

In the hall, Burnett glares at me, and I suck in a breath, determined to hold it together until I'm away from them both. I half-expect Jadick to come after me and argue harder for me to switch rooms, but he doesn't.

Still, I walk quickly.

Burnett holds the outer door for me, and I don't stop moving until I'm in the main corridor, and Burnett closes the door behind me, shutting me out.

Tripp stands nearby, talking to a group of Jades. When he sees me, he breaks away from them and hurries over to me.

"What happened?" he demands.

"Don't ask."

I head for my room, and Tripp falls into step beside me. Still, Grey is nowhere to be seen.

"Okay, where are we going then?"

"I'm getting my stuff and staying with you."

"Uh, not to point out the obvious, but how does Jadick feel about that idea?"

"I don't give two shits how he feels."

Tripp, wisely, says nothing to that.

Back in my room, I deflate, realizing belatedly there isn't any "stuff" to grab. I came here with nothing but the clothes on my back. Other than the bag my mother left me, I'm without a single earthly possession. For some reason, that realization nearly breaks me.

"Fuck!" I kick over the small table and watch as it slams against the far wall.

"Whoa, hey." Tripp grabs my shoulders, steering me toward the door. Or, more specifically, away from anything else I can damage. "What happened in there, Mac?"

His eyes are kind on mine, but I hold back.

"Nothing," I say.

He drops his hands, disappointment flashing. He knows I'm lying, but he doesn't press it.

"And the scouts?" he asks. "Did he say anything about them?"

"No. he obviously knows Guy was stabbed. I'm guessing one of them ran his mouth."

"I don't think so," Tripp says.

"Did you hear something?" I ask, remembering how he was whispering with those Jades.

"They didn't escape. Jadick let them go after they agreed to recruit more of the pack to our side."

I'm not holding my breath on that one. But I'm sure they told Jadick what he wanted to hear to save their own asses.

"Do you think anyone knows we were in that room?"

I can't help worrying that I've somehow screwed myself out of my bargain. Without our deal, I have nothing. Especially after finding out the scouts are those two assholes. They want to help me less than Jadick does. And if the pack doesn't fight on our side, what will happen to my mother? To Levi?

"I think if he knew for sure, he wouldn't have searched us and let us go," Tripp says.

"You're right," I agree, but deep down, I'm not so sure.

Jadick's playing a game with me, but it's not necessarily the same one I'm playing with him. The problem is I have no idea how either game works.

"He wants me to move into the office across from his," I say.

Tripp frowns. "To sleep there?"

"Yes."

"What did you tell him?"

"What do you think?"

He grins. "I bet that went over well."

"Listen, if I stay with you, it'll make you a target. He's going to be pissed. So if you don't want to—"

"Give me some credit, Mac." He slings his arm over my shoulder and pulls me in for a quick hug. "Come on. Let's go get you settled in your new space." He scoops up my extra clothes and tucks them under his arm. Then he extends his free hand. "Roomie," he adds.

I take his hand in mine as I grab the bag my mom left me and let him lead me out. "Thanks," I tell him.

"Don't thank me yet. I snore, remember?"

I nod at the clothes he's carrying. "That's what the dirty socks are for."

CHAPTER 15

ripp's room, it turns out, is one in a series of small alcoves carved out by dividers that look like they were stolen from a container store. A very likely scenario, considering where we are. The dividers offer a small semblance of privacy but do nothing to block out the noise coming from the other "rooms" around ours.

"How many bedrooms are there in here?" I ask as he leads me through a maze I'm very sure I won't be able to navigate my way out of alone.

"Probably sixty or so," he says with a shrug.

"That's insane. The mall's huge. There's so much room to spread out."

"Jadick ordered everyone to stick closer together." He tosses the words almost carelessly over his shoulder as he leads us through what used to be a large, wide-open department store. But I can't help wondering why he'd order something like that.

Is this all so Jadick could shove me down that far hallway alone? Is he so worried about what will happen if I'm tossed in with everyone else? Or does he simply not care about anyone else's circumstances so long as they don't impact his?

Finally, Tripp motions for me to enter one of the spaces. It's not much bigger than a cubicle, but there's a cot wedged against the far wall with just enough room for another beside it.

He dumps the clothes on his mattress and then starts for the door again.

"Where are you going?" I ask.

"I'll grab your cot and bring it back," he says. "Stay here."

His voice takes on a note of authority, but I roll my eyes. "Yes, sir."

I mock salute, and he shakes his head as he disappears back into the maze.

With nothing else to do, I sit on the edge of Tripp's mattress and listen to the conversations floating in from the nearby quarters.

"...Levi put him in charge for a reason," a female voice is saying.

"Levi didn't put him in charge," replies a male. "That asshole grabbed power from a vacuum."

The voices aren't familiar, but their words have my full attention.

"What, did you want the Quinn girl to step up?" the female asks with a derisive snort.

"Which one? The mother or daughter?" the guy challenges.

They both laugh.

I listen to their footsteps as they shuffle out into the maze. Their words stay with me, though, long after they're gone.

More conversations swirl.

Someone asks about dinner.

A fight breaks out over a stolen toothbrush.

Someone says, "I love you" with no sarcasm.

There's a camaraderie in the chaos of so many bodies forced to live so close. And even though I'm smack dab in the center of it all, I am very aware of how separate I am from these people. They're connected. To each other. To their cause.

I'm connected to no one.

Even my relationship with Levi—such as it is—doesn't contain the same kind of bond these people share. Levi and I are mates, and that should count for something. Maybe it does. It's the reason I'm trying so hard to free him after all. But at the end of the day, the Jades are his people. They're the ones he's fighting for. The ones fighting for him.

I just hope they're worth it.

Because when I'm done, they're all Levi will have left.

"Hi."

I look up to see an older gentleman standing in the narrow opening. He's wearing worn jeans and a baseball cap with a fish on it.

"Hi," I say warily.

"You're Levi's girl."

Levi's girl. I swallow hard at how warm those words make me feel.

"I'm Mac."

He nods. "Jim. My mate, Amelia, and I came away from the compound with you."

His scent finally registers, and the small stirring of my wolf confirms his words. She remembers.

"It's nice to see you again," I tell him honestly. Mostly, I'm glad he's alive. That they made it when so many others didn't.

"We owe you for helping to get us out of there," he says.

I stare at him. "You don't owe me anything," I finally mumble.

"You led the way around Kari's scouts. Without you, we would have met them head-on."

I shake my head. "You would have figured it out."

He cocks his head, studying me. Something about his expression suggests he wants to argue, but he merely shakes his head. "You officially one of us now?"

"What?"

He gestures to the cot and the small room. "You sleep here. You eat here. You fought for Nely, and you're fighting to take down the Clemons alpha. Sounds like a Jade to me."

"I'm..."

His words stun me. My sudden burst of emotion makes it impossible to form words.

Up until now, I've felt only their hate and disgust, but the way Jim is looking at me is nothing like that. If anything, there's an openness. A friendly acceptance I haven't experienced in so long it clogs my throat with unexpected emotion. And I find myself wondering if I haven't missed this shred of acceptance that exists scattered among them.

Tripp returns, saving me from answering.

Jim doesn't bother saying goodbye, just shuffles off to give Tripp enough room to enter, dragging the cot behind him. I lift my feet and tuck them underneath me so he has space to shove the narrow bed into our shared space. When he's done, he flops onto it.

"These halls are narrow as hell."

"Are you that out of shape?" I tease.

He sits up, glaring. "I can still kick your ass, Quinn."

"Yeah, right."

Before our sparring can devolve into a wrestling match—which would undoubtedly destroy this entire department store town—a figure appears in the doorway. My body tenses, fully expecting Jadick to have come for me. But instead, I see Grey, grumpy as ever.

"Are you here to drag me back?" I ask him.

He glances at the two cots then back to me. "I don't drag people," he says simply.

"What about your knuckles?" I ask, and his eyes narrow. "Do you drag them? Or is that just Burnett and Gregario?"

For a second, I think I've pushed him too far. That he'll finally snap and try to kill me. But he just scowls deeply and then says, "I thought you'd want to know Jadick's team just returned from Blackstone."

"Team?" I ask.

"The extraction team he sent for Vicki."

He sent a team?

I sit up straighter. "And?"

"No sign of her."

"What do you mean no sign of her?"

"Our spies reported the only prisoner being held at the alpha house is Levi."

"That doesn't make any sense. Where is she then?"

"That's all I know." He looks like he wants to leave but then changes his mind. Instead, he shoots Tripp a look I don't understand before glancing back at me again. "Are you sleeping in here now?"

Something about the way he asks the question makes it sound like he doesn't approve.

I shrug. "I figured I'd let Tripp babysit me for a while. Give you a break."

He frowns. "I don't take breaks." Before I can think of an answer for that, he adds, "I'm across the hall if you need me."

Sure enough, he disappears into the room across from ours.

"Grey. What the hell do you want?" a voice asks.

"I'm moving in."

"The hell you are—"

The response is cut short by growl and a grunt. A moment later, I hear, "Fine, just stay on your side."

Tripp and I exchange a look.

I can see the question in his eyes. The one that wonders why Grey is so intent on protecting me himself. Unfortunately, I don't know the answer either.

"You think you need protection from me?" Tripp asks, and his question is direct enough to startle me.

I almost blow him off, dismissing his question entirely. But then I look around and realize, at some point along the way, I started trusting my former friend again. Or maybe I never stopped. Either way, the only way to move forward is to be honest. At least about this.

"Someone drugged me back at the compound," I say. "Or tried to."

His eyes bulge at my words. "What?" His voice rises.

I shush him, wondering if Grey is listening. Actually, I'm positive he is. But I push on, anyway.

"Before we were taken, Levi told me only two people had access to my food while I was a prisoner." I pause and then add, "Jadick and you."

He stares at me, but instead of anger in his eyes, I find only disappointment. Somehow, that's worse. "And you actually suspect me?" When I don't answer, he huffs. "You really think I could do something like that to you?"

I bite my lip. "I don't know."

"I don't fucking believe this. That's why you've been so distant with me? You thought I tried to drug you?"

"Whoever was in charge of my care back then left me locked up alone without food or water for days," I say, temper rising as I remember the hell they put me through.

Tripp's hurt morphs into fury. "I never knew," he says, his voice deadly quiet now. Rage ripples off him. I can feel it from where I sit across the tiny space.

The voices around us have gone quiet. The more I think about what I'm saying, the more I realize this might have not been the smartest place to have this conversation. The Jades already distrust me. Airing my dirty laundry might just make things worse.

But Tripp is clearly unconcerned as he pins me with a look. He doesn't bother lowering his voice at all as he says, "Whatever they did to you—No. Whatever Jadick did to you, I'm sorry. But it had to be him. Because I would never do anything to hurt you. And I'm just sorry as fuck that you don't know that into your bones. That you could ever doubt me."

My eyes fill with hot tears at his words. Because he's right. I should know it. I should have no doubt about Tripp's loyalty.

"I do know," I say weakly. "I mean, I do now."

"Look," he says, "Jadick has been trying to ice me out for weeks. Months. But now, with you, he's trying to wedge himself between us. And it's fucking working. Don't let him do that, Mac. Don't let him isolate you or gaslight you into thinking he's the one you can trust. He's a snake, Mac. Don't forget that."

"I know."

The silence is deafening now. As if the entire room is listening in. And considering they're all shifters with impeccable hearing, they probably are listening in.

"Maybe we should talk about this later," I say, but Tripp grabs my arm.

His expression is fierce. Loyal. "I will never betray you, Mac. I swear it. Do you believe me?"

"I believe you," I say quietly.

But I don't promise the same in return. I can't. And the reality of that makes me sick. Before he can see the truth in my eyes, I turn away and crawl over the second cot toward the door.

"Now what?" Tripp asks.

"Now we find out where the hell my mother is."

HUNGER GNAWS at my stomach as I follow Tripp back through the maze. A few Jades nod hello as we pass them in the narrow walkway. The rest scowl or curse—or ignore me completely. I tell myself it's to be expected. Levi brought me here as an enemy, a prisoner, and now I walk among them like I'm trustworthy.

I'm not.

"They'll warm up," Tripp says as we step out of the store and into the open corridor.

I shoot him a look. "Why should they do that?"

"Because we're all on the same side."

"Just because we want the same things doesn't mean we should trust one another."

He doesn't answer.

I sense movement behind me, and from the corner of my eye, I'm not surprised to see Grey shadowing us. Maybe it's for the best. The more witnesses I have, the less I have to worry about someone trying to kill me. The list of those wanting to try is growing by the day.

We make it nearly to the atrium, where the smell of food is drawing me like a siren's song, before Tripp stops.

"What?" I ask when he gestures toward a storefront.

"You want to know about your mom, this is the best place for answers."

I glance inside and spot several Jades loitering around a single arcade game. Pac-Man, I realize. An innocent enough game. But the threats being called out are not.

"Twenty bucks on this asshole to choke in the first thirty seconds," a man says.

I almost laugh until I hear the response.

"Thirty says I'll choke your mom if you don't fuck off," says another voice—this one familiar and disgusting.

Dirk.

And with him are two of the asshole Hellions from the alley behind Inferno.

I step inside the small shop, every instinct pushing me to start knocking heads together until every last one of them is laid out on their backs, maybe even without their tongues still attached. But then I remember my wolf is still out of reach.

I grit my teeth as Tripp steps up beside me.

"Pike," he calls out sharply.

The group of men turns as one, eyeing us with varying levels of hostility.

A large man wearing a Hellion jacket steps out of the group and faces us. The others part to give him room, but they crowd in to make it clear whose side they're on. Dirk is front and center, glaring back at us.

"What the fuck do you want, Thompson?" Pike asks.

"You just got back from Blackstone," Tripp says. "We want to know what you found."

Pike and a couple of others exchange a look I can't read. When he turns back to us, he crosses his arms and relaxes his expression. "I don't have to tell you shit."

His gaze lands on me then, his eyes roaming as if exploring my body. As if he has the right to. Or he'll just take the right even if I refuse. It reminds me of that night in the alley with Dirk. How they all tried to gang up on me. Use what they saw as their brute strength against mine. It triggered me then, and it triggers me now.

With a roar, I close the distance and slam my fist into Pike's smug face.

He bends at the waist, hand cupping his eye where my knuckle collided with bone. His uncovered eye glares back at me with murder shining inside it.

"You bitch," he snarls.

Then he attacks me back.

"Whoa, hold up!" Tripp's yell is lost to the roar of a dozen more men hurrying to join Pike. Fists fly. I catch a wild punch in the chin, and my knees buckle. Instead of making me retreat, the pain ignites my fury. I shouldn't be this easy to beat.

What the hell is wrong with my wolf?

I fight back, kicking and dodging and using my nails.

My training goes out the window. Without the strength of my beast, I'm nothing compared to these men, and if they figure that out, I'm dead. The harder I fight, the less I care about dying. I just need to take a few of them with me.

Someone produces a knife.

I can't see who. There's no time. It's all I can do to stay out of the way of the sharp end. Another hand juts in, grabbing the wrist of whoever holds the blade and twisting sharply. The knife-wielder doesn't let go, but in the end, that's his mistake. I glance up in time to see Grey turning Dirk's hand around and then shoving the blade into Dirk's gut.

Dirk curses as blood leaks from beneath his shirt.

The others work into a frenzy at the scent of blood in the air.

This fight just reached a whole new level.

Someone calls my name, but I ignore them.

A fist slams into my temple, too fast and out of sight for me to see it coming until it's knocked me fully sideways.

Reeling, and with a migraine exploding behind my eyes, I know I've pushed too far. Black dots swim in my vision, and dizziness threatens to suck me into unconsciousness. If I do that, I'm dead for sure.

Struggling to remain conscious—and out of the way of another hit—I stumble back directly into a body. Jerking away is no use. Strong arms come around me, holding me fast. I kick awkwardly, trying to make contact with a kneecap, but the angle is wrong. Or I'm wrong.

I miss completely and only end up nearly tripping myself.

Rage courses through me, and my thrashing increases. I should be better than this. I *am* better than this.

"Relax, Mac. You're safe now."

I stiffen as Jadick's voice registers against my ear.

A second later, he's shuffling me to the side, and I find Tripp reaching for me instead. In this moment, I trust him a hell of a lot more than I do Jadick, so I let him tug me behind him as Jadick steps forward to address the crowd.

Around us, security is already rushing in and pulling the remaining fighters apart. Mostly, it's just five Hellion guys trying to pound Grey—all of which are failing at the attempt.

"Everyone stop!" Jadick's voice booms as he stands before us all, confident, cool, and obviously fully expecting everyone to obey his issued command. In this moment, he looks every inch the alpha. But it's not flattering. In this moment, he's Crigger. Ruling by fear and by force.

Still, it works.

The remaining fighters break apart, all of them breathing heavily.

"Whatever this is about, it's over," Jadick says, and I'm too surprised he's not going to demand the details to argue with him. "Suit up and get to your Protocol B exit points," he adds.

The men look at him, startled.

"Shit," Tripp swears under his breath.

"What is Protocol B?" I ask.

But Jadick's already pulling me away and down the hall. "I'll tell you on the way," he says.

"On the way where?"

"Anywhere but here," he snaps. "We're leaving."

CHAPTER 16

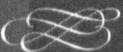

ripp tries to follow us, but Jadick screams at him to get to
his exit point.

"I'm not leaving her," Tripp snarls, marching up to Jadick to face
off with him.

Jadick glares back. "You know how this works, soldier. Abandon
your exit point and you're abandoning your own people. Is that
what you're choosing right now?"

Tripp doesn't answer.

I watch his chest rise and fall with angry breaths. Finally, he
shakes his head. "If anything happens to her—"

"She's safest with me," Jadick snaps impatiently.

Tripp looks over at me. "I'll see you at the rendezvous," he says,
clearly torn.

I nod, still confused.

Finally, Tripp runs off in the opposite direction, and we start
moving again. A killer headache pounds in my head, but I ignore it
and pull away from Jadick's iron grip. Or attempt to. I don't get far
before he grabs me again and practically drags me away from the
crowd. In the atrium, a security team is shouting orders, but the
only thing that sticks out to me is their repeated use of "Protocol B"

to anyone not already running toward wherever it is they're supposed to go.

The energy is hectic. The security team looks strained. Or nervous.

"What the hell is going on?" I ask.

"We're leaving," Jadick says, still as vague as ever.

"Are we going to Blackstone?"

I can't keep the hope out of my voice, so I don't even try.

He shoots me a withering look. "You'd love that."

It's not an answer, but I'm starting to think I won't be getting one.

We reach the office door, and Jadick shoves me through. In the short hall, he goes left into the first room. The one where he frisked me earlier. Being back here puts me on edge, but he's not paying attention to me.

He rifles through the desk drawers and shoves a few small items into a duffle bag. A notebook. A pocket watch. A gun.

I watch, trying to figure out what has him spooked enough to abandon this place. The only time we've done it before is when the compound was attacked. I freeze in horror, thinking of Guy and Lenny with a creeping sense of dread.

Jadick zips the bag just as Burnett and Gregario appear in the open doorway behind me.

"We're ready," Burnett says.

"Good. Let's go," Jadick tells them. He rounds the desk and reaches for me again.

"This is crazy," I say. "What happened to make us run? I thought we had a plan. The scouts—"

"The scouts gave us up," he hisses, rounding on me so sharply I step back.

"How do you know for sure?"

"Our perimeter checkpoint was just slaughtered," he snaps. "Your brilliant fucking idea to turn them to our side backfired. I'm getting us out before a repeat of the compound makes escape impossible."

He shoves me toward the door where Burnett manhandles me toward the back hall. From there, I'm hustled into the conference room, and Gregario pushes me out of the way just as Burnett yanks the large projection screen straight off the wall. Behind it is a hole cut directly into the cement. Burnett sits in front of it and then uses both legs to kick it hard enough to knock loose the drywall enclosing it.

The entire square flies off then breaks into pieces as it hits the asphalt on the other side. Fading sunlight streams in, and Burnett wastes no time crawling through the opening that's just big enough to allow him passage.

Gregario jumps up, shoving me forward, and I fall into line behind Jadick who's already hurrying to be the next one out. I'm too shaken to resist. The pounding in my head hammers to the beat of my heart now.

A broken heart.

The threat of my own death doesn't produce so much as a drop of adrenaline. But this? Almost killing an entire tribe of people because everything I do backfires—twice? This sends fear racing through my bloodstream like a dam has broken.

In the dying daylight, I look around, trying to get my bearings.

We're in an abandoned parking lot in an area bordered by trees. No other Jades are in sight, and I have no idea if that means they've all escaped through another exit or if Jadick's just that selfish and brutal to have abandoned them already.

"Hurry up," Jadick snaps, and I start to follow out of pure instinct but then hesitate.

"I can't shift," I say, worry snaking through me. "I can't run from here."

"We're not literally running," he says as if I'm being slow.

An engine revs, and I see an SUV careening around the corner of the outer wall then lurching to a stop before us.

Grey's in the driver's seat.

For some reason, seeing him here is a relief. I feel safer with him, and that's probably going to get me killed eventually. Burnett

385

hurries to pull open the passenger door and Jadick climbs inside the backseat.

I hesitate, thinking again of Tripp and wondering why I don't see other Jades exiting the building. Instead of joining Jadick, I begin to back away.

Then Gregario is there, shoving me toward the car. He crowds in behind me, wedging me between him and Jadick with zero access to either door. Burnett climbs into the front passenger seat beside Grey, his broad shoulders taking up more space than most. Of the two, I prefer Gregario. Mostly because he didn't try to flatten me with his fists. Yet.

"Go," Jadick orders.

The moment the car door shuts behind us, Grey accelerates, and we speed diagonally across the empty lot toward the road.

"Where are the others?" I ask, again looking for signs of the others leaving like we are. But as far as I can see, the lot is empty other than us.

"On their way out," Jadick says. He's looking down at his phone, which he's angled away from me so I can't see the screen.

Already, the sky is darkening to pink with the setting sun. It'll be dark soon. And then what?

"Where are we going?" I ask.

"Somewhere safe."

"Is that where my mother is?"

Finally, he looks up at me. "What?"

"I know she isn't Kari's prisoner." I watch his expression as he continues to text. "I know you're lying to me about her not checking in, too."

A small twitch of his eye gives it away.

My anger flares. "Was it all a way to manipulate me then?"

No answer.

His silence only serves to confirm my fears. Of course he was manipulating me. Hadn't he been the one to say that love was a weakness? And he'd made sure to exploit mine.

"You better be taking me to her," I say as if I could actually back up my unspoken threat.

He glances over at me then goes back to his phone. "You'll see her soon."

I stifle a scream, my hands balling into fists in my lap. Suddenly, Grey jerks the wheel, and I'm thrown against Jadick, but for once, he doesn't even seem to notice me. Then Grey's straightening out the wheel again as we finally hit a main road full of evening traffic.

I straighten, pulling my body away from Jadick's, and glance around us for some sign of an imminent threat. But there's nothing out of place among the other vehicles coming and going on the four-lane road. Nothing like the compound with its cave-in and utter destruction.

Maybe Jadick's intel was wrong. Or maybe he's lying again. Manipulating us all—

Boom.

The car swerves as the force of an explosion hits us from behind.

Grey's eyes flick to the rearview as he grabs the wheel, gripping it to maintain control. I twist in my seat and see a plume of black smoke rising above the trees. Behind them stands the mall. Or it did.

My breath sticks in my chest.

I turn back around slowly and meet Grey's eyes in the mirror.

"Son of a bitch," Gregario mutters from beside me.

"Find out if everyone got out," Jadick says, and I'm surprised to hear him so worried for others. Maybe there's hope for him after all. "We're going to need every damn soldier we have now," he adds, and I shake myself for even thinking he's capable of real empathy.

Up front, Burnett's phone dings with a text. He swipes to read it, and I watch as his entire body tenses.

"What is it?" Jadick asks.

"Good news," he says, though I don't believe that for a second. Not when every drop of energy rolling off him screams the opposite. "Your package is ready for delivery."

"That *is* good news." Jadick leans back into his seat, instantly relaxed.

Whatever this package is, it's important enough to make him forget his people could, at this very moment, be dying or dead. Another explosion sounds, this one quieter now that we've put more distance between us and the mall.

No one even looks up. Their apathy is horrifying.

All I can think about is Tripp.

No, not just Tripp.

I think about Frankie and Nely and even Lorenz. Did they all really get out?

Or were more lives lost just now because Jadick's determined to think only of himself?

"And the safe house?" Jadick asks.

"Still secure," Burnett says.

"Good. We'll regroup there. Wake me when we arrive."

He leans his head back against the seat and closes his eyes. I stare at him, disbelief and indignation heating me from the inside.

"You're going to sleep?" I demand. "Now?"

He doesn't crack an eye as he answers me, his voice dangerously clipped. "I am, and you should too. When we get where we're going, there will be no rest. Not for you."

His words are mildly threatening. Or maybe it's the silky sweet way he says them that has a trickle of unease running down my spine. My fear makes me snarky.

"If I say no, are you just going to drug me again?"

His eyes open, and he lifts his head to look at me. "Again? You think I drugged you?"

"I know you did."

"And when did this alleged drugging occur exactly?"

"When I first came to the compound. When Levi held me in that room."

My voice wavers.

After the last few days with Tripp, seeing him be here for me, I can't imagine anyone else being behind it anymore, but the way Jadick's looking at me now...it throws me off balance. He's not simply denying the accusation. There's a wistfulness to his expression; a darkness that shakes me to my core.

"Listen carefully, Mac. I don't want you unconscious for what I plan to do. When I make my move, I want you wide awake. Do you understand me?"

My stomach hardens until it feels as if I've swallowed a stone.

When I don't answer, he closes his eyes and returns to his reclined position. No one else in the car says a word. I can feel Grey's eyes on me again, but I don't look up. Not for the entire ride. I don't sleep either.

IT'S past midnight when Grey finally pulls into a dimly lit motel. The sign reads Pine Hill Motel in neon letters, three of which are blinking unsteadily. Instead of parking in one of the spaces, Grey pulls around back and parks in one of the Staff spaces. I don't recognize the other two cars already here, but that doesn't mean they aren't ours. Hope worms its way into my chest against my will.

Grey cuts the engine and the lights.

We all get out.

Part of me expects Gregario or Burnett to grab me, but they don't. Jadick knows I won't run. Not just because of our deal, either. He knows I need to see for myself who made it here.

I follow Jadick and the others toward the motel where we take a metal stairwell that's so caked with gum and who-knows-what-else that I can't bring myself to touch the railing. We climb to the second floor where Jadick turns the knob and lets himself inside the first door we come to. Gregario looms behind me with an unspoken yet clear command that I should enter too.

Inside, the air smells damp and musty.

The walls were once green—maybe a calming mint—but they're so faded now it's a disgusting shade of pea soup. I eye the single queen bed with growing trepidation.

Jadick does a quick sweep of the closets and bathroom and then turns to face us.

"Go check on the others," he says, looking past me to Gregario. "Get me a head count and a list."

"Got it."

"Burnett, find Frankie, and tell her I want a full debrief."

"Will do."

The two disappear back outside.

Grey lingers just outside the open door. Again, I refuse to meet his eyes. There's a very good chance if I do, I'll find pity, and that would only make me lose it. I can't afford that. Not now.

"Sir," he says when Jadick doesn't offer any orders.

Jadick looks up—glued to his phone again already. He seems to realize Grey is waiting for him. "Find us something to eat," he tells Grey.

Grey grunts out a response, and I wonder if he actually intends to do as he's told. But then he's gone, and Jadick and I are alone.

"Close the door," Jadick says.

I do it, mostly because, if I play nice, maybe I'll get some answers.

I refuse to fully play his game, though. If we play anything, it'll be on my terms.

"What's the plan?" I ask.

I'm not sure what I expect from him. Silence maybe. Or smug platitudes. But at my question, he tosses his phone aside and closes the distance between us faster than I can react.

His hand closes over my throat, and he slams me against the wall. My head *thunks* hard against the rotting drywall, sending a few specks raining down. Jadick's eyes are lit with fiery rage as he stares down at me.

"The plan," he says, so close I can feel his hot breath, "is none of your fucking business."

"What..." The moment I try to speak, his hand begins to squeeze, slowly closing my windpipe. "...did I do?" I rasp.

"What did you do?" he repeats. "What did you *do*?"

He squeezes hard one final time then lets me go, moving away to pace.

"You sabotaged me, you fucking bitch."

His distance isn't comforting. Not even with the relief of a full breath in my lungs. His movements are jerky. He's unpredictable—and caged.

Not a good combination.

"How did I sabotage you?" I ask.

"Those scouts were set to help us," he says. "And after five minutes with you, they ran straight back to Kari to rat us out the moment they were free."

"You have no proof it was them."

"Who the fuck else knew where we were?" he roars.

Guilt snakes through me, squeezing like Jadick's hand. Stealing the breath from my lungs.

"I didn't—"

He rounds on me, breaths labored. "Don't you even dare deny it, Mac. My patience only goes so far."

"I was going to say I didn't know it was them. When I went to see them."

"When you defied me, you mean."

"I wasn't there to defy you." Lie.

My heart beats faster as I try to decide whether he knows my plan to replace him with Levi.

"I was there to help," I say.

He pauses, studying me with narrowed eyes that make it crystal clear what's happening: I get one chance to convince him. That's it.

"Recruiting them to our side was my idea," I say. "Using them to recruit the others, sparing their life, all of it."

"I remember." His voice is soft and slick.

"Well, I remember us making a deal that puts us on the same team. If I'm going to be your wife, that makes me your equal. But then you locked me up like a common prisoner instead of letting me help you."

The word "wife" tastes bitter in my mouth, but I shove past it.

"I only went to see them to convince them of our idea. To remind them everything that's at stake. And because I didn't know if you'd already done it. You left me in the dark, so I took matters into my own hands."

"You can see how well that worked out."

"Yes, well, how was I to know Kari picked the only two assholes in the world who hate me more than she does? The minute they saw my face, I knew I'd made a mistake." Jadick's eyes narrow. "The point is it was an accident. I didn't sabotage you. Not on purpose."

"Why do they hate you?"

I pause and realize his question is sincere. "You have to ask?" He doesn't answer. "Let's see. Because my mother is the bounty hunter who arrested Guy's father once? Because I'm a Romantic? Because they're bullies who like to torture weaker prey. Take your pick."

He doesn't answer at first. I can see from his expression that his rage has cooled, but I know better than to assume anything.

"They underestimate you then. You are not weak, and you are not prey."

I don't argue, but it's hard to keep from pointing out weak prey is exactly how he treats me too.

Besides, he's already talking again. Lecturing me. Reminding me of my mother in the way he's talking down to me. "As much as I like your plan to turn the pack to our side, I've learned not to expect people to do as you ask. There's too much darkness in our hearts for that. If we want to gain their loyalty, we will have to do so by bending them to our will. By force."

He pauses, and I can't help but feel as if he's challenging me, checking to see if I'll argue.

I don't.

"From now on, we do it my way," he continues. "If you can agree to this, we will do it as equals. Together. No more prisons." He steps closer, dark eyes searching mine. "Deal?"

"Deal." I clear my throat, forcing the word out despite the revulsion coiling inside me. He's wrong. Being mated to Jadick will be the worst kind of prison.

He leans in to kiss me, and I flinch, jerking away. "That's not part of our deal," I say. "Not yet."

"Fair enough," he says on a sigh. He gestures to the bed. "Get some sleep then."

I remember his words from earlier. About how there won't be any rest for me when we get where we're going. My body goes cold as I realize he meant to seduce me. "I want you wide awake when I finally claim that kiss." His voice drops to a whisper. "And claiming your mouth is only the beginning."

Bile rises in my throat, and I force it down.

Jadick smiles serenely and heads for the door. "I'm going to meet with Gregario and see who made it so far."

I open my mouth to tell him I'll come too, but he cuts me off. "I'll come get you when Tripp gets here."

It's the best I'll get. And I have a feeling rocking the boat now will only cause me more problems in the long run.

"Thanks," I say, my voice hollow.

"Of course." He stops at the door and adds, "And Mac? You aren't a Romantic anymore."

CHAPTER 17

*N*o one wakes me, contrary to Jadick's reassurances. With groggy awareness, I peel my eyes open to see light already streaming in around the edges of the curtains. Apparently, sleep came for me despite my best attempts to resist. A quick glance down at myself reveals all my clothes intact. Relief floods me. Despite Jadick's promise about wanting me awake, I'm too on edge to dismiss anything. Rolling to the mattress edge, I sit up and put my boots on the floor. Underneath me, the bed is still made, though the duvet is rumpled from the hours I've spent on it.

In the dim hours of dawn, somewhere between awake and asleep, I swear I heard the sound of Tripp's voice outside. But now that I'm fully alert, I'm not sure if I dreamt it after all.

Pushing to my feet, I go to the door and wrench it open.

Grey is there, leaning against the railing that overlooks the parking lot. He stands sharpening a knife with a metal rod, his movements methodical and practiced. No one else is in sight.

"Where is everyone?" I ask.

He glances up then uses the tip of his knife to point toward a door at the end of the hall. "Tripp's in there."

I mumble, "Thanks," and then practically sprint for the door he pointed toward.

Pounding on it, I call out, "Tripp? It's me. Open up."

"Kinda early for that," Grey calls from behind me, but his voice lacks any real heat.

I ignore him and pound on the door again. "Tripp!"

The door opens, and I fling myself at my friend.

Tripp catches me with one arm then the other, staggering back a step at the unexpected momentum.

"Whoa," he says against my ear. "I'm here. Where's the fire?"

I pull back and glare at him. "You weren't here last night."

"Yeah, I was busy escaping an explosion," he says wryly.

I huff. "I was worried."

"Am I in trouble for nearly getting killed?"

I roll my eyes. "Whatever, I'm glad you're okay. Wait. Are you okay?"

A closer look reveals a welt along the underside of his chin. I grab his face, yanking it upward so I can get a better look.

"What the hell happened?" I demand.

"Did you not hear the word 'explosion'?" he asks.

"Was anyone else... Did everyone get out?" I ask.

"Everyone got out," he says, and the relief I feel makes my knees buckle.

Tripp's arms tighten around me. He leads me to the bed, and I don't sit so much as just give in to my bent knees.

"I stayed until I knew for sure," he continues. "That's why I didn't get in until just now. But I checked in with Grey a lot to make sure you were safe. He stayed outside your room the entire night."

"Probably because Jadick had me watched," I say. "He pretended like I'm not a prisoner anymore, but we both know that's bullshit."

Tripp gives me a look that means there's more going on here. "No, Gregario was ordered to stand guard, but Grey stayed too. I asked him to keep an eye out and report anything."

"Like what?"

"Mac, when was the last time you shifted?" His forehead creases with concern.

"Not since before I was shot. Why?"

His frown deepens. "Do you feel your wolf at all? Is she accessible?"

"She's there," I say slowly. "But the venom is too. Until that's run its course, I'm not quite at full strength. Why are you asking me this?"

"What if it's not just the venom?"

"What do you mean?"

"I mean, what if Jadick—"

"Get the fuck away from her."

Jadick's voice is angrier than I've ever heard.

I turn, confused at what he thinks is happening here.

"What—?" I begin, but Tripp cuts me off, standing with hands balled into fists.

"She came to me," Tripp growls. "And I'm not going to lie for you anymore. I know the truth. I know what you're doing to her."

"Lie about what?" I demand.

"You have no right to question me," Jadick roars.

Whatever's going on, the violence exuding from them both is making me crave a more open space. This small room—and me wedged between them in it—is suddenly way too crowded.

"Will someone tell me what the hell is happening?" I demand.

"Sure," Tripp says, eyes flashing. "Jadick?"

Jadick looks about two seconds away from tearing this entire shitty motel to the ground. Without thinking, I step between them, pressing my hands to Jadick's chest. He's the wild card here. If I can get him to back up, this won't turn into a shit show. Maybe.

I press harder so that his gaze flicks to me, ignoring how intimate it feels to be touching him this way.

"Outside," I order when our eyes meet.

To my surprise, he listens. It's not until I follow him out into the breezeway that I realize why he's doing as I say.

"Detain him," Jadick says to his men waiting behind us, and I see Gregario and Grey surge forward, pushing past me and into Tripp's room. The door slams behind them, and immediately, yelling breaks out from inside.

"You won't get away with this," Tripp yells, and I go still, remembering those exact words from Crigger's lips as he lay dying in that warehouse.

But that was Kari, I remind myself.

Yeah. And this is Jadick.

"Walk with me," he says before I can rush in to help Tripp.

His hand closes over my wrist, dragging me along.

I let him, needing to know what has Tripp so upset.

Jadick marches us past the room where I slept and down the stairs toward the parked SUV. Halfway across the parking lot, I plant my feet and yank away from him.

"Where are we going?" I demand. "And what did you ask Tripp to lie about?"

"We're going to Blackstone," he says. "My men are in place, and it's time to rescue your pet. Unless you've changed your mind."

"Levi's not my pet. He's my mate."

He closes the distance, and I flinch away, barely managing to hold my ground as he looms in front of my face. "I'm your mate, Mac. Don't fucking forget it again."

"What did you ask Tripp to lie about?" I ask again, refusing to back down even if it means delaying our departure.

He straightens, putting a little more space between us. Just enough that, when we breathe, we're not using the same oxygen. It's still way too close. Especially considering I can still hear the sounds of fighting going on in Tripp's motel room. Every crash sends my unease up another notch, but I don't let it show on my face.

A few other doors open, and Jades peer out, faces concerned at the sounds of the scuffle.

"Tripp thinks I've done something to mute your wolf," Jadick says, and my attention snaps back to him hovering before me. "That it's more than just the poison."

His words startle me. Mostly because I've spent half my time wondering who drugged my food that first time they held me prisoner and then the rest of it beating myself up for not being strong enough to rescue Levi on my own.

Not to mention my conversation with Tripp before. His warning that it's been Jadick all along. Damn. I should have seen this. Or at least suspected.

"And did you?" I ask.

"Why would I want a weak mate?" he asks as if the accusation is ludicrous.

It's not an answer, but without Tripp standing here to back it up —and without proof—there's nothing to accuse.

When I don't answer, he gestures toward the car. "Shall we?"

Another sound above me draws my gaze. Tripp's door opens. Gregario steps out. His lip is bloodied, but otherwise, he's unharmed. He meets my eyes with zero flickers of interest. A dead stare for a dead heart.

Then he descends the stairs and joins us.

Jadick holds the car door open, and I try not to think about how he's, once again, making me choose. Tripp or Levi. Fight or flight. Freedom or love.

I don't think about it. I just get into the car.

GREY DOESN'T RETURN from Tripp's room, so it's just the three of us in the SUV. Gregario drives. Jadick and I sit in the backseat together. Our car ride reveals a few more details of Jadick's plan but not many. Despite his reassurances that I'm his equal, we both know he's running this show without me. I'm simply his trophy. Kari used me, Levi wanted me, and now Jadick has me. It's as simple as that.

Actually, it's not simple at all.

Without my wolf and without Tripp—or even my mother—I stand zero chance of beating Jadick. Even Grey is absent. According to the bits I catch from Jadick's side of phone conversations, Grey remained behind to guard Tripp, who is no longer welcome with the Jades and will be detained until the alpha takeover is complete.

Jadick's "men" as he called them earlier are apparently mostly made up of the Hellion biker club. I don't know many of them personally. Only Dirk and Pike and the assholes who joined in our brawl before we left. I don't trust a single one as far as I can throw them. But Jadick's game isn't about trust. It's about usefulness.

Once they've outlived theirs, I have a feeling I know what he'll do to them.

Hire some bounty hunter like me to bring them in for slaughter.

I wonder if that's what Crigger was doing with Dirk that night.

Whatever the Hellions have done to "get into place," it's worked well enough to get us into town. Less than two hours later, we cross into pack territory and then, a half hour later, into Blackstone itself —all without incident. At the town limits, Jadick's phone rings.

"Yeah," he answers.

I listen, trying to decipher who's calling and why. But without my wolf senses, I can only hear his side of things.

"Good," he says. "No, we're coming in now." He glances sideways at me then adds, "There was a hiccup, so we moved up our timeline."

From the other end, I can hear a female's voice but I can't make it out.

My thoughts drift to what Jadick said about muting my wolf on purpose. Making me weak.

"No, just stay put until everything's in motion," he says, and I refocus on the conversation. "Mac's doing great," he adds.

I stiffen.

Why is someone asking about me?

"Is that my mother?" I ask just as Jadick says, "Very good," and disconnects the call. He glances at me.

"This will all be over soon, Mac. And when it is, your mother will be returned to you unharmed. You have my word."

He turns away from me to look out the window, signaling he's done with this conversation. I stare at the smooth skin of his cheek and fantasize about ripping it open with my claws.

Bloody, slashed skin oozing…

I comfort myself with the silent promise that I'll make my dream a reality. If it's the last thing I do, I'll get my strength back, and I'll use it to make sure he can never hurt or manipulate anyone again.

He's right.

This will all be over soon.

Despite my nerves and the incredible weight of what's at stake, a wave of nostalgia washes over me as we drive through downtown. It's shocking considering I spent nearly my entire life hating this town. But now, returning after everything that's happened is making me feel a strange sense of connection. If not to the people, then to the land itself.

We pass the town hall where a sign stands that reads: Blackstone, population 1598. Est. 1836.

But that's a lie.

Our pack has lived on this land for much longer than that.

And our numbers are much lower these days.

Unless you count the Jades that are sneaking back in as we speak to battle it out with the ones who've chosen to stay. The mateless against the mated.

Rebels versus Romantics.

We're about to see if our alpha was right all those years ago about rejection making us stronger.

"Do you ever think about Lacey?" I ask.

Jadick looks over at me, startled. "What?"

"Lacey. You must miss her. She was your mate."

"She was my fated. Not my chosen."

He makes it sound like he's comforting me. Stroking my ego, even. He thinks I'm jealous of a dead girl?

"Yes, but the loss cuts deeper when a fated dies, doesn't it?"

"I never claimed her."

"Would you have if she'd lived?"

His expression shutters. "Why are you asking me about her?"

I shrug. "I heard Thiago had her killed just to hurt you. I was wondering if it worked. If being a Romantic made you weaker like your father believed."

His mouth tightens. I've struck a nerve.

"My father was wrong about a lot of things," he says quietly. "But I was never a Romantic."

It's not until we're idling at a red light at the base of the hill that it dawns on me how empty the streets are. No traffic. Not even a pedestrian.

I kick myself for not being more alert, but my wolf barely stirs even when I berate her.

Dammit.

The light turns green. Gregario drives the speed limit, no more, no less. But he's tenser now. Stiff and silent with anticipation. So is Jadick.

We're close.

This is it.

We drive straight to the alpha house.

Kari's army either lets us or has been otherwise detained.

There's no one to stop us from pulling right up to the front door, but Gregario drives only to where the straight-a-way begins to curve and stops.

I look at Jadick, but he's staring through the windshield at the alpha house.

His house.

Once upon a time, it had been a plantation home. Southern antebellum charm drips from the white columns that frame a large front door. Below that, long, low steps beckon like a white marble carpet to greet us. The steps, like the porch, wrap all the way around. To the right, a sharp corner cuts away before a tall fence rises up for privacy. To the left, the steps flow with the gently bending shape of the house where a side entrance is barely visible from where I sit.

Those steps and that side door are the last places I saw Levi.

My shoulder twinges as the memory threatens to suck me under.

Kari shooting Thiago. Taking Levi. Shooting me.
I hate how I've returned, but at least, I've finally made it.
Somewhere inside this house is my mate.
I'm coming, I think, hoping like hell it's not too late.

CHAPTER 18

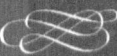

A breeze tickles my cheeks as I get out of the car and step up beside Jadick. Gregario steps in front of us, but Jadick nudges him out of the way.

"Kari Clemons, I challenge you for the role of alpha," Jadick calls out to the empty yard.

My heart pounds wildly in my chest as his crisp words ring out sharply against the quiet.

A beat of silence follows as we wait for a response.

My muscles are coiled tight, ready for an attack. I scan the rooftop, searching for snipers or some other underhanded tactic. But there's only the three of us standing drenched in sunshine and pre-meditated murder.

When Kari doesn't appear, Jadick twitches restlessly beside me. I wonder suddenly if her entire strategy is to ignore us. It's brilliant, honestly. Because the worst torture I can think of for someone like Jadick is to pretend he doesn't exist.

But then the door opens, and Guy and Lenny walk out along with four other security guards armed with guns. My rage finally has a visual target. I glare at them with what I hope is the force of my threat against them comes to life. But then my attention is fractured. Pulled away to someone even more terrible.

Kari.

Her hair gleams in the sun, her skin glowing and her eyes alight with what I can only imagine is a hunger for our heads on a plate. But even though I know logically that she hates me—that she's the monster we're here to slay—her face is too familiar to fear.

I hate her as much as I once loved her. And I think I might love her still.

In this moment, I realize it's a good thing Jadick doesn't expect more from me than this—a trophy draped over his arm.

He has to be the one to destroy Kari. And for the first time since it all began, I finally believe he intends to do it.

"Hello, brother," Kari says, her voice dripping with disdain as she faces off with Jadick.

"I challenge you, sister, for the role of alpha. Do you accept my challenge?" he asks.

She grins. "I've lived for nothing else."

Hope drives my anticipation to a crescendo. My normally cool nerves kick into overdrive. Adrenaline courses through me, filling my veins with enough strength to close the gap I've been struggling with for weeks.

I don't need my wolf. I just need Jadick to fucking win so this adrenaline can carry me to wherever they've tossed Levi.

I'm not leaving here without him, no matter what my bargain with Jadick demands.

"I'm ready when you are," Jadick says.

At his words, Kari's men raise their guns and aim them at Jadick's chest.

My breath catches.

"Or," Jadick adds, "do I overestimate your sense of honor?"

"Honor?" Kari snorts. Her gaze flicks to me for the first time then quickly back to Jadick. "We're long past honor, aren't we, brother? Years of torture at your hands. A lifetime of pain and beatings. A childhood absent of love. Full of hatred even from my own bloodline." She gestures to the guns. "You're a fool to expect anything less."

"They won't follow you for long," Jadick warns. "Not if you win like this."

I try not to think about the hypocrisy of his argument. Mostly, I try not to think about what will happen next if Kari tells her men to fire.

"I don't need leadership advice from a guy who runs away from his problems," Kari says. "And what's this?" she sneers at me. "Are the two of you friends now? Or did you sell your soul to him in order to get your precious mate back?"

I shudder, wondering how the hell she can know me so well when I don't know her at all. Or maybe I do; I just refuse to admit it.

"Jadick and I want the same thing," I say coldly.

"Ah, you're both in love with Levi then." She smirks.

"We both want to see you bleed," I say with a snarl.

Her smile vanishes. "You've allied with the devil, Mac."

"A little hypocritical, don't you think?" I snap at her.

She studies me then looks back at her brother. "We'll see," she murmurs.

And then to her men, she says, "Aim."

My breath stalls. My chest squeezes tight. The bitch is really going to gun us down like this. I don't know why I ever expected more from her. She's shown me her true self, and I've yet to really believe it.

Behind me, a noise draws my attention. I glance back, not wanting to take my eyes off Kari and her mercenaries, but the noise is loud, and the possibility of another threat is too great to remain still. What I see makes me forget all about keeping my eyes on the enemy.

Black Moon pack members converge, a few walking down the road on foot with cars full of them following slowly behind. Most pour from the woods.

Wolves.

In all shapes and colors.

Witnesses.

I look at Jadick.

He ignores me, grinning back at Kari, satisfied.

"You brought an army?" she demands, eyes narrowed. "After all your bullshit about wanting a fair fight?"

"These are not my soldiers," Jadick says. "Yet." Kari glares at that. "These are Black Moon pack come to pledge their loyalty to the new alpha."

"Who told them to come?" she demands.

She glances from Jadick to her own men uncertainly.

"I did," Jadick says. At Kari's confusion, he adds, "My alpha call is strong enough to reach them. Even without the crown on my head, they can hear me. What does that tell you about the rightful heir, sister?" She doesn't answer, and he pushes her harder, taunting her with the reminder, "Pack law says my challenge must be met by the alpha only. With the pack as our witness, what do you think they'll do when they see you cheating your way to the top?"

I can feel Kari's hesitation, and as it stretches into indecision, I know she's realized the guns are no longer a smart option.

With a sharp nod at her men, she says, "Put them away."

Jadick looks focused now. Ready.

"Come and fight me," he urges her.

"Gladly." A fire rages in her eyes as she makes her way down the steps. Over her shoulder, she orders her men, "If Mac so much as twitches a finger toward the fight, shoot her."

Bitch.

The crowd closes in until a circle surrounds us. Jadick nods at Gregario, and he grabs my arm, pulling me back to join the others on the fringes. In the center of the space, Jadick and Kari face off.

Kari's claws are the first part of her body to shift. A second later, she's a wolf, landing lightly on four paws and shaking out her sandy coat until her fur stands on end. She swipes at Jadick, who shifts a second slower. But his attack begins the moment he's taken the form of his beast—and it doesn't stop.

I have no idea what I'd expected. Part of me wondered if Jadick had some trick up his sleeve. Some way to get out of this physical altercation. He's deadly, but something about him always seemed unwilling to engage.

I was wrong.

He's relentless in his determination.

And so much stronger than I'd anticipated.

Maybe that's been his strategy all along. By not fighting Kari, he offered an illusion, a rebuttal to her claims of violence. How could a man so unwilling to fight her be guilty of the abuse she's accused him of? But it's perfectly clear now. The way he dominates. The way he tortures and plays with her even as he fights for the upper hand.

In less than five minutes, he draws first blood. A short but deep-looking gash on Kari's shoulder.

She makes a sound of pain but then shakes it off.

Her cry slices through me. Another reminder of what Jadick is to her. What he's made her become in order to survive him.

They clash again, their grunts and growls vicious now.

Kari slashes her claw across Jadick's snout, and the shallow cut bleeds immediately, dripping down his mouth and into his own black fur.

I stand stiffly beside Gregario, rigid with anticipation.

There is no good winner here. Neither deserves to live after what they've done, but I root for Jadick anyway. He's the only one who will give me what I want when this is over.

Kari is swift and cunning—a better fighter than I ever knew. Another thing she hid from me. But Jadick is brutal and merciless. Quick to exploit a weakness. As I well know.

When he can reach it again, he swipes at the same place he's already injured her. This cut slices twice as deep, and on the heels of Kari's cry, she stumbles. Her leg barely holds her weight now. She limps, trying to compensate, but the injury is clearly setting her back.

Jadick circles her.

It's only a matter of time now, but there's no honor left in his attack. He's playing with her. It's disgusting, no matter what I think of my former friend. He is exactly what she's accused him of being: a monster. *Her* monster. If nothing else about our friendship was real, this is. Kari bearing the brunt of her family's evil treatment. No wonder they drove her to such lengths. No wonder she's beyond caring about anyone but herself.

In the center of the crowd, Kari's eyes are exhausted—and resigned.

She does everything but lie down at his feet.

Still, Jadick doesn't kill her.

Not yet.

His advance is slow, his gaze on the crowd. He wants us to know he's already won. That killing her at his own leisure is a luxury he's earned. He wants us to see it as power. Instead, I hate him far more than I ever did. Only a monster kills something too weak to stop it.

He does a full lap around Kari, playing to the crowd, who's going wild for this show. Our pack has never shown their blackened hearts so fully as they do now. Their cheers, growls, and howls aren't quite supportive of Jadick, but they also don't mind another Clemons in the dirt. So, it's close enough, and Jadick preens for them.

Finally, he loops back around to where Kari stands, head hanging, body heaving with labored breaths. Blood drips from the deep wound on her shoulder, her fur matted with it and caked with dirt.

She looks beaten.

Jadick looks like he's already won.

He's so convinced of it, in fact, that he never sees her coming. She waits until he's standing over her, still playing to the crowd, and then makes her move. She launches herself upward where his throat is just above her head and latches on. Her teeth sink through flesh, and I don't need my wolf's instincts to know the bite will be fatal if she manages to hold on.

"Kari? Kari, is that you?"

The voice is female and full of urgency.

I don't recognize it, but Kari immediately releases Jadick. She turns, searching wildly for whoever spoke.

"Jadick." The woman's voice comes again, this time with recognition.

He, too, is searching the crowd.

Everyone around me does the same.

Halfway across the circle, onlookers are jostled, and two figures push their way to the front. A woman steps into view, and the shock of recognition startles me despite the fact that I haven't seen this woman in years. Brown curly hair hangs down her back. It's longer than when I last saw her. Wherever she's been, it's done her good. She looks healthy. Cheeks and hips filled out. Clear eyes that are nearly unmarked by the harsh life she once led here. But the same deep lines I remember from before are still etched into her forehead and the corner of her eyes. Worry lines. Evidence she isn't one of us —not really. Even after ten years gone, Marilyn Clemons is still the picture of gentleness.

She is pure-hearted; nothing like the rest of us.

She is the antithesis of her children.

Jadick and Kari both gawk at her, their glowing eyes wide with shock.

The crowd is hushed, but that doesn't last long. Within seconds, murmurs go around, and a few people press in to get a closer look at the late alpha's wife.

Then a second figure is there, shoving them all back.

"Back up." Vicki Quinn. Safe and sound and looking like she's ready to do damage. "Give her some room, or I'll move you myself," she threatens.

My mother is a force. Her reputation precedes her, but even if it didn't, there's no doubt she means every word she's saying.

Marilyn Clemons approaches her children slowly. A shepherd come to gather her evil sheep.

"Oh, Kari," she says, dropping to her knees and putting an arm around Kari's bloodied shoulders. Kari, still in wolf form, nuzzles in close for a hug, and Marilyn's eyes close as emotion overtakes them both. A tear squeezes out of Marilyn's closed eyelid and slips down her cheek.

Then she looks up again, smiling at Jadick.

He shudders, his body suddenly losing its shape as he shifts back to human form.

"Hello, mother," he says.

But he doesn't move to embrace her. Instead, he looks down at his sister.

"Yield," he says, his voice ragged and raw. In human form, his throat bleeds profusely from her bite. But he doesn't seem to notice or care. "Yield, and I'll let you live."

Kari snarls up at him.

"Fight me, and I'll kill you both," he warns.

Marilyn flinches, but she doesn't look quite as surprised as she should.

My jaw, however, drops open.

The crowd shuts up.

I cast a glance to where my mother still stands very near where Marilyn kneels with her daughter. Vicki's gaze is locked on Jadick, her hand hanging stiffly at her side. My eyes lock on the long blade she has strapped to her hip, and I realize with a start she's not here to help reunite a broken family. She's here to break it some more should Jadick order her.

This is where she ran off to.

And this is why Jadick didn't tell me.

He marches over to where my mother stands and yanks the blade free from its sleeve. Then he walks back to where Kari waits beside Marilyn. He leans in, and before any of us know what's coming, he slits Kari's throat wide open.

Marilyn screams.

Jadick grunts.

Kari's wolf falls limp in his arms.

Blood pours from her wound. Angry, thick, red-black blood that doesn't just leak from her opened body; it coats her instantly.

Jadick steps back, letting Kari fall unceremoniously to the ground.

Marilyn reaches for her, but my mother is already there, yanking her back.

Fury and shock root me where I stand.

"I am your alpha now," Jadick announces to the crowd. "And like my father, I will rule with strength and power. An eye for an eye—that is the Black Moon way."

Her throat for his. That's what he means.

The crowd understands.

They go wild for it.

The alpha bond—which I never felt for Kari—washes over me. It's not so much a bond as a leash. A way for him to bend us if he chooses. And the crowd seems drunk with it now. As I watch them all cheer his victory, my stomach rolls with the sick realization Kari was right. I've allied myself with the devil. It can't be helped, though. All the angels are gone.

CHAPTER 19

I don't know when the Jades arrive or where they were hiding during the carnage. It's like, one second we're alone with the frenzied pack while Jadick performs his hostile takeover, and the next, Jade security is everywhere. Lorenz leads a team of at least thirty, and they waste no time surrounding the crowd then driving them back. I listen as he gives orders for people to return to their homes, their businesses, their lives.

"Your new alpha will make a statement once things are put in order at the alpha house," he assures people.

I watch as they obey him, struck by how strange it is to imagine returning to normalcy. How easily they walk off and do exactly that.

I have nothing normal to return to. Not ever.

My gaze lands on Kari, who lies bleeding on the pavement. Alone.

Nearby, Marilyn has been pulled to her feet. She isn't restrained, but it's clear she's not free either. My mother escorts her toward the house where Jadick has already headed as well. Gregario walks at his side, head bent as he listens to his master. Burnett is lining the old guard up by the door, including Guy and Lenny, making them kneel, ready to pledge loyalty and submission to their new alpha.

The space on my right is wide open. Across the yard, nothing but trees. For a second, I feel the urge to flee into them.

No one's watching me.

In the chaos, I've been forgotten.

But somewhere in that house is Levi. He's all that matters now.

"You okay?"

I startle at the sound of Frankie's voice and then look up as she grips my shoulders, shaking me loose of my harried thoughts.

"I'm fine," I say. "Just... what the hell."

"Get inside," she says grimly.

"Is Tripp—"

"He's fine. You need to get inside before Jadick forgets to uphold his end of your deal," she says pointedly.

Nodding, I start for the door, but when I reach Kari, my feet won't go any farther. She looks up at me, her eyes glassy. She's weak with blood loss.

We don't speak.

I try to find words for what I feel, but there are none.

"Mac."

Jadick calls my name, and I let that be distraction enough to move me. Kari watches me go. I feel her hot gaze burning holes in my back as I leave her behind and take my place beside her brother.

My face feels strange. Tingly almost. It takes me a moment to realize I'm fighting the urge to cry. Kari was someone I moved heaven and Earth to save once. Now, I've left her to die, and even though she might deserve it, I hate that I'm doing it.

I hate her.

Mostly, I hate myself.

Lenny and Guy don't say a word to me as I pass them on the front steps. If Levi weren't such a priority, I'd make time to stop and request their heads on a platter. But that will have to wait.

When I reach Jadick, my shoulders are stiff, but my eyes are dry.

"Where's Levi?" I ask.

"We're waiting on the house to be cleared, and then we'll go have a look," he says.

I shove past him and through the open front door.

"Mac," Jadick calls sharply behind me.

"I'm done waiting," I tell him.

The house is cool, raising goose bumps on my skin as I stride past the hollow foyer. Kari has removed every single piece of décor that once stood here. The marble statues, sculptures of Clemons' in their wolf forms. But she apparently hasn't made time to redecorate, so now, only blank walls and smooth granite floors remain. My footsteps echo as I march through it all.

My instincts lead me right back to the room where they brought us before. It's a glorified medical wing with single occupancy rooms furnished with hospital beds and all the machinery to monitor a patient you've drugged into unconsciousness.

At least, that's how they looked when I was here last.

I find the room they stuck me in the last time and shove the door open.

Empty.

Across the hall, Levi's old room is empty too.

My heart pounds.

I continue down the hall, pushing doors open and peering inside.

Dark, empty spaces are all I find.

At the end of the hall, I push through a door I've never used before. This area has always been restricted even when I used to visit Kari as a kid. Down the stairs I go, faster and faster. Part of me wants to slow down, to prolong the torture of discovering they've actually put Levi down here.

It's a dungeon.

There's no other word for it.

Kari told me stories, but I always thought she exaggerated out of hatred for her father.

Now, I see she wasn't doing it justice at all.

Bare cement walls surround me. Roughened cinderblocks coated in grime and spider webs. There's no outer door sealing the cells. It's unnecessary, I realize, because the prisoners will never be strong enough to escape anyway.

Manacles are mounted to cell walls. Rusted iron with decades' worth of blood and sweat and grime caked on that no one ever bothered to clean. Why would they? This place isn't intended for health and comfort.

One by one, I pass the empty row of cells.

The last one is occupied, and if I didn't know he was here, I might not recognize him. Bloodshot eyes are barely visible around his swollen lids. His hair and body is covered in dried blood, dirt, and whatever else this place has coated him in. I nearly gag at the stench of sweat and feces permeating the air and step closer, my gaze roaming over him.

His leg is sliced open in a dozen places. Nothing too deep. Just enough to bleed him. His chest is worse, though. The cuts aren't clean. They are jagged, open wounds that ooze yellow.

Worse, they look days old. Which means he isn't healing.

What I smell is sickness. And whatever chemical they've given to mute his healing.

"Levi," I breathe, my hands gripping the cold iron bars.

He looks back at me, haunted and hollow.

"You can't fool me again," he says flatly.

My heart breaks as I realize he thinks I'm an illusion. Kari used me against him. Another reason she let me leave in the first place. Rage makes me tremble as I think of all she's done to him here.

I hope she bleeds out on the front lawn.

I hope she's already dead.

"Levi, it's really me," I say, voice cracking.

He turns away, staring blankly at the wall instead of at me.

I want to scream. Instead, I fumble with the lock. My strength is nowhere near recovered enough to break through it. Looking around wildly for some kind of key, I see only cinderblocks stained in blood. My vision blurs with it.

I choke back a sob, my helplessness threatening to suffocate me now.

To get this far only to come up short—it's maddening.

"Here, let me."

Hands reach past me for the lock. Jadick steps in to help me do the thing I know he must loathe. I don't look at him, though. I look at the deadbolt. A key slides into the mechanism and twists. The click of the lock springing free sends a jolt through me. My body wakes up. My brain shuts down.

Shoving Jadick aside, I fling the door open and rush inside, dropping beside Levi as if we're racing against time. We are. We always have been.

"Levi," I say, tears streaming down my cheeks.

He looks at me, still unsure.

I press my hand to his bruised cheek.

"You're real?" he asks in childlike wonder. The hope is unmistakable in his haunted brown eyes, and I snatch it, holding onto the feeling for us both.

"I'm real," I breathe, and to prove it, I press my lips to his.

He makes a sound against my mouth. A groan and a gasp twisted together into startled clarity. In an instant, I'm snatched away. Hauled to my feet and then shoved against the bars.

Jadick leans in, his face inches from my own. "You don't kiss him anymore, Mac. Or did you forget?"

"Let her go," Levi roars.

Except the roar is more of a plea.

It breaks me. Or it would if I weren't already broken.

"Get your hands off me," I nearly spit at him. "We had a deal."

"The deal is to free him," Jadick says. "Nothing more. Or did you forget that too?"

My stomach roils, and it's tempting to vomit all over Jadick's pretty shoes. But that wouldn't help my case. Kicking his ass wouldn't help either, and unfortunately for me, that's not an option anyway.

Footsteps interrupt us. Gregario and Lorenz appear.

"Get him upstairs," Jadick tells them. "Clean him up."

They file into the cell, and I immediately struggle against Jadick's hold. But his hands are strong, and they don't ease up. I'm pinned to the bars hard enough that the metal rod at my back sends pain through my spine.

Over Jadick's shoulder, I watch as the two Jades grab Levi under his arms and haul him up. He groans and tries to fight them, to get to me, but he's too weak to make any progress.

"Levi, it's me," Lorenz says. "I'm not going to hurt you. We're going to help."

But Levi doesn't care. Not while his tortured gaze is locked on the way Jadick's restraining me. I watch as Lorenz and Gregario pull him down the hall. They don't even have to subdue him. Within seconds, his strength wanes, and he stops struggling, his body limp with exhaustion.

The two men all but carry him from the dungeon.

"Jadick, don't do this," I whisper as they disappear upstairs with my mate.

"You belong to me now, Mac. That was the deal."

"I don't belong to anyone," I growl.

"If that's true, you'll understand why you must let him go now. Your part in this is finished. He's free."

He's not wrong. Dammit. But I can't just walk away. Not without closure. Not without an explanation. Levi deserves that much.

"He won't feel free," I say, "Not after he finds out what I've done."

"That's not my problem."

He's not going to budge, I can see it. But I can't let this go.

"Give me tonight," I say, hanging my head. "One last night. To explain. To say goodbye." My cheeks burn with the agony the words cause me. And a shame I can't explain even to myself.

I expect him to refuse me. Instead, he says, "And what will you give me?"

My head snaps up.

Our eyes meet. In his gaze is pure triumph. Everything's for sale. Even me.

"What do you want?" I hear myself ask.

No, Mac.

The words whisper inside my head.

I ignore them.

"We'll present ourselves to the pack tomorrow," he says. "You'll stand by my side. You'll kiss me like you've promised. They'll see our alliance. What I want from you is to make them believe it."

"Why wouldn't they believe it?" I ask, confused.

I expected him to demand sex. My body on a platter. He's stared at it hungrily for long enough. But I should have known. It's not that he doesn't want me. But with Jadick, even sex takes a backseat to politics.

It's all about winning.

Besides, once we're married, I have a feeling my willingness will no longer factor in, anyway. He'll take what he wants from me until there's nothing left to give. And even then, he'll find a way. Isn't that what Crigger did with Marilyn?

"Surely you've recognized by now what Levi has turned you into. You're an inspiration, Mac. A symbol for true love. But you're no actress. The truth of your feelings shines through as plain as the nose on your face. What I want from you is to convince them. When we stand together tomorrow, you will kiss me like you want me. You will put your hands on me like my body is the only one you desire. You will let me touch you like I own you. Like you want this alliance more than you want him."

"You want me to sell it."

"I want you to stick your tongue so far down my throat the rebellion forgets Levi ever pined for you. Or that you ever came to rescue him. I want you to kiss me like you kiss him."

CHAPTER 20

The only person alive more disgusting than Jadick is me. My skin crawls with the emptiness of having my soul snatched away. No, not taken. Sold. I let it go willingly for the price of this—my hand on the brass knob of Levi's door. One night with him. It's all I'll get. And it will never be enough. But it's more than adequate for the destruction I'll cause while I'm here. If I were a better person, I'd walk away. Let it end now. Before it begins. But I'm not better. I'm so much worse. My heart is blacker now than when I started. It will be blacker still tomorrow.

I open the door.

Levi looks up from where he sits on the edge of the bed; a large-four poster monstrosity that would have taken up my entire living room. But that house across town isn't my home. It never was. The bloodshot eyes staring back at me from across this plush bedroom—that's my home.

And I've come to burn it down.

The room is full of shadows, dark except for the muted after-noon light stealing in through the open blinds. A sea of soft gray carpet separates us, and where Levi sits, apparently trying to lace up an old pair of boots someone found for him, a single yellow ray of sunshine slants across his body—a teasing of happiness against the melancholy.

It's just the room, I tell myself.

This room was sad before we got here. The third floor of the alpha house is reserved for guests that Crigger, when he was alive, would have rather avoided. And now Jadick has shoved us up here too, probably hoping to forget what we'll do inside it tonight. Until tomorrow when he can blot it out with his own body.

But I don't let myself think about that. Instead, I focus on Levi.

He's showered in the hours since I've seen him. The hours I spent pacing downstairs until they let me come up.

Now, the scent of soap drifts toward me. I inhale and feel strangely stronger than I did before. More steady in my own skin. He must feel the same because, at the sight of me, he stands and walks over, his untied boots dragging their laces behind them. His sweatpants are slung low on his hips, his abs drawing my gaze like a starving man to a meal.

Up close, I see the bruising and cuts remain where the blood and grime has been washed clean from his face and neck. His eyes are wild—dark orbs that are entirely too small for the storm of emotions hiding inside them.

When he reaches me, his roughened hand cups my cheek. "You're real," he says, brushing his thumb over my skin.

It's not a question, but the truth is, "No," I am not real. Not for him. Not after tonight.

I press my lips together, trying to hold back tears. The effort is futile, though. They stream in silent tracks down my cheeks. One after the other after the other. Soldiers lost to war. Defeated.

Levi swipes at them with his thumb, and then suddenly, he's grabbing me and crushing me against his chest, tightening his arms around my body, holding me closer than his own breaths.

It's too much. I lose it. Sobs wrack my body, shaking me until I can't do anything but ride the wave of my own emotions. Pain, relief, loss, love. It's all there, fighting to get out. Levi holds me, running his hands over my hair, soothing me with soft words.

His embrace is gentle, his words tender. I haven't seen this side of him in years, and it only makes my grief worse. This is what I'm losing. This is what I've given up.

He's alive, I remind myself.

I still hate me.

Maybe I shouldn't have come.

When my cries are spent and my knees are too weak to hold me up, Levi guides me toward the bed. We sit side by side, and he angles himself to face me. With strong hands, he smooths my hair out of my face, tucking it behind my ear.

"You have no idea how much I've missed you," he says.

Every single word breaks me down.

"I never stopped fighting to get back here," I tell him.

"Tell me what happened," he says. "Tell me everything."

But, of course, I don't.

"Tripp got me out and took me to the safe house," I say instead. "A mall a few hours from here."

"In Wythe. I figured."

I hesitate. "Not Wythe. Green Hills. Apparently, you were fed wrong intel to protect the location."

His eyes darken. "Whose idea was that? Wait, let me guess. Jadick."

I don't answer.

He lets out a breath and then nods at me to keep going. "Then what?"

"Jadick took charge."

His eyes darken. "Yeah, I figured that too."

"He beat Kari," I say quietly. "Earlier today. Slit her throat on the front steps."

"Is she dead?" he asks.

"I don't know. She was pretty bad when I came looking for you."

He doesn't respond to that. I can't tell if he wants her to be dead or if he wants her to stay alive so he can kill her himself.

"Where's Tripp?"

I hesitate. "In a motel somewhere outside Burke."

He frowns. "What's he doing there?"

"He's been detained."

His expression darkens. "For what?"

"Talking shit, I guess." At his confusion, I add, "He accused Jadick of slipping me something to mute my wolf or prolong my healing—"

"Healing from what?" His concern is instant and eclipsing of everything.

"I was shot," I say, touching my shoulder where the wound is still tender to the touch. "You don't remember? Outside on the steps when Thiago—"

"Right. Yes." He shakes his head as if to clear it. His frown remains. "You aren't healed yet?"

"No." I sigh. "My wolf is still out of reach. I can't shift, and I'm still pretty weak."

"You think Jadick drugged you?"

"I don't know. Tripp thinks so. Tripp thinks it was Jadick trying to drug me and manipulate me from the start."

"And Jadick locked him up for it." His voice is grim.

I nod.

He's quiet for a moment. I can see him thinking through all the pieces that have changed places on the board since he was left here. My stomach clenches as I wait for him to guess which place is mine now. But he only asks, "Am I still a prisoner then?"

My eyes widen. "No. You're free."

He doesn't respond, but he doesn't seem sure about my words.

"What did Kari... What happened to you here?" I ask when the silence begins to prick at my conscience.

He looks away. "I'm sure you've guessed the answer to that already."

My stomach knots as my eyes graze over the many cuts and bruises on his body. His bared skin only offers more of a chance to notice the damage they did to him.

Torture.

"You never gave up our location," I say, my throat tight as I imagine it.

He looks away. "I couldn't, not when I knew you were there."

I don't deserve that kind of loyalty.

"Levi..."

He leans in, bringing our foreheads together. His hand slides around the back of my neck, cupping my head. It feels like a prayer, this moment together. Like a dream. Now I know what he meant about this not feeling real.

"Mac, you have no idea how much I worried... How much I hoped you stayed out of her reach. All that mattered was your safety. You were what kept me going. Hell, it's the only thing that kept me sane. If that's what I am."

I lift my face to his, unable to help myself. His skin is soft where I press my lips to his cheek.

"You kept me going, too," I whisper.

"After a while...my injuries—the pain—it messed with my head," he says, his voice hoarse now.

I draw back, watching him as he struggles to explain.

"I wasn't sure what was real anymore," he tells me. "Or who. Sometimes, I thought you'd come to me, but it only turned out to be Kari or one of her men. After that, time didn't register. Reality felt ... removed. I am ashamed to admit that I would have broken down and told them whatever they'd wanted to know if it weren't for you. I would have sold out everyone in those moments. Every Jade who relied on me for safety..." He hangs his head in what I realize is shame. "Knowing you were there with them—that's what kept me from breaking."

"That's not something to be ashamed of," I tell him. "I only wish I could have been here sooner. Jadick kept putting me off, and my wolf wasn't strong enough to come alone, and I couldn't—I couldn't—"

"It's okay. Shh." He pulls me close again, and this time, I can swear I feel him shaking too as we cry. For each other. For ourselves. For the people we used to be and never will be again.

"It's going to be okay," he says, and I don't even let my brain think about how untrue those words are.

Instead, I kiss him.

There's no room for healing or care. No thought to his wounds or mine. Only this need. I can't tell him he's wrong. It's selfish of me, but the words just won't come. So, I kiss him. And I love him with my body hard enough that, hopefully, it won't matter to him that this will be the only night we'll ever have.

It will matter, of course.

Tomorrow.

But for tonight, I give him all I can and pretend it will be enough.

Levi's tongue sweeps into my mouth, and it's everything yet still not enough. Desperate for more, I rise up onto my knees, crawling onto his lap and wrapping my arms around his neck. He groans as I settle on top of him, my core pressing directly against his already hard length.

"Mac," he says, voice ragged, eyes piercing right through to the tattered remnants of my soul.

I lean in to kiss him again, but he stops me. "Wait. Let me see you first. I need to touch you."

He peels my shirt off and tosses it aside. Then my bra. It falls to the carpet without making a sound. Or maybe I can't hear it over the rushing in my ears. Levi stares at me for a long moment, my skin tingling with the weight of his gaze. He stares at my shoulder wound, still pink and inflamed where the skin is finally beginning to heal over. After a long moment, he looks lower, to my taut nipples.

Then he touches me.

His fingers brush my skin, and I shudder. He smiles softly. I smile back.

He traces near my wound and frowns, but then his fingers trail lower, and the frown is replaced by concentration. And need.

His thumb is rough against my already hardened nipple. The moment I feel his hands, a fire ignites in my core. I lean into his touch, arching my back to beg for more. His hand grips my breast, squeezing. Then he moves to the other. And then his mouth is closing over me, sucking and nipping, and I grind into him.

He groans, and the gentleness of the moment is eclipsed by desperate desire.

His face is buried between my breasts as I rock into him.

It's not enough.

"More," I demand. "Please, Levi."

He cups my hips and lifts me off him, tossing me onto my back against the soft mattress. His movements reveal no trace of pain or injury as he crawls over me, looking down at my half-exposed body like it's only the appetizer. His gaze roams lower, and his hand follows, unbuttoning my jeans. Yanking them down my legs. Tossing them aside.

My core aches until I want to scream with the need for him to touch me. To fill the void inside me.

The smart thing would be to stop wanting him. But I don't claim to be smart. Instead, I let the wanting take me over. Then I don't have to think about tomorrow.

Levi lowers himself over me, his mouth claiming mine in a hot, plunging kiss. I run my hands over his back and down his hips, shoving at the sweats separating us. His lips curve at my efforts.

"Not yet," he says.

With a trail of soft, slow kisses, he makes his way down my body. He lingers over my breasts then again along my abdomen, his breath tickling the sensitive skin of my thighs. When his mouth closes over my center, I buck off the mattress, gasping. The sensations blind me, and I forget everything but this moment.

His tongue is masterfully erotic against my clit.

I can't breathe, but I no longer need to. All I need is this.

My orgasm rips through me, loosing a moan that comes from deep within me. Levi doesn't stop until my legs tremble from the aftermath of what he's done with my body. I grip the sheets as he rises up on his knees before me—and then I grip him.

His hard length barely fits in my hand. His taut body remains perfectly still as I stroke him back and forth.

"Mac." My name on his lips is a plea.

It makes me feel powerful in a way I never have before.

Me, ruling over Levi Wild.

He groans and suddenly pulls out of my reach, shaking his head. "You're going to kill me," he says—a terrible joke considering, but his sexy smile is teasing.

"I need you," I say.

"Do you?" His smile turns villainous as he lowers himself over me. "Tell me about that, Mac. What do you need?"

His breath is hot against my ear, the whispered words making me ache for him.

He strokes a hand down my hip and then dips his fingers between our bodies, sliding them through the slickness he's created. My back arches, my hips rocking to meet his very talented fingers.

"I need you," I pant. "Now. Please, Levi."

"I'm here," he whispers, and then his hand is gone and he's sliding his cock inside me, filling me, stretching me.

I gasp, my pleasure taking off like a rocket.

He goes slow, letting me get used to the size of him, but I rock harder and faster against him, urging him onward. Going slow gives me time to think, to remember what this is. I don't want to do either.

"Faster," I beg.

And he gives me exactly what I want.

Hard and fast, he rocks into me, sending me higher, drawing sounds from me I've never made before.

"Come for me, Mac. Now," he orders, his voice taking on an edge on the last word.

A command.

And I do.

With an abandon I've never let myself feel before, I come apart right there in his arms. The pleasure sends me soaring, and I don't bother to stop the cry ripping from my lips. Levi silences me with his kiss, swallowing my screams. And then he's groaning around our tangled tongues, his own release stiffening his shoulders as he comes too.

My wolf stirs again, stronger than before. This is what she needed, I realize. Him. Her true mate. I hope that means she's coming back to me now.

When our bodies are still again, Levi eases back and looks down at me, his hands on my face tender once again.

"You have no idea how long I've wanted to do that," he says.

"I think I have some idea, actually."

He grins.

This man who was tortured for days and days grins like it's nothing. My heart squeezes with the love I feel for him in this moment.

"I'm sorry it took me so long," I say, a lump in my throat.

"Don't," he says firmly. "Don't ruin this moment by reminding me of all that. You're here now. We're together. And as soon as my wolf is able, I'm claiming your ass. I'm not letting you go ever again."

My throat closes at his words. Hot tears burn my eyes, and I look away, but not before his face pinches in concern.

"Whoa, what's wrong?" he asks, shifting his weight to ease off me. "Are you hurt?"

"No," I choke out.

Not on the outside.

"Mac," he says, "talk to me."

And I should. Now's the moment to tell him what I've done. To say goodbye.

"I just want to feel your arms around me," I say finally.

Levi rolls onto his side, draping his arm across my body and curling me tightly against him. He sighs, and I can feel the contentment radiating from him. The peace. I tell myself he deserves one night of it at least. But deep down, I know it's an excuse.

"I love you, Mac," he says against my hair.

"I love you too," I tell him and then let him drift off to sleep.

Once, Levi told me he was my villain.

Tomorrow, I'll be his.

CHAPTER 21

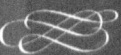

*L*evi is softly snoring when I climb out from underneath him and tiptoe around to retrieve my clothes. The plush bedroom is bathed in the shadowy gray of pre-dawn. Despite the darkness, Levi's skin gleams where he's thrown off the covers during the night. I stop and stare for a long time, memorizing the cut-out of his muscled biceps and the hard line of his jaw. I never want to forget what he looks like when he sleeps.

Finally, I dress, unsure whether I want him to discover my escape. If he does, I'll be forced to explain, but as it is, there's no chance of kissing him one last time. Of seeing him look at me like I'm his whole world.

"Mm, you can't escape me again," he says, his voice slurring with sleep.

I freeze, my hand on the knob. But when I turn back, his eyes are already closing again. His heavy lids are impossible to keep open, thanks to the wolf healing still working its way through his wounds. He'll be out for a few more hours yet. Still, this is my chance to do the right thing.

To tell him what I've done for him.

"Levi," I say, taking a step toward him.

"Mac," he returns lazily.

But the words won't come. Instead, I say, "Do you trust me?"

His eyes slide halfway open. "Of course," he says with no hesitation, but he's more awake now.

"I want you to remember that trust," I say, my voice cracking.

He watches me through narrow slits. Sleepy. Hurting. And completely in love with me. My heart cracks into a thousand pieces as I watch sleep drag him away from me.

"I love you," I whisper.

Then I wait.

But he doesn't stir again as I slip out.

I tell myself it's for the best. Goodbyes are not my forte.

In the hall, a figure moves, and I tense. Near the stairs, my mother beckons me forward. I exhale, joining her.

"How is he?" she asks.

How is he? As if she didn't run off and do Jadick's dirty work without telling me. As if she never sold me out to the monster himself. As if I didn't nearly get murdered, beaten, and blown up since we last saw each other.

"He's healing," I say.

When I start to move past her, she stops me.

"And you?"

I bite back all the angry retorts. They'll do no good with a woman like her. Our eyes meet, and I let her see it in my gaze instead.

She flinches.

"I have to meet Jadick."

I shove past her, and this time, she lets me go.

"You're doing the right thing," she says.

I don't turn around.

Downstairs, security roams. Gregario is the first to notice me. "Jadick's waiting for you," he tells me, but I don't answer, startled to see Grey coming through the front door.

"Hey," I say, ignoring Gregario and hurrying forward.

Grey stops, his expression as impassive as ever.

"Where's Tripp?" I ask.

"He's staying with his mom."

My eyes narrow. "You make it sound like he had a choice."

He shrugs. I want to be angry with him, but it wouldn't change anything.

I sigh. "Levi's upstairs," I say.

Grey's eyes flick to the stairs then back to my face. "How is he?"

Gregario comes up beside us. He doesn't say a word, but he's also clearly waiting for an answer. It gives me hope that Levi still has at least some of their loyalty.

"Healing," I say. "Physically, it'll be a few days. Mentally…"

Grey nods.

Gregario looks ready to shove me toward wherever Jadick is waiting.

"Will you stay with him?" I ask Grey.

"I'll stay close," he says.

I nod before following Gregario down the hall. It's the best I can do for him now.

Jadick is already waiting for me when I walk into the alpha's office. Just like the rest of the house, this room has been stripped of anything that made it Crigger's space. Trinkets, gifts from allies, trophies… gone. Even the books have been cleaned out. All that remains now are a large mahogany desk and a wall of empty book-shelves to match.

Jadick stands at the window, hands folded behind his back as he stares through the glass. The sun will be up soon; the sky is already growing lighter. And then time will speed on ahead whether I like it or not.

Jadick waits to speak until Gregario pulls the door shut behind him, leaving us alone.

"We will make the announcement after lunch—"

"I want Tripp here."

435

He turns to look at me. "You're not in a position to make further demands."

"You're wrong. After that announcement, my leverage is basically gone. Right now? You still need me to stand beside you. To sell it."

He doesn't respond.

"Bring Tripp back," I repeat.

"He's lying. I didn't drug you."

"I know that."

He studies me, uncertain. "How do you know?"

I don't want to tell him my suspicions, so I say, "It doesn't make sense. You want a strong mate. Someone who can hold her own, especially now when you need to appear untouchable. You want me to help you win them over. I can't do that if I'm weak."

He relaxes. "I'm glad you see the truth."

"Tripp's only trying to protect me."

"There are consequences to baseless accusations," he says. "Especially against the alpha."

"Then punish him," I say. "Give him bathroom duty for a month. Make him taste test all your food. But he doesn't deserve to be exiled."

"This is why I chose you." I blink, surprised and immediately wary. His smile is too nice. Too soft. "You're wise, Mac. You get people. And in turn, they respect you."

"You still think I'm more liked than I am."

"You still don't understand how others see you."

I cross my arms. "I don't care how anyone sees me."

"Yes," he says, sure of himself. "You do."

His certainty pisses me off. "Are you going to bring him back or not?"

"I'll do as you say." I feel a sagging relief as his next words hit me, "As long as you'll do the same."

I tense again. "What does that mean?"

"I'd like you to meet my mother."

I stare at him. "Why?"

"I think you'll like her. And she'd like to meet you."

"Do I have a choice?"

"Of course," he assures me. "You always have a choice."

I roll my eyes. "Like I had a choice about our deal?"

"I didn't force you," he says with a shrug, and I have to swallow back a scream. This is insane. He is insane.

"Come on," he says, crossing the room and opening the door for me. "I think you're really going to enjoy yourself."

Resigned, I follow him down the hall to the family wing. In the far northeast corner of the house, Jadick pushes open a door and motions me through.

Glass lines two of the four walls with a coating that helps block the worst of the sun's rays while trapping the warmth inside. Plants line the space with a scattering of chairs and loveseats in the center.

Marilyn Clemons sits in a high-backed wicker armchair. A throne fit for the returning alpha queen. She looks up from a book laid open in her lap and offers us a tight smile.

"Hello, Jadick," she says.

"Mother. This is Mac, my fiancé. I thought you two could get to know one another before the engagement is made public later today."

He doesn't move to approach her, and I remember the cold disregard he showed her yesterday on the steps. Despite the fact that he's brought her home, there's no love in his heart for the woman who raised him.

Still, she nods. And I see in her eyes what I feel swimming in my own.

Neither of us has a choice, not really.

"Very well," she says.

"I'll come back for you when it's time to prepare," Jadick tells me.

Then he leaves me alone with the matriarch of this horrible, disgusting family.

Instead of continuing the conversation, Marilyn returns to her book.

I take that as a sign not to bother with conversation, and instead of joining her in the sitting area, I wander the room, studying the plants. Some are herbs, but most are tropical exotics. Flowers in bright shades of pink and yellow growing from stems that sport thorns bigger than my thumbs.

It's disturbing and fascinating, this collection.

I catch the sound of a book closing and then, "So. You are to marry my son."

Marilyn's words startle me, and I whirl sharply, eyeing her over the top of the cactus I've skulked around. "Yes."

"Why?"

Her blunt question speaks volumes about how she sees her own son. I step around the foliage and make my way over to where she sits. "Because I promised."

"I see." She glances out the window, her thoughts seemingly a million miles away. "And what has he promised you in return?"

I don't answer.

"Whatever it is, I hope it was worth it."

"You sound like you don't approve."

"I had the distinct misfortune to be born into a cursed pack," she says. "And instead of escape like I'd dreamed of all my life, I was made queen of that pack. Not a day went by that I didn't wish for another fate. There was nothing I wouldn't trade for another life."

"Is that why you left?" I ask. "Traded your children for a better life?"

"Desperation makes bad men evil," she says. "You'd be wise to remember my son is willing to do whatever it takes to win."

"I'm not sure that's a trait you should be proud of."

She looks up and cocks her head at me. "If I asked your mother about you, wouldn't she tell me you do the same?"

I open my mouth, close it again.

She's not wrong.

But it's not the same either.

"For me, winning means saving lives, not ending them," I tell her.

"We're all the villain in someone's story, darling."

Her words make me think of Levi. My chest threatens to crumble in on itself with the pain of what I've done to him.

"I'm the villain in plenty of stories," I tell her quietly.

"Then you're a perfect match for my son."

MARILYN and I don't talk much after that. I spend the rest of the morning perusing the plants and trying to focus long enough to read one of Marilyn's books. They're all romance novels with meek little damsels for the heroine. I get only a few chapters into each one before the protagonist's lack of wherewithal pisses me off. It's not that I think she should save herself instead of letting her white knight do it for her. The very belief one can be saved at all is what has me tossing the book aside as far too unbelievable to enjoy.

The room heats to stifling as the sun rises.

A literal greenhouse and Jadick has left me here to cook.

Finally, the lock clicks, and the door opens.

Marilyn and I both look up as a gust of air conditioning sweeps into the room from the hall. My mother looks from Marilyn to me.

"Mac," she says. "It's time."

In this moment, I hate her more than I ever thought possible.

But refusing to get up won't stop what's coming.

I push to my feet and walk away from Marilyn without a word. I have no idea what Jadick expected for our time together, but the whole interaction feels pointless to me. Sliding past my mother into the hall, I make sure to bump her shoulder. Hard. Her expression tightens, but she doesn't comment.

"I'll return for you shortly," she tells Marilyn then closes and locks the door behind me. "This way."

She leads me up the stairs to a second-floor bedroom. I slip inside behind her, feeling like a prisoner in my own body.

"This is for you to wear," she says and holds up a dress.

It's silver with shimmering fabric and spaghetti straps. The style couldn't be farther from my tastes. But I steel myself against my reluctance and snatch it from her.

"Mac," my mother says, her voice already weary, and we haven't even begun. "I know you're upset, but you don't have to take it out on me."

Of all the things she could have said, these words trigger me most.

I whirl, glaring at her with a heat that could scorch the sun. "Why shouldn't I take it out on you?" I demand. "When you're the one who orchestrated this whole thing."

"What a ludicrous thing to say."

She huffs as if I'm ridiculous. Not to be taken seriously. It's that dismissal that only infuriates me more.

"It's pretty insane," I agree. "To think my own mother has helped trap me into this situation rather than help me avoid it."

"You're hardly trapped," she says, still acting as if I'm being dramatic.

"What would you call it?" I shoot back.

"Your future is much brighter than it was a few weeks ago," she says.

I stare at her, incredulous. "You call being blackmailed into marriage with a monster 'brighter'?"

"Being mated to Jadick ensures your survival," she says, her temper finally showing through.

"Except I'm not Jadick's mate," I remind her. "I'm Levi's."

"And Levi is the number one enemy of the pack right now."

I stare at her. "You don't care about anyone, do you? Especially me."

"I care about only you," she says, her tone suddenly vicious with emphasis. She takes a step toward me, her voice low like a threat. "You are the only thing that matters to me, Mac. And every single day of my life, I am fighting to preserve you. Your future here in this pack, on this Earth—sometimes happiness must be weighed against survival. I thought you would have learned that lesson by now."

"Rejection is protection?" I say with disgust, "Is that it?"

She blinks and says nothing.

"You aren't doing me a favor by pushing Jadick toward this." She opens her mouth, a denial in her eyes, but I cut her off. "I heard you. That first night in Green Hills. When you thought I was sleeping. You told him to do whatever it took, and then you stepped aside, abandoning me to his trap. Knowing what it would take for me to accept his offer. You're just as much a monster as he is. Except worse, because I thought I could trust you."

The pain in my chest is a literal stab as I say the last few words.

"You don't know anything," she hisses, surprising me with her viciousness.

"I know you sold me out. Used me as the payment to save my own life."

"I had to consider all options," she snaps, her voice rising right alongside mine.

"So you sold me off to Jadick? That was the option you chose?"

"That deal I made with Jadick saved your life. Without it, you would have died."

"You don't know that—"

"I do!" Her outburst is driven by something I can't name. "You were dying, Mac. You have been for a while. When Levi rejected you, you never did the same to him. Did you ever stop to think how that affected your wolf? Have you learned nothing from the ways of our pack?"

I blink, surprised by her point.

"A rejection isn't complete unless it's done on both sides. But you never did reject him, did you? And so your wolf has hung suspended from that half-bond for years. And you've wasted away slowly. Sick with grief. And then you saw Levi again, and it all came back. He still loves you. His wolf still wants you. And the mate-bond is still possible because you left it open."

Shock washes through me, and I take a step back, trying to absorb what she's saying. It makes sense. I know all of this. Have seen it firsthand. But I was so caught up in my own feelings—the grief, the hate, the loss... I didn't even see it.

"You would have died from losing Levi," she says quietly. "I did what I had to do in order to save you."

"How does selling me to Jadick save me?" I demand.

"Forcing you to reject Levi saves you."

"Well, your plan won't work. I'm not rejecting him."

"Not yet," she says, and I realize where this is going as she says, "When you kiss Jadick and announce you're taking him as your mate to the entire pack… that's the rejection."

I stare at her in horror.

"That's why I left. He asked me to hunt down Marilyn. So we could use her against Kari to give him the upper hand in the fight. With your life hanging in the balance, I couldn't refuse him. But I never wanted you to go through this alone."

"I've always been alone," I say coldly.

She flinches but otherwise ignores my words. "Before you even think about refusing to go through with it," she goes on, "know that Jadick is counting on that. He's already given the order to kill Levi if you so much as hesitate out there."

Of course he has. And I know for a fact she'll follow that order too.

The way she's orchestrated it all. How stupid I've been. And now, it's too late.

My mother sighs, either in defeat or resignation. She looks at the dress I'm still clutching in my closed fist. Then she looks back at me, and the sadness I see in her expression startles me into silence.

"I'm sorry, Mac. I know the pain of rejecting one's mate," she says quietly. "And while I don't know if it makes us stronger, I know you'll survive it. That's what matters to me, Mac. You being alive. Without that, your chances of finding happiness don't even matter."

She swallows hard and shakes her head.

"Maybe you'll understand someday; maybe you won't," she goes on. "But I stand by my actions. I made the best choice I could, given the circumstances. And I won't ever apologize for saving your life."

I don't know what to say to that. She wants a "thank you" or something like it, but I can't summon gratitude. Not now. Maybe someday, like she said.

For today, I let her walk out and close the door, leaving me alone. If I want to find a way out of this future she's forced on me, I'll have to do it without her help. But first, I have to kiss the enemy.

CHAPTER 22

Still trembling, I put on the dress. My mother's words echo inside the room long after she's gone. I've gone cold from the reality of it all. Wishing I had more time to figure out another way. But I'm out of time. And there's no more waiting.

The knock comes all too soon.

"Come in," I call, but the knob is already turning before the words are even out. I look up from my own reflection in the long mirror, expecting my mother again. But it's Jadick who opens the door and steps inside the bedroom. He looks distinguished in a black suit and slick hair. Almost respectable. Or honest. But the look in his eyes is unmistakably dangerous. He's a snake—and he's starving for a meal.

"You look delectable," he says, eyeing me.

"This dress isn't my taste," I say, turning back to the mirror with a frown.

He strides up behind me, so close I can smell his cologne. It's overpowering, not unlike his personality.

"It's perfect," he says simply, eyeing the scandalously low-cut bodice and wire-thin straps. There's not much holding this dress up. I feel naked. But I think that's his whole idea.

His hands land on my shoulders, and I stiffen. He ignores my reaction, smiling at me from over my shoulder. "Ready?"

"My hair," I begin, but he waves me off.

"Leave it down. I like it wild." He winks at me and then turns away. A good thing considering the face I make at his innuendo.

At the door, he stops and turns back expectantly.

I look back at him, wondering if he knows my acceptance of him will be a rejection of Levi. But of course he does. He's counting on it. I take a deep breath and force my feet to carry me toward him. I'm not overly concerned about integrity or keeping my word. But I'm not stupid enough to think he'll let Levi—or even me—walk out of this house should I try to change my mind now.

There's no going back.

This will ensure my survival—and Levi's—but it's going to hurt like hell. Good thing I'm no stranger to pain.

The house is empty as we move through it. The only sound is our footsteps and the rustling of my awful dress as we make our way down the stairs and through the grand foyer. Near the door, my eyes catch on a statue that wasn't there before.

It's a wolf nearly as tall as I am. Made of alabaster all except for its onyx eyes that seem to watch me as I pass by. It's a gross representation of wealth—and the exact sort of thing Jadick would pick out.

"Just think, all of this will be yours soon," he says, misreading my interest in the thing.

He's lying, though. Jadick might marry me, but he'll never for a second let me think that any of his fortune is mine. My future is looking a lot like Marilyn's past, and it's terrifying me.

The sun is high overhead when we emerge onto the steps of the alpha house. My eyes land on the crowd that's gathered. Jades and Black Moon wolves standing shoulder to shoulder for the crowning of a new king.

Heat warms my bared arms and flushes my cheeks. I force my chin high as I walk beside Jadick, my arm tucked into his. The crowd's eyes are lasers burning into my skin. Near the front of the crowd, I spot Frankie. A few rows back are Lorenz and Nely. Beside them, Grey and Tripp stare back at me. Tripp's expression is frozen in horror. He's finally realized what I'm about to do.

I don't see my mother. Or Levi. I exhale, relieved I won't have to look at them while I do this.

Then a side door opens, and both of them stroll out. It's the same exact spot where I was forced to leave Levi behind. The same place I stood when Kari shot me. A rush of emotions well within me. At the same time, I feel the weight of Jadick's gaze burning into my face though I refuse to look. I force the emotion back, refusing to let it show on my face. I have no doubt Jadick planned their arrival this way just to prove a point.

From across the distance, Levi's eyes meet mine. Then they flick to where my arm is tucked through Jadick's.

Levi falters.

I watch as the color drains from his face. His eyes narrow, and shock gives way to fury. He takes a step toward us, but my mother stops him. She leans in, whispering something into his ear. His expression tightens, his jaw working back and forth.

I can't take it anymore; I look away, my body flushing with fiery heat. Shame burns me worse than the summer sunshine ever could.

"Come," Jadick says, pulling me toward the crowd.

I have no choice but to go.

"Welcome," he calls out, and the pack quiets. Already, the alpha power behind his voice is enough to make him heard without needing a microphone. "Yesterday, you all watched as I defeated my sister and became your alpha. Today, we welcome back the brothers and sisters who once left us in search of a better future. The Jades, who stand among you, fought bravely against my sister's rule. They are to be rewarded and treated with respect. Some of you have called me to condemn their behavior as traitorous. But I refuse to punish them for defecting when, in the end, they brought me back to my rightful place. We are all one pack now, one people. And I will not allow a single division among us."

I catch sight of the Jades' expression and realize something's

447

wrong. Lorenz and Nely look uncomfortable, but Frankie looks outraged.

"By now, you've all been notified of this. In fact, if you're standing here, it's because you've chosen—wisely, I might add—to pledge your pack loyalty to me, your true alpha."

It takes me a minute to realize what he means. The Jades. He's converted them all back to the pack. He's made them swear themselves to him. Worse, he's stolen Levi's pack out from under him.

My blood goes cold as I realize it means Levi really is all alone now. My hopes for making him the alpha are crushed to dust. The only thing I have left is the mate law. Any moment now, Jadick will announce the law is void. That anyone can choose anyone.

That will have to be enough.

It will at least be something.

"To show you I mean peace between us all," Jadick goes on, "I want to present to you Mackenzie Quinn."

The crowd's attention shifts to me, and I force myself to put aside my panic. To think. Murmurs go up, speculation and judgment. Jadick cuts through their humming like a blade falling across my throat.

"It's my pleasure to announce to you that Mac has agreed to be my wife."

The murmurs cease.

Shock is a scent in the air.

The Jades look confused then suspicious. Tripp's face crumples in disappointment, which makes my eyes burn with unshed tears. I blink them back, refusing to fall apart while on display.

Far to the right, I can hear Levi's growl echo in the silence. My mother snaps something at him, and he stills. I don't turn to look. One glance at his face and I'll come apart.

Jadick tucks me in close, smiling at them. Then at me.

I try to look away, but he snags my chin, drawing my face up to his. "Now's the time to fulfill your bargain, Mac." He murmurs the words through a display of teeth. A smile, a snarl—there's no difference.

His voice drops to a silky whisper as he strokes my hair. "Unless you've changed your mind about wanting Levi to live."

Bastard.

I lock gazes with him, and his smile deepens. "Kiss me, Mac. And don't forget to make them believe you."

He's breaking people with this show he's forcing me to put on—and he knows it.

Refusing is futile. It's also not an option.

Out of the corner of my eye, I see Gregario and Burnett standing like sentries against the wall. To everyone else, they probably look like they're here to protect Jadick from anyone crazy enough to try to hurt him.

I know better.

They're here to punish me if I refuse to play this game. Not to mention where my mother stands ready to end Levi if I refuse this.

I don't think, and I damn sure don't let myself look at Levi. Before I can think of any more reasons not to, I kiss Jadick.

Jadick's mouth is soft on mine at first, and I tell myself it's harmless enough. But then I remember his words. "Make them believe it." And I know I need to do more than a chaste peck.

Bile rises in my throat as I let my lips part. Jadick's reaction is instant. A growl rips from deep in his throat, and he crushes his mouth to mine. Passion then obsession then domination—I feel it all wash over him in an instant. His hands grip my shoulders then slide around to encircle my waist, pulling me flush against him.

The crowd goes wild.

Through the roaring in my ears, it's impossible to tell if they're cheering for or against this. Jadick doesn't seem to know either. Or he doesn't care. His attention is solely on me.

I feel his arousal immediately and have to brace myself to keep from pulling away.

Maybe if I pretend it's Levi—

Jadick's tongue shoves into my mouth, taking what I'm only offering begrudgingly. His kiss is not a request. And I meet his demands with just enough compliance to hopefully save my own life.

"Sell it, Mac," he whispers between kisses.

So, I do.

Wrapping my arms around him, I let my hand slide up the back of his neck and tangle in his hair. He plunders my mouth, clearly enjoying our performance and the audience who watches.

It's disgusting.

I'm disgusting.

By the time I pull away, we're both panting, and Jadick's slacks are tented.

My stomach rolls with nausea.

There's a strange sort of settling in my gut. Like a cord snapping free. My eyes fill with tears as I realize that must be what was left of my mate bond with Levi.

Gone.

Our rejection complete.

Through teary eyes, I catch sight of Jadick, wondering if he felt it too. He smiles stunningly for the crowd, his gaze sweeping over, over, over—until it lands squarely on Levi.

Before I can stop myself, I look over.

Levi's stare is a stinging slap, his dark eyes raging with betrayal. Jadick's arms still firmly around me are all that keep me from staggering back at the force of it. I try to breathe, but no air fills my lungs.

Even when he rejected me all those years ago, he never looked at me with such hate. I've just destroyed him—by setting him free. The look he wears says he wants to kill Jadick where he stands, but more than that, I think he might just kill me too, given the chance.

And all I want is to let him.

"My fiancé and I have one last announcement." Jadick turns back to the crowd, apparently satisfied with the damage he's done to my true mate.

I struggle to focus, but it's all I can do to remain upright. My knees threaten to buckle. I didn't think it would be this hard. Or hurt this much. Is this how Levi felt when he rejected me?

"Mac and I are not fated mates, but we're choosing each other for the good of the pack—and the strength of our future children. I think choice is important. Especially when it comes to one's mate."

This is it.

The thing that will make it all worthwhile.

"In the interest of choice and the strength that comes with it, there is one law that I must stand behind as we forge a new peace between our newly re-united peoples."

My blood goes cold at his unexpected words.

This isn't part of the plan. I stare up at him, horror mounting.

His smile slips, his expression hard and calculated as he says, "Romantics are hereby outlawed. Those of you who've chosen your fated have twenty-four hours to either reject one another or leave pack lands forever. After that, your choice will be labeled a crime, and you will be punished accordingly."

Gasps sound.

My knees buckle. Jadick doesn't spare me a glance, only hoists me up so I won't collapse. The picture of love and affection to anyone watching.

"Our enemies will be looking to exploit our vulnerabilities. And I will not lead a weakling pack into their own demise. There will be no fated mates in the Black Moon Pack. Not while I'm your alpha."

The Jades react immediately. Cries of dissent mix with curses and threats.

The Black Moon pack members aren't much calmer, though some of them seem to be happy about Jadick's decision.

I stare at Jadick, stunned.

The realization of what he's done—what he's used me for—is a sickening blow to what's left of my pride. He's just condemned the pack to another lifetime of pain and misery. Not only that, he's forced me into rejecting my true love. My fated mate. And I've just sealed that rejection with a kiss.

The story concludes in book 3,
To Keep A Wolf!

TO KEEP A WOLF

BOOK 3

CHAPTER 1

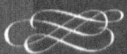

A layer of cold sweat is all I'm wearing against my skin. Even as I think about the possibility of getting dressed, nausea rolls through me. Not because clothes disgust me but because of what I'll have to do if I wear them. Leave this room. Perform the lie. Further betray my people. Thinking about it now, I'm forced to lean over the toilet as my stomach tries to empty itself. The problem is that it already has. Dozens of times. Now, all that's left to purge is my own regret. I don't see that leaving me anytime soon, though.

The world is darker today—because of me. Because of the deal I made. The deal I was forced into. Promising myself to a monster has consequences I didn't fully understand. Not until I stood on the steps of the alpha house and watched Levi's world crumble. But worse than watching Levi's hope snuffed out is knowing I've condemned an entire pack to a future even darker than our past.

Remembering how Jadick betrayed me, condemning Romantics instead of freeing them, my stomach twists again, and I heave.

Nothing comes out.

I slump back down, my knees pressing painfully into the cold tile floor of my bathroom. My hair is a sweaty, matted mess. And my muscles have never felt weaker in my life. Struggling with the movements, I manage to pull a fresh shirt over my head. My shower, finished mere minutes ago, is already rendered pointless, thanks to the fresh wave of sweat and sickness that's taken me down to the floor all over again.

I thought being poisoned with venom—three times, if we're being technical—was bad. This is so much worse.

My vision swims. Partly from the tears I can't seem to keep from spilling and partly because the sickness gripping me is a total bitch.

It's the rejection.

All this time, I'd thought I'd felt the worst of it. The pain of Levi walking away from me was brutal, but this is something else entirely. My body hates me for what I've done. My wolf won't even speak to me when I call on her.

Dying would be easier.

Maybe then, I wouldn't have to watch as my stupid decisions bring about the destruction of an entire generation… Because if this is what it feels like to reject your fated mate, I have truly doomed us all.

There's no strength in this.

Only pain and misery.

I deserve it.

A knock sounds at the bedroom door, eliciting a groan from my hoarse throat.

"Go away," I croak, but the words are way too weak to be obeyed.

Sure enough, whoever it is pushes into my room. It's easy enough considering Jadick had my lock reversed so that it only works from the outside. Still, visitors have been kept to a minimum since they stuck me here after the engagement was announced. Meals are brought up on a tray and brought in by security guards that I'm positive remain stationed just outside the door at all times. I've seen no one beyond them and my new fiancé. Even my mother has been absent, though I'm not sure whether that's by Jadick's order or her own decision. Last we spoke, I wasn't exactly encouraging of future visits.

From where I sit now, I can just make out a masculine shoulder as the current visitor kicks the bedroom door shut behind him. His scent hits me first, and I feel a ripple of unease as I recognize it. He is not a welcome guest right now. In fact, I almost would have preferred Jadick himself.

Instead, it's Tripp, my best friend—or maybe former best friend, especially now—who strides across my plush bedroom and stops to stare down at me. My stomach sinks at the disappointment and accusation reflected in his light brown eyes. "Mackenzie Marie Quinn."

My full name. Damn.

His tone is sharp and just reproachful enough to hit me right in my heart. Tripp and I have always called each other on our bullshit, but I'm not sure I can handle that right now. I look away, hanging my head. Before I can formulate a response, my stomach revolts, and I'm forced to lean over the toilet again.

While I dry heave, Tripp comes closer, pulling my hair back out of my face.

The kindness of his gesture makes me feel even worse.

"Thanks," I say, miserable, as I slump back against the wall, but Tripp's sympathy dries up the moment I'm not preoccupied with the business of vomiting.

"What the hell, Mac," Tripp growls.

I bring my face up and note the way his eyes are narrowed. But my senses are too strung out to read whether he's pissed *at* me or *for* me. I'm going to assume the former, though.

"I know everyone's pissed," I begin but then stop again as a wave of dizziness takes over. I lean on the toilet seat for support and wait for it to pass.

Tripp hesitates like he wants to say one thing but, instead, decides on another. "What's wrong with you?" he demands.

"The rejection," I mumble and then press my hand to my mouth while I try to decide if my stomach has somehow found a scrap worth expelling.

Finally, I exhale.

False alarm.

"How long have you been like this?" Tripp demands.

"Um. What day is it?" I ask, trying to do the math in my fuzzy, sleep-deprived brain.

Instead of answering, he reaches for the hand towel and runs water from the sink over it. When it's drenched, he wrings it out and then crouches beside me. He lifts the cold, wet towel toward my forehead, and I flinch.

He pauses, his angry look draining away, replaced by a softness that makes me want to curl into a ball and never come out again.

"I'm not going to hurt you," he says quietly, and I relax.

Slowly, he brings the towel to my forehead and wipes. Then my cheeks, my nose, my chin, my neck. The cool dampness is a balm to my sweaty, sticky skin. I breathe out a sigh of—not relief but something close to it.

"Do you feel as bad as you look?" he asks.

When I glance up, his lips are twitching. I snort. "Worse."

"Damn, girl."

He sits back, sizing me up in a different way now.

But I don't wait for him to come to a conclusion.

"How are you here?" I ask. "I thought you and Jadick were on the outs."

He gives me a look that says "understatement," and it really is.

"You could say that." He shakes his head. Jadick had been beyond pissed to learn Tripp had accused him of drugging my wolf in order to keep me weak while he manipulated me into marriage.

"Grey called me after the announcement. Told me what happened with your wolf."

"Wait. What do you mean *what happened with my wolf?*"

"The connection. To Levi?" At my confusion, he hesitates. "Your mate bond made you feel what Levi felt...? Did no one explain this to you?"

I shake my head.

He sighs. "Apparently, your mom put it together, and Grey overheard when she said something to Jadick after your ... announcement was made the other day." He frowns at the mention of that particular event but then goes on, "Your bond with Levi was stronger than we all realized, and that made your wolf susceptible to the drugs they gave him while Kari—"

Even though he stops himself, I flinch at the reminder of how Levi was tortured while he'd been held captive here.

"Anyway." He clears his throat. "As his wolf was muted by the drugs and the torture, yours was too. Because of your mate bond."

Our mate bond. Right.

I try to take comfort in the fact that no one was poisoning me directly (this time), but all I can think is how much I want that connection with Levi back again. A connection I didn't even know we shared. One that I severed the moment I publicly accepted Jadick as my fiancé. My future mate.

"Now, I'm back in," Tripp says with a shrug, "but I'm on bathroom duty for a month. Your bathroom," he adds, glancing pointedly at the opulent room that currently smells like vomit and B.O. "Evidently, you've been making a mess."

My shoulders sag. "I'm sorry," I say, but he waves me off.

"Shut up, Mac. Does Jadick know how sick you are?" I simply look at him until he sighs. "Right. Stupid question. And your mom?"

"Haven't seen her."

He doesn't say anything else. The silence between us is like a pressure building.

"He was supposed to rescind the law," I say, desperation creeping in now. I haven't spoken aloud about that moment since it happened. Doing it now is like ripping the doors off a house of horrors. "You have to know that's why I did it. I never would have agreed to marry him without a reason."

The anger he walked in here with resurfaces. "The problem is that you think your reason was good enough."

"What would you have done?" I shoot back, and he scowls.

"My point is you always think you have to do it alone."

"Look around you. I *am* alone."

He shakes his head. "You didn't have to be."

I look up at him, heart thudding. I have no right to ask, but I can't help myself. "How is he?" The words are no more than a whisper.

His expression is carefully blank. "I wouldn't know."

"What do you mean? You're his best friend—"

"He disappeared as soon as your little announcement was made. No one's been able to locate him. Much to Jadick's irritation."

I exhale, relieved that he's safe. But then I consider Tripp's words. "He's out there alone. And probably sick like me."

Tripp's eyes narrow. "And whose fault is that?" I look away. "You took his pack from him, Mac."

"Not me. Jadick—"

"Jadick used you, but it only worked because the Jades trusted you. That betrayal is something you have to live with."

I want to argue. To tell him there's no way; the Jades hate me. But deep down, I know he's right. I got them here. Even if it was because I promised them Levi. In the end, they followed me. And they did it with the hope I helped kill the moment we were done putting Jadick on his throne.

"I know," I say, eyes filling with tears again.

He gives me a once-over, and while there's friendship in his gaze, I see disappointment too. I don't know which one is winning. "When your insides stop trying to get outside, maybe you can get your shit together and make it right again."

I start to answer, but then my stomach twists, and it's all I can do to get over the toilet in time. Tripp holds my hair again. With his other hand, he rubs soothing circles over my back.

"I don't deserve it," I say when I'm back against the wall again.

"What?" he asks.

"You being nice to me."

"No," he snorts. "You don't. But that's not how friendship works."

"Are you my friend?" I ask, hating how vulnerable I sound. But the truth is, if the answer is yes, he goes on a list of exactly one.

"I've always been your friend, Mac. Even when you thought I wasn't."

CHAPTER 2

Two days later, champagne-colored gauze envelopes me. A full skirt that's both wispy and confining as hell swishes at my ankles. Beneath the formal dress I'm wearing, strappy heels threaten to bring me down where I stand. After five days of non-stop vomiting, my body is wobbly even without the threat of stilettos. It would be ironic, for sure; surviving so much venom and violence only to be taken out by a pair of shoes.

Part of me would be glad it's all over. After all, I've rejected my true mate only to chain myself to the most evil, disgusting man I've ever known. Condemning my entire pack to a future like the one I'm enduring now. What else is left for me to fuck up, anyway?

Apparently, this party tonight if this dress is any indication.

It's the least "me" thing I've ever worn. But I guess that's fitting. Because I've never felt less like myself than I do now.

"Knock, knock." A voice at the bedroom door draws my attention, and I look up from where I'm sending my heels a death-stare. Instead, I aim it at my new fiancé, who doesn't wait for an invitation to let himself in. Jadick is dressed in a black and white tux, his dark hair perfectly styled. Gold cuff links bear the Clemons family crest, a small reminder that his family is embedded into the very fabric of this town like the threads in his coat.

His eyes light up when he sees me, and he enters the room with all the intimacy of a couple in actual love.

Bastard.

"You look stunning," he says.

"I look like a prize horse," I say darkly.

He chuckles.

Chuckles.

Like this is all so amusing.

I glare at him, considering my options for weaponry. My bedroom is sparsely furnished, though, as if he knows the risks of giving me anything that could cause bodily harm. A hairbrush, plastic with blunt edges. Make-up. A wardrobe some girls would kill for. Me? I'll kill for a lot of things. Freedom. Love. Morality. Survival. But not clothes.

The only other item left at my disposal is the clock on the night-stand. It's a definite option.

"A stallion, maybe," Jadick says, still going with my non-joke.

My glare turns acidic. "Don't ever call me that again."

"We'll come up with something else," he says, not bothered in the least by my animosity. "I do like the idea of pet names."

"How about I call you 'dictator'?" I ask with mock sweetness.

His amusement hardens. "Careful, Mac. Someone might hear you talk like that and question whether or not this is true love."

I snort at that. It's so ridiculous, it doesn't even deserve an answer.

He walks up behind me, and our eyes meet in the full-length mirror. His fingers reach for my cheek, but I flinch away. At that, his eye twitches, his gaze narrowing as all traces of a smile vanish.

"How are you feeling today?"

Sick.

Stupid.

Heartbroken.

"Empty."

"Good." He beams as if that's exactly what he's hoped for. "I need you well and smiling for tonight's festivities."

"And if I throw up on you in the middle of dinner?"

"You'll be punished accordingly."

I don't miss the glint in his eye, the sadistic bastard. He wants me to insult him. To give him a reason. He's made it clear he likes it when I resist him, though how far he'll take that little game is yet to be determined.

Something tells me he likes the chase. And that's exactly why I refuse to run.

"But I think you'll behave," he says, his fingers trailing lightly over my shoulder and down my arm.

"You obviously don't know me as well as you think," I say, rigid against his light touch, "Besides, I thought you picked me for my rebellious spirit."

His expression darkens. "Spirit, yes. Rebellion, no."

His words trigger my rage, which I suspect is his purpose.

"You really think you've won, don't you?"

His brow lifts in silent challenge. "You're here, aren't you?"

"I'm here because it's the only place I can fight you from. You went back on our deal. You said you'd rescind the law—"

His hand closes around my throat so fast I have no time to react. He shoves me backward until my shoulders hit the wall with a thud that makes me wince. His eyes are intensely focused, daring me to fight back as he leans in and snarls, "You're here because I allow it. Because I wish it. Don't confuse my interest in you for devotion. I'm not some whipped fated mate you can manipulate. I'm not him."

"No," I agree, my mouth moving faster than my brain can stop it. "You're not half the man Levi is."

His hand releases my throat and whips across my cheek.

The flash of pain is instant and sharp. My face is driven sideways, my hair falling into my eyes. For a moment, I don't move, absorbing the pain. Paralyzed by the hate that follows.

"Don't speak of him again," he says viciously.

He strides toward the door, adjusting his jacket as he goes. "I'll give you a moment to collect yourself before you join me down-stairs. Don't make me come back to retrieve you."

Then he's gone, shutting my bedroom door behind him with a soft click. The sound of it echoes much worse than if he'd slammed it. It's a reminder he can get to me anywhere. That this house is his, not mine. I'm not safe here. I never will be.

But I didn't stay so I could be safe.

I stayed to fight.

He might have kissed me, but he won't keep me.

CHAPTER 3

We ride to the party in silence. The car smells like Jadick's late father and our former alpha, Crigger—a fact I don't bother to mention as Jadick's mood seems to have already soured enough from sniffing it at all. Or maybe it was my little dig earlier about him being half the man Levi is.

My face still stings, but I ignore it, unwilling to give Jadick the satisfaction of seeing me suffer. It took another layer of makeup to cover his handiwork on my cheek, but it was worth it. Tripp was right. I have to fix this. I'm the only one who can.

Tonight's event is apparently a mixer for all of the new leadership Jadick has appointed. He seems put out about having to drive across town to the hall he's rented, but from the bits I heard him exchange with Gregario, he refuses to host at the alpha house until he's "made it his own."

I wonder if, deep down, his reluctance to open up the alpha house stems from knowing Levi's out there somewhere. Then again, it's been nearly a week since the announcement—since my rejection —and no one has seen or heard from Levi since he somehow escaped.

Maybe he's just ... gone.

Off to start a new life somewhere else. Somewhere far from me and all the ways we've hurt each other.

That thought is enough to sour my mood.

The car stops, and our driver, a new guard I don't recognize, hops out, circling around to open Jadick's door, not mine. Next to me in the backseat, the young alpha resembles his mother with his dark features and slender frame. But he has his father's streak of cruelty. One look into his hollowed gaze and I know there's nothing he won't do—no one he won't hurt—to get what he wants. Just as Marilyn predicted.

Sliding out, Jadick stands and then turns back, offering me his hand.

I sigh and reach up, placing my hand in his as I slide across the seat and out.

At the contact, my stomach roils, but I swallow hard and shove it down. My disgust is nothing new, and despite my threat earlier, I really don't want to throw up again. My throat is still raw from the last few days. And I really need to keep something down if I'm going to regain my strength enough to figure out how to fix this.

Once I'm standing, Jadick tucks my arm into his and leads me toward the doors. I let him, concentrating on remaining upright in these heels. With any luck, I can use them to impale my fiancé before the night is over.

"Darling," he murmurs close to my ear, "smile."

Gritting my teeth, I rearrange my expression as we pass through the doors and greet the first faces inside. It's not a smile, but it's not resting-murder-face either.

I look around at the guests already gathered in the foyer. Many are faces I recognize, which doesn't help my attempts to seem friendly since none of them are allies. Burnett is here along with Gregario—both in ill-fitting suits. They've been promoted, according to the small talk I heard on the way over. In charge of alpha house security and pack security accordingly.

Their new ranks mean I don't see their faces lurking outside my bedroom door anymore. But their constant hovering presence will make things harder when I bury my heel in Jadick's throat.

That's a problem for future Mac.

Now, they barely look at me as they grunt a hello to their new alpha. Moving past them, Jadick sweeps me from guest to guest, introducing me or reminding me who these people are. Most aren't friendly to me, their keen stares mostly sizing me up to see what kind of ally I will be for them. They're not here because they love Jadick or the idea of his rule. Dripping in jewels or other shows of money, I get the feeling this particular crowd is here for one thing: power.

"It's nice to see someone from the bottom rise to the top," says the mayor, a round-waisted man with bald spots and a bad comb-over. His suit looks expensive as does his diamond pinky ring. "So inspiring," he tells me.

I bite back an angry retort, very aware of Jadick's expectations of me.

Instead, I fake smile and let Jadick lead me away from the asshole. Tonight is about sticking it out. Not sticking my heel in the mayor's throat.

In a glittery black dress, Marilyn stands in the far corner with a small entourage of guards backing her. The men flanking her are covertly dressed in suits, but it's clear they're here to make sure she doesn't say or do anything that contradicts the "reunited mother-son story" vibe. We swoop in for a quick hello where Jadick practically glows when Marilyn tells him he looks nice (in a bored tone). I roll my eyes at the starved look he wears in her presence and am too happy to move on when he pulls me away.

Still, the guests are mostly a blur of small-town politicians and founding families. Not a single person here seems interested in changing the direction Jadick has us headed. In fact, the only other face I see here that doesn't disgust me is Grey.

His presence here tonight surprises me, and the fact that he's posted at the doorway and dressed as a Clemons guard is even more shocking. Even after staying behind to guard Tripp on Jadick's orders, I had come to consider him an ally of sorts during our time in Green Hills. But his being here tonight means he's clearly pledged himself to Jadick.

He stands near an emergency exit halfway between the foyer and the hall where we'll all sit down for dinner and listen to Jadick give a speech about the future.

Tonight, Grey wears a black uniform slightly nicer than the usual tactical-wear. But his blank, impenetrable expression is stoic as ever. Looking at him now, you'd never know all we've been through together. Including the fact that he killed someone for me.

I glance behind me to see Jadick locked in conversation with a man he called Bordeaux who is apparently the new decorator for the alpha house. Words like "ambiance of power" and "masculine tones" reach my ears, and I roll my eyes.

Using the distraction, I make my way toward Grey, stopping far enough away to keep from being obvious. I can feel his eyes find me, but when I look over, he's staring blankly at the far wall. Still, now that I have his attention, I'm not sure what to say.

He's always been loyal to Levi, and that probably means he hates me more than ever.

I finally settle on, "Hi."

Unsurprisingly, he doesn't answer.

"Have you seen him?" I ask.

Still nothing.

"Because I remember asking you to look after him, and we both know you'll probably do a better job than I can." My expectations for a response are dropping fast, but I push on. "Anyway, I hope he hasn't been as sick as me. I hope he's okay. I hope…"

I hope way too much, obviously.

My eyes catch on Jadick, who's shooting me glances now.

I have literal seconds left.

"Anyway, tell him…"

I have nothing to say that will fix this.

"Never mind," I mutter and start to move away.

Grey steps forward, almost in my path. His hand brushes mine, and he steps back again. Something crisp pokes my skin, sharp edges, thin layers—I look down and see a small slip of paper. Curling my fist around it, I run my hand through my hair and tuck the scrap into the front of my dress as deftly as possible.

Then Jadick is coming toward me, and I freeze, waiting to see if he noticed my movement. He only gives me a sharp look that melts away as he grabs my arm and turns to the small crowd beginning to fill in around us.

"Don't wander," he says against my ear.

I don't bother to reply.

Everyone else makes their way to a table and begins to settle in for dinner.

"Come, darling," Jadick says, taking my hand and leading me toward the front of the room. "The alpha sits at the front."

I don't look back at Grey again.

When we're seated, dinner is brought out in courses. The meal is extravagant. Escargot. Scallops in wine sauce. Japanese Kobe steak. A display of power, I realize, as the guests toss compliments at Jadick. Through it all, a live string quartet plays classical melodies and tasteful cover songs.

It's a complete show.

Or the warm-up to one, anyway. Jadick is clearly the main event.

When the last dessert—a molten chocolate lava cake that I have to admit is divine—has been cleared away, Jadick pats his mouth with his napkin and then pushes to his feet. He bends down and presses a kiss to my cheek then makes his way to the stage. I don't miss that he chose the same cheek he slapped earlier. And I have no doubt he didn't miss that detail either. But he has the attention of the crowd now, and murmurs reach me about how sweet we are together.

My dinner threatens to come up.

I swallow hard and focus on the fantasy of Jadick tripping up the stairs onto the stage. No such luck. He strides to the podium, centering himself in front of the microphone. Then, he waits for silence. And damn if he doesn't get it.

His minions hush as we all wait for him to speak.

"Good evening, and thank you for coming." Jadick beams out at the room, and I tuck my fists into my lap. "This night is first and foremost a celebration. Taking my rightful place as your alpha has easily been the most rewarding experience of my life."

Gross.

"You're all here, not only to witness the start of a new era for our pack but to be part of it. A leader is only as strong as its people and I can see your strength as I look out at you tonight. Unfortunately, not everyone in this town shares your support. Since the first Black Moon wolf was made, we have been divided and weakened by the call of fate against our own hearts. For generations, finding our strength in rejection has been our pack's burden to bear. It is the biggest threat to our way of life, to our future."

I have to work hard to keep from rolling my eyes. He's the only threat against our pack now. The obviousness of his hypocrisy might be funny if it weren't so dangerous. Worse, the rest of the room is listening to what he's saying. Agreeing instead of calling him out.

"But no more," Jadick's voice booms loudly enough that I startle. He's on a roll now, his eyes alight with whatever evil point he's building toward. "We bow to no one and nothing, including the hands of fate. As your alpha, I am committed to clearing a path toward a future of strength and power—and, above all, choice."

A few cheers go up. Surprise surprise, the sycophants like that idea.

"My father believed in the strength of our pack. The power of choice and free will, especially when it comes to choosing our mates. And I believe we can achieve that strength without rejection."

My head snaps up at that.

The others look at each other in confusion.

His words are a contradiction to what he said on the steps of the alpha house just days ago. And I can't figure out where it's going. But then his next words confirm he's not somehow veering toward peace. If anything, he's careening farther and farther away from it.

"When I am finished, we will no longer have a mate to reject. Fate will not rule us like some imposing god. It will be your choice, always. Alliances will make us strong, not weak. And we will never be swayed by our baser instincts again."

Cheers—louder this time than before.

They don't understand, but they don't care. They want the power and strength he's promised them. His pretty words are eerily close to what I want to hear, but I know better than to trust him.

Jadick has something up his sleeve.

Before I can decide what it is, he's motioning for me to join him. I blink, only to realize the guests are clapping anew and Jadick is looking at me expectantly.

Shit.

I stand and make my way to the stage where Jadick pulls me in close to his side. The guests cheer for us—for him. He answers them by leaning in and kissing me. It's chaste, but I nearly lose it and punch him.

The crowd goes wild.

He turns back to them, soaking up their adulation.

"We look forward to seeing you all at the wedding," Jadick calls, and then he's pulling me off the stage and into the wings where Gregario ushers us out a side door to the waiting car.

My attempts to get Jadick's attention go unanswered until we're closed inside the car.

"What?" he demands when the door closes.

"What were you talking about in there? About free will and choice and strength? What are you planning?"

His smile is smug. "You'll see, darling. Don't worry. We're both going to have what we want."

I doubt that.

One of us might get what we want. But for that to happen, the other must lose everything. I just hope I get to be the one to take it all away.

At home, Jadick hands me off to a guard to be escorted to my room. He claims he keeps them close for my safety so I'm not alone if I get sick, but we all know the truth: I'm a prisoner here. This is my future; to be guarded night and day until I can fulfill whatever purpose Jadick has decided I serve. Maybe someday, he'll cast me off and let me go. Until then, I'm at his mercy. It's a cage I chose.

I wait until the guard closes the door behind me. The moment I'm alone, I dig into my bodice for the slip of paper Grey gave me earlier. Its existence is the only reason I didn't attack Jadick in the car for that stolen kiss onstage.

Gripping the paper between my fingers, I spread it out and read the bits of words scrawled there. Whatever I was expecting, it wasn't this. Or maybe it was exactly this. I don't know, but after a third read-through, my heart is pounding, my thoughts are racing, and the nausea that's plagued me for nearly a week is finally fading as adrenaline takes over.

The handwriting is Grey's. But the message is, without a doubt, Levi's.

Do you trust me?

That answer is, without a doubt, I do.

CHAPTER 4

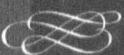

The following morning, I sit propped up in bed, pretending to watch the local news coverage of our dinner gala last night. The TV is muted, though, so all I have are the headlines running along the bottom, all of which paint Jadick as some kind of prodigy savior for our town. The screen flicks to a commercial just as my bedroom door clicks open, and my mother slips into my room along with a tray of breakfast. Surprise ripples through me, though I don't let it show on my face. Not that it matters. She doesn't look over at me as she moves silently across the thick carpet and sets the tray on the table under the window. Instead of retreating, she takes a seat in the chair beside the tiny table.

"You look pale."

I give her a withering look. "I've been a bit indisposed."

Her gaze softens but not by much. "The rejection," she says quietly. Her discerning glance rakes me over. "It's done then?"

I choke back a stream of obscenities. "Yes, Vicki. It's done. Great job sabotaging my choices in life. Again."

Her eyes narrow. "I saved your life," she says. "And since when do you call me Vicki?"

"Since you stopped acting like my mother and became just someone I know who sometimes betrays me."

She looks like she wants to take a jab back at me for that one. Instead, she reaches for a piece of toast and begins to butter it. "Any news on Levi?" she asks, and my heart skips a beat.

I flushed the note. She can't know.

I keep my hostility firmly in place as I say, "Even if there were, do you think I would tell you?"

"You don't trust me," she says, and I snort. She ignores that and goes on. "I'm not without feeling. I have sympathy for his plight. He's alone out there. Probably sick like you."

"Levi can handle himself," I mutter.

She gives me a look I can't dissect. Then she takes a bite of the toast. "You should eat."

"What do you care?"

"You're my daughter, Mac."

I don't answer.

"Jadick wants to see you," she says.

When I look up at her, she's staring at the toast like it contains the answers. Or maybe the problem.

"He sent you to check on me?"

"He wants to know if you're going to keep your word."

"Why should I?" I snap. "He broke his."

She sighs, and when she speaks again, her voice is quiet. "He's up to something." She looks over at me, and an obvious apology is written across her features. A weighted exhaustion that's full of remorse—and worry. I've never seen her look so unsure.

"I know," I say, and, for once, my words are not infused with anger. Not for her, anyway. For a single second, we're not on opposite sides.

"He's trying to use you. Against the pack, sure, but it's more than that, and I don't know what."

"Jadick's not the only one."

"What is that supposed to mean?"

"It means you're just as bad as him. No, worse. You're just like Kari. Pretending to love me and then betraying me."

Her cheeks flush red. "You might not agree with what I've done, but it's hardly a betrayal. You would have died after Levi... I protected you. The only way I could under the circumstances."

"And the people who tried to kill me?" I snap. "Where were you when it came to protecting me from them?"

"What are you talking about?"

"Oh, no one told you? That's right, you left to run off and track down Jadick's mommy, so how could you have known?" I can't help the sarcasm that twists my tone. But her confusion turns fast to anger. She clearly had no idea.

"Who tried to kill you?" she asks.

"Which time?"

I'm probably taunting her, but I can't bring myself to stop. She hurt me. And this is the best I can do.

"Relax. I'm still standing. And you're still the mother of the bride."

She doesn't answer right away, and when she does, I'm not sure whether to be relieved or disappointed that she's already moved beyond the fact that I was nearly killed. "Jadick's planning something. We need to find out what."

"You're the one who wanted this. You figure it out."

"I did what I had to do for our survival. But this... he's keeping secrets. I just can't figure out what his goal is anymore."

I recognize her tone. It's the one she uses when she's puzzling out a mark. A bounty she can't find or a problem she can't solve. And for a moment, I'm tossed right back into that space too. Riding shotgun in her Jeep, helping her track down the creatures of our world who don't want to be found.

I might hate her methods, but my mother always triumphs in the end.

"You want me to keep playing his game," I say.

"I want to know what he's really doing."

"Then find out." I lean forward, tossing back the covers. "Use my time with him as the distraction you need. Find out everything you can. Because I have no intention of going through with this marriage."

"His new security won't talk to me," she muses, forehead creasing in thought.

"Then find someone who will."

My words are clipped, my patience exhausted. She doesn't argue as I climb out of bed and stride to the bathroom. By the time I emerge from my shower, she's gone.

THE GUARD outside my bedroom is new. He grunts more than he uses words, and the air of hostility clinging to him never fades despite the fact that I follow him willingly through the house like I'm his prisoner. Outside the door to Jadick's study, my guard pauses and glares.

"The alpha will see you now."

He doesn't wait for my answer before pushing the door open and stepping back, grunting for me to enter. The moment I step through, he pulls the door closed behind me with more force than necessary.

Jadick looks up from behind a large desk, brows raised at the noise.

"Someone's not happy about babysitting duty," I say.

"You're not a child, Mac."

For some reason, that makes me snort.

He pushes his chair back and stands, rounding the desk to where French doors open to the extensive back gardens. "Walk with me?"

He offers his hand, which I ignore, but in the end, I step up beside him. After nearly a week of being confined to my room, he's offering a walk in the sunshine and a chance to find out more about what the hell those vague promises meant last night.

This is my chance for both. I won't ruin it.

He pushes the doors wide, and even though we're shoulder to shoulder, there's no mistaking who's leading as we stroll outside.

Despite all of the reasons to be a stressed-out mess, I find my wolf relaxing as I inhale the scent of the outdoors. Freshly cut grass, the dirt being turned over as flower beds are weeded. It's exactly what I needed to ground myself amid all the chaos. And just for a second, as I close my eyes and draw a deep breath, I pretend it's all going to be okay.

Way too soon, that illusion is shattered.

Jadick tugs my arm and draws me farther into the gardens. Once, this space belonged to me and Kari. After Marilyn left, Crigger, Theo, and Jadick never stepped foot out here, which meant Kari and I were safe to play and laugh and run and pretend she didn't come from a family who killed or abused everything in its path. Once, it was a place of comfort and happiness for me.

Not anymore.

Everywhere I look now, I see proof everything is absolutely not okay.

Employees and organizers bustle around us, the hum of activity heightened as people begin to spot us strolling past their handiwork. On my right, summer heat bakes the beautiful hedge rows, not to mention the gardeners assigned to revive them where Kari let them languish. Everyone and everything is sweating out here.

"The guests will come through there," Jadick says, his words jolting me back to the present moment with a painful tug.

I follow his gaze and find a series of statues lining the pathway from the front walk to the back of the garden. White tulle lines the edge of the path, herding visitors in the right direction. Fitting that everything is secured and tied off.

Imprisoned; like me.

"Guests?" I ask and realize belatedly he means wedding guests.

I look away, my gaze roaming over the gardens again. Noting all of the statues interspersed among the hedgerows that wind like tiny mazes. The design is a sort of Greco-antebellum just like the alpha house itself. Jadick has already ordered former artwork and décor to be brought up from the basement—whatever Kari didn't destroy, anyway.

Crigger always had a thing for Greek art. Nude sculptures with huge dicks, that sort of thing. Kari used to joke it was his version of a lifted truck. "Compensating" she'd call it. I almost smile now as I watch a marble statue of some unnamed Greek hero being wheeled back to its original place near the center fountain.

The workers pause to look over at Jadick uncertainly.

The alpha grunts his approval, and I shake my head. He is his father, through and through. I pray I don't have to find out for myself whether he's compensating too.

Farther back, where the gardens border the forest beyond, two pillars have been erected about six feet apart, white gauze dangling limply from each one in the non-existent breeze.

"What's that?" I ask, pointing at the place where the columns stand.

"That's the altar," he says, and my heart skips a beat.

"Altar?"

"For the wedding," he prompts. "I thought you'd appreciate an outdoor ceremony. And this way, the entire pack can be present to witness."

"Great," I say with zero sincerity.

Jadick leads me down the path toward the archways where I can see for myself all of the space that's been made for seating. He's right. At this rate, the entire pack will be able to attend this horror show. For some reason, I think of Levi.

Will he be here? When the time comes, does he have a plan to avoid this horrific outcome Jadick's so intent on? Or will he sit by and watch it happen?

Do you trust me?

I want to. When I got his letter, I did. But now... standing here in front of Jadick, I'm not quite sure if I can.

"Your heart is racing," Jadick comments.

I can feel his eyes on me, searching. He's enjoying whatever he sees there.

I force my gaze to his. "Marriage is a big step," I say.

"Would you like to practice?"

"Practice?" I repeat, wary now.

"The ceremony. The end is my favorite," he whispers, crowding me until I'm forced to back up or subject myself to his kiss. Again.

"No," I say, grimacing when my hips hit the low wall bordering the next section of gardens.

Jadick leans close. "You may now kiss the bride."

I place my hands on his chest, pushing him away. He bears down harder, clearly warming to the idea of a fight. It's his favorite way to have me, and I've played right into it.

His head dips lower. Closing the distance.

I cringe, shoving him, but it's no use. He's stronger than I am. I hate that.

I hate him.

Movement over his shoulder distracts me. My gaze flicks that way and lands on a face so familiar and heart-stopping I forget to fight back at all.

Jadick's mouth lands on mine just as, beyond the hedge rows, Levi's face contorts with understanding. Then Jadick's closeness eclipses my view. His lips shove harshly against my own.

I shriek, bringing my knee into Jadick's groin before I can think it through.

He doubles over with a grunt then stumbles back.

My unobstructed view is a victory. But when I look again, Levi is gone.

Maybe he was never there at all.

Jadick snarls, straightening and pinning me with a look I know I should fear.

"You will show me some respect," he spits.

"I respect those who deserve it," I snap back.

He grabs my arm, squeezing until I have to bite back a cry. Dragging me toward the house, he doesn't stop until we're back in his office. Then he shoves me across the room, letting go so that I careen into the book shelf. I catch myself and whirl just as he slams the French doors shut, sealing us inside.

Alone.

I brace myself for whatever punishment he intends to dole out. Backing away, I feel for anything on the shelf behind me that might help. My fingers close around a cylinder-shaped object. I grip it and plant my feet.

Jadick saunters forward. He's not hurrying, not now that he knows we won't be disturbed. When he reaches me, he leans in close and inhales deeply against my jaw.

"You smell good enough to make me want to forget, you know."

I remain still, heart pumping with the need to attack.

"Forget what?" I ask.

"Everything. This farce of a fucking wedding. The sacrifice you'll make after." He leans close and licks me from the base of my throat all the way to my jaw.

It's disgusting, but my mind is too caught on his words to be properly disturbed.

His hand comes up to grip my jaw. He bends so his face is buried against my chest. He kisses my collarbone as if I'm breakable.

"You're exquisite, Mac. Ripe for disposal. And yet, desirable enough to keep."

I don't know what that means. But time's up for asking. His head dips lower, his free hand coming to meet the fabric of my shirt, drawing it down to expose my breast.

I shut my brain off and swing as hard as I can.

The object in my hand meets Jadick's skull—and sticks.

I draw myself away, slipping past him as he screams. My feet propel me toward the door. I catch a glimpse of him as he yanks the weapon free; a small globe with a spear stuck through it. His blood drips from the spear.

It's not enough, but it's all I can do.

Flinging the door wide, I notice my guard from earlier is gone. Not that it matters. Jadick isn't going to let me get far.

Behind me, Jadick is moaning and hissing and gathering himself, probably to bash my skull in. I inhale a short, shallow breath.

Then, I run.

The halls are a maze of gleaming floors and bewildered guards.

They don't move in time to stop me. Maybe it's the surprise. Or maybe we all know I'll never make it beyond these walls. Either way, their reactions are too slow, and I speed past them before they can grab me. I can't decide if that's preferred. My wolf wants the challenge of a fight, but I know I'm not ready for that yet. Not when I'm still recovering from the rejection.

Behind me, Jadick screams my name.

I turn another corner.

And another.

This part of the house is darker. No one has bothered with lights or guards.

Motion sensors beep my presence.

These are worse than guards.

I can't fight technology.

Another turn, this one down a dead-end hallway.

Shit.

I have no idea where I am. This is not a part of the house I've ever seen. And the running has ruined my sense of direction. Somewhere behind me, Jadick's voice rings out.

"Mac!"

He knows I'm still here. Somewhere.

And he loves the chase.

I cannot let him catch me. Something about his words before, though—they haunt me: *the sacrifice you'll make after.*

A door looms at the end of the hall, and I don't even hesitate. Pushing my way through, I stumble into a darkened room and then shove the door shut behind me.

In the far corner, something moves.

Blinking furiously, I wait for my senses to adjust. To tell me what —or who—else is in here with me. It has no windows, and something tells me whatever they're using this room for, it's not meant to see the light of day. Ever.

A sound like sheets rustling steals my breath. I freeze, surveying the shapes as they come into focus.

A long, low table is shoved against the far wall. I can't see what's on it from here.

In the corner, the rustling sound comes again.

A bed.

I take a step toward it. Then another.

I'm stopped when I reach the bars of a cage.

It's enclosing the bed. Making it impossible for me to reach whoever lies on the thin mattress inside.

I hear more rustling. And then, "If physical torture won't work, why the hell would he think psychological torture will?"

The voice is weak, barely more than a whisper, but the sarcasm remains, and I nearly stumble over at the shock of hearing it.

"Kari?"

"Who the fuck did you expect to find?"

I blink, squinting harder into the darkness. Slowly, her shadowy face comes into view. Blonde hair matted to her head in hardened tangles. A face nearly unrecognizable through the bruises. And a throat haphazardly bandaged against the knife wound Jadick left her with last week.

My eyes fill with tears, and I decide not to analyze why until this is all over. I shouldn't care that she's here. Still breathing. I don't.

"I thought you were dead," I say in a strangled voice.

"Relax, you'll get your wish soon enough." She tries to adjust her position but then grimaces and gives up.

"How are you still...?"

"My dear brother has kept me alive."

"For torture," I say grimly.

"For information."

That gets my attention. "What information?"

She barks out a short laugh that clearly causes her pain. Blood leaks from beneath the bandage at her throat. It's disgusting. And justified.

My feelings are a tornado inside me. I don't even know where to begin.

"Did he tell you to play stupid when he sent you in here?" she asks.

"Jadick didn't send me."

"Right. Let me guess then. You came to help me escape."

Her tone is so cutting I wince.

"I'm not here to free you," I say, eyes narrowing.

"Give me a fucking break." She manages to roll her eyes, though her expression is pinched from pain. "You've always been the naïve one."

"What the hell does that mean?" I demand.

I have minutes—seconds, really—before Jadick bursts in and ends this reunion. Then, he'll do who-knows-what with me. And Kari. Well, I'll never see her again. I don't need a crystal ball to know I wasn't supposed to see her now.

"My brother has always been the worst of us, Mac." Kari's words rattle me. Maybe because I sort of believe her. But then I remember what she did to Levi. To me. My heart hardens, and I grip the bars, squeezing the cold iron against my hands.

"You're one to talk," I say. "You played me for years. *Years*. Grooming me. Using me. And then you betrayed me. For what? This?"

"I saved you," she says, her tone vicious.

I step back, fury driving me. She's not worth getting caught for. She's not worth whatever Jadick will do if he finds me here.

"You're a liar. And you deserve all of this and more."

I turn to leave, done with whatever need for closure drove me here in the first place. My strides are long and purposeful. I have no idea where to go next, but I know there's nothing left for me inside this room.

"He's going to kill you, you know."

I let go of the knob.

Slowly, I turn back, hating myself for letting her words get to me. "What?"

"The wedding is a smokescreen. It's the wedding night you should worry about."

I snort. "I can take care of myself."

"If only that were true."

Rage heats my blood, and I turn for the door again. "Go to hell, Kari."

"He's found a witch."

A witch. Frankie's words come back to me. She said he was looking for a witch, a hex, named Rina. Something about the curse of our pack. If he's found her...

I glare at Kari through the darkness. "What does that have to do with me?"

"It's what he wants you for, Mac. What he's always wanted you for. Blood. Death. You're just a sacrifice."

"What?" Her words make no sense, but a ring of truth echoes inside them that keeps me from telling her she's crazy.

"How is this such a hard thing to grasp?" She makes a sound of frustration. "He doesn't give a shit about this wedding or the Jades or anything else. He wants to finish what my father started. And he needs your blood to do it."

"Does this have to do with the curse?"

"Of course it's about the curse. It's always been about that stupid fucking curse."

"What is he going to do?" I ask.

"Perform the ritual that will end the existence of fated mates."

My heart thuds as I think back to dinner and the speech Jadick gave. The promise of a better future for our pack—without fated mates to deal with. "Why?"

"Why what?" she snaps.

"Why bother? Our pack already rejects our mates. It's the law. And he's alpha now. Everyone already follows him. Why bother with the ritual? What else is in it for him?"

"So naïve," she says, clucking her tongue. "Why does any asshole do anything? Power, of course. Mates are the only thing more powerful than the alpha bond, and he knows it. Without it, he'll have absolute authority over every wolf here. No one will ever question him because no one will be strong enough to do it. He'll secure his place as alpha—forever."

Stalking back to Kari's cell, I peer in at her, breathless. "Tell me how to stop him."

She looks back at me, and her expression softens. I think, for a second, it might be affection. That maybe some part of our friendship was true for her. That maybe she regrets hurting me so badly. But then I realize the softening is pity.

"Oh, Mac," she says as if I'm pathetic for even asking. "You can't."

CHAPTER 5

Kari's words hit me like jagged glass, cutting into the wounds she's inflicted on me since the moment she stopped pretending I mattered.

"Why is Jadick keeping you here?" I ask. "What information does he want?"

"Honestly, it's like you're not even listening."

My hands ball into fists, but I bite my tongue, waiting.

She sighs—or tries to. Her wounded throat makes it sound like a wheeze. "Under a black moon, we split ourselves. Rejects and Romantics. We call ourselves cursed—"

"I know the story," I snap.

"You think you do," she says. "The truth is that the only curse we carry is one brought on ourselves. The rejections break us down a little each time. And our connection to our wolves gets weaker with each new generation. Soon, our wolves will vanish completely, and our pack will go extinct."

I stare at her, shock giving way to indignation. "Jadick knows this?" She shrugs. "And he's still going to end fated mates?"

"He thinks it's a lie. Another loophole. He thinks doing this will give him strength and power."

"He's an idiot."

She snorts. "Preaching to the choir."

"But…" I shake my head to clear it for all the good it does. "What does he want from you?"

"The bones of our ancestors," she says, sobering now. "They are the missing link from the past to the present. The only other item he needs to make his black magic work."

Her gaze on me is steady. My heart pounds.

"And you have them," I say.

She doesn't answer. Her eyes reflect pain beyond the physical.

"He would have killed my father," she whispers. "Even if I hadn't. It was the only way to get the bones he needed." Her eyes shimmer with tears. "Everything I did was to protect us."

I can see it—her belief in that truth. Even if she became a monster to do it.

"Don't let him have me." She clears her throat, blinking until her eyes are clear and resolved and devoid of the emotion that goes with her plea. "Don't let him have the information."

"Why me?" I ask quickly. "What is it about me that he needs?"

Voices rumble from outside the door.

"We don't have time for this," Kari hisses.

She's right.

Seconds left to decide if I'll give her what she wants. What we both want, really.

Kari tosses the covers back and pushes to her feet. Swaying, she makes her way to the bars until she's close enough to grab them.

"Mac," she urges. "Just fucking do it already."

I step back and glance around the room, not even sure what I'm looking for. My eyes catch on the table, the items scattered there. Something silver glints, and I lunge for it. A short blade.

My hand closes over it as the voices outside grow closer.

They've found me.

I look back at Kari. "I still hate you," I say, emotion rushing through me now at what I'm about to do. What she's demanding of me. And dammit, what I want. "I'll always hate you."

"I know," she says, somewhere between sad and cruel as she watches me cry for her.

"You tortured Levi, not because he had information you wanted," I say, "but just to weaken me. So I couldn't come for you."

"Of course. You could have killed me," she says, eyeing the knife as I approach her cage.

"I'm going to kill you anyway," I choke out.

She nods. "Get on with it then."

At her words, my wolf stirs—finally—and she's been trapped too long for me to talk sense into her now.

Screw the voices outside.

I use the knife to pick the lock. When the mechanism springs free, I toss it aside. Behind me, the doorknob rattles. I ignore it and shift as I move into Kari's cage.

My wolf doesn't even break stride as my human bones give way and my flesh sprouts fur. Kari waits in silence as I come for her. She doesn't try to fight me off, and I don't even hesitate.

My wolf's teeth sink into her throat, and I taste blood.

Something lands on me from behind, and I'm thrown off Kari and onto the floor of her cell. My wolf yelps at a sudden pain in my side. I'm back on my feet in moments. Kari's lifeless body stares back at me from the floor. I turn away from her and launch myself at the guard who dared try to stop me. His bloodied knife dangles from his hand. He hasn't shifted, and I can see this tiny space won't let him even if he tried.

But it won't be an advantage for long.

I ram him with my shoulder and run for the open door.

In the hall, three more guards come running toward me. They raise weapons aimed at me.

Guns.

I falter, throwing myself sideways to avoid their bullets.

The gunshots roar in my ears, too loud up close.

I brace myself against the discomfort my animal feels at such volume and keep going, shoving past them, knocking them down as I go. My wolf is full of adrenaline, desperate to get out and

495

somehow also reveling in the chase they're giving. She's been caged too long, and now she wants only to be free—and to punish all those who would try to take that freedom away.

Her determination is a special kind of rage.

I've never felt more powerful or more threatened in my life.

Left and right then left again, I do my best to backtrack into the area of the house I can navigate. Guards startle at the sight of me in wolf form. Twice, they get off a shot before I'm out of sight. One of the bullets catches me in the ear. I yelp and keep going, determined not to stop until they make me.

Pain lances through my ear, and blood drips toward my eye.

I blink, shaking my head to clear it, then run for Jadick's office, envisioning myself crashing through those French doors. It's closer than the main entrance and hopefully less guarded.

Slamming the door with my hip, I barrel into the well-lit space just as a horrific boom splits the air. I glimpse Jadick standing in front of the doors, a gun raised. But the boom has thrown me off, and I fall—no, am driven—sideways. I land on the rug with a heavy thud, thanks to the momentum carrying me.

My wolf contorts in pain as we land.

By the time I'm prone against the scratchy rug, I know I've been hit. The pain that radiates from my left shoulder is paralyzing. My wolf howls.

A shadow looms over me, blotting out the light.

I look up to see Jadick standing over me. A bloody gash mars the left side of his head with dried blood coating his temple and cheek. The upper half of his face is swollen, and I take some satisfaction from seeing my earlier handiwork had an effect. He stares down at my wolf, his lip curling in cruel enjoyment.

The gun hangs limply in his hand now, and I brace myself for him to use it again. But he merely stands over me and watches as my injury takes hold. Blood seeps through my vanilla-colored fur and onto the floor.

Footsteps rush in. Heavy boots that are suddenly muted by the carpet as they reach us. Breathless soldiers, wide-eyed and then wary when they spot me.

"Nice shot, boss," one of them says.

Gregario.

The bastard.

"Apparently, I'm the only one in this house capable of hitting a moving target," Jadick snaps at him.

My eyes blur with the pain. Or with the blood loss. Confusion and pain whirl inside me. I can't be dying. One bullet can't do that. But then I recognize the familiarity of the burning in my veins.

Venom.

He's shot me with a poisoned piece of lead.

It's not the first time I've been poisoned. Or even the second. But it is the thing that's kept my wolf from rising all these weeks. Jadick knows it too, which is exactly why he chose it, of all things, to subdue me with.

His eyes glitter as he watches my wolf realize what he's done.

Something in me snaps.

Ignoring the agonizing burn of the venom, I rear my head back, twisting my wolf body around, and bite Jadick's ankle. He doesn't see it coming and reacts a second too slow. My teeth crack through his bone, and he screams.

The tang of his blood fills my mouth. Nothing in the fucking world has tasted sweeter. I decide right here and now to finish it.

Screw the pack and the deal and anything else.

I'll kill the alpha myself.

I release him only long enough to reach higher and bite again.

This time, his calf. It's fleshier than his ankle. I rip into it, wincing at the stabbing pain in my shoulder as I move. Security presses in around us. Gregario. Who knows who else. I don't see them.

I see only red.

Death.

Jadick Clemons' swift end.

Something slams into me with the force of a truck.

Screams sound, ringing in my ears, as I am driven away from Jadick. He stumbles back and through the sea of wolfish bodies pinning me to the floor, I see a trail of blood from Jadick's leg as he's dragged to safety.

I writhe and twist, trying to break free of the massive paws grinding me into the floor. But every maneuver is met with more snapping teeth and sharpened claws against my sensitive flesh.

Finally, the pain is too much and the venom too widespread, and I feel my grip on my beast fading. A scream builds in my throat, frustration more than anything, but I swallow it down. In the next moment, my fur has receded, and my limbs are human again.

I am no longer a deadly, powerful beast. I am simply Mac, a poisoned human-shaped prize. Nothing more.

The wolves who were pinning me back off, though not by much.

My naked body is on full display for a room full of Jadick's soldiers.

And they make no attempt to look anywhere but at my exposed skin.

Assholes.

The burning in my veins is more than just poison now. It's a promise to kill them all before this is over.

In the corner, slumped in his desk chair, Jadick draws ragged breath after ragged breath. Our eyes meet, and I pour every ounce of the hatred I feel into the glare I give him. He does the same, though his is twisted with... desire.

It's disgusting, but I refuse to flinch away.

Not this time.

Instead, I let my gaze travel lazily to where his leg is bleeding and ripped open.

Then I look up at him again and smirk.

His face flushes redder than before. He leans forward as if he's going to get up and march over here but then tenses when he remembers his injury. Bracing his arm on the desk, he says, "Take her upstairs. Two guards on the door and four more on the stairs. No one in or out but me."

"And the wound, boss?" Gregario asks.

His eyes gleam most of all as they rake over my naked flesh. He seems most appreciative of the blood coating my shoulder and upper arm. It's sick.

"Leave it," Jadick tells him.

Gregario drags his eyes from me to his boss, confusion pinching his brows. "You don't want us to patch her up?"

"Did I fucking tell you to patch her up?" Jadick snaps.

Gregario frowns. "Sir, the wedding ceremony is tomorrow—"

"Where was she?" Jadick interrupts. He looks to one of the other guards. Someone hanging back near the doors. "When you found her, where was she?"

"Sir, she was in the prisoner's cell."

The room is silent now. Tense.

"And the prisoner?" Jadick demands.

The man clears his throat. "Dead."

Jadick's silence might as well be a roar. He looks back at me, brutality twisting his features so that, for once, the monster he carries inside him is exposed. He knows what Kari told me. He knows I understand what will happen tomorrow. And he knows that, in this moment, knowing doesn't change a thing.

He'll still use me.

I'll still die.

It'll still all be for nothing.

"Don't clean the fucking wound," he says softly, looking only at me. His victory is grotesque. And my failure has never been more evident. "No point anyway, is there?"

CHAPTER 6

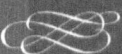

*J*adick stalks out the moment his orders have been delivered. His leg hasn't stopped bleeding, and I take comfort in his obvious discomfort as he limps out. Burnett and another guard follow him, but everyone else lingers, still waiting. And watching. Or, more accurately, leering at the naked woman bleeding all over the rug. Bastards. I'd cover up, but there's nothing handy. Instead, I hold my chin high and glare daggers at them, committing their faces to memory. A mental murder list of everyone I'm going to kill before this is over.

Someone near the back whistles, and the others laugh.

My fists tighten.

My vengeance *will* include them—or I'll die trying.

Finally, the men seem to realize it's time to move me.

"Show's over, folks," Gregario announces, a sly grin spreading over his face as he takes a step toward me.

I'm not surprised when he offers to carry me to my room. Even in my poisoned, pain-filled state, I make myself threatening enough that he backs off. In the space he leaves behind, I realize the only other option left is to get up and walk naked past the dozen men crowded into the doorway.

It's no worse than having them all staring down at me now. Or it shouldn't be. But the idea of turning my back on them, so exposed, and injured, makes me hesitate. Jadick's already told them not to help me heal. Who knows what other liberties they think that affords them?

Before I can make myself move, a thin blanket lands on my lap, tossed haphazardly by someone I can't see over the crowd. And maybe I should worry about the fact that someone just showed me kindness, but I'm too desperate to care. Clinging to the cashmere throw, I scramble to my feet before Gregario can order them to rip it away.

"Move," I snarl with a confidence I don't feel.

Despite my thundering heart, the soldiers part to let me pass, and I keep my chin high as I march toward the stairs. Guards follow at a distance. Their presence is a solid sensation behind me, but I don't look back.

Instead, I force myself to walk.

Past the hall where I just ended the life of a former friend.

Past the sunroom where Jadick's mother called me a monster, no better than her own fucked up son.

And in the very opposite direction of every door that leads out of this forsaken prison.

I've never had to willingly retreat like this before. The humiliation chokes me, but I comfort myself by imagining all of these men dead at my feet.

It works until the pain of the venom makes thought impossible.

Upstairs, the air is cooler. It feels soothing against the poisoned flesh burning me from the inside out. By the time I reach my room, I'm coated in sweat, and the walls are spinning before my eyes.

My breath comes in gasps, but I refuse to give in. Not here. Where Gregario can still touch me under the ruse of helping me.

"Mac!"

My mother's voice is shrill, very near to a scream. She rushes up the steps behind me, but the guards at my back block her before she can reach me.

"Take your fucking hands off me," she warns them.

They release her but keep their feet planted.

"No visitors," Gregario tells her. "Boss's orders."

She glares at him. "I'm her mother, asshole."

"Take it up with the alpha," he says.

She looks like she might just break him in half, but, in the end, she backs down. Glancing past him to me, she says, "I'll see you soon."

Then she retreats.

At the end of the hall, I clutch the doorknob and push my way into a space I can only hope will feel safe until I can regain my strength.

The door slams shut behind me, sealing me in and those assholes out. For now.

In the solitude, I concentrate on my breathing. On remaining upright long enough to stumble to my bed.

Jadick wants me to fight. He's never hidden that fact before. Up until now, I've refused to bait him by giving him that fight. But after what Kari told me, I'm not stupid enough to bide my time any longer.

Jadick thinks he has me cornered. He thinks he's trapped me like a little mouse he'll toy with until he's finally bored and done.

But I'm done playing his game.

Now, I'll play mine.

Unless, of course, the venom takes me first.

SLEEP IS A CLOYING, suffocating thing. I toss and turn, unaware of the passing of time. Someone enters my room at some point, but my fever makes it impossible to recognize who or what has joined me. Hands press against my cheeks. I can't fight back, nor can I summon the energy to respond. A voice murmurs words that are garbled in my clogged ears. My wolf is nothing more than a ghost inside me, hiding from the poison.

My senses fail me, and then I'm sucked away from consciousness, lost to the storm.

When I wake again, my brain is foggy, and my eyes are swollen nearly shut.

I can't remember how I got here. Or where here is.

All I register are screams.

The sounds are muffled through my closed door. The light through the window is gray—making it impossible to decipher time of day. Or which day I've woken to.

It could be dawn. Or it could be storm clouds.

All I know is someone is hurting.

I hope it's Jadick.

Or one of his men.

Or all of them.

Another scream sounds, echoing in muted horror through the alpha house.

I try to sit up, but the pain drives me back again.

Gasping, I realize my eyes have flown wider as I sense movement beside me. Hands. Pressing against my shoulders. Cupping my cheeks. Lips. Trailing over my burning skin.

I try to scream, but the hand closes over my mouth.

Through heavy-lidded eyes, a face swims into view.

Recognition slams through me, but even this feels like a lie. A product of the poison.

It's not him.

It can't be.

He left me. No, I drove him away.

"It's all right." Levi's words nearly break me. Not the fact that he says them when they're so obviously a lie but the softness in his tone. The way he seems happy to see me. The fact that he came for me at all.

I break down, sobbing and nearly choking with the effort.

Levi makes it worse by reaching for me and pulling me into his arms.

He's holding me.

After I rejected him.

This is the worst kind of dream, really.

I'd rather die than hallucinate this.

"She's a fucking mess," someone else says.

Tripp.

His matter-of-factness cuts through the haze of hallucination. It's my first clue that this might be real.

Pushing Levi away, I lean back so I can look at them both.

They look down at me, faces full of concern. Levi's expression is softer, though still full of intensity. Tripp, however, is a splash of cold water as he curls his lip and scans my body.

"You look like shit," he announces. "Again. What the fuck, Mac? You can't stay out of trouble, can you?"

It's real.

I sob again, wincing at the pain the movement brings.

"Whoa, kidding," Tripp says.

Another scream sounds, and Levi tries to soothe me, but Tripp is all business.

"This is not a cuddle sesh, bro."

"Grey didn't tell us the fucking bullet was laced with poison," Levi hisses.

"For real?" Tripp leans in to look at my shoulder then swears.

"I'm going to kill Jadick," Levi says.

"Later," Tripp says. "We stick to the plan until she's safe."

"We need to get her the fuck out of here," Levi says, lifting me into his arms. "Now."

"You don't have to fucking tell me," Tripp mutters.

He starts for my bedroom door, but it bursts open before I can tell them how crazy this is. That they're here at all. That they think they can just walk out the front entrance like Jadick won't kill them on sight.

Grey stands in the open doorway, chest heaving with labored breaths. Otherwise, he's in one piece. "You have two minutes to get down the back staircase and out the staff exit through the kitchen," he says. "After that, I have to try to kill you again."

"Try being the operative word," Tripp says.

Grey doesn't bother to respond. He's already gone.

"We have to move quickly," Levi says, looking down at me. "It's going to hurt."

Somewhere in the house, something crashes. Furniture maybe. And glass.

I cling to Levi, not caring whether my grip is too tight or my helplessness is too humiliating. "Go," I gasp. "As fast as you have to. Just don't stop."

He nods and looks at Tripp. "Lead the way, Janitor Tripp."

Tripp's out the door like a shot.

He knows the way, thanks to his bathroom duties, and he moves like a shadow. Like he and Levi trained to do for so long after defecting from Crigger's authority years ago. Even with me in his arms, Levi glides softly from shadow to shadow. His footsteps make no sound as he and Tripp make their way down the back stairs and through the staff halls.

No one stops us.

I have no idea how that's possible.

This place is like a prison. But today—tonight?—in this unreadable gray light, Levi and Tripp are ghosts.

And now, so am I.

We reach the kitchen, and another figure comes forward from the shadows.

I nearly scream until I see their face.

Frankie Dyer.

Her gray-blonde hair is combed back as usual, and her steel-blue eyes are unwavering. She's always been a badass since the moment she marched up to me and shut down the haters back at Levi's compound. But in this moment, that steel is intensified.

She tosses Tripp a set of keys that he snatches effortlessly out of the air.

"Truck's parked at the end of the drive," she says then glances at me. "Get your ass healed, Mac. And then give 'em hell. Do you hear me?"

"Yes, ma'am."

I mumble the words, but she's already gone, slipping back into the house where she'll continue to pretend loyalty to the man we all want to kill.

But that's for another day, apparently.

"This way," Tripp says, motioning for Levi to follow.

We slip out the side door, and I find myself underneath a heavy gray sky full of rain clouds. In the distance, thunder rolls. Or maybe furniture has just broken again, I can't be sure.

We're halfway across the stone-paved drive when the door bursts open behind us. A trio of soldiers pours out—all of them wearing the alpha guard uniform. I stiffen, recognition slamming through me as I remember their faces from the leering and catcalls while I bled all over Jadick's office rug.

"Hey," one of them shouts. "Stop."

"What's our other option?" Tripp calls lazily.

In answer, one of them pulls a gun from a hip holster and aims it at us.

Levi curses and hesitates. I tighten my grip on his shirt, terrified he's going to abandon me. That maybe I'm not worth the trouble after all.

"Relax, Mac," he says under his breath. "It's you and me." He pauses and then asks, "Do you trust me?"

He doesn't look at me. His eyes are fixed on the enemy. The target. And something about that focus comforts me. He's going to kill them with me in his arms, and even with the venom burning its way through my consciousness, I have never loved him more than I do right now.

"I trust you," I whisper.

He spares me a glance, eyes glinting. "Good girl. Now hang on."

I do.

He doesn't wait for the men to react before he takes off. Instead of hauling ass down the long driveway, he darts left and slides behind one of the duty cars. It's an SUV like the one I rode in on the day we arrived. Tinted windows. Bullet proof armor.

The gun fires anyway, and the three soldiers fan out. An instant later, Tripp is beside us, looking more annoyed than anything.

He catches my eye and winks—and then he's gone again.

One of the soldiers cries out. A body falls with a *thunk* on the stone drive. Levi spins out from around the hood, using me as a weight to gain momentum. My heel shoves into the guard's gut, and it drives him back, thanks to the force Levi's put behind it. I wince, biting back a shriek of pain at the way the impact ignites the poison inside me.

The man is knocked off balance, and Levi wastes no time kicking out against his kneecap. Something snaps, and the man yells as he goes down. Levi kicks the gun from his hand, and it skitters away.

Tripp picks it up and chucks it right back to Levi, who adjusts his grip on me so that he catches the weapon midair with his free hand.

He fires at the third soldier just before the man can barrel into us.

The bullet tears a hole through his chest and drops him immediately.

Then everything is quiet again.

"You okay?" he asks me.

I ignore the pain each movement causes. I'm alive. So is he. That's what matters.

"Yes."

"Let's get you out of here," he says.

Levi and Tripp begin moving, slower this time, wary as we make our way down the drive. We use trees, cars, and anything else we can as cover. But whatever chaos has broken out inside seems to be enough to keep Jadick and the rest of his men distracted.

Against every fear I have of being caught, we make it to the truck Frankie left for us.

An old pickup with more scratches than paint and a dented hood. Tripp lowers the tailgate, and Levi climbs up into the bed with me still clutched in his arms. A pile of blankets has been tossed down, and I brace myself because no amount of bedding is going to be enough to cushion my body against what's to come. But I have no other option.

From the house, a howl sounds, echoing against the velvet-gray sky.

My blood runs cold at the sound.

"That's our cue," Tripp says, his earlier cheer suddenly gone. In its place is an urgency I can practically taste on my own tongue.

Quickly, Levi lowers us both to the bed of the truck so that we're flat on our backs and tucked out of sight. Tripp slams the tailgate back into place and rounds the truck, climbing into the driver's seat and starting the engine.

I bite my lip, knowing this is going to hurt like hell against my already tortured body. Levi turns and reaches over, pulling me onto my side to face him.

His breath hits my nose, and I drink it in, my eyes burning with tears that suddenly have nothing to do with the poison coating my veins.

"Hang on to me," he whispers, using his own hands to wind my arms around his body and latch them into place against his back. Then he does the same to me.

The truck revs as Tripp hits the gas, and we lurch forward. My breath catches at the suddenness of the motion, my hands fisting in the fabric of Levi's shirt. Our eyes meet and hold through every pot hole and every lurching turn as Tripp drives us out of Blackstone and toward a freedom I never thought I'd have again.

"Don't let go," I whisper to Levi.

"I never did."

CHAPTER 7

Instead of pain from the jostling, I am sucked into a nothingness that feels dangerously easy. Poison. Pain. The urgency of running for our lives. None of that matters here. None of it can touch me.

Touch.

My attempt to remain in the darkness is eventually interrupted by a pair of hands.

They sweep across my skin, tucking my hair behind my ears. Running in circles across my back then pausing along my shoulder where Jadick shot me. I tense, bracing myself for pain even in this half-consciousness. But the hands move away, trailing lightly down my arms. Over my hip. Tucking underneath my prone body.

In the next moment, I'm lifted up and out of the truck. Out of the darkness and into the light. A dim glow that feels familiar. Or maybe it's the familiar scent.

Like a memory.

The hands lay me down again, this time against something softer than the unforgiving truck bed. A real bed then. A mattress, anyway. Despite its softness, I don't bother opening my eyes. I'm not ready to return to the world.

Though, the hands are nice.

They don't leave me. Resting carefully against my ribs as whoever they belong to speaks to someone else. I listen as their deep voices murmur quietly.

Their even tone is soothing, the familiarity comforting. Their words float over me, but I can't bring myself to react. It's too much.

I've hurt too long.

"...should have come out of it by now."

Tripp.

He's worried.

I want to tell him to chill, but that would require moving my lips. An effort I'm not ready to make.

"The bullet was dipped in venom." Levi sounds furious. "That makes three times in two months."

"Four, actually," Tripp corrects.

"What?"

"She was stabbed in Green Hills. Long story. Relax, the asshole's dead," he adds, and Levi blows out a breath.

"Thanks."

"Not me," Tripp says. And then, after a pause, "We never should have left her."

Levi doesn't say anything.

"Grey said Jadick really took her down a notch with that gunshot wound," Tripp says quietly. "Apparently, he refused to let the docs treat her for it."

"I heard the story," Levi says in a hard voice. Like he doesn't want to hear it again.

"What you didn't hear is that Jadick made her walk naked and covered in a thin blanket all the way back to her room while Gregario and those asshole guards just stood back and watched."

More quiet. This time, I'm pretty sure it includes teeth-grinding.

"Why does he want to marry her?" Levi asks. "It doesn't make any sense. He doesn't give a shit about her."

Tripp sighs. "Who knows? But none of it changes the fact that he needs to be taken out."

Levi grunts at that.

I want to tell them. That Jadick has found a witch. That he's planning to use me for some kind of ritual-murder that will ensure fated mates are a thing of the past for our pack. That all he needs now are the bones of his ancestors to make it happen. But words won't come. Awareness is too far out of reach.

Eventually, Tripp asks, "You think the herbs will be enough this time?"

Levi's quiet for a beat too long before he says, "They'll have to be."

I listen to the sounds of rustling and movement. Then, something cool is pressed to my wound. A bottle of water held to my lips. I drink, and that seems to appease some of their worry.

But then I feel the ether reaching for me, and I let it carry me away again.

When I wake, the air reeks of something bitter and rotten. I wrinkle my nose, coughing against the acrid odor. Leaning over the bed, I feel the contents of my stomach roil with the depth of my gagging.

I vomit until there's nothing left.

Beside me, the mattress moves, and a chiseled body leans over me, holding a shallow pan beneath my mouth. It's not necessary, but I don't bother trying to say so.

When the coughing subsides, I force myself to breathe through my mouth, and finally, against my best judgment, I open my eyes and look around.

We're in a van. Levi's van, if memory serves.

I have no idea how he managed to get it back or where it's been. Where he's been.

Living in the van from the looks of it.

The mattress is the only clear space, and that's because we're currently on it. Besides that, clothes and various gear litter the front two seats and the console between. A short counter is wedged against the wall behind the driver's seat. It's stacked with trash and takeout wrappers. Bottles of water, most empty, have been tossed or wedged underneath the seats.

The smell isn't coming from any of that, though.

In fact…

I sniff again, following my nose—

The smell is coming from me.

"I think I'm going to—"

Levi shoves the pan underneath my face, and I vomit again.

Except, there are no contents.

I dry heave until my ribs ache.

"What is that smell?" I croak, and Levi sighs.

"It's the herbs," he says, but he removes the poultice from my shoulder and crawls over to toss it out the van door. Yanking the door shut, he stops short of returning to bed. A bed we have been apparently sharing until now.

Our eyes meet, and words fail me.

Dark hair hangs over his brow, framing magnetic brown eyes that hold me captive. His jawline is covered in stubble, a new look for him. Rougher, somehow. I have no idea how he can possibly be sexier than I remember, considering how mouthwatering he's always looked. He is, though. Sexier. It's in his eyes. This hunger— like a heartbeat that pulses only for me.

The dark shadows beneath his eyes only accentuate the need in his gaze.

He's fucking beautiful.

It's nearly unbearable, being here, looking at him. Close enough to touch. After everything. My stomach churns as heartbreak and joy threaten to choke me.

"I might throw up again," I blurt.

His eyes widen, and he reaches for the pan but I shove it away, my cheeks burning because, wow. Not the way I want to break the tension.

"I'm okay," I assure him. "False alarm, I guess."

He lowers himself to the edge of the bed, careful to keep his distance. "You sure?"

I nod. "Where's Tripp?"

"He went to make contact with Grey and Frankie. Let them know we made it out."

We're alone then.

And instantly, the knowledge of that makes it awkward. Or maybe it's the fact that I never thought I'd see him again. Not like this. Alive. Alone. And without some threat of violence hanging over us. All of the things I laid awake and imagined saying seem to slip away from me now.

Instead, I glance out the window behind him and see that we're parked in a wooded area. Secluded. Somewhere overhead, sunlight streams through thick branches, the light already waning toward afternoon. Through the front windshield, I spot a picnic table and a fire pit.

"Where are we?" I ask.

"A campground outside of Lynchburg," he says.

"No phone service this far out?" I ask, thinking of Tripp's absence. Is he gone out of necessity for the mission or because Levi told him to get lost?

"We aren't carrying cell phones for tracking reasons. Tripp ran into town to buy a prepaid phone to make the call. We're safe out here. No one will mess with us."

He's calm, clearly unconcerned with being followed. Then again, I was probably out long enough for them to drive in circles to be sure. Still, my nerves are a bit shot where Jadick's concerned. And the roiling in my stomach is making it hard to chill out.

Or maybe that's due to the fact that he keeps emphasizing how alone we really are. Levi and me. No distractions. For once.

Nervous, I rub a hand absently over my abdomen, and Levi's gaze flicks to the motion.

He frowns. "Those herbs are strong. They're going to make you queasy for a while."

"What kind of herbs?"

"Aconitum. It works like an antidote to the venom. It binds the toxin in your blood and helps eliminate it quickly."

I snort. "I've got the eliminate part down."

He offers a weak half-smile. "You're alive."

"Barely."

His smile drops. "Mac."

He looks like he wants to hug me. Or maybe even kiss me. My memory flashes to the truck bed where he held me close and cushioned me against every bump and dip in the road. My heart cracks as I realize he's doing the very thing I never did for him. He's forgiving me.

"I don't deserve this," I whisper, my eyes filling with hot tears.

They spill over, streaking down my cheeks, one after the other. Sin after sin. Wrong after wrong. Failure after failure.

Levi softens, and it's the softness that breaks me.

I let out a sob and then choke another one back. He picks me up, pulling me into his arms until I'm curled into a ball against his hard chest. I ignore the discomfort of my own body and, instead, focus on the comfort of his. He rocks me, soothing and whispering and patting my hair. He doesn't try to stop me from crying, which is good because there's no holding it back even if I wanted to.

By the time I can breathe again, his shirt is tear-stained, and my cheeks are flushed. But I'm a bit lighter. Able to breathe again.

I also have no more excuses.

Slowly, I pick my head up off his shoulder and meet his eyes. My cheeks burn with shame as I force the words up and out of my throat.

"Levi, I'm so sorry."

Saying it out loud brings the threat of more tears still.

"No apology necessary," he says.

His response brings me up short, and I blink up at him.

"You have nothing to be sorry for," he says.

"I rejected you," I say, confused and determined to convince him how horrible I've been. "And didn't tell you what was coming. The deal I made—"

"You saved me," he says, cutting me off. "You did what no one else could. You stopped Kari and saved my life. And you did it without unnecessary bloodshed between the packs. I owe you my life, Mac."

"You don't owe me anything," I say, but my argument feels weaker now.

He smiles. "Are we fighting about whether we should be fighting? Because there's a certain irony in this moment, and I just want to point out that I didn't start it. For once."

I swat his arm, and he grins.

"You're impossible," I tell him.

"It does feel impossible," he says quietly. His smile drops away, but his eyes still sparkle with something. "You and me. Here. Back in this van."

Butterflies dance and dip in my stomach as I think of the last time we were here.

"It's like we get a do-over," he says.

"Is that what you think?" I ask wryly. "That we can just pretend everything that happened after we left this van—after you *kidnapped* me—never happened?"

"I mean, not everything. That night we spent at the alpha house was pretty amazing."

I fight a smile. "I'm going to hit you again."

"I think I could take you right now."

"That's your plan?" I ask, but there's no anger in my voice. "Exert your superior strength over me—again? Hold me against my will —again?"

He leans closer, his gaze on my mouth. "I want to hold you, Mac. More than you can possibly imagine. But I won't do anything against your will. Not ever again."

He holds my gaze, silent.

Waiting for me to accept his words. To accept him.

I inhale, the butterflies in my stomach batting their way up my chest. Into my heart. Some of the cracks there feel like maybe they're not quite so broken after all.

When I reach for Levi, my hand trembles. He catches it with his own hand and holds tight.

"Is that a yes?" he asks.

"It's an 'I need to brush my teeth before anything happens.'" I grimace, but his lips twitch.

"Done." He hands me a tooth brush and then waits while I brush my teeth and swipe a washcloth over my face. When I'm done, he's still there, hovering impatiently.

"What?" I ask.

"You haven't answered my question," he points out, brow lifting in playful challenge. "Is it a yes?"

I drop the washcloth and turn to face him, the bed just behind my knees.

"If I say it is, will you stop being so fucking nice?"

He grins, and then he's on top of me. Knocking me backward onto the mattress and lowering his mouth to mine. His kiss isn't nice at all. It's the opposite of nice. It's delicious and fiery and fierce and rude—his tongue plunging into my mouth without waiting for permission.

My skin heats, but this isn't poison.

This is healing.

I wrap my legs around his so he can't escape.

Never again will Levi get past me. He's mine now. And I'm his. I don't care what Jadick's stupid engagement deal says. I don't belong to that monster; I belong to this one.

Or I plan to.

Levi's mouth demands more, and I arch my back, willing and ready to give it. But he abandons my lips to trail kisses down my throat. He steers away from my wounded shoulder, but he doesn't handle me gently like before. He uses me, takes what he wants, and it's all I can do to press myself against him to give it.

He nips at my breast through the fabric of my shirt, and my breath catches. Then he sits up, grabbing my shirt in both of his hands. With a quick, deliberate move, he rips the fabric away, and I gasp as he slides his hands against my back, unhooking my bra and sliding it from my body.

He stares down at my bared body with a desperate sort of desire. My skin tingles with anticipation. "You're so fucking beautiful," he breathes. And then he's on me again, his mouth closing over my already hardened nipple, his tongue flicking its peak.

Heat pools between my legs, my core aching.

I hook my hands into the waistband of his pants, shoving at them in frustration. His hard length presses into my thigh, and I rock my hips against it, panting as he works my nipple lightly between his teeth.

"Levi," I gasp.

He growls, the sound vibrating from deep in his throat, and then he peels himself away again, and I'm left suddenly feeling abandoned. He stands, his head brushing the top of the raised roof, and smirks down at me. I watch, rapt, as he unbuttons his pants and lets them fall to the floor. He's wearing nothing underneath, and his erection springs free.

I drag my gaze up to his and glare. "Get back here."

But he doesn't move except to arch a brow. "You don't give the orders anymore, Mac."

I scowl, opening my mouth to argue, but he leans over me, his hands splayed on either side of my thighs. "I told you I wouldn't do anything to you against your will. I never said I'd actually do what you tell me."

He winks.

Before I can answer, he hooks his fingers around my underwear and peels them off. I shiver, but not from the cold. From him. The way he looks me over. I'm more exposed now than I've ever been. But I'm not afraid. Not when Levi leans down and runs his tongue over my clit. I buck, arching my hips while also shrinking away. But I have nowhere to go. He does it again, and I think I might break apart. Then, he's kissing and sucking and fucking me with his tongue, and I have no more thoughts to think.

Only the feel of his mouth on my needy body and my building orgasm.

It slams through me even before I can warn either of us it's coming.

A moan slips up my throat, and I let myself soar with the weight-lessness of the pleasure. Levi doesn't stop, only slows until my orgasm has run its course. Even then, his short licks and tiny kisses are a tease that make me want more.

I grab his shoulders, tugging him up to where I lie.

"Levi," I say, and it comes out as a whimper.

His eyes twinkle with enjoyment at that, but I don't care. I'm so far past caring—or winning. I just want him.

"Please," I say.

"Please what?"

I don't even hesitate or argue. There's no denying that he's in charge of this. I want everything he's giving, and he knows it.

"Make me come again," I tell him.

He answers by sliding inside me, pushing farther and farther until I gasp and tense around his length. His arms grip the mattress beside me, and I watch his jaw tense as he struggles to set a slow pace.

But my orgasm doesn't want slow.

I rock my hips harder against him. Faster. My urgency consumes me, the pleasure eclipsing any pain I might have felt from my injuries. Levi's gaze darkens, his breathing shorter and shorter as he increases the pace. I cling to him, legs wrapped tight around his thighs as the pleasure builds.

At the very edge, he looks at me and says, "Now, Mac," as if he knows. As if he can feel it too.

My wolf stirs, the shifter magic rising to meet the moment. The air crackles with tension I've never felt before. A growl rips from Levi's lips, his skin rippling with the beast inside him.

My canines elongate, aching for his skin.

I want to bite him.

To claim him as mine. Fully. Finally.

"Come for me, Mac."

Levi kisses me, and I feel his sharpened teeth scraping my lips. Lightly. Not quite enough to draw blood but still, it's delicious. And more than enough to send me soaring over the edge of bliss a second time. This time, when I let go, every shattered piece of me goes with it.

CHAPTER 8

*L*evi drapes his arm over my bared ribs, pulling me closer against him. He's on his stomach, probably asleep by now, his face buried against the side of my neck. I, on the other hand, am wide awake. My thoughts are a swirling mess. Imagining what Jadick is doing now that I'm gone. Wondering if my mother will be safe without me. Hating that I care. And thinking of how we might possibly salvage such an epically fucked up situation as this one.

I can never go back; that much is obvious. If I do, I'd be giving Jadick exactly what he needs for that awful ritual Kari spoke of. Still, the idea of staying gone leaves me strangely empty. It shouldn't bother me—being forced out of pack lands. Especially considering the alpha now in charge of those lands. But… I can't change the fact that Blackstone is my home. Or it was.

I can't shake the knowing that my mother is still there. Not to mention Grey, Frankie, and every single Jade we've left behind. I haven't seen Nely or Lorenz since Jadick beat Kari, but I know they're out there.

I can't run.

Not forever.

For the first time in months, I'm safe. And yet, all I can think about is getting back to the danger.

"What are you thinking about?"

Levi's voice is low and silky smooth. I shiver at the delicious way it rolls over my skin. When I look over, he's angled his head up so his eyes can find mine. But he's still lying cozily against me.

I try to move, but he responds by throwing his leg over my torso, pinning me. "Uh-uh. Answer the question." I scowl, and he rolls his eyes. "You're worse than I am."

"At what?" I ask.

"Being seen."

I don't know how to argue that exactly. But in the end, I don't have to. The van door opens, and I stiffen as a figure moves in the doorway. When I see Tripp climbing inside, my relief is short-lived. Levi reaches for the blanket and pulls it over me just in time to avoid giving a full show.

"Gross, you two." Tripp wrinkles his nose and takes a hard right, dumping himself into the front passenger seat. "Get a room."

"The van is the room, bro," Levi tells him pointedly.

Tripp casts his eyes to the ceiling. "No way. Absolutely not. This is now a studio apartment, and I am the third wheel residing in said apartment. There will be no shenanigans while I'm present. Is that clear?"

Levi pretends to think about it.

Tripp turns back, an incredulous glare scrunching his features. "I'm serious," he says.

"Yeah, yeah," Levi says, not nearly convincing enough.

Tripp throws a candy bar at Levi. It hits him in the shoulder, but he just snatches it and rips it open, offering me a bite.

I shake my head, pressing my lips together to keep from smiling.

This is something I could never explain with words, but it's the thing I've missed most in the last few years. My heart aches and fills at the same time as the guys continue their banter. Arguing about dinner choices. Where to put the dirty laundry. What music to play.

It's exactly what I need to heal my worst parts.

"...what do you think, Mac?" Tripp asks suddenly, and I blink, trying to catch up.

"About what?"

"Tacos or burgers for dinner?" Levi asks, and I can hear it in his voice, the amusement and concern rolled into one note. He knows I'm still trying to find my way back to this—to normal.

I start to answer that food is probably not a good idea right now, considering my upset stomach. But then I realize I'm feeling much steadier than I was before. Either the herbs are working—or the sex is. Either way, I could eat.

"Always tacos," I say, and Levi groans as Tripp hoots.

"I fucking told you she would say that," Tripp declares. He slides into the driver's seat and turns the ignition. "Taco Tuesday—on a Thursday—all day," he says.

Levi waits until Tripp's looking at the road and then steals a kiss.

"Busted," Tripp says, eyeing us in the rearview.

"I'll put a dollar in the jar," Levi says, smug.

But Tripp makes a face. "I don't want your sex-money, bro."

"Sex-money?" I echo, "Really?"

"Dirty money," he insists.

"He's not wrong," Levi says. "We are pretty dirty."

My cheeks flush. This is new. Not the banter and the sarcasm. Or the flinging insults. But the sexual references tossed in. It's not territory we've ever covered before. Even in high school, Levi and I hadn't reached this place yet.

But Levi and Tripp slide right into their roles.

Teasing. Laughing.

I join in, grateful for some semblance of a normal life. Even if it is temporary. Part of me knows I should end this little game of theirs. Stop pretending we're not fugitives. Or that I'm not engaged to a monster who will inevitably kill them to get me back. I still need to explain what Kari told me before she... before I put her out of her misery. And mine. But I can't quite bring myself to shatter the illusion. Not yet. Soon.

In Lynchburg, we get tacos and eat in the van, Tripp in the front seat, and Levi and me on the mattress. Somewhere during the process, I sit up and pull away. My crossed legs and tucked body language don't faze Levi, though. He leans against the far wall with his legs sprawled across the pile of blankets, his calf resting against my ankle.

Subtle.

While Tripp regales me with their hilarious camping stories, Levi catches my eye and sends me flirty winks.

My stomach flutters.

It's so stupid. That I feel this butterfly-nerves sensation over him. A guy I chose seven years ago as a crush and then a boyfriend and finally a mate. But it's there, and I find my cheeks heating in a blush and my head dipping in shy embarrassment, which only seems to egg him on.

"All I'm saying," Tripp goes on, "Is that van camping is one thing, but we really need to make a rule that says bathroom breaks need to be done in public restrooms only—or in wolf form."

At my expression, he adds, "I've seen too much of your boy here, and it's not okay."

I laugh and stuff the rest of my taco into my mouth.

"Damn," Levi says, still flirting. "Impressive."

"Imagine what I can do with a burger," I say, except it's muffled and comes out "Imuja wuh Ikiidoo wifuh buhguh."

Levi and Tripp both crack up.

"Did you just make a joke?" Tripp asks.

I chew and swallow. "So?"

"Write that down," he tells Levi. "It's a big day."

"I tell jokes," I say, defensive now.

"Uh, no, beautiful." Levi shakes his head slowly. "You really don't."

"But you're pretty. And you love tacos. And you can fight," Tripp says, ticking off the list on his hand. "So, we'll keep you around."

"Will you?" I ask before I can stop myself.

They go quiet.

And now it's too late to take it back. I've returned us to the present world. To the pain of our past and the uncertainty of our future.

"Will you keep me around this time?" I ask, my voice suddenly small and unsure.

I feel silly and terrified even asking this question. But Levi and Tripp exchange a look, and then they move as one. Levi chucks aside what's left of his taco—what a waste—and Tripp pushes to his feet, launching himself across the space toward me in a sort of Superman move.

I shriek as Levi leaps after him and they both land on me in a dogpile.

Arms come around me.

It's like a bear hug from two toddlers.

"You're not going anywhere," Tripp says, his voice muffled.

My heart warms at their words. And the hug. Even though it's hard to breathe.

After a beat, Levi says, "Okay, enough hugging." He shoves Tripp aside, who, thankfully, is quick enough to land on his feet instead of his ass.

"Wow," Tripp says, "Seriously? I can give my friend a hug if I want to."

"You could," Levi shoots back, "if you weren't both already horizontal."

Tripp pins me with a sour look. "Don't let him go all alphahole on your ass."

"Believe me, the only alphahole here is me," I tell him.

They both laugh at that way harder than necessary.

Assholes.

CHAPTER 9

*L*ater that night, the heat of the campfire warms my face. It's colder here up in the foothills of the Blue Ridge. But the crackling fire in the center of our circle makes it cozy. Not to mention my wolf warming me from the inside out. I haven't thrown up again and am already feeling stronger, thanks to the herbs and the food. My shoulder is slowly beginning to regain function, but I am still mostly one-handed as I try to balance the stick on my lap and shove a marshmallow onto the end without dropping it all.

"Here," Levi says, grabbing the stick to keep it stable until I'm finished.

"Thanks," I tell him and then hold the marshmallow out toward the flames.

Across the fire, Tripp watches me with a contemplative expression.

"What?" I ask warily.

I suspect they've both been purposely trying to keep my mind off things. And it's actually worked—somewhat. It's also reminded me of the friendship I've missed so much over the years. But I keep waiting for them to finally circle back around to the actual elephant in the room.

Instead, he says, "Only toddlers and serial killers like their marshmallows flaming rather than toasted."

I glance at where my marshmallow is just beginning to catch the flame and smirk. "You're obviously uncultured when it comes to making a proper s'more," I tell him.

He snorts, and Levi grins, content to let us argue.

"You have no idea what you're talking about, Quinn." Tripp waits while I inspect my burning marshmallow. Deeming it properly crispy, I bring it toward my mouth and blow out the flames engulfing it.

Levi's right there with the graham cracker covered in chocolate.

Smashing the whole thing together, I trade the stick for the melting treat and bite off half. The heat from the marshmallow makes me wince, but it's worth it.

"Mmmm," I say around the mouthful.

It's possible my eyes roll back in my head a little.

And the nostalgia brought on by the flavors isn't lost on me either.

Tripp just shakes his head at me in mock disgust. "Monster," he says and then goes back to slowly roasting his own marshmallow. It's barely turned brown at the edges by the time he pulls it in and builds his own dessert sandwich.

Two pieces of chocolate. One mostly raw marshmallow.

"You're so weird," I say, laughing as he stuffs the entire thing into his mouth and mimics my noises of appreciation.

"You'll make someone very happy with that kind of simplistic satisfaction," Levi tells him.

"Yeah, if you eat everything raw and your mate never has to cook, win," I say.

"You don't like to cook?" Levi asks, turning to me.

"I don't know. Never tried," I admit. "But I could be into hunting dinner."

He grins. "Yeah, you'd be good at that." He leans in, swiping his thumb over my lip where I've apparently made a mess of my snack. "I wouldn't mind hunting you," he adds in a whisper.

I shudder, and Tripp groans.

"I'm right fucking here," Tripp protests.

Levi snickers, but he doesn't look remotely sorry.

"Speaking of which, how much money do you have?" I ask Levi.

"Why? You want to make another marshmallow run?"

"If we're going to live like this forever, we need a second van," I say.

Levi's grin is devious. "I like where your head's at, Quinn."

"Screw both of you," Tripp says.

"No thanks," Levi tells him.

Tripp throws a marshmallow that hits Levi square in the chest. Levi just picks it up and stuffs it into his mouth, looking triumphant.

"When I have a mate, I'm going to bang her loudly and often," Tripp says.

I laugh.

Levi chuckles.

"In your van," Tripp adds, clearly not getting the reaction he was going for.

"Uh." Levi's smile drops.

Tripp looks like he's won, and I can't help getting the last word so I toss out, "Okay, but you might want to get a new mattress first."

Tripp's disgust makes it clear he's given me the victory on this round after all.

THE NEXT MORNING, the sound of the van door opening jolts me awake. I sit up too fast on my elbows and then gasp at the sudden pain in my shoulder. Tripp freezes at my panic then relaxes, pushing the driver's side door wider so he can slide out.

"I'm going to make coffee," he whispers. "Go back to sleep."

He closes the door softly, and I fall back against the mattress where Levi and I spent the night cuddled together.

I look over at him, hoping to catch a secret glance at him while he sleeps. But his eyes are open and already trained on mine.

The surprise of it makes my stomach flutter.

"Good morning," I say.

"Yes, it is." He pulls me closer, and I suck in a breath as his erection presses against my hip. "How'd you sleep?"

I give him a look that's the opposite of the mood his body is trying to set. "Are you serious?"

"Yeah, why?"

"Tripp's snoring kept me up half the night," I say. "Didn't you hear it?"

"Guess I'm used to it." He buries his face in my neck, and I'm suddenly very aware of how long it's been since I showered.

"Um." As much as my body wants this, my mind can't get past the hygiene issue.

He pulls back and looks over at me again. "What's up?"

I bite my lip. "Can we rain-check this until I've found a shower? And a change of clothes?"

He grins. "You worried you don't smell good enough to eat? Because you do."

His teeth nip at my earlobe, and I jump then melt against him. Okay, maybe—

The van door wrenches open, and I yank back. Levi chuckles as he backs off and we both watch as Tripp sticks his head in the van.

"You two want cream and sugar?"

I blow out a breath, and Levi barks out a laugh. "I was getting sugar all on my own."

"Nope," Tripp says. "Too much information. Get it your damn self."

He shuts the door again, leaving us alone. But the mood from earlier has settled into something else. Finally, after a full day of just *being*, I see Levi's expression shifting toward something more serious.

I tense, even though I know it's time.

"Can I ask you something?" I blurt before he can start.

"Sure."

I hesitate but then shove the words out. "Why didn't you claim me? Yesterday, I mean. When we were... Did you not have, you know, the urge?"

My heart thuds like a hammer against my ribs.

His brow creases. "Is that what you think? That I didn't want you?"

"I don't know." I try to shrug like this is casual. Like it doesn't matter to me more than anything else I've done in my life. Like I'll be fine if he fully rejects me in this moment. "I thought you maybe just decided we're better off apart. At least, in that way. And I mean, that's fine. It's not like—"

"Whoa, it's not fine." He frowns. "Mac, I want you. In all the ways that matter. In all the ways that don't. I want to eat s'mores with you every night. I want to live in this van with you. I want to keep you safe. I want to claim you."

His words send a shiver down my spine. Okay, maybe not the living in the van part. But the rest.

"Then why didn't you?"

"I told you I wouldn't do anything against your will ever again, and I meant it. You need to want this. Us. Mates. It's not as simple as our wolves wanting each other. If we claim one another, there's no taking it back. Jadick will know."

His expression darkens as he says the name.

My fists clench. But I see his point.

"You think he'll do something terrible if he realizes I've rejected him."

"As it stands, you can never go back there," he says quietly. "But your mom... the Jades... If you claim me, he'll feel it. And he won't hesitate to take his anger out on one of them. Just to punish us."

I sigh. He's right, of course. I hadn't thought about it. I'd only thought of how much I wanted him.

"I hate that this is your life now," he adds.

"What? Free?"

"An outcast. A hunted criminal. No home. I want to give you more than that."

"You have," I say softly.

But he doesn't look convinced. Suddenly, he sits up, his expression fierce now. Determined. "Jadick's not one to just give up. He's going to keep hunting you."

"Until we stop him," I say, and Levi nods grimly.

"Exactly."

This is it. The thing I've watched us avoid for the last twenty-four hours. Once we say it out loud, the clock starts. Our life of campfires and s'mores is over.

"I saw Kari."

He stares at me for a beat longer than necessary. Then he gets up and heads for the van door.

"Where are you going?"

"To get Tripp," he says. "He needs to hear this too."

He opens the door and sticks his head out, calling for Tripp to move his ass. A few seconds later, Tripp hurries up with three cups of coffee balanced in his hands.

"Breakfast is served," he says, passing them around.

I take one but don't bring it to my lips. Tripp senses the shift in mood as he climbs in and settles himself in the passenger seat, turning it so he can face Levi and me on the mattress.

"What's up?" he asks warily.

Levi looks at me expectantly.

"I saw Kari," I say again except, this time, they both react.

Levi stiffens, and Tripp's eyes widen.

"She's alive?" Tripp asks.

"Not—Not anymore." I can feel Levi's eyes on me, but I don't look at him. "Jadick was holding her hostage, torturing her for information."

"What kind of information?" Tripp asks.

"The kind involving Jadick's true intentions for me." Quickly, I tell them what Kari told me about using my blood—and death—as a ritual sacrifice to end fated mates forever. "Apparently, Kari killed Crigger because she knew that's what Jadick was planning to do. He needs the bones of his ancestors for the ritual. It's the only thing he's missing."

"Fuck me," Tripp breathes. "This is crazy. Here I thought he just wanted to psycho-love you."

I give him a look. "You're so weird."

"Why you?" Levi asks, interrupting Tripp's reply. "Why does he need your blood specifically for this?"

"I don't know. We were interrupted before Kari could tell me that part."

"And by interrupted, you mean you were shot in the shoulder," Tripp provides.

I scowl.

"You haven't told us how it happened," Levi says quietly.

"I tried to run," I say. "After what Kari said, I just wanted out, so I made a break for it. Made it into Jadick's office where I knew there'd be an easy exit. Only, not so easy. He got off a lucky shot. And then I tore a hole in his leg."

"Whoa, seriously?" Tripp whistles as if impressed.

"I would have torn the whole thing off if he wasn't such a coward who keeps two dozen guards outside his door all the time."

Levi looks tense at the mention of the guards. I turn to him, knowing full well what kind of rage his wolf is feeling right now. "You took out three of those assholes the night you rescued me."

"Good," he says.

"Jadick's injury must be what Grey meant when he said our best shot was coming in that night." Tripp looks thoughtful. "You must have really set him back, Quinn. Nice work."

"I'll feel better when he's dead," I say.

"Can't argue there," Tripp says.

I look at Levi, whose dark expression leaves no doubt he agrees.

"We have to challenge him," I say quietly. "It's the only way."

"Not *we*," he says firmly.

My eyes narrow. "Just because you're an alpha already doesn't mean you have to do this by yourself."

"It's not about being an alpha," he says. "Besides, without pack lands—or a pack—I'm not much of an alpha."

"The Jades still belong to you," I say. "Swearing loyalty to Jadick doesn't change that."

"I'd like to think they'll choose me when it comes down to it," he says. "But in the meantime, we have to be smart. We can't just march in and expect Jadick to play fairly."

I drop my gaze. "That's exactly what he said about Kari." I look down. "It's why he waited so long to come for you."

"Hey, it's okay." He presses his hand to my cheek, drawing my gaze back to his. "He didn't come for me. You did. And I'll never forget that. Even after everything I put you through."

"Maybe we can call it even," I say, and his mouth quirks.

"I'll take that deal."

I blow out a breath. "What next? We need a plan."

"We need a safe place to think," he says. "A base we can use."

"Grey and Frankie—will they fight with us?" I ask. They both nod. "Do you think there will be others?"

Levi and Tripp share a look.

"One way to find out," Tripp says.

Levi nods, and Tripp steps out again. "I'm going to make some calls," he says before shutting the door behind him and leaving us alone.

Levi explains, "A few Jades left when Jadick first gave the ultimatum about the law. We've kept apart because it's safer, but if we had somewhere to go—somewhere safe—maybe we could get them to come to us."

"What about another Jade safe house?" I ask, "Like the mall?"

He shakes his head. "Jadick knew about them all."

He looks angry at himself. But then his eyes lighten with an idea.

He gets up, climbing toward the front. "Where are you going?" I ask.

"To check with Tripp."

"About what?"

"I think I know where we can go."

"Where?"

He doesn't answer as he opens the door and steps out. When he looks back at me, I can see he's hiding something.

"Levi," I begin.

"Do you trust me?"

The question alone is enough to soften me. "Yes."

He smiles softly and then shuts the door, leaving me alone with that speck of trust held delicately in my heart.

CHAPTER 10

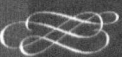

*L*evi drives, and Tripp busies himself in the back of the van with stupid road trip games. Neither one has brought up the things I told them before leaving camp. I suspect we all need time to process it. If Jadick's been planning this for months, maybe years, like Kari's story suggests, it means he played the Jades from the start. It means he's been using them to get to me all along. It's a mind fuck none of us is ready to unravel.

For almost an hour, we look for the alphabet on license plates. It's a far cry from the tense silence of riding with my mother during one of her missions. Still, my thoughts continue to drift back to her as we drive, covering a distance I have no way to measure since I still don't know where we're going.

Levi surprises me by joining in Tripp's ridiculous scavenger hunt antics. He's not one for dumb games like this, but here he is, laughing and calling out the letter X on a road sign. I give him a strange look, and he frowns over at me before glancing back at the highway again.

"What?" he asks.

"I know you're just doing this to distract me," I say.

"Is it working?" Tripp asks from the backseat.

I sigh and settle into my seat. "Sort of."

"We only have two letters left," Tripp says. "Winner takes all."

"All of what?" I ask, twisting around to look at where he's seated on the edge of the mattress. We did our best to clean up as we broke camp, but it's still a hot mess back there.

Tripp shrugs. "The glory," he says simply.

I snort. "The only glory I'm used to getting on road trips like this is spotting the mark before my mother can."

They both fall silent, our game abandoned.

Levi is the one to speak first. "You're worried about her."

It's not a question.

But my good shoulder rises and falls with a non-committal sort of "yes."

"She doesn't know what he's planning," I say.

If she knew, would it change anything? I can't bring myself to ask the question.

"She's still on Jadick's payroll," Tripp reminds me.

I lean my head back against my seat and shut my eyes. "I know."

More silence.

I've ruined the fun.

"She's doing what she thinks is best for you," Levi says quietly.

I can't help but crack an eye at that. "You think she would be on our side if she knew."

"Absolutely," he says firmly. "Your mom is a lot of things, but she loves you, and she's never going to be okay with a plan that involves you getting hurt."

Part of me wants to argue with that. To point out that she willingly helped orchestrate my engagement to Jadick. My entrapment, really. She helped make sure I'd have no choice but to agree, and then she made sure Jadick won the challenge to become alpha. Every action she's taken in the last few weeks has been wholly against what I want.

I don't say any of that. Mostly because it won't change anything. The path I'm on now no longer involves her. In fact, I'm pretty much on my own from here on. Parentless.

A hollow ache forms in my chest, and I blow out a breath. "I guess we'll see."

We cross into West Virginia, turn off the highway, and wind up in the hills on back roads that become too narrow for more than one car at a time. My curiosity piques.

"What kind of secret man cave are you taking me to?" I ask.

"Not a cave," Levi says. His brow furrows. "Well, I mean, I'm pretty sure it's not a cave."

"Why don't you give me the location, and I'll Google Earth it to be sure?" I ask innocently.

"Not a chance."

I huff.

"Mac, you've always sucked at surprises," Tripp says with a chuckle.

"Or maybe it's the surprises that sucked," I shoot back. "Remember my eleventh birthday?"

He groans. "Do not remind me."

"What happened on her eleventh birthday?" Levi asks.

"Tripp bought me a Barbie."

"What's wrong with that?"

"It didn't have a head."

Levi looks both confused and disturbed at once, which is pretty much on par with my own reaction at the time. "What—"

"I wanted her to have something that she could relate to. So I made the head interchangeable with a wolf head. So her Barbie could shift."

Levi tries—and fails—not to snicker.

"Tell him where you got the head," I say.

"From your Twilight figurine collection," he mutters, shoulders sagging with fresh guilt.

Levi laughs outright. "You didn't."

"I thought she'd be stoked. She loved Barbies. And she loved Twilight. Perfect combo."

I can't help it, I laugh too, and Tripp smirks. "I told you we'd laugh about it one day."

"And I told you I'm going to get you back one day."

"Seriously? The statute of limitations on something like that must be up by now."

"Never," I say, eyes twinkling with the promise in my words.

He shudders when I aim the expression back at him. Smart.

An hour later, we've left all semblance of civilization behind. My fingers tap impatiently against the windowsill until Levi grunts at me.

I stop and, instead, rock my knees together, not even trying to appear calm anymore.

Levi only shakes his head at me.

Finally, we wind around a sharp bend, and the landscape opens to the crest of a hill. Long grass blows in a soft wind, mostly wheat-colored weeds where the cooler temperatures of higher elevation and the coming fall have already sucked the life out of the ground. In the center, where the driveway ends, stands a small house.

It's a mash-up of stone and wood. Rustic. Inviting, actually. I'm surprised at how sturdy it looks despite the eclectic use of materials. Smoke wafts lazily from a single chimney, and behind it, thick woods rise up before sloping down the hill and giving way to a view that steals my breath even from here.

"Wow, you can see for miles," I say.

Neither of the guys responds, and it takes me a moment to tear my gaze from the gorgeous view of the Blue Ridge.

When I do, I brace myself for whatever it is they've kept from me.

Then I realize.

The smoke.

Someone's home in that house.

"What is this place?" I ask as Levi pulls the van up out front and cuts the engine.

He exchanges a glance with Tripp then says, "Come on."

I get out when he does, cutting him off at the hood before he can head for the front door. "Who's in there?" I demand in a low voice.

"An ally," he says.

"Why are you refusing to tell me—"

"Mac, just trust us," Tripp says, coming up behind me.

He keeps a safe distance, though. He knows me well.

I look between them, growing more uneasy by the second.

"Levi," I begin, but he takes my hand in his and squeezes.

"It's all going to be okay," he says. "Don't be mad."

"Why would I be mad?"

Before he can answer, the cabin door opens, and a man steps out. He looks the three of us over with the same confusion I feel, but when his eyes land on me, he stills.

His scrunched shoulders fall, and his tight expression drops its guard.

"Mac?"

He takes a step forward then another.

I don't move.

I can't.

His beard is unexpected, but the rest of him—the eyes that seem older and sharper than his years... I've stared at his picture so long; I'd know him anywhere.

Not that I ever expected to see him again.

Emotion bubbles up in my throat, but I shove it down again. I've lived through torture and certain death. I can get through this. Clearing my throat, I pretend this is just another day and force out the words I never thought I'd say aloud.

"Hi, Dad."

CHAPTER 11

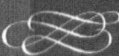

*R*obert Mackenzie hardly looks a day older than he did in the photo I once swiped from my mother; a snapshot of the two of them with me as an infant cradled between them. She swiped it back when she realized it was missing from her night-stand—and I never saw it again. Or him. In fact, I gave up even asking about him when all it ever earned me were curt replies or angry retorts. I never thought I would actually meet him in person. And now…

He's standing in the doorway of what appears to be his house.

It's surreal.

More unsettling than learning Jadick intends to kill me. That was, at least, expected of someone so obviously dark and uncaring. But this—seeing my own father in the flesh living less than a day's drive from where I grew up—is enough to make my stomach churn.

"I can't believe it's really you," he says, still shocked at the sight of me.

That makes two of us, dude.

There's zero weirdness in his expression, considering the fact that I just called him 'Dad' when he so obviously hasn't been one.

Still, now that I've spoken the words and he hasn't proved himself a figment of my imagination, I don't know what to do next.

And it's that uncertainty that has me whirling on my heel and stomping back to the van. I rip the sliding door open and climb inside then slam it closed again.

My breath comes in short bursts, and I can't bring myself to look out the front windshield, so instead, I drop my face into my hands, elbows braced on my knees as I struggle to figure out how to handle this.

Basically, I panic.

I'm a little surprised when no one comes after me. My solitude—and the roaring silence—go on so long that I finally take a deep breath and lift my head again.

Levi, Tripp, and my father are gone from the front stoop.

Casting outward with my senses, I can't find a trace of them anywhere in the yard.

I wait another moment and then warily venture out again. The van door slides closed behind me, and I pause, waiting to see who the noise will bring first.

Still, no one appears.

I debate the idea of going to the front door. My emotions are still a hot, swirling mess and my nerves are frayed from that single moment earlier. Instead of initiating what promises to be a repeat of that, I decide to explore the grounds.

Inhaling the fresh air, I round the house and make my way toward the backyard.

A small garden sits off to one side that looks well-tended. Squash, zucchini, beans, lettuce. Opposite that is a wide tree stump with an axe buried in its center. Against the house, underneath a short overhang, logs are stacked neatly.

He's homesteading. It makes sense considering the closest grocery store is probably miles out. As my thoughts race through what I assume is his life here, a scent reaches me.

Woodsmoke and ... rabbit?

I turn toward the smell and note a smoker set up opposite the garden. Hot coals line the bed beneath it. Above, a self-turning spit revolves slowly. Thin plumes of cooking smoke waft lazily into the afternoon sky.

My stomach grumbles hungrily, but as much as I want to hate this man, I won't take what's his. Or maybe that's my stubborn pride talking.

"You're welcome to help yourself."

His voice startles me, and I bite off a gasp as I turn to see my father standing near the edge of the wood pile. He pauses there as if waiting for me to acclimate to his very presence—which isn't off the mark.

A couple of steadying breaths later from me, he pushes off the wooden stake he's leaning on and strides over. I force my feet to remain planted. Mostly because I can't decide if I want to run toward him or away.

"Rabbit?" I hear myself ask.

"Caught it myself late last night," he says, passing right by where I stand and going straight to the smoker. He opens the hatch and breaks off a small hunk of meat before offering it to me.

"I'm okay," I say.

He looks as if he wants to insist, but in the end, he eats it himself. The silence between us feels full to the point of uncomfortable. He doesn't leave, though.

"Your friends explained a bit of what brought you here," he says.

I stare at him. The comment is so layered, I don't know if he means *here* like this mountain or *here* like this predicament in life. In the end, I guess they're both pretty much the same issue.

"You can stay here," he adds when I don't answer. "As long as you need."

Still, I don't reply. Every word out of his mouth renders me more speechless. Stay here? With him? I don't even know how to feel about that.

"I can't," I finally snap.

His brows lift. "You got somewhere else to hide out?"

"I'll figure something out."

He nods as if he gets it. Gets me.

Impossible.

"What about your mom?"

"She sold me out." I lift my chin. "Did they tell you that's what brought me here? Her betrayal?" He frowns, which I take as a 'no' and push on. "She made sure I had no other option but to accept a marriage proposal from the biggest alphahole that ever lived—a fiancée who intends to kill me on our wedding night in the name of pure toxic masculinity."

"Guess they left that part out," he says, the first hint of a temper working its way into his eyes. "Where's your mother now?"

"In Blackstone. Probably kissing Jadick's ass and promising him all sorts of things now that I'm gone."

"Jadick Clemons is the new alpha then."

"You know him?"

"I knew his father," he says darkly.

"Yeah, well, the apple didn't fall far. And you can thank Mom for helping to put him on that throne."

I expect him to offer up some excuse about my mother's behavior, maybe even defend her, but he ignores her involvement and asks, "Why come here then? Your mother knows where I live. She could find you here if she wanted to."

My hands ball into fists because *she knows where he lives?* What the hell? All this time, she's known where to find him and never mentioned it to me?

Anger works its way to the surface, but I shove it back, noting his watchful gaze. He's weighing my response. Like he can actually read me—a perfect stranger.

"No one bothered to tell me they were bringing me here," I eventually toss out.

When I find Levi and Tripp, I'm going to—

"Yeah, I can see that." He smirks. "If you're wondering where they went, they both ran and hid after spilling some of the story to me."

My mouth opens. "Seriously?"

I glance toward the trees, sniffing, but their scents are too muddled to pick out with the wind blowing crossways.

When I look back at my father, he's grinning. "I've never seen two grown male wolves tuck tail and run so fast. You must be pretty scary when you want to be."

"I'm going to kick their asses all the way down this mountain if that's what you mean."

He shakes his head, still smiling to himself. "You get that from your mother."

The mention of her makes me cringe. But now that he's opened the floodgates, I intend to ride the current.

"I got everything from her, apparently. And not a damn thing from you."

I brace myself for some angry comeback. But his shoulders fall. "Yeah, I can see how you'd think so."

Maybe it's the lack of fight that keeps me from biting his head off, but I keep silent as he walks to the garden and plucks a ripened cucumber right off the vine. Then he walks past me toward the house.

At the screen door, he turns back. "You coming?"

On a sigh, I follow him inside.

The house is simply furnished with an open floor plan. We enter through the kitchen where dark walnut countertops are framed by simple wooden cabinets. The dining table and chairs all look hand-carved from a lighter grain wood that complements the darker tones of the kitchen. Beyond the short breakfast bar, a deep-cushioned sofa is punctuated by an armchair on either end. The seating points toward a screen mounted over the stone hearth.

The vibe is ridiculously cozy, and despite my reservations about, well, all of this, I find myself drawn into the space. I can't help but think how easy it would be to kick my shoes off and sink into that couch, maybe watch mindless TV over a plate of smoked meat and garden veggies.

And that's exactly what he does, I realize, looking up to see my father already watching me. Like he wants to know what I think of the place.

I don't tell him I can see myself being happy in a place just like this one.

"I saw a picture of you once," I say instead. Because it's literally the only relatable thing I have left. "Mom and you sitting together with me in between. I was a baby."

His expression softens. "I remember it. One of the only pictures we ever took. She still has that?"

There's a yearning in his eyes that makes me turn away. "She got rid of it after I found it." I don't look over to see if that bothers him.

"Sure, that makes sense."

His tone is infuriatingly understanding.

I scowl, forcing myself to look right at him, this time with anger. "Does it? Because none of it makes any sense to me at all."

He walks to the counter and plucks a knife from the block. He's half-turned away from me now as he washes and slices the cucumber. Still, I cross my arms, refusing to move toward him.

In fact, maybe I should just go—

"She made me swear," he says on a weary sigh.

I stiffen because I know who he means. And I don't dare do anything to spoil this moment. My mother has never given me even this much. I want more.

"She said accepting one another as mates was a death sentence." *Slice, slice.* "She didn't want that kind of life for you. Taunted, targeted, abused." He looks up, eyes flickering to me, then quickly back down as he makes another slice. "She wanted you to have a chance. So, she made me promise to let her leave and never come looking for her. For either of you. Said if I did, it would only make your life harder."

He stops and plates a few pieces of cucumber. Then he slides it closer to me and goes back to slicing. I stare at the offering. He doesn't go on, and I have a feeling he's waiting to see what I'll do. Whether I'll accept his gift—not just the veggies but his words.

Slowly, I reach over and pick up a slice. Then I pop it into my mouth. The freshness hits my tongue. It's delicious after so much fast food.

"And that's it?" I ask. "You promised, and then you just…let her leave?"

He arches a brow at me. "Have you met your mother?"

I scowl.

He has a point. Even so…

"Your mother and I were fated. Claimed and sealed from nearly the first night we met. Our bond was unbreakable. Or so we thought. But then we had you. And from the moment I laid eyes on you, I knew there was one thing that could get me to let your mother go. Your safety was all that mattered, kid. Still is."

I take another slice of cucumber, eating slowly. "Why did she have to go back at all?" I ask. "I mean, why not stay here together? Renounce the pack?"

"I could desert easily enough," he says with a snort. "I was nobody to them. The product of a fated pairing. I grew up bullied for it too. And that's how I knew your mother was right to spare you from it. But her…" He shakes his head sadly. "She comes from one of the strongest lines in our pack's history. Her parents were warriors. Her father was a beta for years. And she'd already made a name for herself as a hunter. If she deserted, Crigger would look for her. Hell, he did come looking for her."

"He did? She never told me that." She never told me any of this.

"She wanted you to form your own opinions." His smile is wistful, his eyes glazed over with some memory. "But damn, she was a firecracker. Kicking ass with you in that baby sling. She put down half the guards he sent for her right there in the front yard—broad daylight too, which is why she did it in human form. She was a stickler for that."

I snort. My mother has always impressed upon me the need to fight in human form as well as—or better than—I can as a wolf. Now I know where that rule comes from.

"And the other half?" I press. "The guards Crigger sent?"

He looks back down at the cucumber he's finished slicing. His eyes narrow on the knife in his own hand. He carefully sets it aside and says quietly, "I made sure they were no longer a threat."

He killed them. For her. For me.

The knowledge brings with it a whirlwind of emotions I can't begin to name.

"And then she went home anyway," I say, forcing the rest of it aside.

Besides, warm fuzzies over Daddy's protection isn't the issue here. My mother's decision to force him out of our lives is.

"She did what she had to do." He turns to me then, chin raised in a stance I know well—and am shocked to realize didn't, in fact, come from my mother. "We both did."

CHAPTER 12

*L*evi's scent hits me the moment I step outside. With a quick tug, I pull the front door closed behind me and scan the yard. The sun has begun its slant toward the treetops, but there's still plenty of daylight left for me to spot him near the edge of the trees. Across the distance, he meets my eyes. My wolf stirs, a low hunger in my belly that is something I know I'll never stop feeling. Not when it comes to him.

But I ignore it as much as possible as I march over to where he waits. My conversation with my father has left me off balance but not so much that I can't pin my mate with a glare that has him wincing.

"Oh, there you are," he says in a horrible attempt to be funny.

"Where's Tripp?"

"No cell reception. He went to find a landline to check in with Frankie—"

"Did you know?" I demand. Levi's shoulders sag, clearly resigned to the inevitable. "All this time? Did you know where to find him? That he was this close to Blackstone?"

"No," he says firmly enough that I actually believe him.

Something in me softens at that, and I realize my biggest worry was that Levi had kept this from me. That it would be another betrayal. The fact that it's not soothes something that was in desperate need of reassurance.

"When did you find out?" I ask without quite so much hostility.

"Tripp and I did some digging a while back," he says. "Back before Jadick joined us. Back when it was just the two of us and those first few Jades. We knew we needed allies. Resources. I hired someone to track down my parents, and Tripp suggested we look for your dad too."

"Why my dad?"

"Your mom always mentioned he was against the rejection thing like us." He shrugs. "Figured the guy must be a badass to have captured your mom's interest. And fathered you."

I blink, unprepared for the compliment.

"So, you've known his whereabouts for literally years?"

"No. The P.I. came back empty on that one. It wasn't until recently that I learned of this place."

"How—"

"The morning of your announcement with Jadick," he says, and my cheeks heat in shame at the reminder of what I did to him. "Your mother escorted me outside. Told me, when the chaos broke, I should make a run for it. I had no idea what she meant yet. Just before the speech began, she leaned over and rattled off coordinates. She said if shit went sideways to bring you here."

"My mother let you escape?" My shock is overwhelming, and for a moment, I can't make sense of it. Of her. "That doesn't make sense. She sold me out to Jadick. She wanted me to—" I can't say marry "— agree to his terms."

"Maybe she knew that she'd made a mistake."

"Did she tell you what this place was? Who was here?"

He shakes his head. "She never got a chance, but I had a feeling. Or maybe I hoped. For your sake."

"You hoped?" I snort derisively, but he shakes his head, sadness creeping in.

"Whatever his reasons for staying away, he's alive. And he's your blood. That means something, Mac. Trust me."

I catch myself, realizing he's thinking about his own parents. My temper falters. I've completely skipped over that part of his story. "Did you find them?" I ask quietly.

"My folks?" he asks. His expression falls and then hardens. "We found where they'd been buried."

"I'm sorry," I say quietly. After all these years, it's not exactly a surprise, but it's heartbreaking, nonetheless. "Do you know who...?"

"Crigger," he says grimly. "I suspected it back when they disappeared. They'd begun gaining traction. Supporters in their campaign against the rejection custom. And Crigger didn't like that. He chased them off pack lands to cover his tracks or maybe make it not so obvious. But in the end, it was him. Well, Thiago most likely since that was his favorite trigger man back then."

Anger heats my skin as I remember Thiago's cruelty. Yes, it would have been him. Jadick's methods aren't quite so obvious in their destruction. Or, they weren't back then.

Levi watches me carefully, and I realize he's waiting for me to respond. My words don't seem like enough, though. Not after everything he's lost.

"They would be proud of you," I tell him.

His eyes glisten at that.

My heart aches, and I step closer, instantly aware of the emotion he's reining in. When I touch my palm to his cheek, I expect him to pull away. Maybe even change the subject. Levi has never been one for emotional displays. But he surprises me by grabbing my hand and holding it to his stubbled cheek with ferocity shining in his sad eyes. "Thank you, Mac. For the second chance. For everything."

I offer a tilted smile. "Look, this doesn't negate the fact that I still intend to kick your ass for springing my father on me."

He laughs, and the sound of it chases off the lingering grief. For now. I know the loss of his parents will always hurt. Hopefully, he knows he doesn't have to hurt alone. Not anymore.

"I expect nothing less," he says. "Come on. Let's take it to the mat."

~

TWENTY MINUTES LATER, a knock on the van door has Levi and me pulling abruptly apart from where we're tangled up on the mattress. Instead of ass-kicking, I've mostly just been assaulting him with my mouth.

"Yeah," Levi calls out.

I glance over at him and smile to myself at his disheveled hair and unfocused eyes.

"Put your parts back in their own sockets, people." Tripp doesn't wait for an invitation before he pulls the door open and sticks his head inside. "Everyone PG-13 in here?"

"Your mom," Levi tosses back.

"Nah, she's completely inappropriate always," he says, flashing a grin.

I groan as Tripp makes himself comfortable in the passenger seat, rotating it so it faces us. "Guess the party's over," Levi grumbles, grabbing a shirt and pulling it on.

"I think you mean the party can start now that I've arrived," Tripp says, pretending to be hurt.

I roll my eyes and sit up, raking my fingers through my hair to try to tame it. But I know my flushed cheeks make what we were doing all too obvious. "How'd it go with Frankie?" I ask, mostly to take the focus off, well, this.

Tripp's smile immediately vanishes, and unease skitters up my spine. "Not great," he says.

"What is it?" I ask.

"Jadick's gone apeshit over you leaving."

Levi shakes his head. "So? We knew that would happen. The guy's a fucking lunatic."

"Yeah, well, he's also not good at losing." Tripp pins me with a stare that has me one hundred percent sure I'm going to hate whatever he says next. "The alpha house is in chaos. Apparently, dude's on a rampage. He's not going to stop until he's tracked you down and has you back."

"When you say 'track me down'..."

"He's sent a bounty hunter after you."

"Which one?" Levi demands, and Tripp gives him a withering stare.

"I'll give you five guesses, dipshit."

I groan. "My mother."

CHAPTER 13

*A*s the sun dips behind the swaying treetops, the three of us pile out of the van and once again approach the front door. The guys hang back a bit, letting me be the one to step up and knock. A second later, the door opens, and this time, I don't lose my shit completely when I see my father standing before me. It's still crazy. But I've adjusted well enough that I don't panic. Outwardly, anyway.

My mouth is dry, though, and my palms are sweating for reasons that make me feel like a kid all over again.

"We're back," I say lamely, suddenly unsure how to proceed.

He glances past me and gives Levi and Tripp a quick once-over. "They're not even bleeding," he says, gaze returning to mine.

I shrug. "I'm not myself today."

His lips twitch. "I have just the thing."

He lets the door hang open invitingly and disappears inside. I follow, a strange sensation of comfort washing over me as I enter the cabin again, this time through the front door. The space is much the way I left it earlier. Except the kitchen counter now has a spread of cut vegetables that include all the makings of a salad.

"Here." My father hands me a bowl, but instead of salad, I see rice and shredded meat with some kind of gravy poured over it.

Before I can think of a reason to refuse, he's pushed the bowl into my hands and retreated to gather two more for Levi and Tripp. They take their servings with none of the hesitation I feel.

My father takes a seat at the table with a bowl of his own, motioning for us to join him. Tripp is already pulling out a chair. Levi hangs back with me. Quietly, he says, "It's just dinner."

Then he pushes past me and sets his bowl down in front of an empty chair. He sidesteps his own place setting, though, and instead, pulls out the remaining chair, looking expectantly at me. I take a deep breath that makes my stomach growl as the scent of the meal hits me.

I refused him earlier, but I'm way too hungry to do it again.

One foot in front of the other, I make my way over and sit.

We eat in silence for a few minutes, and the awkwardness is only overshadowed by my own nerves. From beneath my lowered lashes, I dart glances at the man seated across from me. A short, scruffy beard covers the lower half of his face. His sandy-blond hair is tousled as if he's been running his hand through it since we last spoke. Short lines pinch at the corners of his eyes like he's been concentrating hard on something and it's left its mark.

Still, he eats with the casual confidence of someone who's never had their food snatched away by bullies. Or been forced to abandon a meal in order to chase down a mark.

I remember his story from earlier. How he helped my mother avoid the hunting team Crigger sent after her all those years ago. How he killed several of them at once to protect me. That picture he painted was one of a lethal warrior. But there's nothing warrior-like about him now. And I wonder if maybe that's his real power; letting people underestimate him so he can push past their defenses.

I wonder if it's mine too.

"Seconds?" he asks, yanking me from my thoughts, and I look over to see Tripp and Levi have already emptied their bowls.

"I wouldn't refuse," Tripp says, and my father waves him toward the kitchen.

"Help yourself. First round is provided by the host. Seconds are self-serve."

"Don't mind if I do," Tripp says, pushing back his chair.

Levi follows, winking at me as he goes.

I pretend not to notice and shake my head at them. "You both eat like savages."

"Keeping you alive is hard work," Tripp quips from where he stands over the stove pot. "Makes a man work up an appetite."

I snort and find my father watching me.

"He's full of shit," I say and then duck my head. "I mean crap," I mumble.

Robert Mackenzie tips his head back and laughs. "I think we're a little past the swear jar stage, don't you?" His brows lift, and I feel my mouth tip upward in an almost smile.

"Guess so."

"No salads then?" Levi asks with a nod at the veggies spread out.

"Figured being on the road has left you with a craving for something more solid," my father says with a shrug. "We can do salads or wraps for lunch tomorrow."

Tomorrow.

The only thing weirder than this day is the idea of repeating it.

"Sounds good," Levi says.

The guys take their seats again and I go back to my food. The meal is simple but pretty good. I suspect the stew meat is the rabbit he was smoking out back, but I don't ask. My wolf doesn't care anyway, and I'm too grateful for a full belly to be picky.

"Well." My father finishes off the last of his food and sits back. He rubs his middle appreciatively, which strikes me as funny considering he's the chef. "Not my best work, but it fills the gullet."

"It's great, Mr. Mackenzie," Tripp says, mouth full of food.

"Call me Rob," my father tells him.

"This is wild rabbit?" Levi asks as he finishes off his second bowl.

A nod. "I set small game traps on the back hillside," my dad says. "It's a little gamy at first, but you get used to it."

Levi nods, his smile soft. "My mom used to make a stew with it. This reminds me of hers."

"Your last name is Wild." Levi nods as my father rubs his chin thoughtfully. "Your mom was—"

"Deanna," Levi says.

"And Ralph," my father adds, snapping his finger as he remembers. "How are they?"

"They died a few years ago," Levi says quietly.

Finished with my food, I set aside my spoon and slip my hand underneath the table to brush my fingers over Levi's knee in silent comfort.

"Sorry to hear it," my father says with genuine sorrow on his face. "I don't get much news of the pack out here."

"They left the pack years ago," Levi says. "So you wouldn't have heard anyway."

"I see. What made them leave?"

"Support for their message grew too strong, and it became dangerous. Crigger had them driven out and then hunted down to silence it."

My father frowns. "Their work being…"

"To lift the ban on fated mates," Levi says, eyes flicking to Tripp then me.

"Ah. And you stayed?"

"Not for very long," Levi says tightly. He doesn't look at me as he says, "I've been working on the same mission myself since high school. Tripp joined me early on, and we began getting pack members out of town, helping them defect so they couldn't be tracked. Our relocation services started with Tripp's mom and went from there."

Pain flashes in Tripp's eyes at the mention of his mother. I feel guilty for not asking about her before now. Sending her away had to be painful for him; they'd been so close growing up. I'd been close with her too. All those times my mother would run off to bag a mark, leaving me home, Tripp's house had been a safe haven. His mom had been like a mother to me too back then. I haven't seen her in years.

And the expression Tripp wears now tells me those years are hurting him.

"The apple didn't fall far," my father says, approval lacing his words and drawing me back to the conversation. "It's a dangerous mission you've taken on." He glances at me and Tripp. "All of you. This situation you're in now—it sounds like your cause was gaining traction. Otherwise, the alpha wouldn't be pushing back."

"That's a nice way of saying he's trying to kill us," I say darkly.

"But you're free now," my father says. He leans back in his chair, assessing me. I want to ask what he sees, but I don't dare. "You're safe. And you're welcome here as long as you like."

Tripp glances at me. "Speaking of safety," he mutters, and my shoulders sag with an invisible weight. I know what he's hinting at. What he wants me to tell my father.

On a sigh, I say, "We learned Jadick has sent someone to hunt me down and bring me back."

"I see." My father eyes me carefully, and I know he's working it out already. Who, I mean. "A bounty hunter?" I nod. "Your mother."

I nod again.

Raw emotion darkens his expression, but he blinks, and it's gone. Interesting. Definitely a better poker face than I gave him credit for. But it helps to know he's maybe more ruffled about my showing up here than I originally assumed. At least, I'm not the only one struggling to navigate the weirdness of it all.

"She'll find you," he says matter-of-factly.

I can't argue it. But that's not the issue with this scenario. It's what I'll do about it when she comes that makes this so incredibly difficult.

"I won't let her take me back," I say quietly. I force myself to hold his gaze, mostly so he can see how much I mean it, and I can see whether he plans to get in my way.

In that quietness, he reads my intent.

"You'll fight her."

"If I have to." The words make me sick to my stomach, but I mean them. I won't go back to Jadick. I won't be dragged to my own death. Not even by her.

My father is silent.

Tripp and Levi exchange glances. I don't meet their eyes, but I can feel their worried gazes cutting to me. Like they want to tell him the whole story. About the Jades and the fact that we plan on fighting back. But I'm not ready to trust him that fully yet.

I stare down at my empty bowl, bracing myself. If he defends her, I'll leave. If he doesn't believe me, I'll leave. If he downplays the danger, I'll leave.

I can think of so many ways he can undermine me right now. So, when he finally speaks, I stop breathing, as if that will stop the stabbing through my heart.

"We should fortify the doors. Set some traps outside. Try to keep her out as long as possible."

My gaze whips up, but he's not looking at me. Instead, he's looking at Levi.

"What?" I manage, but they both ignore me.

"You really think that'll be enough?" Levi asks.

"No," he admits. "But it will slow her down, and hopefully, I can use that moment to talk some sense into her."

Tripp snorts. "Has anyone ever successfully talked sense into Vicki Quinn?"

No one laughs.

My father pushes back in his chair. He rounds the corner to the stone hearth. There's a rustling sound, and then he re-appears, a rifle in his hand.

My eyes widen.

Levi stills, and Tripp whistles. "Hot damn, Rob." Tripp's voice holds a note of awe.

"Relax," my father says, noting my reaction. "It's nothing lethal. Not to her, anyway. I keep a box of tranquilizers in the closet just in case. It'll slow her down long enough we can hopefully subdue her."

"And then what?" Levi asks.

He sounds much more nervous about this than Tripp or even my dad.

"Then we hope she sees reason," Tripp says.

I barely manage to hold back a snort at that. "Yeah, right."

My father looks up at me. "You sure she knows about this whole sacrifice thing your fiancé had planned for you?"

The question rattles me because the truth is I don't know for sure. I assumed, but… meeting Rob has already shown me assumptions aren't nearly as accurate as they might seem. "I don't know," I admit. "She knows Jadick's a fucking monster though, and that's enough for me."

He grunts and then leans the rifle against the end of the counter. "Well then. Let's get this food cleaned up so we can get to work."

CHAPTER 14

We spend twenty minutes tidying the kitchen. By the time we're done, full darkness has fallen. Outside, night creatures are just beginning to sing their songs. But my wolf is having none of the relaxation those soft sounds should bring me. She's on edge.

For good reason.

My eyes dart continually to the rifle propped against the counter.

My thoughts are on my mother.

"He's not going to use lethal force," Levi says so close to my ear that I jump.

Jerking toward him, I scowl. "I know."

He simply raises a brow in answer and then moves away to toss a rag into the sink.

My father and Tripp are both already seated in the living room. I can sense their eyes on me. With a heavy sigh, I make my way over to an empty chair near the fireplace. The hearth is cold though logs are stacked nearby in a tin container. I suspect the chill of autumn starts up here long before it reaches the lower altitudes.

"We could light it," Tripp offers, but when I look over at him, I see my father already shaking his head.

I answer for him. "A fire would mean smoke. And smoke would be a dead giveaway of where we are for anyone searching nearby."

"If Vicki's coming, she already knows exactly where we are," Tripp points out.

I exchange a knowing glance with my father. "She might not be the only one he sends," I say quietly.

"Good point." Tripp leans back as Levi joins us in the empty chair opposite mine.

"Mac's right," Levi says quietly. "Jadick never puts all his eggs in one basket. There are sure to be others looking for you."

"We have the benefit of a strategic location," my father says.

Levi nods. "The hillside out back is pretty steep and hard to navigate. There are a ton of fallen trees and brambles strewn across the easier paths." He cuts a look to my father. "And traps," he adds.

My father winks.

"I thought you said your traps were to catch small game for dinner," I say.

He shrugs. "That too."

Tripp offers a fist bump. "Nice work, Rob."

I stare at their interaction, not sure how to feel. Part of me wants that. To just...sink into this whole situation. Let it be normal. Let it feel good, even. But then I think of all the years he missed. All the times my mom shut me out of knowing anything about him.

I turn away and find Levi looking at me.

His dark gaze is heavy, but despite that, an understanding is reflected in his eyes that helps ease my discomfort. Suddenly, I'd rather be back in that van. Alone, with him. Screw Jadick's wrath. My wolf wants to claim her mate and just be fucking done with it.

"So," my dad says, ending whatever silent conversation my wolf and Levi's seem to be having. "Tell me more about Jadick's plan for marrying Mac."

"It's not so much the marrying as the killing," I say.

"Right. What exactly does killing you accomplish?"

I hesitate, but at this point, there's no reason to hold back. "It's about the curse."

"The one that says we need to reject our mates in order to be stronger," my father says.

I nod. "As you know, Crigger believed that accepting one's fated mate not only made the wolf weak, but it made the entire pack weak too. He claimed it would open us up to enemy attacks. Destroy our pack. Anyway, he apparently brainwashed Jadick into thinking the same thing, and now Jadick wants to do some kind of ritual that would literally remove the existence of fated mates entirely."

"How in the hell is that even possible?" my father asks.

"He's evidently found a witch willing to help," I say.

"And what do you have to do with all of this?"

"It seems I'm the blood sacrifice necessary to make it happen."

My father's eyes narrow into slits. I can feel his anger pulsing now; a glimpse into the warrior he can be. It's there and gone quickly though. By the time he speaks again, he's leashed it and hidden it somewhere deep.

"Jadick sounds a lot like his old man," my father says.

Tripp snorts, "Understatement."

"He's worse," Levi says flatly.

"The fact that he chose Mac..." Tripp says, frowning. He glances at me quickly. "No offense but I don't get it. Why you? I mean, you're not exactly the easiest target. He had to know you'd fight him every step of the way."

"I don't know," I admit. "I've been wondering that same thing, and no one's been able to tell me that. Not even Kari."

"I can't believe she survived that alpha challenge," Tripp says with a shake of his head.

"Kari as in Crigger's youngest?" my father asks.

I hesitate, unsure where to start. "We were close," I say quietly. "Or I thought we were. And then she turned on me and killed Thiago. Jadick nearly killed her in the challenge, but she somehow survived..."

Tripp puts in, "Jadick cut her throat, for fuck's sake."

I look at Tripp, keeping my voice even. "She was injured. Badly. And he made sure she remained that way. No healing. Just on the brink…" I look down at my hands. "She asked me to end it for her."

No one speaks for a long moment.

When I glance at Levi, his face is a mask of undefinable emotions. I can only guess at the roiling under the surface, but for now, he's keeping it hidden. Undoubtedly thinking of the torture she put him through until we were able to free him.

"She was your friend." My father's words startle me, and I look up to see him studying me.

"Yes."

"And she betrayed you." His glance flicks between me and Levi.

Tripp snorts. "You could say that."

I take a deep breath and let it out again. My father's still watching me, assessing.

"She set all this in motion," I say. "She had Thiago kill Crigger. And she kept Levi as her prisoner in order to control me. She knew about the ritual. That I would be sacrificed. She knew what Jadick intends and tried to stop it—in her own way, I guess."

"But she didn't know why it had to be you," Tripp says.

I shake my head. "If she did, she never said."

Across the space, Levi is still as stone. I want to touch him. To reach out and let him know he's not alone in wherever his mind has taken him. But the truth is that he is alone there. The only way to end it is for him to find his way back here.

"It sounds like we need to find out more about this ritual Jadick plans on doing," my father says. "Does he have the bones you mentioned or did Kari keep that one to herself?"

"No idea," I admit.

"In the meantime, can we talk about how we're going to stop Vicki from blowing this damn door down and dragging your ass back to your fiancé?"

Tripp's tone is somewhere between sarcasm and actual fear. I don't blame him. My mother—

A knock sounds on the door, and we all go still.

My wolf strains toward the surface, begging to be let free against whatever threat has found us. I hold her back, glancing between the others who also look just as ready to tear something apart.

"Mac, I know you're in there."

My mother's familiar voice does nothing to assuage my fear. In fact, it only amplifies it.

I send Tripp a look that says *she's already here?*

He sends one back that's pretty much just *WHAT THE FUCK.*

My father stands and strides across the room to retrieve the rifle. My fear courses through me like adrenaline. Levi stands too. There's something wild in his eyes but also completely grounded—in what, I don't know. He walks over and puts himself between the gun and the door.

"You're not taking her, Vicki." His words are absolute.

"I'm not trying to take her," Vicki says, but her voice is strained. Impatient.

I push to my feet now too and step up beside Levi. He immediately shoves me behind him. My father takes a step toward us, but Levi stops him with a glare.

Tripp slides off the couch and huddles beneath the window. He watches Levi like he's waiting for a signal, and the knowledge of what they're capable of together tightens my stomach.

"Then what *do* you want?" Levi asks.

My mother hesitates, and when she speaks again, her voice is heavy with emotions I've never heard her express before. "To apologize," she says and in a much quieter voice, "and to come home."

I look at my father, who blinks, clearly not expecting that answer.

"Why can't I scent you?" I call before anyone can answer her pleas.

"I used a cloaking charm I traded from a witch in Indigo Hills."

"Why cloak yourself at all?" I ask. "If you're not here to apprehend me. Why not let us sense you coming?"

"The charm isn't for you," she says, and the urgency from earlier returns.

"Who is it for?" Levi demands.

"It's—"

A snarl sounds, and then boots shuffle across the yard. My senses pick up a heartbeat, incredibly fast. Too fast. Not human then.

Another snarl, this one familiar: my mother's wolf.

Finally, a new scent hits me.

"Open the door," I say.

Levi tries to protest, but I just move past him toward the knob.

"Whoa, Mac, you can't—"

"She's not lying," I hiss. "There's a tracker outside."

He hesitates a single beat, just long enough to inhale the new scent and decide for himself. It's more than enough time for me to slide past him and out the door. My mother's nowhere in sight; already gone to meet the threat. Knowing it only makes me move faster.

Behind me, I can hear Levi demanding that I wait.

But I press onward, thinking only of the devastating venom that left me poisoned for days the last time I faced one of these assholes. Regardless of whether my mom's lying or not, she doesn't deserve that fate.

I rush out and scan the yard, spotting two wolves near the tree line, locked in combat. The charm spell is still intact because I still can't scent my mother, but the tracker's smell wrinkles my nose.

I take off at a run, shifting as I launch myself toward the fight. My paws hit the grass with grace and agility—and, damn, it feels good to take this form again. For the space of three strides, my wolf's release is nearly euphoric. But then we lock onto the enemy ahead, and everything else fades away.

Behind me, I sense another wolf approaching.

Levi. And the sound of heavy boots rushing behind him.

My father.

Out of the corner of my eye, I catch sight of Tripp's wolf coming in from the side. Watching my back as always. Or maybe this was the signal Levi gave. Either way, he's arcing wide to come in from the opposite side from me.

This tracker is about to regret his decision tonight.

The tracker knocks my mother farther into the trees. She is light on her feet, up quickly, and already facing off again. But she's careful not to get too close to its claws. We both know what will happen if their venom-coated tips break her skin. The tracker understands the advantage and uses it perfectly, stalking toward her until she's backing away. Its back is to me now, unaware of the threat approaching. Perfect.

I eat up the ground, mere steps away now.

Just before I can bury my teeth into its throat, a shot rings out.

It's nothing like the blast of a bullet. Instead, the sound is muffled; more wind and propulsion than gunpowder and force. Something sharp buries itself in the tracker's neck. The tracker jerks and then shakes it off. But another second later, the wolf's body is listing sideways and then abruptly falls over.

I pull up short, huffing with the need to finish what I started. But the damn thing is already out like a light. Up close, I spot the dart my father shot it with, still sticking out of the thing's furry neck.

From the shadows, my mother's wolf emerges, sniffing. She stalks toward the tracker and stops, eyeing the dart. She looks up at my father sharply, her large wolf eyes narrowed. A snarl rips from her lips. Then she sinks her teeth into the tracker's throat and rips it open.

CHAPTER 15

My heart rate is strangely calm when I step out of the shower and dress in the change of clothes I've borrowed from Levi. A pair of sweats and an over-sized tee that says Tactical Elite, We Go Hard. The words distract me from my spiraling thoughts. The idea that Levi wears this is almost amusing. Or maybe it's just my dirty brain that sees an innuendo where there isn't one. The slogan doesn't feel like something he would choose to wear, but then I realize maybe I don't know him like I think I do. I make a mental note to ask him about it, and somewhere in this inner monologue with myself, I wonder how I'm not falling apart.

Sure, my entire upbringing was centered around normalizing violence, especially where my mother is concerned. I've seen her subdue targets more times than I've witnessed it in movies over the years. But killing an unconscious wolf? That's new. Even if it was a tracker.

Whatever happened to her after I left Blackstone has left its mark.

That, more than anything she said, leaves me wanting to hear her story. It also convinced the rest that she isn't a threat to me after all. Even so, I could sense Levi's hesitance at leaving us alone in the house. He made me take the rifle into the bathroom with me, which I promptly stuffed into the linen closet so I wouldn't have to look at it.

Weapons don't bother me, but something about the idea of having to use it on my mom doesn't sit well. If she's going to attack me outright, I'll fight her off with the weapons gifted to me by blood —or not at all.

I towel dry my hair and then hunt around for a brush. I come up with a comb and do my best to make it work on my thick, tangled head of hair. On the upside, the wound on my shoulder is pretty much healed already. And my ear is good as new.

Apparently, the aconitum worked after all.

The house is quiet beyond the bathroom door. Tripp, Levi, and my father are burying the tracker far enough away from the house that anything that might stumble upon and dig it up won't trace it back here—hopefully.

My mother helped herself to the second bathroom, but I can't hear a single movement other than my own.

When I can't put it off any longer, I step out and pad through the house on bare feet. To my surprise, I find my mother sitting at the table with a drink in her hand. She wears a pair of gym shorts and a gray tee that I expect belong to my father though I can't scent anything coming off the clothes or her own skin. The glass she holds is half-full of amber liquid. In the center of the table is a bottle of whiskey. I retrieve my own glass from the cabinet and pull out the chair across from her, the one my father sat in earlier, and help myself to a hefty pour.

She watches me, silent.

I don't let myself look too closely at her expression. Maybe I'm not ready to know the answers to all my questions. Or maybe it's easier to be angry if I don't let her explain.

"I didn't hear you come out," I say.

"The cloaking charm."

"Right. From Indigo Hills?"

"I got it from Clem, the bartender we hunted down last Christmas. Remember?"

"Yeah."

We'd spent the holiday in a dive bar in Laramie. It sucked.

We fall silent, and then, accidentally, we both lift our glasses and drink in unison. Gulp after gulp until our glasses are empty. Like mother like daughter.

Ugh.

The alcohol is a welcome burn against my throat. I don't wait to see if it's enough to take the edge off before I reach for the bottle again. My mother watches me pour and then holds her own glass up for a refill.

I pour for her too, and then we both just sit.

For some reason, I think of the beach trip I'd been secretly planning with Kari—before all of this went to shit. Whiskey tastes better on a beach. Or that's my theory. I wouldn't know for sure.

Outside, I hear the approach of footsteps. All human. They must have shifted back for the purpose of digging. A moment later, the front door opens, and my father walks in. Levi is right behind him.

"Where's Tripp?" I ask.

"Checking the perimeter," Levi supplies.

"Any more problems?" I ask.

Levi's dark glance says he knows what I mean. Any more enemies to kill?

"No," he says, and in that word is exhaustion and suspicion, the latter aimed at my mother. He crosses to me and drops a kiss on my cheek. He smells like freshly turned earth—and blood.

I offer him my glass.

He takes it and downs the double shot then hands it back. "Thanks." The glass is streaked with dirt from his fingers.

"I put some clothes in the bathroom for you," I tell him.

His gratitude conveys in the squeeze he gives my shoulder. "Thanks. I'm going to grab a shower."

He disappears down the hall, and I'm left with my parents, both of whom are staring at each other like they're seeing a ghost. Suddenly, the third-wheel tension is unbearable.

I push back in my chair. "I'm going to check on Tripp," I say.

"No." My mother's answer is quick to the point of forceful. She glances at me, softening as she tears her gaze from the man she supposedly once loved. "Stay," she says softly. "We have a lot to discuss, and I'm afraid it can't wait."

I look at my father, fully aware that I'm considering his wishes over hers in this moment. He finally looks away from her and over at me, his shoulders sagging. "She's right. We should talk."

I sit again.

My father strides to the kitchen and comes to the table with a glass of his own. He grabs the bottle and pours himself a generous double shot. When he lifts a brow at me, bottle aimed toward my glass, I shake my head.

No amount of alcohol is going to lessen this weirdness anyway.

He shrugs and replaces the cap.

I watch while he takes a hefty sip, and then, together, we turn to look at my mother. For the first time I can ever remember, her face flushes in discomfort.

She clears her throat and looks down at her glass.

When she doesn't speak, my own impatience wins out, and I snap, "Fine, I'll start. Why don't you explain to me what the hell you're doing here, and save the bullshit? We know Jadick ordered you to hunt me down."

She drags her eyes to mine. "You're right. Jadick did order me to find you, but that's not why I came."

When she falls silent, I say, "I'm listening."

"Jadick's entire mission as alpha is about erasing the forced will of fated mates." She speaks slowly as if choosing her words carefully. "Instead of breaking the curse imposed on our pack, he's determined to end the very call of fate herself. He thinks the idea that the universe imposes this on us—who we love—makes us weak. That without our own choice in the matter, we—"

"I know all of this," I say, rolling my eyes. "Look, if you think you're going to come here and pretend you didn't know Jadick is a piece of shit before now, you can see yourself out. Because that lame excuse isn't going to work on any of us."

Her expression tightens. "He's planning a ritual," she says, and I stand up, the chair scraping loudly against the floor as I push it back in disgust.

I look at my father. "I'll be in the van. Call me when she's gone."

"Mac, wait."

I whirl away from the door to glare at my mother. "You expect me to believe you didn't know any of this when you sold me out to that asshole?"

Her silence speaks volumes.

"And you come in here acting like you're some angel sent to help inform me of this danger now? When I've already managed to remove myself from it, no thanks to you? Give me a break."

Behind me, the door opens. Tripp walks in and stops short when he sees our standoff. Down the hall, the shower cuts off. Great, everyone's listening now.

"Mac." My mother tries to speak, but I'm done listening to her excuses.

"You're not my savior, Mom. I found out about the ritual and Jadick's intentions all on my own. I uncovered what kind of mess you helped put me in. And I nearly got myself killed in the process. Did you even know Jadick shot me with a poisoned bullet for trying to escape? Did you even care?" I don't wait for her answer before pressing on. "If anyone's my savior, it's Levi and Tripp. They got me out of that house. Not you. And they brought me here where I'd be safe—from everyone except for you, it seems."

"I told you. I didn't come here to hurt you."

"Are you sure about that? Because you led a tracker right to our doorstep."

I don't bother with the fact that she killed it while defenseless. As disturbing as it was to watch, I know she did it because nothing less would stop that thing. And we can't exactly keep it contained in the house.

"It's obvious Jadick doesn't trust you, anyway," I say instead. "That he sent that tracker to follow you. To make sure you got the job done."

"Jadick doesn't want a tracker to kill you," she says. "He needs you for the ritual."

"I'm sure he'll come up with another desperate female to manipulate."

"No one else will work," she says. "It has to be you."

The way she says it speaks volumes, and I stare at her, unflinching. Now, my heart races. Because she knows something I don't.

"Why?" I demand.

"Because," she says, voice rising to match mine, "three branches. Three choices. Three bones of our blood. Reject, Accept, reject. Three times three, so mote it be. That's what the spell calls for. Blood of three generations times three choices."

Her words ring out into the silence, and the potency in them, the certainty in her, stops me from calling bullshit.

Her eyes are hard and knowing. More secrets, then.

"What does it mean?" I ask.

She sighs. "Before you lose your shit, you should know I didn't learn this part until after you left." She glances at Tripp and frowns. "Escaped," she amends.

"What exactly does it mean, Vicki?" my father's voice is like steel; enough so that she flinches as she drags her gaze to his.

"She and Levi are fated," my mother tells him.

He nods. "Yes, I can sense that. But they're not mated yet. Not claimed."

"No. Jadick manipulated Mac into rejecting Levi. Again," my mother adds and then gives him a pointed look that suggests he should know the significance of her explanation.

"Reject, accept, reject," he repeats.

She nods, the hardness in her expression dissolving into what looks like sorrow.

The bathroom door opens, and Levi emerges amid a cloud of steam that escapes with him. Dressed in only a pair of low-slung gym shorts, he runs a hand through his wet hair. My eyes dart to his bared chest. Even in a charged moment such as this one, I can't ignore the attraction I feel.

Reject, accept, reject.

She's right. That's what I've done to him. My heart pangs as I realize it.

When I look back at my father, his brows are knitted as he attempts to work through the layers of whatever my mother is trying to tell him. Finally, he says, "Does this have to do with my parents?"

My mother nods. "And us, I'm afraid."

My father doesn't say a word. Instead, he simply raises his glass and empties it. When he sets it down again, he says, "Shit, Vicki."

"What?" I ask. Something about his reaction has unsettled me. The anger I felt is gone, replaced by wariness. Whatever my mother's claiming, it's real; his stunned reaction leaves no doubt about that.

My mom looks back at me again. "When I first met your father and realized we were fated, I tried to resist. I don't need to explain to any of you how hard the pack would make our lives if we tried to be together. So, I rejected him. But he persisted." Her lips twitched toward a fond smile. "He convinced me, and when I finally accepted him, we ran away together."

I take a step toward the table. "And you had me."

Her honesty is enough to bring me back to the table, but it's my father's face as he watches her tell it that has me taking my seat again. This is the most vulnerable moment I've ever shared with either of them. If they care about the fact that Tripp and Levi are witnessing it, they don't show it.

Neither of the guys say a word, though.

"And then Crigger sent people to hunt us," my mom says. "To find me and bring me back so I could hunt down all his enemies. Just like my father did before me. Apparently, the price of being the best is job security—whether you want it or not."

Her attempt at humor is too dark and horrible to be funny.

She goes on, "When they found us, your father and I did what we had to do to protect you. I considered leaving you here with him, but by then, Crigger knew you existed."

"Why does that matter?" I ask. "I was a baby. Nothing to him."

"You were mine," she says. "And I knew he'd use you to control me if he could."

"You were safer with her," my father says.

"Safer among the violence and abuse of our pack?" I ask, unconvinced.

"Safer where Crigger could see Vicki's loyalty to him went deeper than her devotion to you," Levi says quietly.

I turn to look at him, surprised. And more surprised when my mother doesn't disagree.

"My parents did the same to me," he says. "It was their way of keeping me safe from Crigger's wrath. If they didn't care about me, why should he?"

Tripp huffs. "It's fucked up."

"It is," Levi says, casting a hard look toward Vicki and even my father. "But it worked."

"Yes," my mother says sadly. "It did."

"So, what does that have to do with this ritual?" I ask.

"When I left your father, I did the thing I knew would keep us all safest," my mother says. "I rejected him. Again."

"Three generations times three choices," Levi repeats.

I look from him to my mother. "And your parents?" I ask. "They did the same?"

She nods. "It has to be you. Jadick knows it, and he'll stop at nothing until he has you back so he can use your blood to end fated mates forever. I didn't know the ritual demanded these specifics until two days ago.

"I was furious, of course. Jadick used me. Pretended his marriage would save you—that it would end the curse. That's what he told me. He manipulated me into helping him arrange it under the guise of protecting you. Anyway, by the time I learned the truth, you were gone, Mac. I wanted to leave, too, but I couldn't. Not without raising suspicion. So, when Jadick ordered me to find you, I saw my chance, and I took it."

She glances at Levi.

"I hoped you would remember the coordinates I gave you," she tells him. "And I came here to tell you..." She looks back at me again, raw vulnerability shining in her normally proud eyes. "I'm sorry, Mac. For everything."

CHAPTER 16

hree generations of rejecting and accepting a mate and then rejecting them all over again. That's the legacy I'm part of. Second chance romances. Or, basically, just getting back together with our exes. That's what the women in my family are about, apparently. And now, I'm being hunted down for my blood because of these choices by men who think we don't deserve to live. Would the world ever change?

I was really doubting it right up until the moment my mother apologized. Now, the world feels tipped on its axis. I stare back at her, completely at a loss. Showing up on my father's doorstep shocks me less than her apology, along with the heartfelt—no, *heart-wrenched*—look she wears as she waits for my response.

A response that sticks in my throat and aches in my chest.

"I…"

My words are lost to the ringing of a phone.

We all look to my mother, who pulls a cell from her shorts pocket. She clutches it tightly and says, "It's Jadick."

"The GPS—" Levi begins as she starts to answer.

"It's untraceable," she adds and then hits the button to connect the call.

I hold my breath as she puts it on speaker and says, "Yeah?"

"Did you find her?" Jadick's impatience is edged with irritation.

"Not yet."

He's silent except for his breathing, which is heavy and laced with fury.

"I'm warning you, Vicki," he says finally, his voice deadly calm. "Do not even think about trying to play me. She's mine now, and there's nothing you can do to stop this."

"I just need a bit more time," my mother replies, her voice hardening with all the certainty of the bounty hunter I've watched hunt countless times over. "There are a few other places I think she'll try to go."

"So you say," he says.

"I'll check in again soon," my mother says, unaffected by his threatening tone.

"Make sure you have what I want when you do."

The call ends, and my mother picks up the phone, disconnecting the battery and SIM card before setting the pieces on the table. Then she looks up, glancing past the others to me. My hands are balled into fists at my sides. When I realize it, I relax them and exhale, concentrating on my breathing and cooling the tension and rage in my body.

The sound of Jadick's voice in this room is a reminder that I'm not free yet. Not really. But I will be.

"I accept your apology," I tell my mom. "But it doesn't make up for the past or for helping Jadick trap me in all this. The only thing that will do that is helping me—" Tripp elbows me "—helping *us* put him down."

"You have my word, Mac." My mother's expression is solemn. "I'll do whatever it takes. I only ever wanted to protect you."

"I know you believe that," I say carefully. "But your methods are not welcome here. You do it our way from now on or leave."

"You'll need me if you're going to fight him—"

"Our way or leave," I repeat. "Those are your only choices."

"Don't you mean 'our way or the highway'?" Tripp whispers. "I kind of always wanted to say that."

I give him a look, but he just grins, impervious to my glare.

My mother looks at the others, one by one, and whatever she sees in their gazes must echo my words because she finally looks back at me, nodding. "Deal. What would you like to do now?"

Instead of answering her question, I look at my father. "You didn't ask for this," I tell him. "I understand if you don't want to be involved. We can find somewhere else to—"

"I'm in." He doesn't look at my mother as he says, "I let you go once because I thought it best for you. But I don't intend to ever do it again. I'll fight with you—and for you. Whatever it takes to make you safe."

I shove aside the warmth his words bring. There will be time later to examine how I feel about the man who's just professed blind loyalty and the woman who's finally promised to stop meddling in my life and instead let me be in charge of my own choices. The stirring of emotions is an intense storm I don't have time for right now.

Levi catches my eye, and I see understanding in his gaze. But, as if he knows what I need, he puts it all aside too. "Tripp and I will follow you wherever you go," he says like that answer should be obvious.

"Hell yeah," Tripp echoes.

My lips curve as I glance at my former bestie. Maybe not so "former" anymore. "You want to kick ass together?" I ask because bantering with Tripp is safer. It makes this whole thing less crazy.

"I got your back, Mac and cheese," he says, and I punch him in the arm.

WE TAKE a break from our strategy meeting to allow Tripp and my dad to get cleaned up. While my mom eats leftover stew, Levi asks her for updates on Frankie and Grey and a few other Jades. She offers what little information she has, but it's clear she's not privy to their lives. They don't trust her. I can't blame them.

"What about Nely?" I ask, thinking of the girl who became my almost-friend back at the mall before everything went to hell and I became the enemy's betrothed.

"Gone," my mother says.

"Gone where?"

"No idea."

"And her mate? Lorenz?" I ask.

"Both of them left. Along with most other Jades," she tells us. "Especially those without rank or position in the alpha house."

"They would have defected," Levi murmurs. "This is why we left in the first place."

"Do you know where they might have gone?" I ask Levi.

"There are a couple of safe houses in Rose Hill, right outside Blackstone," he says. "We used them to check in with our spies in town—"

I shake my head, cutting him off. "Those houses were burned while Kari was alpha."

His gaze darkens at that, but after a few blinks, his shoulders sag, and the light goes out. "Then, no. Everything else is compromised. Jadick..."

He doesn't finish. He doesn't have to.

"We need to find them," I say. "If we're going to do this, we need reinforcements."

We need numbers we don't have, but I don't bother to point that out. The fact is we're doing this either way. Saying out loud how horrible our odds are won't help.

"What about outside help?" my mom asks.

"What kind of help?" Levi asks warily.

"Lone Wolf pack. Mafia pack—"

"Absolutely not," Levi says.

My mom is quick to rebut, and by the time Tripp and my father rejoin us, Levi and my mom are embroiled in an argument over whether or not going to other packs for help is wise.

"We asked them to fight Kari for us, and they all said no," Levi says. "What makes you think they'd change their minds now?"

"The fact that magic can remove fate's hand from our lives?" my mom scoffs. "I would think even they would understand a threat like that. Who's to say someone wouldn't try it on their packs next?"

"I'm not going to beg," Levi says, eyes flashing as his temper rises.

"Who said anything about begging?" My mom glances at me, but I don't say a word. I've already told her she has no say in our plans, but I also know we can't beat Jadick alone.

"Have they been like this the whole time?" Tripp asks quietly, coming to stand beside me again.

"Pretty much."

"They're kind of an even match," he says after a moment. We share a look, and he grins. "They're both stubborn as mules."

The conversation at the table cuts off, and both my mother and Levi turn to glare at us.

"Whoops," Tripp says and slides past me into the kitchen for a glass of water.

My father steps into his place, standing close enough for me to feel awkward.

"My money's on Vick," he announces, and something strange flickers in my mom's expression at the nickname.

My father watches her carefully, and suddenly the awkwardness I feel has more to do with the undercurrent of emotions passing between them.

Two decades apart have only seemed to stoke their connection. Gross.

I take a step away, and my father chuckles.

"So," he says, crossing his arms over his fresh shirt. "You two decide how we're going to fight this war yet?"

"No one's decided anything," Levi says.

My mother scowls and looks away.

"But now that we're all here," Levi continues, casting me a look that has me tensing. "I think we can all agree that, at the end of the day, the only way to remove an alpha is to challenge him."

"And you want to be the one to do that," my father says.

"No way," I say, stepping forward to cut this off. "You're not endangering yourself like that. Not after... Just, no."

"Mac," he says, and it's the softening in his tone that pisses me off more than his argument. "I'll be fine."

I scowl at him. "You sound like an idiot."

His brows go up at my outburst. I'm aware I sound like the worrying girlfriend, but I don't care.

"You've already been held prisoner, tortured, and effectively cut out of your own pack." He winces, but I'm willing to say anything to keep him from putting himself in danger this way. "Besides, we all know Jadick's not going to fight fair. He didn't with Kari, and he won't with you. All that matters to him is winning."

"I know, but that's my point—"

"He's going to cheat and fight dirty, and he won't stop until he's gotten what he wants," I say.

"Right, but he's already overplayed his hand—"

"Jadick only cares about himself, and his ego is bigger than anyone I've ever met."

"Which is what I plan to use against him."

Levi's words are drowned out as I continue to argue. "He's sure of himself, and even worse, he has already beaten us at every turn—"

"Mac."

He nearly shouts my name, and I fall abruptly silent, still glaring at him.

"It has to be me, and you know it," he says.

"I don't know anything of the sort," I say.

He looks at my mother. "Did Jadick hold a bonding ceremony to link him to the Jades? Did he claim them as alpha?"

My mother blinks. "No." She frowns. "He asked for sworn loyalty, but that was it. I guess he didn't think it was necessary."

"Because the asshole thinks he already won," Tripp puts in, but there's excitement in his eyes as he sets his water aside and comes forward.

"He probably thinks Levi isn't a threat anymore," my mother adds.

Tripp slides into the empty seat, looking between them. Even from here, I can see it in his eyes: He finally thinks we have a shot. And I know exactly why. It's the same reason my stomach is dropping because it means I can't argue with Levi's idea anymore. And maybe I shouldn't. It's what I always wanted for him anyway. He'd make a great alpha.

"If he never did the bonding ceremony," Levi says, "then the Jades are still mine."

Tripp pounds a fist on the table in victory. "You're still the alpha, my dude. And that means you still have a pack to fight for you."

Levi looks over at him. Then me. "Fight for us," he corrects.

Everyone turns to look at me, and I realize they're waiting for me to agree with this insane plan. "We don't even know where they are," I say.

"We don't need to," Levi says. "My alpha call will reach them, and they'll come."

"And if they don't?" I ask.

"They will." He sounds so sure.

I sigh. "Fine. You'll challenge Jadick."

"The Jades will back us," Tripp adds.

Levi nods. "And when he's gone, we can break the curse once and for all." More certainty. So much that his dark, bottomless eyes seem to wrap around me, assuring me of our victory. Our future.

I don't know how to tell him nothing will ever feel sure for me until Jadick's dead. Maybe even then.

But a noise outside shatters the moment.

We all hear it at the same time, our heads whipping toward the back door as one.

My wolf stirs, and I feel the hairs on my arm stand on end as the noise outside grows louder. Paws padding over grass.

In the darkness, something moves.

Tripp is closest. He's up and out the door before any of us.

My mother and Levi are right behind him and then my dad, careful to keep his body in front of mine, though I'm sure he doesn't think I notice. I call up my wolf, ready to shred right through these clothes and shift the moment I see whatever's stalking its way toward the house.

A tracker, judging from the way the creature prowling the back-yard seems locked onto the cabin. Not to mention the lithe, quick way that it moves through the darkness; cutting through air and space toward its prey.

My heart thrums at the idea that we've been found out.

But by the time I lay eyes on the massive wolf rounding my father's garden, Tripp is already upon it. With a deadly growl, Tripp's wolf explodes from his skin. He rakes sharpened claws over the tracker's snout even before the thing can fully lock onto its new enemy.

Tripp's teeth rip into the thing's throat, speed and fury combining to make my friend just as deadly and swift and strong as the tracker itself.

The sound of teeth against flesh is wet, promising a messy kill. Levi pulls up short, angling back so that he's shielding me from the worst of it.

"Where did Tripp learn to fight like that?" I can't help but ask.

Levi casts me a look. "Training."

Beside me, my father grabs my arm to keep me from getting closer. Annoyed, I try to pull free, but when I catch sight of the carnage ahead, I realize there's no point.

Tripp's wolf rips through the tracker-wolf, laying it out on the ground until it's nothing more than blood and parts. My mother, still human, ventures closer, but she's already been rendered needless.

The dead tracker wolf is no longer a threat.

We all stare in silence at the dead wolf, and my mind races at what it means.

"If Jadick didn't know we were here before, he will now," Levi says grimly.

"Two trackers that won't be returning," my father mutters in agreement. He looks up, first at Levi then my mother. Finally, to me. "We can't stay here any longer."

Regret flashes in his eyes.

"I know," I say, but he shakes his head.

"I told you this was a safe place," he says.

"It's not your fault," I tell him.

He looks sad, though. It makes me wonder what he expected.

"We'll have to leave first thing," Levi says.

He looks at me, waiting. I nod. Still in wolf form, Tripp nods too. The decision is made.

Winded and coated in blood, Tripp steps back and then heads for the hillside. I start after him, but my father stops me. "There could be more," he says.

"That's why I'm going," I tell him, pulling away from him and starting for the woods.

Instead of stopping me, Levi jogs to my side.

"If you try to tell me to wait at home, I'll claw your gorgeous face off," I tell him.

He smirks.

"What?" I demand, still walking.

"You think I'm gorgeous?"

I roll my eyes. "We're possibly surrounded by trackers, and that's what you want to focus on?"

"We're not surrounded," he says.

"You sound really sure of yourself tonight."

His smile slips, and he grabs my wrist, stopping me. "Not sure," he says. "Determined. I refuse to accept anything less than a long, amazing life with you, Mac."

"I want that too," I whisper. "But I can't even think about it. Not until... it hurts too much."

"I know." He squeezes my hand. "I'll think about it for both of us. I just want you to know what I'm fighting for."

I nod, trying to convey the things I can't put into words. We begin walking again, patrolling for more threats, this time hand in hand. Farther out, I can hear Tripp moving along the hillside, hunting. But I don't sense anyone else. Levi seems to be right. Still…

"We can't stay here," I say.

"I know—"

A *ding* sounds, and we both freeze. My eyes scan the ground, and a second later, my wolf senses ping on something half-buried in leaves a few yards away. Levi nods, letting me know he sees it too. Tripp comes bounding over, and I can already hear my parents' footsteps approaching fast from the yard, thanks to their wolf hearing.

Levi picks up the phone and presses a button, illuminating the screen as everyone else hurries up to where we stand.

"What is it?" I ask.

"Tracker's phone," Levi says. "It needs a password to access fully, but there's an incoming text I can pull up without it."

We all wait as he swipes, and the screen shows a video sent twenty minutes ago from an unknown number. Levi hits play, and the screen shows a mess of bloody limbs that's worse than what Tripp just did to the tracker. The camera pans over what was obviously once a person then angles up to show a woman screaming from the sidelines of a small crowd. Tears streak down her dirty cheeks, but through the layer of grime, I recognize her instantly.

Amelia.

Jim's wife. No, his mate.

She is devastated, which makes my stomach drop with a knowing that sickens me. The dead body is Jim. The first Jade in Green Hills to be truly accepting of me. He's also part of a fated-mate pair. Which means Jadick isn't just hunting me. He's hunting every Jade who fled the pack too.

The camera angles again, spinning to reveal who's filming the horror.

Jadick.

He grins, but it's more malicious than happy. Or maybe they're the same where he's concerned.

"Since Mac has deserted her own people, I've decided to expend them as she has so obviously deemed them insignificant. One death every day, Mackenzie, darling. Until you return home where you belong and show us we matter to you after all."

The video ends. Levi curses viciously, and the screen goes dark, plunging us all into shadows. He wastes no time picking the phone apart and crushing the pieces under his boot with more force than necessary.

I don't move.

The others stomp around, muttering vows to kill Jadick for what he's done. Tripp announces a plan to contact Frankie and Grey first thing tomorrow. But I can't speak around the lump in my throat. Grief clings to me, so thick I could peel it off my skin. And a burst of shame.

This is my fault.

No, it's Jadick's fault. But I can stop it. I have to go back. Even if it kills me. As long as I take him with me. This has to end.

It's time to wipe out the Clemons line.

Forever.

CHAPTER 17

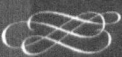

*B*ack at the cabin, I head for the van. The others hang back, chatting about clean-up. Maybe it makes me rude or a bad house guest, but I don't give two shits about the dead tracker's blood and guts coating the back lawn. Not when Jadick's left an innocent life on the steps of the alpha house in much the same way.

"Mac."

I hear my name just as I'm rounding the front of the house.

I keep walking.

"Mac, don't walk away from me," Levi says when I don't respond.

I turn to face him, noting the dark angles of his features accentuated by the shadows. His eyes soften at the sight of me, though it only seems to emphasize his predatory side. He's angry. Not at me. But even so, his fury is a taste on my tongue, and the grief inside me wants to swallow it whole.

"Talk to me," he says.

"Where are the others?"

"Cleaning up."

I don't answer.

"It's not your fault, you know."

Something in my expression must convey that he's hit the bull's eye with those words because he reaches for my hand, snagging it before I can pull away.

"Come on." He leads me toward the van and slides open the door, motioning for me to get inside. He follows and shuts the door behind us. It's not enough to be soundproof, but at least there's some modicum of privacy here.

Levi sits beside me on the mattress.

"Jadick's the killer. The monster. He is the one to blame for this pain. Not you."

His words are firm but tender enough to rip open the wound I've been holding closed since the moment I saw the video's horrors.

"It's just… when is it too much?"

My voice breaks, so I shut my mouth, swallowing hard against the wave of emotion. If I don't talk and don't breathe and don't touch anyone, maybe I can hold all of it inside me—

But then Levi yanks my hand to pull me close and folds me in against his chest, and the dam breaks. It's not tears. More a rush of feelings I've kept at bay for, well, maybe forever. My breaths are labored despite sitting still. It's not a physical exertion; it's an emotional one. Fury, rage, helplessness, it's all there. The best I can do is swallow down my own screams that threaten to come with it. Instead, I breathe deeply against Levi's chest, my shoulders wracking with silent agony. This is more than grief. This is helplessness and rage. I want nothing more than to take my emotions out on the one who deserves it most, but without that option, apparently sitting like this, nearly hyperventilating while I feel through it all, is the one thing my body can do to purge the fury.

Levi holds me tight, brushing a hand down my hair.

He doesn't speak, and I sink into the comfort of his silent soothing.

Finally, I catch my breath. When I pull away, Levi's lost all traces of the battle-ready expression he wore earlier. Instead, there's no sign of stress or worry or problems. There's only this: him and me.

"I hate that I'm always falling apart around you," I say.

"I love it," he says, and I glare at him.

"You love that I'm a sobbing, helpless mess in your arms?" I ask, an edge to my voice.

"You weren't sobbing this time," he points out, which only makes me glare harder. His smile turns sheepish. "Okay, that came out wrong. I love that you feel safe enough with me to let your guard down. That's how I know you've really forgiven me."

"Of course I've forgiven you. I told you—"

"I know what you told me. But you're still mad I'm going to challenge Jadick." His brow arches as if to contest that fact.

I only scowl. "Why should you get to have all the fun?"

He chuckles. "Look, we're both going to have to accept that we're letting the other one expose themselves to danger before this is all over."

"Are you saying you're not going to fight me about the fact that I'm going with you?" I ask.

"I mean, fighting is my second favorite thing to do with you," he says, grinning. "But no. I get it. We're equals in this."

I exhale.

"We have to go back before he kills any more of them," I say quietly.

"I know." He grips my elbows and pulls me in again, pressing a kiss to my forehead. It's a chaste gesture, but even so, my blood stirs with need. I'm suddenly aware of the fact that we're alone. On a bed. But I'm also aware that we're in a van parked out front of my father's house. And both my parents are way too close for me to let my guard down just now.

Levi eases back, a knowing twinkle in his eye. "I guess this means I'm sleeping on the couch tonight."

TRIPP RETURNS LATE, startling me out of the suspended place between awake and asleep where I always seem to float. The van door is a soft click, and then his scent reaches me instantly, but my heart races anyway. "Sorry," he mutters, climbing into the driver's seat and shutting the door behind him.

"What are you doing?"

"Levi snores," is his explanation, though, since Tripp is the one who snores, we both know he's only using it as an excuse to check on me.

He settles into the chair, reclining it as far back as it will go, and folds his hands over his middle.

"Who's on watch?"

"Rob." His voice is sleepy.

I consider going back to sleep, but after a few minutes, it's clear my mind isn't interested. Instead, I sit up, noting Tripp's chest is a steady rise and fall. Already asleep. Lucky asshole.

As quietly as possible, I get up and climb forward, using the passenger door to exit the van. Tripp stirs, eyes opening to meet mine through the window where I stand.

"Take the bed," I say.

"You sure?"

"Yeah."

I turn away but not before I hear, "Thanks, Mac."

My steps are silent as I pad around the house in search of my father's scent. It takes me a few minutes, and I realize he's masking it with the direction of the wind.

When I get close, I hear his voice joined by my mother's, and for some reason, I hang back, listening.

"You think the plan is reckless." My mother's voice is matter-of-fact though softer than usual.

"I think our daughter should be protected from danger instead of running toward it." My father sounds gruffer than he has with me.

I know it's wrong to eavesdrop, but I've never heard my parents interact before. It's too strange and fascinating to turn away just yet. I need to know what they're like together. Or maybe it's me just waiting to see if my mother means her apology—and her loyalty.

"Removing her was never an option," my mom replies.

"Of course it was," he says more forcefully than I expect.

I stiffen, wondering if my mother reacted too.

She doesn't answer, and he adds, "The past is done, but I'm not going to let you make all the decisions anymore. She came to me, and that means I'm in this now too."

"You have every right to be involved," she says, and honestly, her words shock me. I expected a fight or some kind of resistance, but there's only regret and kindness in her words now.

"Tomorrow, we all go together," he says.

"All right."

More softness from her. It's so weird.

"You look well, Vick," my father says.

"You too, old man."

My mom's teasing is a shock. And my dad's reply, "Not too old to get my hands on you," is even worse.

My nose wrinkles.

I start to back away. No way do I want to walk in on whatever's happening now. Or about to happen.

"Would you?" my mom asks, dead serious. Vulnerable, even.

I stop moving again, my heart aching at her tone.

"Would you really still put your hands on me, Robert?"

"Vick," my father whispers, chastising. "My hands ache for you. Always. That will never change."

Right.

Time to find somewhere else to be.

Parents, it turns out, are gross.

CHAPTER 18

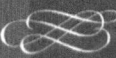

$\mathcal{A}$ hand on my arm pulls me awake, and I sit up, fist balled in a half-swing. Levi blocks it before I can hook his jaw.

"Whoa there, killer. Easy."

"You scared the shit out of me."

I sit back against the tree, its rough bark digging into my back through my thin shirt. The early morning chill isn't enough to pierce my core warmth, but the dew has left my shirt and pants damp.

I move a little to chase away the stiffness of a night spent under a tree.

"You slept out here?"

"Tripp needed a bed."

"You could have come inside."

"He said you were snoring."

He doesn't look sorry. He also doesn't look convinced.

"Someone needed to keep watch," I say, defensive in the silence.

"Your dad was doing that."

I snort. "Not unless you count watching my mother." As soon as the words are out, I make a face. "Gross, forget I said that."

Levi laughs. "They had a reunion, huh?"

"I know nothing," I lie.

I wish I didn't.

"After everything that's happened," he says, "this is what will scar you for life. Your parents' sex lives."

"Don't ever say parents and sex again."

He grins and pushes to his feet, offering his hand to me. "Come on, breakfast will help you forget."

I doubt it, but I let him pull me up anyway.

Except that, the moment I'm on my feet, I find my body pressing oddly close to his. And his expression shifts from light amusement to something darker—and desperate. His breath hits my face, and I don't even think about it. I just push onto my toes and taste his tongue with mine.

His reaction is instant. Strong arms grip me, circling my back and crushing me to his chest. His mouth on mine is ravaging. I don't bother to wonder how he knows this is what I need.

Nothing soft. Nothing gentle.

Just this.

The force of his need pressing against the nerve endings in my body that so desperately crave a feeling other than my own panic and fear. We're leaving today. Headed right back into the mouth of the beast. Who knows what we'll find—or if we'll walk out again.

I just want one more moment where none of it matters.

Levi's hands travel to the waistband of my pants, and I shimmy my hips to help him pull them down my legs. Then his fingers are at my already wet core, slipping into me and drawing a moan from my throat. His lips find mine, swallowing my sounds as he pushes one finger into me then two.

I nearly crawl up his body with pleasure, clinging to him in my half-dressed, half-aware state. His other hand grips my ass, squeezing, and I lose patience. Yanking on his own pants, I tug them down until his hardened length springs free. I barely get my hand around it before Levi pulls his own fingers away from me and instead cups my ass, lifting me to meet him.

I wind my legs around his body, barely breaking our kiss as he lowers me and slides into me quickly enough to make me shudder with the shock of it.

"Too much?" he asks, and I pull away to look him in the eye.

The concern is too real, too much of a reminder of what we'll face when we're finished here, so I shake my head.

"No," I tell him, nearly pleading with it. "Don't stop."

He drives into me, over and over, until I see stars bursting behind my eyelids. His breath is heavier now, and I can feel the sweat clinging to his skin as he pushes us both closer and closer to the edge with this hard, fast rhythm.

My own pleasure builds toward some pointed edge, a cliff I can't stop myself from falling over. My canines lengthen to pointed tips, aching to bite. To claim. Levi's teeth scrape along my throat, and I know he's thinking the same thing. I hear myself moan his name—a prayer to fate herself—and then I'm flying, my orgasm sending me soaring far above this world and its pain.

Levi doesn't let go, though. His body shudders as he finally comes, and then we soar together.

By the time we make it back to the cabin, everyone's up and moving. My parents barely say a word to each other over breakfast. It's awkward but not in the way it felt awkward in the woods last night. I start to wonder if I maybe missed something, if maybe things took a turn in a way I didn't stay to hear. But I'm damn sure not going to ask. No one asks about Levi and me, either, even though I'm sure they can guess what we've been up to. Tripp takes one look at us—more like one sniff—when Levi and I walk in together and looks down at his food again, though not before his eyebrow arches with pure teasing judgment.

Levi ruffles his hair as he passes, and Tripp slaps his hand away, both of them laughing.

"Morning," my father says, sharp eyes missing nothing.

"Morning," I return.

"Anything out there last night?" Levi asks him.

My father's gaze darts left, stopping just short of my mother. "Nothing," he says.

"Good," Tripp says, and the conversation ends there.

A moment later, my dad says something about loading the supplies and disappears out the back door before I can ask what supplies and where they're being loaded. My mother goes back to her coffee and toast, clearly pre-occupied.

I force myself to eat a few bites of the eggs Levi puts in front of me before my stomach turns to lead. He doesn't push me to eat more and, instead, simply slides the plate over to himself and finishes it off.

"You need to eat, Mac," my mother says.

I turn to her, ready to argue, especially if it means an outlet for my nerves. But Levi stops me, covering my hand with his. "She did," he says, his voice clipped.

Before my mother can reply, he shoves back in his chair and takes our empty plates to the sink. To my surprise, my mother lets it go.

When the dishes are cleared and rinsed, we all file outside. None of us has any bags to carry, which is just a nod to the sad state of my life as a fugitive. The idea of staying in one place, even if that place is Blackstone, is appealing enough to make me long for this to all be over. But then I catch myself. Too much has happened for me to think it'll be that easy. Or simple.

I look at Levi, who's organizing the inside of the van so we can all ride together. My heart aches to think that, when this is over, we might still have a chance together. But my heart doesn't dare let hope win out.

I look away—just in time to register the sound of a vehicle. A second later, it rounds the side of the house, and my father drives into view. A Jeep, this one much older and dirtier than the one my mother drives. It has no doors and no roof. The thing looks straight out of a safari—if that safari had taken place thirty years ago.

My father grins from the driver's seat as he pulls to a stop in front of the van.

"She started right up," he announces, clearly proud of the fact.

"I can't believe you kept it," my mom says, eyeing the Jeep like she's seeing a long-lost friend.

"Had her parked in the trees, covered with camouflage. For emergencies," he adds.

My mother wanders closer, running a hand over the hood appreciatively. They share a look. "This thing's been through it, huh," she says, a sort of smile playing at the edges of her usually serious mouth.

"Still going too," he tells her.

She nods as if this is some kind of good omen. Maybe it is. I hope it is.

"What do you say?" my father adds. "One more trip together? Kicking ass, taking names?"

My mom hesitates. It's clear she's not excited about being alone with my dad.

I step up, the words tumbling out before I can stop them.

"Actually, I think Mom and I should go together," I say.

My mom turns to me.

"If someone spots us, they'll think you found me and are bringing me in," I tell her. "The van's less conspicuous. They can follow behind and track us to make sure no one tries to intercept."

"She's got a point," Tripp says, but Levi says nothing.

I know he wants to tell me it's safer in the van. But I also know he won't, not after our conversation earlier.

My mom nods. "All right."

"When we get to Blackstone, we'll find a place to lie low and call the pack," Levi says.

"Good," I tell him. "In the meantime, I think Mom and I should find the witch." Levi looks like he wants to argue. "If we can remove her from the equation, he can't do the ritual."

"You're the key here, Mac, not the witch," Levi points out.

"I think Mac has a point," Tripp says, surprising me by taking my side. "Jadick's been looking for a witch for a while now. It's clear his idea rides on her presence. We remove her, and he can't try this again with someone else."

"If he's dead, he can't try it again at all," Levi says darkly.

I suppress a sigh. "You're right," I tell him. "This is just a back-up. A failsafe. Besides, it keeps us from sitting on our hands while we wait for the pack to show up."

"Fine," he says, "But no wild goose chases. We can't afford to be spotted."

"I can help with that," my mom says.

Everyone turns to her.

"You know where he's keeping her?" I ask.

She hesitates, guilt creeping in. "I suggested our house. Told him it would be the last place anyone would look."

I stare at her, not sure how to respond. Returning to Blackstone is one thing. Seeing my house again, full of all those memories…

"What will you do with her?" my father asks.

My mother frowns, and I remember what she did to the tracker last night. "We're removing her from the equation. Get her out of the house. Find a place to stash her where Jadick won't find her," I say firmly, catching her eye. "That's all."

She scowls. "Fine."

I start for the Jeep. My father climbs out to relinquish his wheels to us. As I pass him, he stops me and presses a phone into my hand.

"Take this," he says. "It already has all of our numbers, and we have yours."

I don't bother asking him where he got it; my dad seems prepared for pretty much anything, and I already love him for it.

"Thank you," I tell him, and then, before I can overthink it, I hug him quickly.

He steps back, his cheeks flushed but his smile genuine. "Go get 'em, girl."

"One problem with this master plan," Tripp calls. "Mac, Jadick's ultimatum about taking lives is all about you showing face.

610

Anything short of that and he'll make good on his word, and you know it."

He's not wrong.

"That just means he'll need to see us," I say, considering.

"Not an option," Levi growls at the same time my father says, "No way."

I sigh. "We'll grab the witch, stuff her in the back, and haul ass past the alpha house." Turning to Levi, I add, "By then, the pack will be arriving, and you can intercept Jadick when he comes for us. We won't even stop driving."

His tight expression makes it clear he hates the idea of letting me get so close to Jadick. Even my father's face is flushed red now. But there's no other way, and they both know it.

"A drive-by. I like it," Tripp says.

"Fine," Levi grinds out.

"Dad?" I ask and then suck in a breath at the fact that I just used that word.

He seems to realize it, too, and some of the resistance goes out of his expression. "We can try it your way," he allows. "But if he gets too close, I'm blowing his head off, fuck the rules of engagement."

Tripp lets out a whoop.

Even Levi looks inclined to agree.

I let out a breath and climb into the passenger side of the Jeep. "Fine by me," I say.

The "supplies," which are basically a shit-load of weapons my dad has saved up, are off-loaded into the van, and in a few minutes, we're ready to go. Levi steps up beside me, his dark gaze intense with all the emotions this day has already wrought.

"Be careful," he says quietly.

"Kick some ass," I tell him, refusing to acknowledge how many lives are at stake today. Including his. Ours.

He leans in and kisses me. My face flushes with warmth thanks to our audience. But no one reacts. Well, unless you count Tripp's shrill whistle a reaction. Levi doesn't look away from me, though his mouth does curve in a small smile at Tripp's teasing.

"Call me when you have the witch," he says then trudges back to the van.

Tripp moves in beside me then. "You have any kisses for me."

"Kiss my ass, Tripp."

He shrugs. "Not what I had in mind but—"

"Tripp," Levi growls, and my friend hurries toward the van, wearing a big grin.

I roll my eyes, but something in my gut loosens at his easy teasing, which I suspect was his goal all along.

Levi starts the van, its engine idling a hell of a lot softer than the Jeep's. My dad throws the last of his bags—I really want to ask where he got so many weapons—into the back and shuts the door. I watch as my mom walks over to him and gives him a peck on the cheek. "See you on the other side," she says.

His eyes widen, and he stops, staring after her as she climbs into the Jeep beside me, and we drive away.

CHAPTER 19

My mother drives like we're already being chased, which actually doesn't surprise me. It does, however, irritate me considering she's the one who encouraged Levi to keep us in sight while they followed.

"Mom, they're not even out of the driveway yet. Slow down," I say.

She doesn't respond, nor does she take her foot off the gas.

Warning bells sound in my mind. I look over at her, noting the white-knuckled grip she has on the steering wheel.

"Mom," I snap. "If you try to betray us, I swear I will—"

"Relax," she says, still not slowing. "I'm not betraying you. I'm saving them."

"What the hell does that mean?"

She takes the next corner fast enough that I have to grab the bar above my head to keep from being shoved against her.

I debate the wisdom of reaching over and yanking the wheel, a move that will surely cost us the Jeep considering there's no way we won't hit a tree. But I also refuse to let her do what I think she's doing.

"The witch can't do the ritual without you," she snaps, and it takes me a full breath to realize her intention.

She's not double-crossing me for Jadick's orders. She's doing the opposite.

"If we don't go back to Blackstone, he can't hurt you."

"Mom," I say, but she just keeps driving, blowing straight through a stop sign.

"Mom," I say again, louder now.

Her chin juts out stubbornly.

Moving fast enough that she doesn't see me coming, I reach over and grab her face in my hands, turning it so she's forced to look at me. She tries to wrench free, but I don't let her. Finally, she's forced to slam on the brakes.

The tires screech, and we're both driven forward as she comes to a sudden stop.

In the silence, I see her fear reflected in her usually hardened eyes.

"I know you're scared," I say.

"I'm terrified," she hisses.

Anger.

I'm used to that.

"This will work," I say.

"It's a shit plan, Mac." I don't answer, and she sighs, settling back against her chair. Her eyes are on the road, but she makes no move to start driving again. "I've never gone for a mark with such a shitty plan, and that's usually just one on one combat."

"Hey," I say. "Two on one."

She grimaces. "Right."

"I can't leave those people to die," I say quietly. "Even if you can."

She twists in her chair, looking at me again. "You think this is easy for me?"

"I don't know. Is it?"

"Running is easy," she mutters and then says more darkly, "Fighting is easy. But only if I know I can win." No argument there. "Risking you," she adds, "is the hardest thing I'll ever do."

"Was that true even when you made that deal with Jadick for my life?"

"Without his help, you would have died."

"You don't know that."

Anger flashes, but she exhales, letting it go before saying, "You're right. I don't. What I do know is you're alive, here, now. And I'm done interfering."

"You are literally trying to drive me off into the sunset against my will," I point out.

She scowls. "Fine, I sometimes interfere. I can't help it. You're my daughter."

I laugh. It's brittle, but it's something, I guess.

She looks at me warily as if she's thinking the same thing.

"We're sticking to the plan," I say.

"It's a shit plan," she says again.

"It's a shit plan," I agree.

She stares back at me, searching my face—for what, I don't know. Finally, she blows out a breath and straightens in her seat. Behind us, the rev of an engine roars closer from around the bend.

In the side mirror, I see the van speeding toward us. It lurches to a stop beside us on the narrow, winding road. From the driver's seat, Levi glares at my mother. Tripp leans out the open window toward us.

"You tryin' to set a new record or what?"

My mom taps the wheel. "Just seeing what this baby can do."

Tripp glances at me, and I nod, letting him know we're all good. He turns and says something to Levi and then waves us forward. "Let's do it."

My mom eases off the brake, and we head down the road, this time at a speed that doesn't threaten to toss me around the seat. As we drive, I can only think about how true it is: this is a shit plan. But it's the only one we've got.

Blackstone is three hours away, according to my mother.

Even this far out, we don't stop for gas. Not at a station, anyway. When Levi gets low, he signals for us to pull over, and he refills using a red can stashed in the back of the van underneath the mattress compartment.

"How's it going?" Levi asks when I wander closer to where he has the can propped up to the fuel opening. Both sides of the road are lined with trees. It smells like open fields and pine out here. Like nothing in the world could be this wrong. For once, I appreciate staying off the major highways. My wolf is better out here. More sure of herself.

"Fine," I say. Knowing what he really means, I add, "She wanted to kidnap me and run me out into the hills where no one would find us. Let you guys have all the fun."

He grunts. "Not a bad idea."

"Don't start," I warn.

"I'm just saying," he says, clearly having fun with it now. "Your mom and I finally see eye to eye on something."

I roll my eyes. "Have you guys heard back from Frankie?"

His half-smile vanishes. "No."

"And Grey?"

"He's with us, but he's staying put for now. He can do more good on the inside."

I don't bother to speculate about reasons for Frankie's silence. None of them can possibly be good for any of us.

"I've put out the call though," he says. "For the pack or, at least, the ones who ran off when Jadick took over."

"Is that a good idea?" I ask, startled. "I mean, won't Jadick sense it and figure it out?"

He shakes his head. "If he never bonded with them, he has no way of knowing. And if they've put distance between themselves and Blackstone, the sooner I put out the call, the better. Time is not on our side."

I tense at that. He's right. We have no way of knowing what time yesterday Jadick executed Jim. Or what time he'll do it again today if we're not there to stop it.

"Do you sense anyone close?" I ask.

"Not yet."

I turn away as he finishes up, capping the red can and the fuel tank.

"They'll be there," he says to me, and I glance at him, giving him what I hope is an optimistic smile. But it feels more like a grimace.

In minutes, we're back on the road, and I start scanning the horizon for some sign that the Jades have found us. But traffic is light, and no one flags us down as we pass through town after tiny town.

When we reach the outskirts of pack lands, we pull over again.

The guys off-load weapons where my father has apparently cataloged our options and divvies them up between him and my mother. I don't bother to listen to his explanation of what's what. My mom taught me to fight with my hands—or claws—or not at all. I'm not going to change it up now.

Levi and Tripp crowd in close, though, taking guns and tucking them into various hidden parts of their clothes. We're all loading back into the cars when someone calls out for Levi. A female voice, still distant, though I spot her quickly.

Across the road, an abandoned gas station sits with one end partially collapsed inward, thanks to years of rotting and disrepair. Just beyond the edge of the overgrown parking lot, a figure hurries toward us.

My wolf sight locks onto her, and my eyes widen.

"Nely?"

I start for her, but my father grabs my elbow.

"She's a friend," I say, but he doesn't let go.

Levi and Tripp hurry across the road, and apparently my dad decides that's enough of a reassurance. He lets me go, and I race after them, catching up just as they all reach one another.

Nely is breathless, sweaty, and exhausted if the bags under her eyes are any indication. But the sight of her boosts my hope in the plan.

She's answered Levi's call.

More are coming, I know it.

"Where are the others?" Levi asks.

Nely shakes her head. "Still being watched," she says as she finally begins to catch her breath.

He frowns. "They're in Blackstone?"

"They're waiting for you," she says, her eyes landing on me. "Glad to see you're still out here causing chaos."

I flash her a smile. "I was bored."

She shakes her head. "So, what's the plan?"

I start to answer her, but my mom steps up beside me, nudging me silent. "We should keep moving." She scans the horizon as she speaks, and I stiffen, realizing she's right. We're too exposed out here.

"Good idea." I look at Nely. "You can ride with us."

"Actually, why don't you ride with the guys?" my mother says. "Mac and I have an errand, and then we'll meet up. They'll fill you in."

"Sounds good." Nely nods, and we all start for the cars.

"I'm glad you found us," I tell her as we walk.

Her relief matches my own. "I'm glad you were out here to find."

MY MOTHER WINDS around the back roads outside of town, slower now that we're close to our destination. I try to read her, but she's back to the silent, stoic Vicki Quinn I've come to know so well. Giving nothing away, especially comfort or camaraderie.

We have Nely, though, I remind myself.

And that means we have the Jades.

They're waiting for you, she'd said. And that means we have the numbers we need to take on Jadick's loyal warriors.

This is going to work.

It has to.

Grabbing the witch is icing on the cake.

When we make the turn that will finally separate us from the others, I glance back to see Levi watching me from the van.

Here we go, I think to him.

Don't fucking die, I think he'd say back.

But from the driver's seat, he doesn't move or react other than to wrap me up in that glittery, dark stare of his. It's potent enough that I feel his presence with me until long after they've passed out of view. Traffic is light in this part of town. Or maybe it's this time of day.

Early.

My mother and I lived in the outskirts for two reasons. First, it's cheap, and second, it's the farthest you can get from the alpha house without leaving pack lands. Unfortunately, there are plenty of other Black Moon wolves with reasons for wanting less oversight. Our neighborhood isn't the best even in daylight. The only advantage is that most of its less reputable residents will still be sleeping off the previous night's consequences for at least another couple more hours.

We pull into our driveway without spotting another soul.

I look up at the sagging roof sloping down to meet the single-story structure. Chipped siding and crooked shutters aside, it's not the world's worst house. It's just not a home.

My mom parks and unbuckles, moving quickly as she climbs out.

"Come on. We've got minutes before that asshole figures out we're here."

I climb out and hurry to catch up as she stalks toward the door. Darting glances left and right, I look for movement, but there's nothing. The street is strangely empty.

"I can't believe he doesn't have guards posted—" I start.

"He does."

A body drops from above me.

I jump back, just barely avoiding a collision. Out of the corner of my eye, I see another and another do the same. Guards. On the roof. Smart.

My mom yells at me to put them down and get inside. My heart registers the danger and possible adrenaline, and then my instincts kick in with years of training, not just to fight but to react calmly in the face of a threat.

I inhale.

Exhale.

Then I look up and smile when I see who's left their perch to try and stop us.

"Hello, Gregario."

CHAPTER 20

I bare my teeth at the monster who is second only to Jadick on the list of people I want to kill today. He looks back at me like I'm his number one. My attack is instant, absolute, and lands a right hook against his jaw hard enough to send him reeling. He recovers and comes for me, using all his body weight like a linebacker. I spin aside and shove him, sending him against the house.

A shot rings out, and Gregario's body jerks forward, careening into me. He grunts, a crimson stain blooming on his shirt where a bullet has torn through the back of his shoulder. But as he slams into me, I know the injury isn't enough to stop him. He's using its momentum to get to me, and by the time I know it for sure, I'm pinned beneath him.

His shift to wolf is slow, thanks to the bullet, but his bones pop and fingernails give way to claws that rake down my cheek in our struggle.

Pain slices into my skin and then heat.

Blood.

The idea that he's drawn first blood fuels me. He's still human with otherworldly claws protruding from gnarled fingers.

Avoiding their sharpened points, I bring a knee up and into his groin. He groans and goes limp. I push him off me then roll, slipping my arm around his throat until it's locked tight enough to cut off his oxygen. He thrashes, struggling, but I don't loosen my grip.

Another shot.

I watch as another of the guards is brought down by the small, near-silent gun my mother carries. One more to go.

Gregario continues to kick and fight.

My mother drops the third guard and then looks over at me.

She tosses me a gun, but I ignore it and, instead, release his throat long enough to grab a blade one of the others dropped during the fight. With my fist wrapped tight around the hilt, I drive it into Gregario's throat as he lunges up at me.

Gregario gasps and falls back as blood leaks from the wound around the buried blade. Then he goes limp.

I finally let him go and scramble to my feet. My mother walks over and aims her gun at his head.

"He's already—"

He gasps for air, so suddenly, I let out a strangled scream.

My mother pulls the trigger, putting a bullet through his brain. He falls still again.

Dead. For real this time.

I exhale, wobbly, relieved, dumbstruck.

"Let's get the witch and get the fuck out of here."

My mother has never sounded more unruffled.

That makes one of us.

I follow her into the house, braced for another attack. Inside, it's quiet as death, which puts me more on alert. The familiar pictures, scant though they may be, send a wave of nostalgia through me. It's not that I *want* to be here or even feel connected to this place. But I can't help all the years' worth of memories washing through me any more than I can stop breathing.

The couch where I ate cereal on weekends and watched cartoons while my mother slept off her injuries from a night of hunting. The dining table where Tripp and I carved our names into the wood on the underside out of sheer boredom.

My throat tightens at the memories.

The living room is empty, though. No witch.

That brings me back to the moment.

My mother and I exchange a look. The witch would have surely heard the commotion outside and come to investigate. The fact that she's hiding is only going to prolong our presence here. And make her more difficult to procure.

My mother motions for me to stay behind her, and we continue on toward the kitchen. Beyond that are two small bedrooms, no back door. She has to be here somewhere.

The blood spatters catch my eye a millisecond before the smell reaches me.

I stop, yanking my mother backward just as a knife sings through the air, burying itself in the wall where my mother just stood. A figure moves faster than any wolf I've ever seen. Lithe and limber, nothing more than a blur of long hair and an even longer blade clutched in each hand.

Marilyn rounds the corner and sends blades flying—one at each of us.

My mother shoves me aside, catching a knife in the thigh for her efforts. I slam into the wall and then sidestep as Marilyn launches herself at me with a crazed shriek.

She lands close.

Too close.

I see her eyes, glassy and wild. Her hair, tangled. Her clothes, coated in blood. My next move sends me into the kitchen, drawing her away from my mother. I grab the knife still stuck in the wall as I spin into the space and nearly lose my footing in the puddles of blood on the floor.

"Marilyn, stop this," my mother demands.

Sliding toward the dinette, I catch myself on the back of the vinyl chair. Then I spin, wielding the knife as Marilyn chases after me.

She dodges my attempts with the blade and punches me square in the face so hard I see stars. Then the knife is gone from my hand, and I can only twist violently sideways to avoid a deadly blow.

Over Marilyn's shoulder, I catch sight of my mother. She's on her feet, braced against the doorway. The blood stain on her pants is growing, but the knife is clutched in her hand. She holds the blade instead of the handle, loose between her fingers and thumb. I see her intention a second beforehand and duck. The blade hisses through the air, burying itself in Marilyn's back.

Marilyn screams, arching against the sudden pain.

I use my boot to shove her backward, and she slips in a puddle of blood, going down hard on her hip.

I stand over her, stepping on her hand when she tries to swing on me again.

"What the hell have you done?" I demand.

The witch's body is splayed out in front of the sink. What looks like multiple stab wounds are slashed through her skin. I glance over once then away again quickly. It's horrible. Worse than anything we've done.

"I did what I had to do," Marilyn says at my feet.

My mother limps closer, careful to keep her footing in the ever-growing sea of witch blood.

"You stopped him," my mother says, and I can't tell if she's relieved or disgusted or both.

"I'll stop you all," Marilyn says. "The monsters must be sent to Hell."

I shudder at her words. The way she doesn't even seem to register what she's done. Or the brutality in how she's done it.

"I never should have brought you here," my mother says. She crouches beside Marilyn, regret and concern tightening her features.

Marilyn looks up at her, smiling. "I told you I would make you sorry you dragged me back to this hellhole town."

"You did," my mother says.

Marilyn sniffs and then winces in pain as my boot leans harder on her hand.

"Where's Jadick?" my mother asks.

"Planning his wedding, of course." She glances at me. "His bride is dead, though."

I shudder at the insanity in her eyes.

"Mac isn't dead, but you're headed that way. Let me pull that knife out so you can shift and heal."

Marilyn laughs bitterly.

"No healing exists in a place like this," she says. Another blink and her eyes clear. "He knows you're here," she whispers. "He already knows."

My mother frowns, but she doesn't look particularly concerned.

A ripple of unease shoots through me as she turns her attention to me. "Your mate won't survive what waits for him now."

"What are you talking about?" I demand. "What is Jadick planning?"

"She's just talking nonsense," my mother says.

She moves toward the door, but I crouch, grabbing Marilyn's hand. "I'm nothing like him," I say. "Tell me what he's done so I can make it right."

"Right?" she scoffs. "There's nothing right about him. About you. And he's already won."

"I can stop this," I insist.

"Did you know I went to see an oracle?" she asks, and the question is so off-topic I can only stare at her.

"Mac, let's go." My mother hovers in the doorway, favoring her injured leg. But I don't move to join her.

"What does an oracle have to do with anything?" I ask.

"Three times three," she says. "It told me things. Dark, twisted things. My son cannot be saved. His heart is cursed. And now, yours is too. She told me."

"She lied," I say, releasing her hand angrily.

"A pack of lies," she whispers, falling back into her own blood. "A pack of black hearts—all of you. The only way to win is to die."

The sound of the tranquilizer gun jolts me.

A dart lands in her shoulder, and Marilyn thuds against the floor.

I look up sharply at my mother, whose mouth is set in a hard line. "The only way to win."

Neither of us bothers to finish the sentence.

"She could be a problem when she wakes up," I say.

"She'll either leave, or she'll seal her own fate," my mother says. "Come on. Let's go."

Outside, neighbors have finally emerged to investigate. A small crowd has gathered in the patch of deadened grass where Gregario and the other guards lie. My mother still holds the gun at her side as she motions me past the onlookers and back toward the Jeep.

Between the gun in her hand and the bullet holes in the dead men, no one tries to stop us.

"Mac."

I look up as my mother tosses me the keys, barely managing to snag them out of midair.

"You drive. I'll shoot."

"Deal."

I climb in and get us the hell out of there—forever.

We pass three black SUVs on the way to the alpha house. The first two don't react to the sight of us, but the third hits the brakes hard. I watch in the rearview as it spins in a reckless U-turn before racing toward us again.

"We have company," I say.

"I see it."

My heart pounds. Not at the tail we're trying to outrun but at what could have happened to the others. If Jadick knows we're coming—

I don't let myself think about it now.

I take corners on squealing tires, weaving deftly in and out of traffic until the vehicle following us is forced to fall back.

Finally, I turn onto the road for the alpha house and give it gas.

The circular drive is punctuated by the house, and for a moment,

I think maybe Marilyn was wrong. Levi stands on the steps of the house with Jadick only a few yards away. They're alone, facing off like two alphas about to fight for the title. Hope soars. Maybe Marilyn was just crazy after all. But then I slam to a stop and see them.

The Jades.

On the roof. Bound and shoved to their knees. Behind them, guards await the order to push them to their deaths. And I realize this is how he executed Jim in the video.

This is what he plans to do to all of them.

No wonder they never came when Levi called.

Jadick already has them.

Marilyn was right.

He's already won.

CHAPTER 21

I scan the yard, but Tripp and my father are nowhere in sight. Neither is Nely. The van is parked in the grass several yards away, but the door hangs open, revealing an empty interior.

"Mackenzie, so good of you to join us," Jadick says. "And Vicki, perfect timing. The guests of honor are here. That means the party can finally begin."

"Let them go." My voice is flat, but I don't move from the Jeep. My thoughts race, trying to form a plan. Anything to distract him—

"If that's what you want." Jadick shrugs and looks up at the row of prisoners and guards. "Send one down—"

"Wait!" I leap out of the truck, rushing forward. "No. that's not what I meant."

Levi grabs me, stopping me before I can get closer to the asshole orchestrating all this.

"Calm down," he says, his voice low in my ear. "It's handled."

I stiffen at that. Tripp. My father. Nely. They're on it. They must be.

Straightening, I look back at Jadick.

"Isn't that how you meant it?" he taunts, smiling broadly.

"When you left, I assumed—we all did—that you no longer cared what happens to your own people. So, I acted accordingly."

"Fuck you."

"In good time."

Levi snarls, and now it's me holding him back.

"Vicki, you've been busy."

Jadick's comment draws my eye, and I see my mother has climbed out of the truck. The blood on her pants is evident, but the limp is better. Already healing, thankfully.

"I have." She holds up the gun, inspecting it casually in her hand. "Four shots fired. Four bodies down." She looks up at Jadick, eyes narrowing. "Guess I've still got it."

Jadick simply lifts a brow. "Four of mine compared to dozens of yours."

My mother cocks her head at him. "Is that what you think? Are all of these lives not equal? To yours? To your mother's?"

Jadick stiffens, and I smile smugly, watching as he tries to decipher what my mother means. Clearly, he doesn't know what his mother has done. And that means he doesn't know the witch is dead yet. Watching him realize he's not as good as he thinks is a lovely bonus.

He presses the button on a handheld communicator and says, "Find my mother. Bring her to me."

The reply that comes back is almost instant. "Sir. She left two hours ago. She said you ordered her—"

"Fuck!"

He throws the communicator against the house, and it breaks into pieces.

I smile wider.

"Is that your way of saying your mother's life is worth more to you than one Jade?" my mother calls.

"I'm going to kill you," he seethes. "If you hurt her. If you put a hand on her—"

"She hates you," I say, "Did you know that?"

"She will come to understand what I've done for her," he says. "As will you."

"She would rather die than live here with you."

"You don't know anything about family," Jadick says, an edge of cruelty working its way back into his voice. "You have only your mother, who clearly cares more about her own gain than your life."

"At least, my mother didn't say I'd be better off dead."

My words find their mark. Even if he recovers quickly, I see that it bothers him. That he clearly brought her back here out of some sense of twisted affection or familial bond. It's sick. And kind of sad. But then I remember how Marilyn would kill me if given half a chance, and I remember what kind of people the Clemons' really are. What exactly they're all capable of.

"You can have her back, though," I say. "If you let them go."

"Don't attempt to manipulate me," he snaps.

I glance up at the rooftop. The Jades are still there. The guards haven't moved. My chest tightens. I don't know what else Jadick has planned, but I know we're running out of time to get control of this.

"I'm simply making an offer," I say. "Like the one you made me."

"Everyone's come to make an offer," he taunts. "Levi here thinks I'll lower myself to actually fight him. And poor Mac thinks she can bargain her way into a new deal. Unfortunately for both of you, this union is pre-ordained, and nothing will change that now."

A vehicle approaches from the street, engine gunning as it careens down the drive and pulls to a sudden stop beside us. The driver gets out, but instead of moving toward us, he hurries up to Jadick and whispers in his ear.

Jadick's face flushes red.

He looks from his messenger to me and then to my mother.

Clearly, he knows the witch is dead. I wonder if he knows Marilyn is the one who killed her.

"You think you've won, but you've only—"

"Oh, for fuck's sake." My mother raises the gun. "You talk too damn much." She points the barrel at Jadick and fires.

I tense, helpless to stop my mother's reckless act, one that will surely plunge this scene into chaos—and worse, cost lives. But as she fires the gun, she pulls the barrel up sharply. The bullet unleashes itself on a trajectory that soars high over our heads. Less than a second later, one of the guards standing on the rooftop is blown backward off his feet as the bullet tears through his skull.

No more darts then.

The other guards react, screaming and attacking the Jades.

Unaffected, my mother fires again.

I don't get a chance to see who she hits before Levi grabs my arm, tugging me urgently and yelling about taking cover. I glance at my mom, who's re-aiming at another guard. Before she can get a shot off, a guard on the far end of the row is shoved roughly forward until he's tumbling over the edge of the roof, arms flailing. His body makes a disgusting sound as it hits the concrete walkway below and sticks. The rest of Jadick's men are screaming at the prisoners, threatening death if they so much as move.

My heart thunders in my chest.

Levi and I backtrack to the SUV where Jadick's men have abandoned their post to rush into the house at Jadick's orders. Undoubtedly headed upstairs to gain control over the chaos on the roof. Above me, Jades have begun to get off their knees and fight back even with their hands tied. My gaze catches on two figures, neither guard nor Jade, racing around and cutting the ties on the Jades' wrists and ankles.

Tripp pauses long enough to salute us with dramatic flair, and then he rejoins my father as they free everyone and battle the guards.

My heart swells.

Across the concrete, Jadick screams for more backup to no one in particular and then rushes for the house, only to pull up short when a second falling guard nearly flattens him. He scrambles backward and then turns sharply, disappearing into the three-car garage behind him.

"Levi," I start, tugging on his sleeve.

"I see." He glances back, making sure I'm right behind him before turning his attention back to the garage—and the distance separating us from it.

Scanning our backs, I note movement. Far down at the other end of the drive, two more SUVs pull in. I glance back to my mom, who's still firing at the guards stupid enough to get close enough to the roof's edge.

"Mom," I shout.

Our eyes meet, and I point to the incoming vehicles.

Her expression hardens. "Where's Jadick?" she asks.

The third garage door begins to lift, and I see her gaze catch on the movement. "Go," she says.

"What about you?" I ask.

Her eyes burn with intensity as she pops out the empty cartridge and loads another. "I'll find you," she says. "Go."

I don't tell her goodbye. Or that I love her. Or any of the other thousand things I could say. Hopefully, there will be time later. There has to be.

Levi grabs my hand, and together, we race for the garage.

Inside the garage are three parking bays. The first two are empty. The third holds two small ATVs, each only big enough for one person. The garage door on that side is wide open. A third ATV whines loudly as it races across the lawn beyond where we stand. I catch sight of it just before it disappears over the hill.

Urgency drives me, and I hurry to one of the remaining ATVs, climbing in.

"Mac," Levi says, but I just grab the three-point harness and buckle myself in.

"Mac," he says again as I turn the small key and the motor comes to life. He stands over me now, blocking my exit, and I finally look up, an argument ready on my lips.

But he only holds out a helmet. "Put this on."

Relieved, I take it and shove it on.

Levi climbs onto another ATV and buckles in.

I take a steadying breath then square my back against the seat and punch the gas pedal all the way to the floor. The ATV shoots forward. I grip the wheel, using it for direction and also to hang on as I whip out of the garage and across the patch of concrete drive before careening onto the grass.

Levi is right behind me.

Down a short embankment and then up again, I drive a path that slices sideways across the hilly yard. Ahead, I catch sight of Jadick's ATV as it disappears around the corner of the house. With the gas pedal held to the floor, I aim straight for him.

Above me, the rooftop of the house shows my father battling three guards at once. My stomach tightens, but I force my attention back to the turn coming up. My dad can handle himself. I have to believe that and clear my head for what I'm about to do.

By the time I reach Jadick's ATV, it's empty. Through my helmet, I hear the muffled sound of Levi's ATV as it pulls up beside mine. We park and climb out, facing a tall hedge that separates this part of the grounds from the back gardens. It's too tall for me to see over, but there's nowhere else Jadick could have gone.

"He's in there," I say, already starting for a small opening where the back and side walls meet.

The gap is barely wide enough for a single person, put here only for the gardener's access. I know because Kari and I used it more than once to sneak in and out when we didn't want her brothers or father to know we were here.

Levi grabs my arm, stopping me. "Mac, we can't just run blindly in there after him."

"He's going to get away," I start.

"How?" he asks, and the question stops me. "He was getting away, and instead he parked here and ran back inside."

"You think it's a trap?"

"Damn right it's a trap."

I huff. "Even if it is, we can't just stand here and do nothing."

"Your parents and Tripp are already inside," he says quietly. "Why not let them handle it?"

I stare at him, searching his depthless eyes for whatever he's not saying right now.

"And you," I prompt. "Let you go handle it. Everyone but me."

"I have to challenge him—to end this," he says, and I can tell from the anguish he wears that he hates to ask this of me. But he hates the idea of me getting hurt even more. And I soften because I feel the same about him. But—

"I can't sit back and do nothing. Not where you and I are concerned," I tell him. "I tried that, and look how many years we wasted apart. Look how many lives are being lost because of this mess. I'm going with you."

He looks like he wants to argue, so I add, "Jadick wants us all to believe that loving our fated mate makes us weak, but I think he's wrong. You make me stronger. Together, we can beat him. Apart... I'm not going to find out."

His gaze burns into mine, and I bite my lip, wondering if he's going to argue it further. Instead, he pulls me in and kisses me with an intensity that steals my breath. Then, just as quickly, he's releasing me and stepping back, his hand sliding from my arm to my hand. Gripping tight, he says, "Together."

I smile, wobbly thanks to the toe-curling kiss. "Together."

Hand in hand, we slip through the hedge and into the garden to find the serpent that waits within.

CHAPTER 22

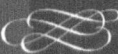

The garden is a simple maze with multiple paths, all leading to a center fountain depicting none other than a naked Greek god of a man—Jadick's favorite décor. Ugh. Luckily, the low hedge rows make it easy to spot anything taller than four feet. Unfortunately, that includes a fair number of marble statues— more nudes, of course—along with shrubs carved into spiraling patterns that swirl upward. Bordeaux has been busy. On the far right, the house rises up. From this angle, I can't see the rooftop battle that's clearly still raging from the snarls and gunshots still ringing out. My wolf senses movement on more than just the roof now, though. Worry spikes again at the thought of my parents and Tripp up against the evil Jadick has bred here, but I don't let myself think about that. Not when I need to focus on this.

Sweeping my gaze right to left, I spot the archway set up in the very back, and my stomach sinks.

"He's there," I say, pointing.

"You see him?" Levi asks.

"No, but that's the site he built for the ritual." I can't bring myself to say *wedding*. "Something tells me he's there." And waiting for us, I realize. Or, for me.

My hands turn clammy because it's obvious Jadick is luring us here—and that he must have a plan. That means we haven't caught him as off-guard as I'd hoped.

"Let's go," Levi says.

From the hardness in his tone, it's clear Levi has realized the same thing.

We turn away from the house and make our way through the maze toward the archway. The beams have been strung with vines and flowers. Honeysuckle and something else that makes my nose wrinkle. A rotting sort of scent that I can't readily name.

We creep closer, our steps silent against the stone path.

Levi is rigid and ready to pounce. I can see the bunching of the muscles around his neck and shoulders as he leads the way. Braced for a fight. We both are.

Behind us, the sounds of the fight on the roof continue. Screams and grunts that punctuate the silence in a way that drives my need for action. Adrenaline pumps through me, strangely calming as we round the final bend and reach the archway.

Jadick stands beneath it, his back half-turned to us as he fusses with several items set on a narrow table. He doesn't seem bothered by our presence. Nor does he seem worried about the fight Levi is about to start with him.

In fact, when he looks up, his gaze lands solely on me.

"There's my bride."

His words are the spark that ignites the explosion. Levi lets go of me, his beast rippling beneath his skin.

"Jadick Clemons, I challenge you," Levi says, voice trembling with rage. "For the role of alpha. A fight to the death—"

"This is all incredibly predictable," Jadick cuts him off. "And honestly, boring."

"Pack law states you must accept my challenge," Levi says.

Movement behind me sends me whirling. I stop when I see Burnett and a few others advancing toward us. They don't attack, though the sneer Burnett sends me says he wants to.

I look back at Jadick where Levi still waits for his challenge to be accepted.

"I am law here," Jadick says, eyes glittering with the conviction of his words. "And I say whether this challenge is worth acknowledging."

He sets aside the blade he's holding and rounds the low stone platform that separates us from him. Not a platform, I realize with a jolt as I finally pay it attention. An altar. Complete with metal rings for binding wrists and ankles. At each corner are a small pile of bones. I sniff, noting the same bones have been tied off to the vines amid the honeysuckle. Gross.

Are these Crigger's bones?

With a shudder, I fall back as Levi takes a step forward. The guards at our back aren't enough to faze him. He came here for this moment, and it's not hard to see he's determined to have it.

But Jadick stops, looking past Levi to me again. "You would have made a formidable mate, Mac."

"Are you going to fight me or not?" Levi demands. He's barely hanging onto his human form now. Jadick refocuses his attention on Levi.

Finally, he sighs. "All right then. Let's get it over with. I have things to do."

That's all Levi needs to complete the shift and launch himself at the Clemons heir. Jadick barely manages to get into his wolf form before Levi's massive paws land on him, shoving him backward.

They go tumbling across stone, their fur catching on the sharper branches jutting out of the hedges. Levi's teeth rip a chunk out of Jadick's shoulder, and Jadick responds by nipping back. Their movements are fast and lethal, each drawing blood, one from the other. But it's easy to see Levi's stronger. Jadick's movements begin to slow. Levi's blows become more severe.

Jadick makes the mistake of looking over at me. His eyes rake me over like he's looking for something. Disappointment flashes. And the distraction costs him.

Finally, Levi pins Jadick hard enough that Jadick can't get free.

My heart plummets, and I brace myself for the final blow. The kill that will pronounce Levi the winner, the alpha of the Black Moon pack.

A shot rings out, and before my brain can fully register the sound of the gun going off, my body jerks forward. A chunk of flesh is torn away as a bullet rips through my biceps.

I try to put my arms out to break my fall, but only the left hand obeys. My right arm hangs limp, and when I hit the ground, I scream as pain bursts from my insides.

Levi's wolf howls. I don't need to look up to know it's him. I feel his anguish in my own body, separate from my own pain though no less potent. And then I feel the agony cut short.

Jadick uses the distraction to his advantage, knocking Levi aside and pinning him instead. A second later, I'm seized by a sense of pain so much greater than my own injury has caused.

Levi howls again, this time much softer and more desperate.

Then, he's silent.

Footsteps sound as boots march over to where I've fallen. With a groan, I fling myself onto my back in time to see Frankie coming toward me. Relief floods me, and I exhale, summoning the strength to form words around the pain and the blood loss.

"Someone shot me," I say through clenched teeth. "Find them and stop them."

"I've found them," Frankie says, strangely neutral as she steps up and aims her gun at my forehead. "But I can't stop until I've finished it."

My eyes widen, and I realize way too late what's happening. Frankie's finger begins squeezing the trigger, and I shut my eyes, bracing for the end.

But it never comes.

A grunt sounds and then a shuffling of limbs.

I reopen my eyes in time to see Frankie tackled to the ground by a familiar figure dressed in black. Grey lands on top of Frankie as he wrestles the gun from her hand.

"Mac's not mated to Jadick, you idiot," he hisses at her. "Killing her won't harm him."

"But—the kiss. They claimed each other," Frankie says.

"This isn't the way," he grunts.

"It's worth the sacrifice."

"It's not," he roars.

She manages to yank away, and he rears back, plowing his fist into her face. She goes limp long enough for him to grab the gun from her then immediately begins fighting anew to get it back.

"Frankie, stop," I scream, but she's lost to her own rage.

"He can't get away with this," Frankie says, spit flying from her clenched teeth.

I recognize the look she wears as one Marilyn wore earlier. There's no thread tying her to reality. Only her own twisted sense of justice. And what she must do in order to achieve it.

"Stop her," another male voice orders Grey.

My father rushes toward us, a few guards giving chase behind him. But he ignores them, his expression urgently locked on Frankie and the threat she poses.

"Put her down if you have to," my father yells at Grey.

"No," I protest, but even I can see it's going to come down to Grey or Frankie.

Skin rippling with the change coming over him, Grey tosses the gun to me with a grunted, "Here," and by the time I've managed to grip it in my hands, he's already shifted and sunk his teeth into Frankie's throat.

She shifts beneath him, legs jerking as he severs her artery. When she stops moving, she's a wolf. And I can only stare in shock for a long moment as Grey steps away and looks at me, his wolf covered in blood.

Before I can respond, a shot rings out. Dazedly, I look down at the gun I now hold, worried I'm the one who fired it, even though I never moved to do so. Someone screams.

My mother.

The sound of her shrill voice, so full of terror, snaps me out of my reverie. I look up again and see my father clutching his chest. Blood leaks from a wound there. On his face, I see confusion, then horror, then pain register. Until finally, he drops to his knees.

Behind him, I see a guard—Lenny—pointing a gun. My mother screams again, this time a battle cry. She launches herself at Lenny, knocking him to the ground. His gun slips away as she rolls on top of him and wraps her hands around his throat. He thrashes, but she doesn't let up, taking her vengeance on him.

My father falls to his side and looks over at me. "Finish it," he says in a strained voice, blood leaking heavily from the bullet wound in his chest.

Pain guts me then. Terror for what I'm about to lose just as I finally found it.

I open my mouth and close it again as words fail me. The shock of what's happened is overshadowed by movement. People are running this way through the garden from the direction of the house. I tense and then realize with a start that they're all Jades.

Hope rises swiftly—but then just as quickly is dashed again as I see the guards and other Black Moon pack members close at their heels. They don't make it much farther before they're forced to turn and fight again.

I hold tight to the gun still in my hand, and Grey and I share a look.

"Go," I tell him.

My shoulder is already beginning to heal at least enough for the bleeding to have slowed. And maybe even enough to aim this gun properly.

I lift it as Grey takes off for the Jades.

"Jadick, stop," I scream, pointing the gun at Jadick's wolf.

He looms over an injured Levi, clearly ready to deliver the killing blow now that Frankie and my father have been dealt with. My heart thunders with terror as I note the blood and deep gashes torn into Levi's fur. Levi's eyes are open, but he doesn't move when he sees me with the gun.

Jadick stalks away from Levi, headed my way. He shifts as he walks, coming toward me with the dark, lethal gaze of someone who's won.

I curl my finger around the trigger, waiting to make sure I have the clear shot. But his mouth only curves upward as he steps directly into my line of fire, each step bringing him closer to his end.

"It's over. You'll never hurt anyone ever again," I say just before an arm snakes around my throat from behind and I'm yanked hard enough to send the gun flying from my hands.

CHAPTER 23

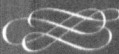

"*N*either will you," a masculine voice whispers, the animosity so familiar it sends a shiver down my spine.

My racing heartbeat pounds in my ears. Burnett's scent burns in my nostrils, and I struggle against his hold, to no avail.

Tripp appears from the direction of the fighting, his clothes stained with blood. "Let her go," he growls, advancing on Burnett.

But I nod at where Levi lies alone and helpless in the dirt. Tripp curses and rushes to his friend, crouching to assess his injuries. My gaze darts to Jadick as I try to come up with some plan that will allow Levi to escape with his life. And my father, too, if it's not too late.

My eyes land on Frankie's wolf, and my wolf nearly loses it. She would have done anything to keep Jadick from ruling this pack. Including killing someone she cared about. The knowledge of that leaves me bereft.

Soldiers emerge from the chaos of the fighting near the house. They carry a body between them, and my heart lurches. My mother —bound and gagged. Blood leaks from multiple wounds, none of which look lethal, but the fury in her eyes says she didn't make it easy for them to take her. Hopefully, she took Lenny out first, the bastard.

She's dropped unceremoniously in a heap at Jadick's feet. Her grunt is muffled and bitten back like she'd rather die than make a sound against what's happening to her.

"Tie her to the left post," Jadick orders.

She's yanked up again and dragged to the left side of the archway then tied to it.

"What are you doing to her?" I demand.

"Only what is required for the future of our people," Jadick says. His voice is flippant, easy. He's enjoying this—even my shock is entertaining.

"It's me you want," I say.

"You're not wrong." His lips twitch. "Alas, the ritual requires three generations to sacrifice their blood, which means you, your mother, and—" He motions to the archway where movement catches my eye.

I go still, shocked to see a woman walking toward us. Her gray hair is long and full, caught in a braid that hangs down to her waist. Bracelets jangle at her wrist, and a flowy skirt swishes along the ground as she emerges from the shadows. She looks right at me with a gaze so piercing the air between us ripples.

Magic.

He's found another witch.

"Hello, Mac. My name is Rina."

Her voice is friendly, which somehow makes all of this so much worse. Does she not understand what she's here to help do? I don't bother to reply. Not when Jadick is practically glowing with anticipation.

Instead, my disbelief gives way to a brokenness that threatens to buckle my knees right where I stand. All of it. For nothing. For this.

To have come so far and then fail is…

"Rina here is the original witch who cast our curse." Jadick's voice holds a note of triumph. "I'd given up looking for her, and then, boom, out of nowhere, she comes to me two days ago and volunteers to complete the ritual with her own blood."

"Blood?"

"Turns out she's the third generation," Jadick says.

My mother looks ready to spit nails.

"I don't understand," I say.

Jadick looks radiant as he delivers the words, "Rina is your great-grandmother."

"What?"

His words are a punch to my gut. Shock, disbelief...

I look down at my mother, who refuses to meet my eyes. She's too busy staring at the woman as if she's seen a ghost.

"Vicki, you should have called me," Rina says quietly. "I would have come sooner."

"I think your timing is perfect," Jadick says. "And don't forget your oath. You swore to me in blood that, after today, our curse regarding mates is done."

"I haven't forgotten," she tells him.

My jaw drops. "You're working with him?" I demand. "Even though we're your family?"

Rina doesn't answer. Levi, however, snarls. He's recovering, which is good, but I know one wrong move will trigger Jadick to punish one of us for his attempt. I look over in time to see Tripp shoving Levi back down again. I know it's for his own good, but seeing my mate on the ground and my own bloodline standing over it all like a traitor is more than I can bear.

I bring my elbow back into Burnett's ribs, and he grunts, his arm going limp. I start to land another blow, but Jadick's voice stops me.

"Fight back, and I'll finish him," Jadick warns, his words snapping me back to the present moment.

I stop fighting.

Burnett releases me long enough to lift me off my feet. I'm carried and then dropped unceremoniously onto the large slab of stone beneath the archway. My struggles to get up are met with vicious hands that shove me back down again. A rope is produced, and my wrists and ankles are quickly secured.

Panic bubbles up, threatening to choke me.

I can't move. I can't run. I can't fight.

Instead, I scream.

It's cut short with a stinging slap across my face.

I look up into Burnett's cruel eyes and promise myself that, even in the afterlife, I will come for him. He won't outlive my wrath, nor will he ever, for one day of his awful life, have peace. Not after this.

"Mac," Tripp calls sharply.

I drag my gaze over to where Tripp kneels beside Levi. My wolf howls inside me, and it's all I can do not to bite through these ropes and run to him now. Even if they kill me for the defiance of it all. But then I look at my friend—really look at him, and the urge to give it all up for something so futile is shoved back. Tripp's expression reflects my own horror, but there's none of the sad acceptance in him that I can feel in me.

He looks grimly determined—to do what, I can't figure out.

We've tried it all.

Nothing has worked, and yet he doesn't look beaten.

"Mac," he says again, more gently this time.

I blink, trying to focus on what he's not saying.

His gaze darts to something on my left then quickly back to my own confused stare.

"You can do this," he says.

I almost laugh at his words. Instead, what comes out is a sound I can't name. A grating of my voice against my throat.

He's wrong. I tried to do this, and it only ended in bloodshed.

Jadick clicks his tongue. A sound of impatience I intend to ignore, but no one's ever ignored Jadick Clemons successfully. I know that now.

He marches over, grabbing my still-healing bicep, the one Frankie just shot, and squeezes to the point of pain. My instinct is to shrink away, but thanks to the ropes holding me, I have nowhere to go. Instead, I grit my teeth rather than give him the satisfaction of a scream. Still, when I look up at him, I can see the glitter in his eye that says he knows he's pushed me to the brink. And he'll push me further still.

"That was a sad attempt at prolonging the inevitable, Mac. But we're not finished here."

He positions himself just so beneath the archway.

"We're ready," he snaps at the witch.

Rina takes a deep breath, and I find myself fighting hope that she'll refuse. But she merely begins uttering an incantation. As if she didn't witness our attempt at an insurrection before beginning her ceremony. Her voice wobbles slightly; the only clue she's uncomfortable with the turn this night has taken. After a moment, it steadies again, and I feel the slither of magic as it creeps over my skin.

Gather ye, brother to brother,
Beseech we as one, the Great Wolf Mother,
On this night, we break with fate,
Under a black moon, we reject all mates;
What was once whole is broken again
What we've healed we now un-mend.
Generations before us,
The third branch becomes the source,
Accepted and cast off,
A queen and a pawn.
Her blood as an offering,
Her choice the softening.
Ripe and ready,
True and steady,
Great Wolf Mother,
A sacrifice and another,
Death of your desire,
Born of your decree,
As we will it underneath the black moon,
So mote it be.

She nods at Jadick. I watch as he picks up the crooked blade from the table and turns toward me, using his free hand to grip my wrist. My body reacts, struggling to get free, but the bindings pulled taut against my limbs are unyielding. Jadick brings the knife down against my forearm, and I gasp at the sudden sharpness of the pain.

Blood pools then begins to run from the wide gash.

Rina comes forward, placing a bowl to catch the blood, and the drip-drip-drip is a disgusting rhythm, a song heralding everything I've fought to stop.

I breathe, shoving back the panic at seeing such a large wound opened. It won't be long before the blood loss hits me. Especially after the gunshot that's already left me weakened. Once I lose consciousness, there will be no coming back.

Rina's expression is grim but also clear. She knows I'm finished.

This is it.

The spell will be cast, and my life will be lost, all so Jadick can manipulate fate.

I glance at where Levi lies in the grass. His eyes are open and trained on me. The unexpected awareness jolts me, and I inhale a sharp breath as a thousand unspoken words pass between us.

A lifetime, really.

One we'll never know for ourselves.

An entirely different path, a destiny we'll never meet.

If blood loss wasn't threatening to end me, the loss of a future with Levi would.

My heart cracks, and in the empty places, I feel the magic itself begin to take root. It's a black hole, eclipsing. A current, eddying. And the presence itself is such an invasion, I shove back against it. My back arches, and I let loose a scream that echoes into the tree-tops before being swallowed by the stars.

The guard beside me grunts, and I look over to see some sort of altercation happening just beyond where I've been laid out.

A hand shoving toward Burnett's belt.

Tripp's face lurches closer just before it's smashed by the butt of a rifle.

As he goes down, his eyes flick to mine. Desperation flashes, and he hurls something toward me.

The tiny vial sings through the air, and I only barely manage to open my hand in time for it to land against my palm. Tripp falls to the ground with a muted thud, and Burnett's there, planting his massive boot against Tripp's neck to keep him from getting up again.

I want to scream for my friend's life, but the vial is hot in my hand, and time is too short.

My eyes flick to the poison I now hold.

The venom Tripp just risked his life for.

Then I look over at where Levi still watches me from the same place Jadick put him down. He hasn't tried to get up again. He won't. I know it as surely as I know he's the one who told Tripp to get me this venom.

All that poison.

All those times it almost killed me.

I glance sideways to see Burnett still looming over Tripp. On my other side, Jadick's slicing my mother's arm open and filling a bowl with her blood. He hasn't noticed my prize.

Directly beneath the archway, Rina repeats her incantation. Three times, she'll say the necessary spell before the magic is complete. Our eyes meet. She offers me a secret smile, urging me to drink. Like she's known all along it would come down to this.

When I look back at him one last time, Levi rises onto his elbow and nods.

I blink, a single tear escaping down my dirty cheek. A goodbye and a thank you.

"I love you," I mouth.

"I love you too, mate."

His words reach me even as low as he speaks them. And somehow, they give me the strength I need to do what comes next.

If I can't stop Jadick, I'll stop him from using me. It's the best I can do. And maybe it's always been where this was headed. Maybe there was never a chance of breaking the cycle without breaking me too.

The only way to win is to die.

Marilyn's words echo inside my head, urging me on.

With fumbling fingers, I manage to uncap the vial, and then, with an awkward wrenching of my body against the hard stone, I manage to lean down so that my mouth reaches my bound hand.

Tipping up the vial, I bring it to my lips and upend it until the bitterness explodes against my tongue. This is nothing like the venom I've been injected with before. This is so much worse.

The warm liquid is a death sentence.

I drink it all.

CHAPTER 24

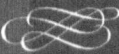

Someone screams, and it's urgent enough to make Jadick take notice of what's happened. He looks at me sharply, eyes dancing over my face then down to my hand—the empty vial still clutched there—and finally, back to my face again, which is already beginning to burn with the effects of the poison I've ingested.

My heart skips a beat and then races. My head hammers with what feels like a two-by-four being slammed into my temples. This poison—it's so much more potent than anything I've felt before.

The fire it brings is instant and consuming.

My lungs seize, and I jerk with the effort of trying to draw breath.

Dots dance across my vision, and I fall back against the stone altar, paralyzed by pain.

"What have you done?" Jadick breathes. He grabs the vial and holds it up. "Poison? Where? I ordered all of this destroyed. No one was to have this here tonight."

Tripp looks up at Burnett.

Jadick notices, and his eyes narrow, but then Grey steps forward, smug. "She'll end this. On her terms," Grey tells Jadick. "And there's not a damn thing you can do about it."

"No," Jadick roars.

He drops the knife and the bowl of blood. It splatters at his feet, which feels like a victory in itself. Ignoring the loss, he grips my shoulders, shaking me until I can't see straight. His mouth moves, but I don't hear the words over the roaring of flames inside me.

Then he looks at the witch, eyes wild. "Don't stop," he orders, and I realize she's done exactly that.

"The poison," she begins, but he's not hearing any of it.

"She has still given her blood," he insists, lurching for the bowl again. He holds it under my mouth, letting the drops fall in one by one. "Don't stop the spell," he orders her.

"She has poisoned her blood," the witch says calmly. "She is compromised. This ritual demands pure blood, or the magic will reject your request."

Jadick turns back to me, eyes blazing with a fury I have to wonder doesn't somehow burn him like the poison is burning me.

"Jadick," I say, the word a choked sort of whisper.

His eyes narrow. "Just hold on and fight it," he grinds out. "You've done it before."

But I shake my head, a smile curving my lips despite the blinding agony.

I reach for his collar, grabbing fistfuls of the fabric and drawing him down to me.

"What are you—?" His anger and confusion are all the invitation I need.

Yanking him close, I plant my mouth against his, pushing all the venom I've held in my mouth past his angry lips. Holding myself against him so that the poison seeps in before he can reject it. The fire fuels me. Or maybe it's the magic.

I can feel the moment it hits him. The way his body stiffens. The locking of his muscles in protest.

He tries to wrench away. But I don't let him.

With magic swirling and poison igniting, I kiss the wolf to death.

Jadick staggers backward the moment I release him. He falls, clawing at his mouth as his lips flush bright red then immediately begin to turn blue. He gasps as if his throat is clogged, and I fall back, watching with paralyzing relief as Jadick slowly suffocates.

The poison is a relentless spiraling, though, and before Jadick has stopped jerking against the invisible force stealing his life, black dots dance before my eyes. I blink them away, determined to see this.

Someone yells, the words unintelligible to me.

Beneath the archway, Rina begins speaking again, but her words are lost to my ears.

Then bodies are surging forward. A hand grips my shoulder, but I'm no longer aware of any sound I make against the pain.

A face swims into view.

Tripp.

"Mac," he mouths.

Then he's gone again.

Hands appear.

Another vial is tipped to my lips. Its contents empty themselves down my throat.

Rina, the witch, stands over me. Her gaze is calm though intent. Lines of concentration appear on her forehead as she waits for my death.

The fire inside me continues to consume.

My wolf howls, writhing as it slowly dies.

"..not working," Rina says to someone else. She sounds sad, and I wonder if I should just stop fighting and let myself go.

"...blood," a familiar voice snarls.

Levi.

He stands over me, back in his human form. His handsome face is streaked with blood, but the desperation he wears is clearly for me as he rakes his eyes over my face. His hands cup my cheeks, and he leans in and says, "Don't give up on me."

He crushes his lips to mine.

I fight him, terrified of the poison still clinging to my tongue.

But Levi's grip is like iron, and he climbs up on the stone altar, pressing himself against me until I'm consumed by him.

By us.

My wolf stirs, and Levi's grip on my hip tightens. He kisses me harder, his tongue swirling against mine with no sign of succumbing to the poison.

Rina's voice lifts, growing louder with some incantation she's uttering. I don't hear the words, nor do I care. If I'm dying today, I'm going out in a blaze of passion.

Levi's mouth is a balm to the fire burning me up from the inside. And then, suddenly, I gasp as his teeth pierce my delicate throat. Blood rushes to meet him. But he's already backing away and urging me to bite him too. I open my mouth to protest but find my teeth already lengthening for his skin. My wolf—she wants him. Any way she can get him.

Levi's throat is at my lips.

I bite, sinking my teeth into the space just above his collarbone.

The fire inside me is chased away, replaced by a heat much more enjoyable. My wolf slams herself against my skin, desperate to break free. Levi climbs off me, urging me to sit up. The moment I do, I feel the magic of our mate bond rooting inside us.

The poison is no longer a threat. Even without shifting to complete the healing, my wolf is strong and whole, and nothing of its destruction remains. Even my arm is healed.

When I look back at Levi, I know why.

Worry, fear, hope, elation, love—they pour into me. Levi's gaze reflects every single feeling, and I know whatever bond I thought we had before has just increased ten-fold.

Are you okay?

Levi's voice in my head has me yelping in surprise. When I've regained control, I stare at him.

I can hear you in my head. How?

His brow lifts. *Magic.*

Rina—?

I start to look at her, but his answer stops me.

No. Not Rina. Us.

I don't understand.

We're mates, Mac. Our bond is strong.

But the poison. I should be dead—

Jadick was wrong. Love doesn't make us weaker. It makes us stronger.

Are you saying love healed me? I can't help the sarcasm as I say the cheesiest words ever. *Your kiss was that powerful?*

He sends me the mental equivalent of a smirk. *Are you saying you don't like the idea of a little sexual healing?*

I shake my head. *Whatever.*

Fine, the antidote might have had something to do with it. The point is you're safe now. He leans in, his wolf nuzzling me again.

And my mother? My—My father??

Vicki's fine, they both are.

Relief floods me then. The idea of losing my dad to a war I brought to his doorstep would have been a loss too big to bear.

What about you? I suddenly remember Levi's injuries.

Healed. But what matters is that I have you, Mac. And look. We get a do-over after all.

I soften at that, still reeling at the idea that we can hear each other this way. I try to remember how long it's been since our pack could communicate this way. Decades, for sure. When I look over, I catch Rina watching me.

Her expression is softer, too, like she knows what we're saying to each other. Impossible.

Before I can work through it all, a rumbling comes from the gardens at our back. I look up to see my father stalking through the crowd of wolves gathered there. His shirt is torn and stained with blood, and he grimaces as he walks, but he's on his feet, breathing, fighting, looking like a force to be reckoned with. And that is enough to make my heart swell with love.

As he approaches, Black Moon pack and Jades alike all part for him.

He wears a sword strapped to his back like some kind of

medieval hero. Guns are strapped across his chest and down his legs. He's not injured that I can see.

I exhale as he approaches.

"You okay?" he asks me.

I nod, and satisfied, he hurries over to untie my mother. The moment she's free, she hurls herself into his arms.

"I thought you were—" She doesn't finish as she chokes on her own relief.

"I know," he assures her.

She sobs quietly against his shoulder, which is a definite first, but their embrace is short-lived as she turns to Rina.

"This is not okay," she hisses.

"Isn't it?" Rina asks, unruffled by it all. "Isn't it all more than okay?"

My mom's face flushes.

Before she can answer, Burnett pushes to his feet where he'd crouched to check Jadick's vitals one last time. When he turns to us, his face is ashen.

"He's dead," Burnett says, half-shocked, half-lost at the news.

"And you're fired, buddy," Tripp says cheerfully.

He brings an elbow up and slams it into Burnett's face. "Whoops," Tripp says gleefully.

Burnett growls, ready to fight, but Levi steps between them, baring his teeth.

"Stand down," Levi orders.

I can feel the alpha energy radiating from Levi, but Burnett doesn't bow. My wolf strains to act. Mostly, to rip Burnett's heart out for daring to defy an alpha. But then I notice Burnett's gaze flicking to me as if waiting for a command.

His eyes widen, and I freeze as I realize what's happening between us.

Energy like nothing I've ever felt before winds its way around me and then reaches for him.

A tie binding us.

A rope stretching across the distance that—

No!

My wolf tries to resist, but the alpha bond has already taken root.

I snarl, shaking my head and tossing my body as I struggle to fight it off. But deep down, I know it's too late.

"Mac," my mother says, her voice hushed. "I feel...are you..." The thread reaches for her too. She takes a step toward me and then drops to one knee, bowing her head. "I swear loyalty to you as my alpha."

Immediately, my father does the same. He draws his sword and lays it out on the ground before him. "Mackenzie, I swear loyalty to you as my alpha."

The sound of his deep voice rings out in the silence.

Behind me, voices rise, and I turn to see other pack members dropping low in a show of deference and respect to their new leader. One by one, the Black Moon pack swears their loyalty. And then Burnett drops to one knee, muttering an oath of loyalty. To me.

CHAPTER 25

ozens of wolves profess their loyalty to their new alpha, and instantly, the invisible thread that tethers me to only my mother and father multiplies. A connection tethering us all forms so quickly that even my wolf is dumbfounded. For a moment, no one speaks. They're all waiting—probably for me, though I have no idea what to say or do next. In the weighted silence, Levi steps close, eyes searching mine.

"Hail the new alpha," he says.

I wince, but his elation isn't teasing at all. It's simply happiness.

"How do you feel?" he asks when I don't answer.

"I don't know," I admit. "I'm alive."

His expression softens. "You are more than that."

Instead of answering, I look at the others. Tripp and Grey stand close by, and I notice their posture is angled toward Levi. "You're still Jades," I say, wrapping my head around all this.

They nod. Tripp shrugs. "I mean, I could be swayed for the right number of tacos."

Grey smacks him.

I look down at where my mother still kneels.

"You're okay with all this?" I ask her.

"Ask me again after I've taken orders from my own daughter," she says, but there's a glimmer of unmistakable relief in her eyes. And something else I never thought I'd see. Pride.

Rather than acknowledge it, I look at Rina, who watches us with a soft smile.

"Thank you," I tell her.

"I didn't do much," she says with a wink.

But I don't believe her. Turning it all over in my mind, I suspect she's done a great deal, mostly where we couldn't even see it happening.

"We should clean all this up," I say, a little uncertain.

Levi leans in and whispers, "Maybe let them all get off their knees first."

"Oh." I look around, startled to realize the pack is still kneeling. And waiting. Shit.

"Uh, you can rise," I call out.

Out of the corner of my eye, I see Levi fighting a smile. He's enjoying this, and why shouldn't he? We've won. We're alive. And the Clemons' line of alphas is done.

Still, there are enough questions unanswered and problems to solve even in the midst of our victory. Even without Jadick, we're still prisoners, thanks to the curse.

I square my shoulders as the pack gets to their feet. The Jades continue to look to Levi, but at least, there's no more animosity between the two groups.

"Now what?" I ask.

Levi shrugs. "Whatever you want."

I have no idea what to do with that. For as long as I can remember, there was an expectation for me. A duty to perform. My time has never been my own, not where the pack is concerned. Looking out over the others, I realize it's probably been the same for them.

And suddenly, instead of feeling overwhelmed by this new title and responsibility, I see the opportunity in it.

"You're all free to go," I call out.

After a beat, some begin moving slowly toward the garden's exit. Others remain, looking uncertain. I try again. "I mean, you're free to go forever."

Everyone stops and looks back at me, eyes wide. Even the Jades mumble uncertainly now.

"Uh, Mac, that's not how this whole alpha thing works," Tripp says in a low voice.

I ignore him, determined to make this right any way I can.

"Look, we came here today to fight for you because we saw the injustice and the oppression that came with the Clemons line of alphas. Fated mates or not—the choice should be yours. And so should your choice of which pack to belong to. For decades now, you've been forced to remain here. Those who left were hunted down and dragged back. That ends now. Apparently, I'm your new alpha."

Tripp snickers.

Even Grey looks slightly amused.

I cast a glance at Burnett, who, despite his oath of loyalty, still puts me on edge.

"But I don't have to be," I add. "If you want to go, you're free to do so. I won't stop you, and no one will come looking to bring you back either."

A weighted silence hangs, and then, slowly, people begin to move again. But a voice interrupts.

"And us?" a female calls out. "What happens to the Jades now?"

I see Nely standing at the front of the crowd of Jades who've come together in a separate group. Levi catches my eye, and I wait for him to address them, noting the sense of connection between him and them through my new alpha awareness.

"Same goes for all of you," Levi tells them. "You've given up everything for this moment, but you don't owe us anything for that sacrifice either."

His words make me think of Frankie, but I purposely turn away from where some of the pack members have come forward to collect her and the other dead or wounded.

"If you want to go, you're free to do so," Levi adds.

Murmurs go around, and then Nely asks, "What if we want to stay? What happens then? There are clearly two packs on land made for only one."

Levi hesitates. It hits me then—two packs, two alphas. Nely's right. It's never been done before.

"Well?" Levi prompts. "What do you say?"

I blink when I realize he's talking to me. "About what?"

"Nely's right. If we're going to truly end this, one pack makes sense."

"Oh."

"Don't agree too quickly," he adds.

"I just… It doesn't seem fair to re-burden the Jades with a curse they escaped when they defected."

"Mac, do you not feel it?" he asks, cocking his head to study me. "The curse is gone."

"I…" I look at Rina for confirmation. "But the ritual was incomplete. Doesn't that mean the curse still stands?"

"The curse remained as long as a Clemons ruled this pack," Rina explains. "Now that a new alpha has been chosen, the curse is finished."

"I don't understand."

"I suppose time has a way of erasing—or changing—our stories." Rina raises her voice, including everyone in what she says next. "A century ago, my mate was the alpha of these lands."

My jaw drops. Nothing she said could have shocked me more. And not only because she's just admitted to being over a hundred years old either.

Rina continues, "We were the strongest pack in the entire country then, with a bloodline that offered a mate bond like no other wolves in our history, thanks to my magic. Back then, my husband's second was Arthur Clemons. Unfortunately, Arthur had a thirst for power we didn't see coming until it was too late. With the use of black magic, Arthur challenged my husband and won. Soon after, I was banished, both for being the mate of the former alpha and for being a witch."

"That's where our distrust of witches comes from," I realize.

She nods.

"And that's when you cursed us," Levi adds quietly. There's no judgment in his tone, though. Only understanding.

Rina sighs. "It wasn't my proudest moment. Or most mature. But yes. The curse meant, as long as a Clemons was alpha, their mate bonds would be weakened. As a loophole, Arthur decreed mate bonds were forbidden. He thought by refusing your fated mate, the pack could still be strong. He demanded it, in fact." She glances at my mother and then me. "But he was wrong."

"You broke the curse when you killed Jadick," Levi tells me.

"I don't know what to say," I admit. "When I drank that poison, I thought for sure we'd failed." Levi winces, but I turn to Rina. "When you said you'd made a blood oath to Jadick to end the curse..."

She smirks. "Didn't I keep my word?"

I shake my head. "You put an awful lot of faith in us."

"I put faith in you, Mackenzie. And it was rightly placed."

My mom steps up and slides an arm around my shoulders. "It was," she agrees. "Thank you," she tells Rina.

"The women of our family were brave in their choices," Rina says. "I'm glad to see those choices have made you stronger. Our people were always meant to lead this pack. You put things right again and have given me peace."

"The Mac pack," Tripp says, and a few cheers go up.

I glare at him. "Absolutely not."

"Right." He ducks his head.

Levi tugs my arm, obviously entertained. "So? One pack then?"

"Please don't make me choose, Mac," Tripp puts in.

Grey shakes his head.

I hesitate then look back at Rina. "You were banished because you were an alpha's mate," I say. "With no authority of your own."

"Back then, it was tradition that the male ruled the pack," Rina says.

"Well, times are changing, and so are we. If we combine the packs, we do it as dual alphas. Equal in title and authority."

Levi grabs my hand, squeezing it tightly. "I wouldn't have it any other way."

EPILOGUE

The memorial is crowded. Even with the winter chill still lingering into early spring, the entire pack has shown up for what is unquestionably a historical event. Despite our early arrival, I haven't seen Levi in hours. From the moment the guests began to arrive, we've been pulled along for small talk, introductions, congratulations, and, of course, commendation for the way we've handled the alpha house. Or, as my brain will forever refer to it, the Clemons house.

I couldn't live in it.

Not for a single fucking day.

As soon as the dust settled on the events leading up to my becoming alpha, Levi and I knew two things: First, we'd never try to tell anyone who to love, and second, we'd never live in this damned house.

In fact, I didn't even want to leave it standing.

Now, seven months later, it's not.

The house itself was taken down two months ago, and since then, a memorial sculpture was erected along with markers for each member of the Clemons family. I might not want to live in a house full of violent, painful memories, but I also didn't want to forget.

The future was about not repeating the past.

I intended to show everyone where we'd come from so they knew exactly where we weren't going to go.

Now, I stand before the fifth gravestone. None of them are buried here. Rina asked for one thing when she left us that day: to be gifted the bones of her enemies. I didn't ask why because, frankly, the dark request suggested an answer I probably didn't want to hear anyway.

I gave them to her without argument, and she'd taken them away to rest elsewhere.

She hadn't returned since.

Now, these markers are for their memories, not their bodies. I'm okay with that.

On my left are the first four names: Crigger, Jadick, Thiago, Kari.

Directly in front of me is Marilyn.

"I knew it. You're still worried she'll return."

I look up at the sound of Tripp's voice. He steps up beside me, leaning lazily over the railing. "Even if she does, this doesn't belong to her anymore," he adds.

I sigh. "I'm not worried she'll take it. She doesn't even want to lead the pack."

"Then what's the problem?"

"Marilyn was just as much a victim in all this," I say. "I guess I just want to know that she made it out too."

"You and Vicki left her in your kitchen, and when the team went back to retrieve her, she was gone," he reminds me. "That means she made it out."

"Yeah," I say. "You're right."

He straightens, puffing out his chest. "Say it again for the people in the back."

I smirk at him. "Make me."

He snorts. "You want to throw down, Quinn, we can go right here, right now."

"Why not? I still haven't kicked your ass for that Twilight-Barbie scandal," I tell him.

"Whoa, no one is throwing down today." Nely steps between us, glaring at both of us in equal measure. "I swear, you're both children."

Tripp grins.

"I'm a babysitter," Nely mutters to herself. "A glorified freaking babysitter."

Lorenz steps up behind her, planting a kiss on her cheek. "A gorgeous babysitter, though."

Nely rolls her eyes. "Stop trying to get in my pants."

"No, Lorenz is right. You're definitely the prettiest second we have," I deadpan.

"Hey," Tripp protests as Nely grins.

"The boss has spoken," Nely says smugly.

"Look, there can't be two seconds. That's just fourths. Or third."

"Actually, I'm third, remember?" Lorenz puts in.

Tripp groans. "I hate math, but you know what I mean."

"We are not doing this again," I say.

"Stop whining, and just accept that there are now two of everything," Nely tells him. "Two alphas and two seconds."

"In that case, I'm getting two drinks." Tripp stalks off, and Nely shoots me a questioning look before I usher her to go after him.

"Make sure he behaves today," I call after her.

"I'm a wolf, not a miracle worker," she mutters but trails after him with Lorenz in tow.

Alone again, I turn back to Marilyn's placard, contemplating. It doesn't take long before another figure appears beside me. I look up to see Grey standing at the railing, his expression much more contemplative than usual.

"Hey," I say.

Mostly, since everything went down, he's been on his own. In and out of town. More and more distant. Something about the way he faces me fully tells me this is important. The answer to the questions about what's been eating him.

"I'm on my way out and wanted to say thanks for everything."

I blink. "You're leaving?"

His mouth tightens. "I've been called home. Family business."

"Is everything okay?" I try to remember if he's ever mentioned family or where he's even from.

"It will be," he says. "Anyway, I just wanted to say it's been an honor fighting with you and Levi. I never really understood what it meant to be part of…something like this."

"Will you be coming back?" I ask.

"I don't know."

"I see. Well, you're welcome anytime, Grey."

"I know. I just…if something happens and you feel me leave the pack, it's nothing personal. If it were up to me, I'd remain here forever. I'm a Jade in my heart. Or Black Moon."

I smile. "You're a Jade in my heart too."

He turns to walk away, and I can't help but add, "I know it was you. With the antidote."

He turns back.

"Levi and Tripp admitted the poison was their idea," I explain.

"You'd fought it off so many times already," he says. "We knew you could handle it."

"But Jadick couldn't," I finish.

He doesn't answer.

"And the blanket?" I ask. "That day in Jadick's office."

He shoves his hands into his pockets, studying me. "You're a fierce warrior, Mac. It's a rare thing to also have a heart."

"Funny. I've thought the same thing about you."

He doesn't reply as he turns and disappears into the crowd.

When Levi finds me, I'm staring at the placard again, but this time, my mind is a thousand miles away. "Hey." He presses a kiss to my cheek.

"Hey."

"I saw Grey leaving. He said he's going home."

"Yeah, we spoke."

"You think he's okay?"

I hesitate and then say, "No, but I suspect it's something he has to work out on his own."

"I think you're right." He sighs and then lowers his voice to whisper, "Can we be done here yet?"

My lips quirk. "Political events not your thing?"

"Not exactly." *More like you're my thing*, he adds through our mental link.

I do my best to keep a straight face. *We need a rule about no dirty talk while in public.*

I hate rules unless I'm breaking them, Quinn. You know that.

Touché. My mouth twitches with an almost smile.

Speaking of rules, we make them. So, let's decide we're done here. I want to take you home and get you naked.

Home.

It still sounds strange even after all these months. Levi and I bought a place a few miles from here in a part of town neither of us ever lived in before. It feels fresh, like starting over. And it feels like home for the first time in my life. I suspect that has more to do with the person I share it with than the walls themselves. Every time I leave though, I can't wait to get back there.

We're supposed to give a speech, I remind him.

Again with the rules.

I snicker.

"You could make your mom do it," he says aloud.

"Make your mom do what?"

The sound of her voice startles me, and I realize she and my father have snuck up on us while Levi and I have been wrapped up in ourselves.

"Levi doesn't want to give the speech," I tell her.

She leans into my dad, and his arm tightens around her. They've only been together about a month now after circling each other for the first six months before that. It's been kind of hilarious to watch —if it weren't for the weirdness of them being my own parents.

"You want me to do it?" she asks, arching a brow. "Because I will, though I should point out my version lacks compassion and warmth where this wretched family is concerned." She eyes the placard nearby with Marilyn's name on it.

I shake my head. "I'll do it."

My mom offers me an approving look.

"We'll see you out there, kid," my dad says, squeezing my shoulder before he and my mom move back toward the party.

The gardens are done up nicely, considering the season's lack of color. Ribbons and tulle for texture. Evergreens for color.

"Is this too much?" Levi asks low in my ear when we're alone. "Being back here?"

"No, it's just... It looks like a different garden now."

"Or we're just different people."

I consider that. "You're definitely different from the guy who ghosted me in high school," I tell him.

"Don't forget the guy who led a rebellion," he adds.

"Or the guy who kidnapped me and locked me in a closet."

He scowls. "I was never that guy."

I laugh.

"And you're not Mac and Cheese anymore either," he adds, and my laughter turns to a scowl.

"Don't go there," I say darkly.

At their request, Lenny and Guy were welcomed back to the pack. They, along with Burnett, have been watched carefully, but in seven months, all they've done is drink too much and troll for dates at Inferno. Word is, Rita herself has taken a liking to Burnett. I guess there's someone out there for everyone.

"I'm just keeping us humble, babe. Reminding us where we come from. I mean, look at all we've accomplished already."

I sigh, looking out over the crowd and noting the pairs of mates standing together.

He's right. We've accomplished so much these last months. Not just in creating a pack built on more than fear and loathing. But the strength of the alpha bond is in direct correlation with the fated mates who've claimed one another. With each new pairing, our strength grows. Just like Rina said.

Seeing the proof makes me proud enough to make that speech after all.

"Time to do the damn thing," I mutter.

"Right behind you, princess."

I lead the way to the back of the garden. Ground Zero. The exact place where Jadick's life ended and mine began. The place where I learned my true heritage—as an alpha heir and, shockingly, as a witch.

After seven months of looking for Rina and waiting for any sign of my own magical abilities to show up, I've accepted the magic gene must have skipped me somehow. Being back in this space, though, I can't help but notice the lingering effects of Rina's magic that remain. Flowers, despite the impossible weather conditions, bloom in small, quiet bunches of blues and purples. They shudder as I pass by, and I wonder if there isn't a tiny bit of magic inside me after all.

I turn to face the crowd, looking out over the people assembled. It's more than I expected, considering how many left in those early days. But more than half came back—some with people in tow. Family they'd hidden, including Tripp's mom. I see him standing near her, and our eyes meet.

He raises his glass and mouths, "Long live the queen."

I shake my head, and it hits me that we did it.

Sweeping toward a movement at the edge of the garden, I go still when I recognize Rina standing at the far edges. She's masked in shade, nearly swallowed by the trees. Our eyes meet, and I regret having stood up here already, stepping into the spotlight I can't run from when all I want to do is chase her down. It's been nagging me for months, what Marilyn said that day about an oracle she'd seen. And I want to find out if Rina was that oracle. But even as I have the thought, she's already moving back into the shadows, her form rippling with the idea that she can probably just vanish if she wants to.

Just before she disappears, another figure moves in beside her. Marilyn. Clean and calm and quiet. She meets my eyes, a sad sort of frown tugging at her mouth. But her eyes are clear, and when she dips her head at me, I know this is goodbye. Forever. She won't come for the pack. As long as I don't come for her either.

She never wanted this life. And now she's finally free of it. Rina will take her somewhere safe, somewhere she can't hurt or be hurt anymore.

Slowly, I nod back to let her know we have a deal. Then Rina ushers her toward the forest but not before Rina looks over and winks at me. And in this moment, I know my suspicions are correct. About her being the oracle, about what was missing from our pack, about all of it. Levi and I might have been mates before that awful day in this garden, but the bond between us now is more than just our own.

It's Fate.

And what I've hoped all along is true: Love has made us stronger than our enemies, not weaker.

"We might be Black Moon pack, but we're dark-hearted no more," I say to the crowd, beginning a speech that's about freedom and renewal and change and, most importantly, love.

Want more from this world?
Read the series where it all began: Lone Wolf Pack
Or read Grey's story in The Mafia Pack, available now!

ABOUT THE AUTHOR

Heather Hildenbrand lives in coastal Virginia where she writes paranormal and urban fantasy romance with lots of kissing & killing. Her most frequent hobbies are truck camping with her goldendoodle, talking to her plants, and avoiding killer slugs.

You can find out more about Heather and her books at www. heatherhildenbrand.com.

Or find her here:
Facebook
Reader group on FB
Instagram
Newsletter – get a free book when you subscribe!
Patreon – NSFW artwork & exclusive books!
TikTok

ALSO BY HEATHER HILDENBRAND

A Witch's Prophecy

A Witch's Hope

Twisted Tides

The Girl Who Cried Werewolf

The Girl Who Cried Captive

The Girl Who Cried War

The Winter Witch

The Spring Witch

A Witch's Heart

Midnight Mate

Goddess Ascending

Goddess Claiming

Goddess Forging

Kiss of Death

Knock Em Dead

Death's Door

Dead to Rights

Dead End

The Girl Who Called The Stars

The Girl Who Ruled The Stars

Alpha Games

Alpha Trials

Alpha Chosen

Dirty Blood

Cold Blood

Blood Bond

Blood Rule

Broken Blood

One Hour: bonus novella

Imitation

Deviation

Generation

Guarded by the Alpha

Alpha Undercover

Mated to the Wilde Bear

The Bear's Fated Mate

Protected By the Bear

The Badge and the Bear

Tragic Ink: A Havenwood Falls story

Small Town Contemporary Romance (writing as Violet Stafford)

Stay for Summer

The Breakup Bet

www.ingramcontent.com/pod-product-compliance
Lightning Source LLC
Chambersburg PA
CBHW031017030726
47497CB00004B/900